PRAYER FOR ALL SEASONS

KATHLEEN CORMACK

KATHLEEN CORMACK

Published by Kathleen Cormack

Cover by John Cormack

AUTHOR'S NOTE

This is a work of fiction. Names, characters, places and incidents either are the product of the author's imagination or are used fictitiously, and any resemblance to actual persons, living or dead, events, or locales is entirely coincidental. Since the majority of the story takes place in the city of Chicago, Il, certain well known places are used to add authenticity.

DEDICATION

In loving memory of two young men who left us way too soon:
My nephews
John "Duke" Crawford
And
Marchello "Kane" Crawford
I miss you guys. Thanks for all the laughs. RIP

Acknowledgments:

I would like to first thank my Heavenly Father for this wonderful gift. I trust Him to continue His work in me and through me as I write to inspire others. I take no credit at all. I give You all the glory!

To my copyeditor, Sonja Mack: Your hard work in ensuring that all of my "i" s were dotted, and all of my "t"s were crossed is greatly appreciated. It takes time and patience to copyedit someone else's work. Please know that I feel truly blessed that our paths have crossed. Stick around. Book number two is in the makings. It would be an honor to work with you again!

To my husband and best friend John: Thank you for designing a beautiful book cover. You just keep amazing me over and over again; big hug and kiss. Love you and thank you for all of your support!

And last but certainly not least: To all of you who read my book (s). It is my hope and prayer that you will become inspired by my stories. The biggest blessing for me is to know that I have somehow blessed you. Maybe it was a sentence, a verse, or the dialogue between characters. Thank you for allowing me to inspire you and make you laugh. I hope you enjoyed the journey as much as I did.

P.S. Love you, mom; love you, dad.

Kathleen Cormack
kathleen@kathleencormack.com
www.kathleencormack.com

Prologue

Pam appreciated her father's words of wisdom—most of the time. But that didn't mean she always heeded his advice. She decided to just go with the flow and enjoy the remainder of her evening with Jeff. The night wasn't over yet. There was still a chance that he would broach the subject of their relationship himself.

As she sat across from him in his living room, admiring his beautiful and spacious two-bedroom townhome, she couldn't help but stare at him when he wasn't looking. There was nowhere else she'd rather be on this cold, wintry Saturday evening. It might have been cold outside, but inside of Jeff's home she felt only warmth and comfort. The handsome gentleman with the caramel complexion was slowly making his way to her heart.

Jeff was easy on the eyes and, though the saying "Beauty is in the eyes of the beholder" might ring true, Pam was certain that most women would agree that Jeff was fine. There was something unique about the 5'11" ex-amateur boxer. His light-brown eyes alone could spellbind you if you looked into them long enough. He had eyelashes that many women would pay to have. His hair was cut very low, his goatee neatly trimmed. His straight, white teeth were a plus and an absolute must for Pam. She had only one absolute on her list: Her man had to have perfect teeth. Her friends thought that was shallow but respected it just the same.

Jeff's voice was deep and sexy. Some men had either a deep or a sexy voice. But Jeff had both. In fact, his voice was deep, sexy and smooth. It seemed as if his words just oozed down to his lips and then out of his mouth. And oh, his phone voice! It was even more enticing. The first time he and Pam spoke over the phone she was practically wiping sweat from her forehead. After she hung up she ran into the bathroom and splashed cold water on her face.

"Did you enjoy the shrimp gumbo?" His question caught her off guard and she didn't answer immediately. He leaned over and lightly touched her arm. "I hope it wasn't too spicy."

"It was delicious. Couldn't you tell by the way I was smacking?" Pam answered with a light chuckle, using humor to relax her nerves. "Where did you learn to cook such a wonderful dish?"

"Well, when a man grows up in a house full of women, it is

inevitable that he learns to cook." Jeff smiled, obviously pleased that she'd enjoyed the meal.

"But I must confess," he sat back in his chair, "I prepared it very early this morning so all I'd have to do this evening was heat it in the oven. I usually prepare most of my meals that way." Pam was impressed. She had not met nor dated a man as precise as Jeff appeared to be.

"Well, it looks like you have this cooking thing down to an art. You obviously had some really good teachers. You also learned the proper etiquette for neat and tidy because your home is immaculate." Her nervousness gave way to her flirtatious nature. If there was one thing Pam could do well it was turn on the charm. She knew how and when to allow the charming side of her personality to surface, a knack she possessed that many men loved.

"Yes. I guess you could say that." Jeff blushed. "But it helps that I'm a quick learner."

Prayer for all Seasons

1

"I feel like he just blew me off," Tricee mumbled. "Oh, well. Stuff happens."

The Chinese food was cold and so was the raspberry tea, which was piping hot a few minutes ago. This was not exactly how Jentrice, better known as Tricee, planned to spend her Saturday evening. It was just after 8:00 PM and she was dressed in her favorite pair of black sweat pants—her favorite due to their expensive price tag—and a white tank top. She was barefoot, sitting at her kitchen table, just staring at the wall. Tricee had a tendency to allow her mind to wander when she was either bored or disappointed.

Tricee had no desire to live in the past, but after her guy friend called to cancel their dinner plans, her mind conjured up images from her childhood. She'd wished that she could have done some things differently but realized that living in regret offered no benefits. She stopped staring at the wall long enough to pick over the shrimp fried rice and egg roll as she pictured her 5th grade classroom.

Ms. Lambert, who all the students referred to as Ms. Lamphead, had been one of Tricee's least favorite teachers. She would ask her 5th grade class, "What do you wish to become once you are all grown up?" She would ask this question every Tuesday morning at approximately 10:00 AM.

Tricee felt that Ms. Lambert's Tuesday morning question was not necessarily asked out of sincerity. She would observe Ms. Lambert's body language before she asked the dreaded question that made her feel so anxious. Ms. Lambert would place her hands on the big wooden desk and use her feet to push herself back in the brown wooden chair. She would then proceed to walk over to each student and stand beside his or her desk with her feet firmly planted in place. Then she would move on to the next student.

On this particular Tuesday, when she reached Tricee's desk, Tricee suddenly had the urge to yawn. She looked over at her classmate Karl, his thick-lensed brown glasses sliding down his face, and he also began to yawn. Ms. Lambert stood stoically, staring at Tricee intently until she stopped yawning. There was no facial expression, not even a blink of the eyes. "If only she could see herself right now," Tricee thought silently.

"Jentrice, what do you wish to become once you are all grown up?" Before she answered, she glanced over at her best friend, Annette, whom she referred to as Netta. Netta was well aware of Tricee's feelings toward their 5th grade teacher, and although she did not understand why she felt that way, she fully supported her friend's decision. After all, they had been best friends since the 3rd grade. When Tricee answered Ms. Lambert, the words flowed easily from her lips just as she'd practiced, with no hint of nervousness. Her answer did cause a stir among her fellow classmates.

"I don't know what I wish to become when I am all grown up. But I have a pretty good idea of what I do not want."

Ms. Lambert cleared her throat. "I see. Well, please share with the class what it is that you do not wish to become."

Tricee drew in a deep breath and carefully articulated the answer she had prepared. "I do not wish to become an old and lonely woman. And I don't want to be one of those women who suffer sadness because of their boyfriends or husbands."

Four months later, Ms. Lambert approached Tricee regarding her answer. "Jentrice, please stay after class. I need to talk to you."

Tricee became agitated. "But it's the last day of school," she whined.

"It will only take a few minutes," Ms. Lambert replied without looking up at Tricee who was standing at her desk.

"But my mother will be waiting for me," Tricee protested.

"I have already informed your mother that you will be staying for several minutes." Tricee turned and walked to her desk, mumbling.

After the class had been dismissed, Ms. Lambert asked Tricee to come to the front. Tricee proceeded to the front of the classroom where Ms. Lambert motioned toward the desk that was directly in front of hers. Reluctantly, Tricee sat down.

"Jentrice, why did you answer my question that way? Why didn't you just name something you'd like to do as a career?" Ms. Lambert was straight and to the point. The look on her face said to Tricee "You know exactly what I am talking about," which was unfortunate as Tricee wanted badly to pretend otherwise.

"Please answer me, Jentrice. I know you must have an explanation," said Ms. Lambert.

Ms. Lambert was so tall and light that, on the first day off class, Tricee and her classmates all thought that she was white. It was not until she'd overheard a conversation between Ms. Lambert and one of the other teachers regarding the Kwanzaa holiday that she learned of Ms. Lambert's ethnicity.

As Tricee sat looking into the face of the woman who, for her, had made the 5th grade almost unbearable, she had to fight back tears. "I hope I do not end up like my mother. I pray that God will give me a better life."

Later on that evening as she lay in bed, Tricee cried herself to sleep. But before climbing into bed she knelt down on her knees to pray. It had been one of the longest prayers she'd ever remembered praying. It was on this night that she would learn the power of prayer. This would be one of the greatest lessons she would learn as a child.

After several minutes, Tricee's home phone rang, bringing her out of her daydream. She walked into the living room and saw that the caller ID box displayed "private number." She ignored it and proceeded to walk back into the kitchen where she picked up the cold Chinese food and tossed what was left of it into the trash. She left the cup of tea sitting on the table, turned off the light and went into her bedroom. In less than 20 minutes she was fast asleep.

Philippians 3:13—Brethren, I count not myself to have apprehended: but this one thing I do, forgetting those things which are behind, and reaching forth unto those things which are before

2

Friday evening: August 2nd - One year ago

"TGIF," Tricee said to herself as she leaned back in her favorite recliner. "Thank God I'm fine." She chuckled and then sipped from her glass of Diet Ginger Ale. A slice of lime tossed into the glass with her soda was the only way she would drink it. It had become one of her favorite drinks during her college years. Now, almost 15 years later, it was as refreshing as it had been back then.

Although Tricee had many fond memories of the four years she'd spent at Northern Indiana University, like everyone else she knew, she enjoyed the idea of making money. And once she received her M.B.A., her finances increased just as she'd expected.

Her college years had gone well. She received good grades and had adopted good study habits. But when it came to relationships, that had been a different story altogether. Every relationship she encountered during her four years in college had turned sour. It appeared as if every guy she dated was immature, insecure, or just plain cheap. She had tried to be reasonable whenever she met a guy who turned out to be cheap. After all, she realized that being a college student meant that you would be low on funds.

But she had dated two young men on separate occasions, during her junior and senior years, who had been gainfully employed. They were both college educated and, ironically, they both believed in the same concept of dating: an evening at her apartment watching a movie while enjoying a dinner she'd prepared. Tricee thought this was fine every once in a while but not for every date. She thought they both should have known better and made them aware of how she felt when she ended the relationship. "You have the wrong woman. I am not a chef and my apartment is not a restaurant," she'd explained. The guy she dated in her junior year laughed thinking that she was making a joke until he saw her very serious expression. And the boyfriend from her senior year became offended and stormed out of her apartment, never to be heard from again.

After these experiences, she met and dated Brad, the only white guy she had ever dated during college. Their courtship lasted for about a month as Brad, as it turned out, was just not comfortable dating a black girl. He liked Tricee and thought she was attractive and very nice, but he was forever looking over his shoulder whenever they were out. Tricee finally got up the nerve to ask him why he was always looking around, to which Brad replied, "I don't know." One day he suggested that they stay in and order pizza. Tricee agreed. And she noticed how relaxed Brad seemed. It was one of the best dates they had. And since they did not have to *go* anywhere but to the door to get the pizza, Brad was well within his comfort zone.

After Brad suggested that they stay in and order pizza for their next couple of dates, Tricee just came right out and said, "Look, you are obviously uncomfortable being seen around campus with a *sister*, so let's just call it quits and chalk this one up to experience." Brad tried to convince her that he was not uncomfortable, that it was just a brand new experience.

There were no hard feelings. They would still see each other around campus and be cordial. In fact, Tricee never admitted that she was slightly uncomfortable, as well, just not as uncomfortable as he was. Once, while at a theater to view a black film, Brad had been the only white person in attendance. That time it was Tricee who spent the evening looking over her shoulder while Brad, interestingly enough, was focused on the movie. Although she'd tried to make the relationship feel as normal as possible, it had become an inside joke between her and one of her college friends, Dawn.

Whenever she and Dawn would call each other or bump into one another on campus, one of them would ask, "Guess who's coming to dinner?" to which the other would reply, "Not Brad Beckum!" Dawn had been one of Tricee's friends from Atlanta. She was from a very well-to-do African American family, yet she was one of the most genuine people Tricee had ever met. Regrettably, they lost contact after graduating.

Indeed, college had been a fun time. But Tricee would come to the conclusion toward the end of her senior year that balancing homework, working part-time, and trying to date was just not her cup of tea. She would also change her major twice before deciding that a Bachelor's Degree in psychology was her fate. College had required "too much thinking on small details" she once told a friend. And she would sometimes half-jokingly tell some of her college buddies, "The professors are always right, even when they are wrong." She was happy that her college days were behind her. She had adjusted fairly well to the world of work with the exception of a few stressful days, which she came to accept as perfectly normal.

Today had been "one of those days." It had been stressful yet productive and, because of this, Tricee decided to go straight home after work. It was Friday evening and two of her girlfriends had asked her to join them after work for some all-you-can-eat catfish from 7:00 PM – 9:00 PM. She passed on the opportunity. She had voiced her opinion once before to her friends: "If I owned a restaurant I'd set a limit. People can be greedy when it comes to free food." Clara's Soul and Jazz served some of the best soul food in all of Chicago-land. It was a popular soul food restaurant that also had a jazz band that performed on the weekends. As much as Tricee disliked the idea of missing out on all the fun, she was just too tired to change her mind.

Her position as Associate Director of Strategic Partnerships & Programs at H&P University, although rewarding, could also be quite challenging. But she enjoyed her work at the large university on Chicago's south side, one of the top schools in the nation. Her career at the prestigious school began after she'd spent two-and-a-half years in graduate school at Evanston South University, located in Evanston, a Chicago suburb. The two-year program had taken her a little longer to complete as she'd decided to work full time. She worked as a coordinator in the Human Resources department and, after one year, transferred to Evanston's School of Education where she served as an academic advisor for the undergraduate students.

Tricee believed she'd done well for a young, African American female. Her friends described her as smart, funny, and always willing to lend a helping hand. As for the physical, she was often told she was attractive—not that it mattered. And she maintained her 5'6" slender frame by doing yoga and taking fast walks along the lakefront. She wore her hair natural, deciding that natural hair was a far better option than anything else. For her, it beat having to have chemicals applied to her scalp every six weeks or so.

To outsiders and to those who knew her, Tricee was considered a success. But she would often think, *if I had attended graduate school immediately after finishing my undergraduate studies, I'd be further along in my career.* She had chosen to take a couple of years off after undergrad to travel and "find herself," something she thought was typical of many young adults.

One of the reasons Tricee was her own worst critic had to do, in part, with a comment that had been made by her mother, Ruby. She had overheard a telephone conversation between her mother and her Aunt Janice, her mother's youngest sister. Actually, she was eavesdropping, but to admit to that would only make her seem small. Her mother's words were etched into her memory: "I do not understand why Tricee wasted two years doing nothing instead of continuing with her education. She has all the time in the world to travel. She could have been much more successful than she is now." Upon hearing those words, Tricee wanted to yell out, "I *am* successful, no thanks to you!" But Ruby was her mother and she knew that behaving disrespectfully was out of the question. Tricee stood in the doorway feeling like a small child who could not please her own mother.

After her mother's hurtful comment, Tricee was ready to turn and leave the house until her mother, who obviously hadn't seen her standing there, called after her. "You're not leaving already. You just got here." Her mother was behaving as if she had not just said such an unpleasant thing about her. "Besides, we don't live in the same state anymore so it's not like we see each other every day." Ruby had not been to visit Tricee even one time after she relocated to the Windy City. When the eavesdropping incident occurred, Tricee had flown back to St. Louis, her hometown, to visit family and friends.

Whenever Tricee came home, she stayed in a hotel or with Netta, her childhood friend, who had made the decision to remain in the St. Louis area after college. Netta was an attorney for the Department of Children and Family Services, happily married and doing very well. Ruby adored Netta and bragged about her on many occasions. Her constant praise used to hurt Tricee's feelings but, over time, she learned to ignore it. She did have a prayer that she would recite often: *Lord, please heal my wounds and please heal the wounds of my mother. And allow us to enter into a relationship that can only exist between a mother and daughter. Amen.*

But now, on this Friday evening as she enjoyed the view of the lake from her condo on Chicago's north side, she was feeling just fine. Nothing and no one could take away her peace. She had delivered a presentation that had gone over well with her boss, so a merit increase was sure to follow. *Sometimes a little bit of stress is necessary when hard work is involved*, she thought as she danced and swayed through her apartment. Her radio was tuned to her favorite jazz station and one of her favorite artists, Najee, was playing. Her head moved back and forth as she listened to the smooth sounds. She opened her eyes when her home phone rang but decided to ignore the call. Eight minutes later, after the song ended, it rang again. "This has to be someone who knows I am home," she mumbled.

Sure enough, it was her good friend Pam. She spoke excitedly, hoping that Tricee would change her mind and meet them at the restaurant. "Tricee, we're here having a great time and the band is awesome! You need to get over here!" Pam Rhodes, Jackie Latham, and Val Edmonds were three of her closest friends. Since she was an only child they were more like her sisters, and she had always felt that she could talk to them about anything. Their friendship was based on honesty—even if it meant someone getting their feelings hurt over the truth. They were a typical group of women, just trying to enjoy life as best they knew how.

"No, Ms. Lady. My mind was made up at five o'clock," Tricee said. "You ladies enjoy the evening. We'll catch up tomorrow."

"Aw, live a little. It's Friday night," said Pam. Pam had a big heart but she could be a little bossy at times. She was one of those people who, if you did not know her well, you would think had no heart. But that was surely not the case. She was determined to try to convince Tricee to meet her and Jackie at the restaurant but her attempts would fail. Tricee was in for the evening.

"The catfish is delicious! Jackie's on her third plate already! I don't know where she puts it all."

"Is Val not there with you guys?" Tricee asked.

"No, she and Cory had other plans."

Val, the only one in the group who was married, would sometimes have to miss a night out with her girls. But she made certain that it did not occur too often.

"Oh, okay. Well enjoy. And please be easy on the men. I am sure you have one potential candidate already," Tricee said teasingly.

"If he's here, I haven't seen him yet," Pam said, placing her hand on her curvy hip. Some men would describe her as "thick," meaning it as a compliment. Either way, there was no mistaking her 5'5" voluptuous figure for anything but. Jackie, on the other hand, stood 5'9" and had a slender build. She could eat almost anything she wanted without fear of gaining weight. Val's petite frame, at 5'4", allowed her the same advantage. "I have good genes," she'd say. "I have my parents to thank for that."

They were all hard-working women in their 30s doing very well in their professions. They'd reached the conclusion that fun was not only a word, it was a necessity; a much-needed reprieve from hard work. "If you want to remain sane, you have to get out and have some fun," Tricee would say. Her friends could not agree with her more.

"Okay. Call me tomorrow," said Tricee. She was trying to get Pam to hang up. She imagined that Pam had excused herself and stepped outside to call her since she couldn't hear the band.

"It's only 7:30, the night is still young. The band is jamming."

After Pam paused for air, Tricee simply reiterated her thoughts. "Pam, I told you. I am just too tired. I'll have to take a rain check."

"You're just sitting over there waiting for what's-his-name to call." Pam's face broke out into a sly grin. When she attempted to speak again, Tricee politely cut her off.

"I will talk to you tomorrow, Missy. There is always next Friday. Tell Jackie I said to have fun." Tricee eased the phone from her ear. "Goodbye, Pam. Love you."

She snickered as she hung up the phone. *Pam could drive you crazy.* She walked into the kitchen for more to drink.

On her way home from work, Tricee had stopped for take-out. She heated the chicken and broccoli in the microwave then proceeded back into the living room, her plate of food in one hand and a tall glass of diet ginger ale in the other. The phone rang again. "Gee, what perfect timing," she whispered. "Why does it seem that folks always call you when you're about to eat?"

She looked over at the caller ID and saw her mother's name. Her mother rarely phoned on Friday evenings because she knew Tricee was likely to be out with her friends. But the fact that she'd already attempted to reach Tricee on her cell phone twice had Tricee convinced that it must be something of an urgent matter. *So much for my peaceful evening.*

3

It's freezing! Tricee grabbed at her blanket. It was the middle of January, one of the coldest months in the big city. Chicago was well known for its wintry weather. The winter season began in November and lasted until somewhere around April. As far as Tricee was concerned, winter started in late October. She often wondered why she'd ever decided to relocate to the Windy City in the first place. But as soon as winter came to an end, she thought about all that the city had to offer during the warmer months. She'd fallen in love with the place, which made it very easy for her to stay put.

As she lay awake in her bed on this cold Saturday morning, she thought of all the summer festivals and how she would attempt to attend each and every one. She felt that Chicago was, indeed, the place to be if you loved the outdoors. And there were so many restaurants to choose from that, when she first arrived five years ago, she dined at as many places as she could. But that got old fast when she realized she was spending way too much money. She was always happy to see many of her favorite restaurants at the Taste of Chicago, an annual food festival that lasted for 10 days. You had to remember, though, that you were only allowed a *taste* of what the restaurants had to offer, and you really could not complain when you handed over your tickets to the vendors in exchange for your food. Tricee learned that lesson the first time she attended the festival.

Along with the festival was live entertainment to be enjoyed by all. Although she loved the various music festivals, the Gospel Fest was by far her favorite and she'd attended faithfully for the past five years. She loved the music and observing different people from all walks of life getting their praise on! *How wonderful it would be if folks behaved like this all the time*, she would often wonder. She would ensure that her workday ended right at 5:00 PM sharp and that her girlfriends would meet her near the main stage. They would not leave until the last gospel group or soloist, whoever was scheduled, had performed.

With no desire to leave the comfort of her warm bed, Tricee pulled the blanket up to her chin. "Lord, summer cannot get here quick enough," she mumbled. She'd promised Pam that she would accompany her to the Lincolnwood Mall, their favorite mall located in Lincolnwood, Illinois. It was less than a 20-minute drive from her north side condo and far better than shopping downtown. Both Tricee and Pam agreed that downtown was much too crowded for shopping so they avoided it as much as possible. There were a few exceptions, though. If there was something Tricee wanted to purchase and she knew for certain that only a particular shop downtown carried the item, she would make the trip. Now, as much as she wanted to go shopping for a pair of black corduroys, she simply changed her mind. She hoped that Pam would understand. The weatherman had stated that the temperature was going to be 20 degrees, too cold to even consider going out unless you had to.

She decided instead that she would spend her Saturday relaxing and catching up on various projects. She could think of many things she could accomplish that she'd been putting off, not to mention studying the book of Isaiah, as she had been slacking in her Bible study in the past couple of weeks.

Tricee had given her life back to Christ a couple of years prior but only recently began to discuss her spiritual walk with Pam. It was not that she lacked the desire to share her faith, it was just that she believed timing was everything. She knew Pam well enough to know the importance of catching her on one of her "good days." Unlike others, who were at least willing to listen no matter what mood they were in, it was an entirely different story with Pam. And she'd learned from past experience that folks who were new creatures in Christ were generally very excited to share their newfound faith. This wasn't a bad thing, but she could recall becoming a little irritated on a couple of occasions when the newly saved seemed quite determined to force their beliefs upon her. Tricee did not want to be that person. She believed it was all in the manner in which it was presented. She was thankful that a few of the people she'd witnessed to had become born again. And whenever someone would inform her of their born again status, she would quote the scripture from *Proverbs 11:30 – the fruit of the righteous is a tree of life: and he that winneth souls is wise*. She felt that this way, she was only confirming what the Word had already said.

On one occasion after becoming newly saved, Tricee, unintentionally, almost lost the friendship of her friend and neighbor Karen due to her lack of knowledge on effective witnessing. She'd failed to realize that not everyone had a burning desire for the Lord like she felt they should. Her excitement to share His word, during this particular incident, helped her to understand the excitement of those who had once tried to witness to her.

When Karen and Tricee first met, Tricee knew that it had everything to do with fate. They lived in the same building and they both had purchased a condo in the same month. And, incidentally, they'd used the same realtor. They met one Saturday evening in the laundry room not long after they had moved in.

Although Tricee would not describe their friendship as close, she liked Karen a lot and they shared many similar interests. Both women were into yoga and agreed that a fitness routine was an absolute must. Also, they both could spend hours by the lake reading and they both felt it was a great way to spend time alone. They would exchange books and then arrange to meet at a later date to discuss them in detail. Diahann Carroll was their favorite actress. They felt that she was elegant, classy, and very beautiful. The movie *Claudine* was their all-time favorite.

Tricee asked Karen one morning over coffee, "Who is your favorite actor?"

Karen closed her eyes and replied, "Girl, Sidney Poitier."

Tricee almost passed out. One would have thought that she'd just won the lottery the way she let out a loud shriek, causing the older black couple who sat at the next table to jump.

"Sidney Poitier!" she said with her eyes open wide. She had stopped stirring her hot cup of Chai tea, "Oh my goodness! I love me some Sidney Poitier! And talk about handsome!"

They both giggled like two teenagers and commented in unison, "That was one fine man in his younger years." Karen had been amused by Tricee's behavior that morning as it had been a while since she'd met a sister who was so funny.

"Did you see him in *Lilies of the Field*?" Tricee asked. "And what about that movie when the white sheriff slapped him and Sidney Poitier slapped him right back?!"

"I do remember that scene!" Karen chimed in. "But I cannot, for the life of me, recall the name of the movie. I believe it was either *In the Heat of the Night* or *They Call Me Mr. Tibbs*." They spent at least a half hour discussing Mr. Poitier.

"And, oh, how I would have loved to have been one of those nuns starring with him in *Lilies of the Field*," said Tricee, closing her eyes and shaking her head.

Karen stared at her in disbelief. "A nun?! Girlfriend, if I were to star in a movie opposite Mr. Poitier, it would not be in the role of a nun!"

The two women laughed so hard they were in tears. It had been this conversation that helped to seal their friendship.

As the older black couple who had been sitting nearby was leaving the coffee shop, the woman stopped by their table. She whispered softly, "I still feel faint whenever I see that Sidney Poitier on television." She then laughed and nodded discreetly toward her husband who stood by the door. "Roger had better be glad that he got to me first." She winked at Tricee and Karen as she turned to walk away. Tricee and Karen laughed so hard that they were both holding their sides.

Tricee chuckled as she recalled that morning at the coffee shop. Unfortunately, she and Karen, not long after that incident, would have a conversation that would not end on such a good note. It would be a conversation about Karen's salvation that would cause the two women to go weeks without speaking.

She'd attended the mid-week service at her church one Wednesday evening. The message that evening was "Witnessing to Others: Our Role as Servants." She left church that evening feeling the joy of being surrounded by God's love and was eager to share her feelings.

The two were in Karen's apartment the Saturday evening after Tricee had heard the mid-week message on witnessing. She'd felt that the timing of the message had been a sign from above and that it was meant for her to share. She was certain that it had been the prompting of the Holy Spirit and not her own thinking that would lead her to discuss with Karen her need for the Lord. They had just watched a popular minister on television, one known for preaching the "prosperity gospel." They easily discussed their feelings about the minister's message, but the conversation would soon take a turn for the worst. When Tricee attempted to inform Karen of how her life would change for the better if only she'd allow God to take control, Karen became upset.

"Life doesn't become an easy ride, Tricee, just because a person becomes a member of a church." Her tone of voice had been a good indicator of how she felt. Immediately after Karen's comment, Tricee received a phone call from one of the women from church. During her brief conversation, she could not help but to notice the scowl on Karen's face.

The woman had called to inquire if she would be attending the retreat that was planned for the end of the month. Tricee had planned to attend and had considered asking her three girlfriends to join her. She had not yet considered asking Karen, but after their tension-filled conversation and the look on Karen's face as she ended her phone call, Tricee thought it best to forego extending her the invitation.

"A person's problem doesn't disappear just because they can recite a verse or two," said Karen as soon as she observed Tricee placing her cell phone back on the table. She could not wait until Tricee was off the phone. She was more than ready to give her a piece of her mind.

Tricee sat silent. She sipped from the glass of peach iced tea that Karen had prepared. She wanted to make sure that Karen was done before she made any comment. After a few moments of silence, Karen reached over to her coffee table and picked up her latest issue of *Essence* magazine. She began to quickly turn the pages, indicating to Tricee that she was done saying her piece.

Tricee exhaled. "Well, I'm only saying, Karen, that lately you seem to be experiencing some unpleasant issues. First, it was your work. You were complaining just last week about how you were ready to quit. And yesterday you were complaining about the guy you have recently begun to date."

"Excuse me," Karen's neck did a hundred degree turn, "but the last time I checked, these were normal issues that every human will encounter."

Karen emphasized the words *every human* with her neck rolling simultaneously. Tricee knew then that she'd struck a nerve.

Karen's reaction caused Tricee to believe that maybe she did sound more like a lecturer than someone who was trying to witness. She felt that perhaps the Holy Spirit was nudging her to be careful in what to say next.

Karen angrily tossed the magazine back onto the coffee table. Tricee regretted that she'd upset Karen but it had not been intentional.

"All I'm saying, Karen, is that prayer changes things." Tricee stood and grabbed her purse. "I'm sorry that you are upset. Maybe I should just leave." She picked up the empty glass and was about to walk toward Karen's kitchen until Karen stood up to stop her.

"Don't bother. I'll get it." Tricee slowly set the glass back on the table. The two women were now standing face-to-face with the coffee table being the only thing separating them.

Tricee could not help but think how much Karen subtly resembled the model Iman. At 5'11" with smooth, brown skin, Karen rarely wore makeup. And her shoulder-length, dark brown hair was always coifed, even if it was styled in a ponytail. Her long neck appeared to stretch when she was angry and Tricee had to fake a cough to keep from laughing. She was by no means making light of the situation, but the way Karen looked standing there, obviously angry, with her outstretched neck, was surely a sight to see. Tricee was certain that she had not been the only one to ever observe Karen's overly dramatic behavior.

"Thanks for the tea," Tricee said as she gathered her cell phone and new gospel CD that featured different gospel artists. She'd brought the CD with her so that Karen could hear it. But that was not about to happen, at least not during this visit.

Tricee walked to the door and turned to apologize once more. "I'm sorry, Karen."

After this incident, Karen made every attempt to avoid Tricee. They had run into each other a couple of times in the lobby where Karen allowed Tricee to take the elevator while she waited for the next one. It bothered Tricee but she said nothing. She felt it best to give Karen her much-needed space.

But even though that incident had caused a rift in their friendship, it had taught Tricee a valuable lesson about witnessing to others. It had taught her not to assume that others would agree with her beliefs, opinions, or advice, even if she believed that the Holy Spirit was involved. Tricee realized that God uses His children, but that the outcome is sometimes not what we might expect. She also concluded that sometimes listening is all that is needed and she vowed to sharpen her listening skills.

Ever since that conversation with Karen, Tricee decided it would be best to try a different approach, which was simply this: to inform others of how her life had changed since becoming born again.

After reflecting upon that moment with Karen, Tricee glanced at the clock to see that it was now 10:00 AM. She was to get together with Pam around Noon. She climbed out of bed and walked over to her dresser. *Pam is usually very good about calling whenever we have plans to meet.* She turned on her cell phone. It showed two missed calls but neither was from Pam.

I hope she is okay with me canceling. Tricee walked back over to her bed while dialing Pam's number. *She's going to have to be.*

Pam answered on the fourth ring. Tricee couldn't help but to notice the excitement in her voice. "Hey, Tricee! I was just about to call you!" Pam said gleefully.

"Well, I guess I beat you to it. And I might add that you sound pretty cheery this morning." Tricee reached into her nightstand for a bottle of aspirin. "What's going on with you, Miss Thing?"

"Girl, you know I am always happy—well, most of the time. Besides, what is there not to be cheery about?"

"The fact that I am about to cancel our plans for today might qualify as a reason," Tricee said as she began to laugh. "Sorry, I couldn't resist."

"Oh, she got jokes this morning," Pam responded. "Actually, I was going to cancel, as well. My change of plans just occurred last night," she smiled, "and I didn't want to call you so late."

Tricee looked up toward the ceiling. *Thank you. I owe you one*, she thought. She swallowed two aspirins and drank what was left of a bottle of water.

"So there," said Pam.

"I guess the joke is now on me, huh?" asked Tricee. They both laughed. "May I ask what your change of plans might be or am I being too nosy?"

"You're being nosy."

"Okay. Duly noted," said Tricee as she lay back on her bed. "But at least I asked for permission to ask you first." Tricee was certain that Pam's sudden change of plans had something to do with Jeff, the gentleman she was currently dating.

"Aw, girlfriend, you know I don't mind you asking," said Pam. Tricee could hear Pam smiling and feel her exuberance through the phone. "Jeff and I are hanging out this afternoon. He wants to take me to that new restaurant in Old Town for lunch."

"Oh, that's nice," Tricee responded. "Be sure to tell me how it was."

"I will. He also mentioned something about a surprise he has for me. I am not exactly sure what it is but he did catch me eyeing this nice jacket the last time we were together." She shrugged, "But who knows? I guess I'll have to wait and see."

"You guys are getting serious."

"I don't know about all of that. We've only been seeing each other for a few months."

"A few months is long enough. Especially if he is buying you gifts, Pam."

"Who said anything about a gift?" asked Pam. "A surprise could be something other than a gift."

"I stand corrected. Sorry." Tricee made a face. Hadn't she just said something about a jacket? Duh!

Tricee wanted to avoid a tense conversation, especially since she was experiencing a slight headache. She was careful to not come off as if she was being too opinionated. She'd had many conversations with her girlfriends about men and relationships, and they were all quick to voice their opinion.

"I suppose only time will tell," Pam said. "Oh, and get this—this evening he's cooking dinner for us at his place, something he suggested." Pam picked up the beige sweater she was considering wearing. "I just hope the brother can cook because sister girl is not good at preparing last-minute dishes."

Tricee laughed. It was a known fact among the four friends that Pam could not find her way around anybody's kitchen, including her own. Jackie, Val, and Tricee would tease her constantly about her lack of cooking skills. They'd ask, "How are you the oldest of five children and don't know how to cook? Wasn't there ever a time when you were left in charge of your younger siblings?" Pam would respond, "Yes, and that's why someone created hot dogs and peanut butter and jelly sandwiches."

Tricee chuckled. "Yes, that would be an emergency situation."

"We'll end up ordering a pizza and calling it a night."

"Well, it sounds like you have a wonderful day ahead. You guys are spending practically the whole day together. I am sure you will have a nice time." Tricee paused. "But please, girlfriend, do not make the man do anything he is not ready for," she laughed. This was actually her way of telling Pam to not do anything she'd regret later. They both laughed.

"I thought you were a Christian," said Pam.

"I am," Tricee responded. "And I'm human, too."

Tricee was aware of how her friend felt about Jeff, and so were Jackie and Val. They knew that Pam was looking for a long-term relationship and that she wanted that with Jeff. But Pam had shared with them how Jeff had stated on three separate occasions that he was not ready for a committed relationship. The friends all felt that Pam seemed happy enough with her and Jeff's arrangement, and as long as she was happy, that was all that mattered.

Pam told Tricee once that she believed that Jeff would change his mind in time. It was obvious that Pam remained hopeful that things between her and Jeff would soon change. Tricee was not so convinced, and the last time she attempted to discuss with Pam her true feelings about Jeff and how he seemed to want a relationship that benefited him only, Pam made it perfectly clear that she was not interested in her views. She told Tricee, "I know you mean well, but let me deal with this."

"Oh, look at the time! I better get going," said Pam. "It's freezing out. I need extra layers."

"Yes, and be sure to cover your head," said Tricee.

"Yes, ma'am," Pam replied. But before they ended the conversation, she asked Tricee about her plans. "So what's on your agenda for the day?"

"I have several projects to work on—not job-related, just some things I've been meaning to get to." She did not share with Pam how studying the Bible was one of the things she'd planned. That topic would have likely taken their conversation to a whole other level.

"Alrighty then," Pam said. "Do enjoy the day. We'll chat soon."

"Okay, girl. Talk with you later."

After they said their good-byes, Tricee showered, got dressed and then proceeded to the kitchen. She toasted two slices of wheat bread and microwaved some water for a hot cup of tea. Her projects consumed most of the day and she was left with only a little time to study the book of Isaiah. She opened her Bible and began to read. Her kitchen was where she did most of her Bible study. It was one of her favorite spots in the condo, not to mention she liked the idea of being close to the refrigerator.

She took a bite of the tuna salad she'd prepared for lunch, which was now an early dinner, and began to read. Although she felt tired, she was so into the words from this major prophet that she continued to read. She highlighted key verses, something she always did whenever she studied the Word, and made notes in the margin. It was 6 PM by the time she closed her Bible and headed for the living room to watch television. She was surprised to receive a phone call from Pam.

"Hey, it's me," Pam whispered.

"Are you okay?" Tricee became concerned.

"Yeah, I'm fine." Pam did not sound like she had earlier.

"Where are you? Are you with Jeff?"

"Yes...," Pam hesitated. "Hey, I'll call you later, okay?"

"Pam?" Tricee repeated her name but she had already hung up. She dialed Pam's number but the call went straight to voicemail.

Wonder what that was all about? She raised an eyebrow as she headed for the kitchen.

4

Friday evening: August 2nd

"Hello, dear. Am I catching you at a good time?" *Absolutely not!* Tricee had to catch herself from talking out loud. Her mother's voice sounded different but Tricee was none too surprised. Her mother's moods changed like the weather, and whatever mood she was in usually determined the direction of their conversations. They had just spoken on Wednesday so Tricee was not expecting to hear from her again until the middle of next week. Their phone calls were now taking place at least once a week, which was a progression from once every two weeks. And Tricee no longer waited for her mother to initiate the phone calls. Although their relationship was still strained, there had been a little improvement.

"Hi, Ruby, how are you?"

Ruby sighed. She didn't really like that her only daughter referred to her by her first name.

"I'm just fine, dear. How are things at work?"

"A raise is forthcoming. So, of course, that means work is keeping me busy."

"Oh, how wonderful, dear. More money is something we can all use." There was a brief silence. "Do you have any days you can use?"

Her question immediately caused Tricee to become skeptical. "Is everything alright?"

"Yes, everything is fine." Ruby was quick to respond. "A friend from work is visiting Chicago in two weeks." She hesitated and Tricee could hear her exhale through the phone. "She has family there and rarely has the opportunity to visit. She is aware that my daughter lives there so she asked if I wanted to come along."

"Oh." Tricee was stunned. This was not what she'd expected to hear. It was not that she did not wish for her mother to visit—in fact, she thought it might be a good idea—but it was one of those things that Tricee needed to prepare for.

"Bev and I— "

"Bev?" Tricee could not recall her mother ever mentioning a friend by the name of Bev.

"Yes, Bev and I have already booked two rooms at one of the hotels downtown."

Tricee continued to listen in silence.

"It would only be for a weekend. We'd fly in on a Friday and leave early on Monday." Ruby realized that Tricee's silence meant that she was surprised to hear of her plans, and Ruby was now starting to feel uncomfortable with the conversation. She dreaded the thought of visiting her daughter, especially due to the circumstances. But the visit was inevitable. Tricee had no clue as to her mother's motives for wanting to visit so suddenly. She only knew that something did not seem quite right.

Ruby had always believed that life was unfair and that there were just some things that were not easily fixed. One of the things she disliked about Tricee was her inability to accept that life was not always a bed of roses. It seemed to Ruby that Tricee lived more in a fairy land and not the real world. She had once told a friend when Tricee was only 2 years old, "If I had to do it over again, I never would have had this child."

Ruby made the comment after Tricee's father, now her ex-husband, had stayed out late one evening. When Ruby inquired as to where he'd been until midnight, he simply stated, "I went to the bar after work for a drink." It had been the truth but his answer was unacceptable. As far as Ruby was concerned, a man with a wife and a 2-year-old daughter was not supposed to stay out until midnight, no matter where he'd been. It would have been unacceptable for a woman, especially a woman with a small child. So why should a man have a different set of rules to play by? Ruby felt that women received the short end of the stick and that things had not changed much since she was younger.

Ruby had worked full time since Tricee was 13 years old. Prior to working full time, she held a part-time position as a caregiver for the elderly. J.P., her husband at the time, had been employed with the city of St. Louis as a machinist. His salary had allowed him to provide a comfortable living for his wife and only daughter whom he cherished with all of his heart. Pumpkin Spice was his nickname for the brown-skinned little girl who looked a lot like her father.

Everyone who met the Miller family was certain that theirs was a happy one. Ruby and J.P. had done fairly well at keeping others in the dark about the issues that existed in their marriage—

with the exception of one of Ruby's friends. But soon after Tricee turned 11, things in their household became worse and more unpleasant. J.P. was no longer able to keep up the facade. They divorced and J.P. put in a transfer at work and relocated to the state of Kentucky.

Afterward, 11-year-old Tricee asked, "What's wrong? Why don't you and daddy love each other anymore?"

Ruby responded, "We're just not getting along."

She'd shown no emotion, which confused her bright and curious daughter. "But doesn't that make you sad, mom?" She had never seen her mother cry and she found that very disturbing.

After her divorce, Ruby attended a secretarial school, a good alternative in those days to college, and received her certificate in two years. She'd felt she needed more income for her and her daughter and had grown tired of her role as a caregiver. The alimony and child support helped but, for Ruby, it was just not enough. She was able to secure a position as a secretary for one of the local government agencies in St. Louis, working her way up to senior secretary.

Now, at the age of 57, Ruby maintained an active lifestyle. She worked and also volunteered for two community organizations near her home. Not one to attend church regularly—something her daughter was not happy about—she "believed in God" and said that was all that was needed. She never remarried. Tricee was not even sure if her mother dated or if she had anyone special in her life. The topic was one that the two women had yet to discuss but, little did Tricee know, this was all about to change. In fact, a lot of things were about to change for the both of them.

Tricee finally broke her silence. "What time will you arrive?" *I hope you change your mind by then.*

"I believe the flight arrives at 10:05 in the morning, but let me confirm and I will call you back with all of the details."

"I will try to take that Friday off. What date are we talking about?" Tricee was ready to get off the phone. It was 10:40 PM and she was tired, but she decided to ask pertinent questions in order to process the information she'd just been given.

"August 16th. And I am sorry if this is too short of notice," said Ruby, now sounding very tired, as well.

When Tricee did not respond her mother continued to talk. "Jentrice, I need to talk to you about some things, and that is part of the reason for this trip."

"It must be important since it requires you to pay a visit." Tricee sighed. "Can't we just talk about it over the phone?" she asked, feeling a little flustered. "I mean, not tonight but some other time?"

It was not her mother's phone call that caused her to feel uneasy, although it was an unspoken rule between them that Fridays were generally not the best time to call. It was her mother's plans to visit on such short notice that had her feeling anxious. And this important thing she wanted to discuss was not helping. Tricee wanted so much to not allow her mother's phone call to steal her joy for the evening but, for now, that was easier said than done. This Christian principle she was trying to adhere to was not working.

"Mother, I'll call you tomorrow. I need to go to bed." As far as Tricee was concerned, this conversation had run its course.

"Okay, we'll talk tomorrow. Bye, dear." *Click.*

Tricee failed to say goodbye. She just hung up. She sat in her recliner with her arms folded. Her first impulse was to call either Pam or Jackie but she knew the calls would likely go straight into voicemail. They were in a noisy environment and it was unlikely that they'd even hear their phones. Tricee knew from firsthand experience that whenever they went out to this particular place, they would not leave before midnight. Knowing that it was not a great time to call anyone, she still had the irresistible desire to reach out to one of her friends. All she'd wanted minutes earlier was to crawl into her bed.

She reached for her cell phone and thought about calling Val until she remembered what Pam had said earlier about Val and her husband, Cory, having plans for the evening. She thought about Annette, her best friend from St. Louis, and remembered that she was traveling this weekend for work. Tricee was not about to phone Netta to discuss her issues while she was on business.

Netta was attending a three-day lawyer's conference in Houston. She'd informed Tricee about her trip when they'd spoken last week. She'd also emailed Tricee some pictures of the hotel where the conference was being held. Her email had read, *Check out this fabulous place where I get to spend three whole days with a bunch of lawyers. I so wanted my hubby to come along, but being around a bunch of attorneys—even his own wife—would have been too much-lol.*

The four women Tricee could call upon when she needed to vent were not available. She had other acquaintances, but discussing her personal business with them was not an option. Karen was in this category. There were some things she had not revealed to Karen, such as her strained relationship with her mother. And Karen was such a private person herself that she had not shared much of her personal business with Tricee, either. Unfortunately, Karen was not an option for a late-night phone call.

With a sigh and her cell phone resting in her hand, Tricee sent a text message to Pam: *Give me a call tonight—if you can.*

She was now distracted by her thoughts. What did her mother need to discuss? Why did she give only two-weeks' notice for her visit? She believed her mother's plans to visit were in the making some time ago. She believed Ruby was behaving selfishly by not informing her of her plans to visit sooner. Surely, Ruby had to have known how things worked in the working world. A two weeks' notice was fine for an employer. It just didn't seem right to give someone such short notice if you were planning to visit them. And Tricee wasn't buying the "my friend from work asked me if I wanted to come along" story.

Maybe Aunt Janice could clue me in as to what's going on. She thought back to a conversation she'd had with her aunt. It had occurred during Labor Day weekend, four months after Tricee had overheard her mother's unpleasant comment about the course of her professional life. Tricee had traveled home to spend the holiday with family. Her Aunt Janice had volunteered the two of them to do the shopping for the family gathering. Tricee was fine with this because it would allow her to spend some time with her favorite aunt. They were very close as Aunt Janice was more like an older sister. They both understood that whatever was discussed between them would not go any further. And so it was during this particular visit when Aunt Janice broached the subject of Tricee's success.

"Tricee, you have to believe in yourself because depending on someone else to believe in you is not an option. I am very proud of you. You have accomplished so much."

"Thank you, Aunt Janice. It means a lot to me to hear you say that," Tricee had responded with a lump forming in her throat. *If only those words could have come from the mouth of my own mother.*

Tricee knew that her mother shared just about everything with her younger sister so she decided to give her aunt a call first thing in the morning. She would be subtle while probing for information. She hoped that this whole situation would make more sense after she had spoken with her aunt. Maybe her aunt could help her to see the issue from a different perspective and free her mind of these nagging thoughts.

"I need a good night's rest," Tricee said softly. She walked over to her tan sofa with the plush, comfortable pillows, and picked up the remote. Many times she'd fallen asleep right on the sofa, only to wake up during the middle of the night and go climb into her bed.

While switching through the channels, she came across the 1934 movie version of *Imitation of Life* with Claudette Colbert and Louise Beavers. The movie was a classic and a tear-jerker for many who had seen it. It was one of Tricee's favorites. She thought the acting in it was superb. And the 1959 version of the movie included the late Mahalia Jackson, whose voice Tricee had always loved. She had seen both versions of the movie at least five times.

The light-skinned actress in the movie who played the daughter was ashamed of her own mother. This had been discussed amongst Tricee and her friends. "How sad is that? To be ashamed of your own mother?" they'd say each time the movie was being discussed. She tossed the remote to the floor and proceeded to watch the movie only to be interrupted by an interesting thought. *How ironic that this movie would be showing not long after a conversation with my mother*? Was this some sort of a sign? Tricee tried to dismiss the thought. She'd never been ashamed of her mother. They did not always see eye-to-eye but she never denied her own mother. She believed that a mother-daughter relationship was supposed to be the closest relationship on earth. She'd felt strongly that a mother-daughter bond was not meant to be easily broken. It didn't matter that this was obviously not the case for her and her mother. It was just the way she felt.

But the movie had caused her to pause and wonder. Her emotions began to settle and she watched the movie in its entirety. It was 3:00 AM when she finally fell asleep.

Tricee woke up at 7:00 AM having slept only four hours. She sat up on her sofa and glanced around the living room. Her body ached all over. She rose from the sofa, walked over to her cordless phone and called her mother. There were no second thoughts as she dialed Ruby's number. She left a message on the answering machine: "I am sorry for the early morning phone call but I just remembered that I am traveling for work on August 16th. It is likely that I will be gone for a few days, possibly the whole week, so I will not be available when you visit."

5

"Girl, you are my inspiration. I need to set aside time on a Saturday to study," said Val.

"I admit I have been slacking lately. So I made a deal with Father."

Tricee had managed to get halfway through the book of Isaiah. Val called just as she was finishing up chapter 34.

"Now you know we're not supposed to make deals with Jesus," Val said, laughing. "And I love how you refer to Him as "Father." You can just feel the love."

"I'm glad it's noticeable."

"So what was the deal you made?"

Tricee let out a giggle. "It's too embarrassing."

"Then why did you mention it?" asked Val as she shook her head. She could always count on Tricee to make her laugh, even when God was the topic of conversation.

"I'll tell you about it one day, but not today."

"Okay, chickadee. Suit yourself. But in the meantime, let me get off this phone." Val turned and smiled at her husband, Cory. "I need to think about what I'm cooking for dinner before I find myself making deals with Father to send me a new husband."

"This is true," Cory uttered in the background. He smiled as he patted his wife on the backside.

"I heard him," Tricee said, smiling. "Hey, before you go, let me leave you with this." Val was all ears as Tricee quoted the last verse in chapter 34.

"Amen," Val said. "Thanks for sharing."

Tricee had recently purchased a study guide to go along with the book of Isaiah. But until this morning it was still wrapped in its original package. Procrastination and a hectic work schedule were to blame. She had been so busy at work that by the weekend, all she wanted to do was catch up on some much-needed rest.

January was one of the busiest months at the university. Everything from the meetings that had taken place back in November and December had to be finalized by the end of the month. This was to ensure that the executives and CEOs of the participating organizations would not have an opportunity to change their minds. There had been only two occasions when that had happened before and Tricee vowed to do whatever she could to see that it did not happen again, at least not while she held the position.

Her rationale was simple. Most people were motivated by dollars and cents but she was a big proponent of education, which left her feeling elated when new partnerships were developed. Many of these programs provided the students with more opportunities to work in their respective fields prior to graduating. This was a win-win situation, especially for the student.

Tricee rarely allowed her schedule to interfere with her Bible time and she was not too fond of using that as an excuse. Her grandmother used to say, "The Lord gave us His one and only son; we can at least give Him a couple of hours each day." Tricee's grandmother was considered very religious. In fact, she was considered a little too religious by her friends and family. But it was her sense of humor and the way she treated others that made her so special. She lived by the golden rule: Do unto others as you would have them do unto you.

Grandma Eda, her paternal grandmother, had raised Tricee's father and his two siblings in the church. She had them convinced that the angels attended church every Sunday to ensure that they would be there. "The angels come to church on Sundays to make sure the little children are there," she'd say. Tricee's father and his younger brother shared with Tricee once how they had become afraid to miss church. They would spend the service looking around for the angels. Tricee's aunt, who was a year older than her father, would laugh, saying that she'd known as a child that angels did not come to church and that she would ignore her mother's tale. She still teased her two younger brothers to this day for being so gullible.

Although Tricee knew that her 85-year-old grandmother used to be something of a jokester, she took her words of wisdom to heart. It had taken her a long time to accept that she was only human and that God was not keeping score on the number of times she missed studying the Bible. The cold weather today had been a good thing, however. It had provided her with an opportunity to stay indoors and get caught up, just as she'd planned.

She did her laundry and vacuumed her entire condo. She also finally got around to rearranging some of the pictures that hung on her walls. The framed artwork of an African American woman holding a child looked better in her bedroom, so she hung it over her bed. She felt the framed artwork of four African American women getting pedicures by four African American men belonged in the living room for direct observation. It would serve as a reminder to her and her guests that women deserved to be treated like queens. She moved it to the wall right above the sofa.

Tricee had an appreciation for art in its various forms and attempted to support a few of the local artists. One of her neighbors, a young white male in his late 20s, was one of those artists. He was tall and very slender with reddish hair and freckles. He was a history teacher who loved to create art as a side job. He also considered it a hobby and had told Tricee that relaxation was, in itself, a form of art. "I am most relaxed when I am painting," he'd said.

His artwork was beautiful. Tricee did not hesitate to purchase one of his paintings when they'd first met. The piece contained clear blue water with a few clouds scattered above. An eagle was hovering near the clouds. An empty wooden chair sat a few feet from the water, a small open book lay beside it. For Tricee, it was the perfect picture of serenity. She would imagine she was sitting in the chair, alone with the book. Reading did for her what painting did for her neighbor.

The picture hung in the entry hall where it was easily noticed. The only way someone could miss it is if they walked into her condo with their eyes closed. There had yet to be a person who visited her who had not commented on this picture. Tricee believed that you could tell a lot about a person's personality by what they kept in their dwelling, so she decorated her condo to reflect her peaceful nature.

After completing her house chores, she decided to go online briefly to check her emails. Her boss was not shy about sending her emails over the weekend, but Tricee would only respond if it was something really urgent. Otherwise, it could wait until Monday morning. Her boss was a pleasant woman but her one fault was that she had not learned how to leave work at work. Tricee liked her boss and, on most days, enjoyed working for her, but she wished the middle-aged woman from Peru would learn to relax more.

As she checked her email messages, Tricee broke out into a huge grin.

Hi, Tricee. I know it has been a while since we've spoken via cyberspace but things have been pretty hectic here lately. I know that sounds so cliché, doesn't it? However, it is true and I can imagine you must be keeping very busy, as well. I have so much to share with you and I'd like to hear all that has been happening with you. I'll be in Chicago on business soon and would love to get together! Kind regards, Kenzie.

P.S. Are you still seeing that guy you were telling me about? The one who thought he had to touch you each time he said a vowel? LOL

"Ha!" Tricee laughed. *Get it right, Kenzie. It was only two outings,* she thought to herself.

Tricee smiled as she typed her reply. "*Kenzie, it's so nice to hear from you, as always. Keep me posted on your travel plans to the Windy City. Best, Tricee.*

P.S. I stopped seeing Mr. Hands after the second date. ☺

Tricee and Kenzie had managed to stay in touch via email. They'd spoken over the phone three or four times since graduating from college. They met in a psychology class during their sophomore year. Their friendship was genuine. They made a promise to each other to keep in touch after leaving college and their friendship had been strong enough that their promise was kept. It had been at least three months since the two women had exchanged emails so Tricee was elated at the prospect of seeing her college pal.

When Tricee and Kenzie met, they were both naïve college students searching for a comfort zone on their college campus. Freshman year had been all about getting acclimated to their new surroundings, but by sophomore year they were trying to "fit in" with the right group. Neither of them had the answers as to how to make that happen as fitting in had been something one did in high school. But it all worked out in the end as both young women learned the importance of a healthy self-esteem.

When Tricee saw Kenzie strolling into Intro to Psychology on the first day of class, she'd assumed that the goal of the blonde-haired, attractive 20-year-old was to date the star athlete on campus. It was a bad assumption. Tricee told herself that she would never prejudge anyone again; she would allow herself the opportunity to get to know a person first. But she was only 20 at the time, so she allowed herself to excuse her shallowness. She had wondered if Kenzie had prejudged her. She thought it was very likely but they'd never discussed it.

During their time as undergraduate students, the two women

would form a friendship that they described as unique and special. The openness they shared with each other made it so. Kenzie liked to describe it as "fate."

Kenzie admitted to Tricee one day after class as they walked across campus that she was terribly insecure and unsure of herself. Tricee had felt the same way. They would soon find out that many of their fellow college peers had also felt this way. Tricee was not sure of what Kenzie had been told prior to entering college, but she knew what had been drilled into her mind as well as the minds of her friends from high school: *You must work harder than your white peers. Study hard and make good grades. And stay true to yourself.*

Tricee ended up spending several more minutes online, reading articles after checking her emails. She thought about how a lot had changed since college. After reading an article about an incident that had happened recently, she thought again of Kenzie.

She'd learned a lot about herself over the years and her views on certain issues had changed. The many conversations she'd had with Kenzie had taught both of them some valuable lessons on race and the impact race relations had in this country. They discussed everything from guys and the latest fashions on campus to the many stereotypes people held.

Tricee was surprised to learn just how comical Kenzie could be. Until college, the laughs that made you wet your pants had all been caused by black folks. It wasn't that Tricee thought that only black people had the ability to make you laugh, it had just been her experience. Kenzie changed all of that. She had arrived 10 minutes late to class on the first day after the lecture had begun. The only seat available was the one next to Tricee. The seat behind Kenzie was occupied by a white male student who looked as if he had not slept in days. He was literally leaning over in the chair; his eyes opening and closing as he fought hard to stay awake. As soon as Kenzie sat down the young man suddenly perked up.

The activity at the back of the lecture hall distracted the professor and made him look up, an annoyed expression plastered across his face. Kenzie's presence had obviously awakened the student who would lean over every few minutes as if to whisper in her ear. It was now Kenzie who became annoyed. She leaned over to Tricee and whispered, "Who is this greaseball and why is he breathing down my neck?" Tricee had to cover her mouth to keep from laughing. The professor heard the commotion and looked up once again with the same annoyed expression. Tricee found herself laughing out loud as she reminisced.

After the first day of class was over, Kenzie introduced herself to Tricee, all the while trying to ignore the student who had sat behind her. He waited anxiously, hoping to introduce himself, but he would have no such luck. As he came walking toward them, Kenzie grabbed Tricee by the hand and led her out of the lecture hall. Once outside of the building and with an arm full of books, Kenzie began to run; Tricee having no other choice but to run with her. There were a few stares from some of the other students as they watched two women, one white and one black, run hand-in-hand across campus. By the time they were out of the young man's sight, they were both doubled over laughing. It had become official on that warm day in August—Kenzie was, as Tricee would tell her after they stopped laughing, "a bona fide nut." She'd meant that in the best possible way and that was how Kenzie received it. For the next two years, the two women would share many humorous moments.

There was an incident one evening that wasn't meant to be funny, but given the way it happened, Tricee laughed each time she thought about it.

One evening during exam week, Tricee and Kenzie were studying in Tricee's dorm room. Kenzie had become upset after her roommate asked her to "get lost for a few hours." The roommate's boyfriend was coming over and she needed some privacy. Kenzie was forever complaining about her roommate's constant need for privacy. She had called Tricee that evening complaining about her roommate. "I can't believe her inconsideration, not allowing me the option of studying in my own room. Gee whiz, this boyfriend of hers probably won't be around after the semester ends. And why isn't she studying? It's exam week!"

Tricee invited Kenzie to study with her since her roommate preferred the study halls for intense study sessions. For Tricee and Kenzie, this particular study session would turn out to be the most memorable. Tricee sat in front of her computer, shaking her head and chuckling as she recalled the event:

After taking a break from studying, which they'd done for hours at that point, Kenzie decided to showcase her talent for giving and memorizing speeches. Tricee was not prepared for what would happen next. As she flipped through the pages of a magazine, sipping soda that had turned flat, she looked up and saw a bright-eyed Kenzie standing on the desk chair that belonged to her roommate. There Kenzie stood, reciting from memory the "I Have a Dream" speech by Martin Luther King, Jr.

Tricee raised an eyebrow and thought, what in the world is she doing? She wasn't sure if Kenzie was making an attempt at being funny or if she was trying to prove her knowledge of famous African Americans. What is she trying to do? Tricee thought to herself. Show me she's down for the cause?

As Kenzie continued to passionately recite the speech, looking as serious as ever, Tricee realized that she was not trying to be funny nor was she attempting to make light of Dr. King's most famous speech. Tricee did not know if she should laugh or cry, so she did both. The sight of a white girl, standing on a chair, belting out the words that had once been spoken by one of the most prominent African American leaders in history had been a sight to see, indeed. Tricee had laughed because she had not been expecting it and she'd cried because it was touching.

Kenzie also cried after she was finished, which made it an emotional moment for them both. As Kenzie wiped away her tears, Tricee watched her grab more tissue and wipe the seat of the chair in which she'd been standing. Tricee found herself chuckling at Kenzie's small act of thoughtfulness. Wiping away her own tears, Tricee asked Kenzie what had prompted her to suddenly begin to recite the "I Have a Dream" speech. After blowing her nose, Kenzie replied through more tears, "I don't know, but it's such a powerful speech."

This was true. And Tricee could not help but to think how she had not known any blacks, including herself, who had memorized that speech. She knew they existed but she had not met them. To see Kenzie recite that speech had inspired Tricee to learn it herself. And she did, some years later.

Kenzie had shared with Tricee how she had an uncle who had been one of the 250,000 participants to gather in Washington on August 28, 1963, and how her parents had explained why the march was significant. And why her uncle had felt compelled to attend. She was about 6 years old when her parents showed her a picture of her now deceased uncle along with a picture of Dr. King, the man who had helped to revolutionize a nation. Even as a youngster, Kenzie would be in awe of many of the things that her parents would teach her about the important events that had taken place prior to her birth. And they would continue to teach her and make her aware of the important events that would take place after she was born.

If there was one thing that Kenzie's parents had impressed upon her it was that all people should be treated with respect. And if their behavior was unpleasant, it had nothing at all to do with the color of their skin.

Although Tricee had met other nice white people, not one of them had exhibited the qualities she'd admired in Kenzie. Not to say they did not exist; it was just that Tricee had yet to meet one who would impact her life the way Kenzie had.

As she logged off her computer, Tricee received a call from the doorman. She was not expecting anyone so she wondered who had decided to show up unexpectedly.

"Ms. Miller, you have a guest here," the doorman said. His voice was similar to the late singer Lou Rawls. "Jackie." The doorman smiled. "It's your friend Jackie."

Jackie returned the doorman's smile. *He has a nice voice.* She was tempted to flirt a little but decided against it after spotting his gold wedding band.

"Oh, thank you, sir. You may send her on up, please."

"My pleasure," said the doorman.

One of the reasons Tricee decided to purchase a two-bedroom condo, other than not being able to afford a single-family home on Chicago's north side, was the benefit of 24-hour security. There was comfort in knowing that no one could get past the doorman. It could happen, but as long as they were doing their jobs, it was not supposed to. And she had not had a problem since she'd purchased the unit.

Besides, a single-family home wouldn't have been right for Tricee. She was single, no kids, and no interest in maintaining a home. The $216 a month she paid in condo association dues took care of the maintenance and was well worth it. She realized that anything could happen anytime and anyplace, but she felt very secure with her living arrangements and appreciated the fact that visitors had to stop by the front desk first.

"Hey, lady!" Jackie walked in and hung up her coat. It was one that Tricee had not seen before. "It feels nice and warm in here. Remind me, again, why I decided to come out in all this cold."

"I have no idea but I was just about to ask," said Tricee. Jackie laughed.

"Well, first let me apologize for not calling you first. It's sort of rude to just drop in on a person."

"Oh, girl, please! I don't have a problem with my friends coming by unannounced. Besides, if I didn't wish to be bothered, I would just tell the doorman not to let you up." Tricee chuckled. "So what brings you to my neck of the woods? And where did you park?"

"I had to meet Alesia's dad downtown this morning. This is their weekend together; he's taking her shopping for a new outfit for her play tomorrow. He has to have her home tonight though, because I want to see my angel first thing in the morning all dressed up for her play." Jackie gushed at the thought of her 13-year-old daughter.

"Oh, how sweet! She is truly a daddy's girl, isn't she?" Tricee asked.

"Yes, she is! I asked her—well, actually I attempted to persuade her to forego this weekend visit with her dad so that we could go shopping and get prepared for tomorrow." Jackie rolled her eyes to the ceiling. "But she had the nerve to tell me she needs her daddy time!"

Tricee laughed as she and Jackie walked into the living room. "She wants to go shopping with her dad and not her mom—you have to love it!" said Tricee.

"I am so glad she has a good relationship with her father. He tried to talk me into letting her stay for the entire weekend, saying that he could bring her to the play. But I told him he wouldn't know how to do her hair, and I can't risk my baby going on stage looking like who knows what."

Jackie and Tricee both laughed as Jackie continued. "You know, I'll never forget when Alesia was about eight or nine, it was before her dad and I divorced. I had gone out of town for a couple of days only to return home to find my baby's hair looking like Farina from *The Little Rascals*! All I could think about was how it had been a good thing that I was only gone for two days! Girl, I told her dad, 'Don't you ever try to comb my baby's hair again!'" Jackie wiped tears of laughter from her eyes as she recalled her daughter standing before her with braids sticking up all over her head. It had not been funny then but it sure was funny now.

"Okay. I can clearly see how his combing her hair could be a potential problem," Tricee said. "It seems that hair has always been a big issue for women, doesn't it? When will you start allowing her to do her own hair?"

"Not any time soon," Jackie said. "She brushes it and pulls it back into a ponytail and that's as far as it goes. And if she ever asks me if she can get a relaxer, the answer will be no."

Tricee ran her hand through her own natural tresses. "Oh, I can understand that. Natural hair is healthier in my opinion."

"I agree. Anyway, I wasn't ready to go back home so I decided to drive north and check out that boutique on Bryn Mawr, the one down the street from where the train stops. One of the teachers at my school told me about it."

"I know the one you're talking about. And they do carry some really nice things."

"It's different. Not like the clothes you would find at a typical department store." Jackie snapped her fingers. "Oh, I almost forgot! You asked me where I parked. I parked right in the 15-minute parking lot. I winked at the doorman."

"That will do it," Tricee laughed.

Jackie nodded her head and then paused before speaking. "Doesn't he sound like Lou Rawls? Your doorman?"

"Yep," Tricee said. "You want to call the front desk and ask him to sing 'Lady Love?'"

Jackie shook her head and laughed. "Next time," she said as she stood up. "Have you talked to Pam today?" Jackie looked at the artwork on Tricee's wall and commented before Tricee had an opportunity to answer her question. "You moved this into the living room, exactly where it belongs, for all to see." She was referencing the artwork that displayed the four men giving pedicures to the four women.

"It looks better in here. Would you like something to drink?" Tricee asked as she walked into the kitchen.

She hadn't given her conversation with Pam this morning another thought until Jackie mentioned her name. But she couldn't help but to wonder why Pam had called a little earlier, as it was obvious she was not in a position to talk. She'd hung up so abruptly. It had made Tricee even more curious as to how Pam's and Jeff's date was panning out.

Each of Pam's three girlfriends felt that Jeff obviously had some interest in her. They just weren't sure of how interested he was in being in a committed relationship. They wanted to be happy for Pam, seeing as how she believed she'd met that special guy. But sometimes when you're on the outside looking in, you can see things that your girlfriends don't always see, or wish to see. And that was the situation with Pam. They sensed something about Jeff that Pam was willing to overlook.

Tricee came back into the living room with a cup of hot tea and a cup of coffee. Jackie was sitting in the recliner, talking on her cell phone. Tricee gave her a quizzical look. *Oh, no she isn't sitting in my recliner.* She walked back into the kitchen to retrieve a bag of unsalted chips along with a package of trail mix that she placed on the coffee table. She sat down on the sofa, sipped some tea and grabbed a handful of chips, allowing Jackie to finish her conversation. Tricee continued to look at her questioningly as Jackie ended her conversation.

"That was Alesia," Jackie said as she placed her phone back into her purse. "Why are you looking at me like that, Tricee?" she asked as she reached for her coffee and some chips.

"I am thinking how I can't believe you had the audacity to sit in *my* chair," Tricee said. Jackie laughed as Tricee continued, "But I expect such behavior from you."

The two of them shared another laugh. Tricee was glad that her friend had decided to stop by. After such a busy yet productive day, it was nice to relax and enjoy her friend's company, even though she'd meant to have the day to herself.

"I'm sorry," Jackie said. "I guess I forgot that the recliner was off limits." She looked at her watch. "I need to call Pam to remind her about tomorrow morning. You said you two talked earlier?"

Tricee had not mentioned that she'd spoken to Pam but Jackie had been so caught up in their conversation and distracted by her daughter's phone call that she'd just assumed that the two of them had spoken.

"We talked this morning before Noon," said Tricee without going into details. She chose not to mention how Pam had called only a couple of hours earlier, sounding different and whispering. She figured if Pam wanted Jackie to know of her whereabouts, Pam would have to be the one to divulge that information. It wasn't that there were any secrets among them; there had been times when one of them might mention what the other was doing. But in this particular circumstance, Tricee did not feel it was her place to make mention of Pam's outing with Jeff. It would have led the conversation into a whole other place. She would find out from Pam later why she'd called and then suddenly had to hang up.

"I'll call her later. But I should get going. I don't want to have to tip the doorman any extra cash," Jackie said as she began putting on her coat.

"You've only been here, what—30 or 40 minutes? It just seems longer when we start running our mouths," Tricee said.

"True. Thanks for the coffee and the squirrel food, girlfriend," Jackie teased. "Are you sure you won't be able to make it to the play tomorrow?"

"I'm sorry I have to miss this one. I promised to usher tomorrow and we start revival tomorrow evening. There's just too much going on at church right now." They stood by the door as Tricee lightly touched the collar of Jackie's coat. "Is this new?"

"It is," said Jackie. "It's my X-mas gift from my brother."

"Nice," Tricee said, admiring the knee-length, wool, off-white coat. "It makes you look like a first lady."

"Classy and sophisticated?" said Jackie. Tricee nodded. "Well, say one for me in church tomorrow." Jackie opened the door just as Tricee's cell phone rang. Tricee walked over to it to see who was calling and decided to ignore the call. Jackie looked at her friend curiously, noticing the expression on Tricee's face.

"So what are your plans for the rest of the evening?" she asked.

"I am just going to relax. I don't have any plans," Tricee answered.

"I have been meaning to ask you," said Jackie as she attempted to find out whose call Tricee was ignoring, "How is your friend from church doing? What's his name?"

Tricee made a face. "I have several friends, acquaintances from church." She knew exactly who Jackie was referring to, however. And he had been the one whose call she was ignoring.

Tricee did not see a reason to start up a new conversation, especially one that involved men. The topic alone would have Jackie staying for at least another hour. Fortunately, Jackie decided to leave well enough alone.

"Girl, you know you can be so secretive at times," Jackie

said.

"Girl, you know you can be so secretive at times." Tricee wiggled her head as she mocked her friend's voice.

"But I love you anyway," Jackie said, chuckling with Tricee as she reached over and gave her a hug. "I'll talk to you tomorrow to let you know how the play went."

"Yes. And please give Alesia a big hug and a kiss for me."

After Jackie left, Tricee picked up her cell phone expecting to listen to a voicemail but there wasn't one, much to her surprise. She considered returning the call but decided against it. Besides, there was a good chance the phone call had something to do with her possibly being asked to meet for dinner, to make up for the dinner that he canceled a few Saturdays back. While Tricee understood that plans could go awry sometimes, leaving no other choice but to cancel, she did not believe in being too available.

She had been looking forward to getting out on that particular Saturday evening. They'd had plans to go to a movie and then to dinner afterwards, but instead she ended up ordering Chinese food and staying in, feeling a little disappointment.

Her cell phone would ring again just as she was walking into her bedroom. She glanced at the phone and saw that it was the same person who had called earlier, but again, she decided not to answer. *If it's important and he really wants to talk to me, he'll call back.* And with that she went into her bedroom and grabbed two *Essence* magazines and a novel that she had gotten halfway through last week. Then she went into her kitchen, boiled some water for more hot tea, sat at her kitchen table and began to read. On this particular evening, it was a perfect way to spend a Saturday.

Proverbs 31:25 – Strength and honour are her clothing; and she shall rejoice in time to come.

6

Saturday morning: August 3rd

"What's eating Tricee Miller?" Jackie sipped the strong cup of coffee that the waitress set in front of her. "The last time I saw *that* look was when you'd heard the series *Soul Food* was being dropped from the network."

Tricee, Jackie, Val and Pam were having breakfast at Pancakes 2 Go, one of their favorite restaurants. Actually, it was one of Tricee's favorite places, but she had succeeded in getting her girlfriends hooked on the banana pancakes.

"Oh, I didn't see your text until this morning," said Pam after sipping from her glass of orange juice. "Sorry for not calling you last night. Is everything okay?"

"Everything is fine. I'm just a little tired." Tricee placed a forkful of pancakes into her mouth. She'd phoned her Aunt Janice this morning to probe, but she didn't have any information at all on why Ruby had suddenly decided to pay her daughter a visit.

"Oh, did you end up having a hot date last night after blowing us off?" Pam teased before taking a bite of her pancakes. "Umm, yum, yum." She closed her eyes and shivered. "These are so delicious."

"Pam, can you try not to be so demonstrative when you're eating?" Jackie laughed. "You act as if you're eating a big ol' juicy steak."

Pam closed her eyes and took another bite. "I don't know, ladies. I think I might need to be alone for a minute."

Val chuckled, rolling her eyes to the ceiling at Pam's remark.

"So how was the jazz band last night?" Val glanced over at Tricee although her question had been directed at Jackie or Pam. She could sense that Tricee had something on her mind.

"They were fabulous," Jackie said. "It's too bad you and Tricee couldn't join us. Pam and I had a great time."

Pam chimed in, "Yeah, we had fun! There were these two guys trying to flirt with us. I had to contain my laughter because

Jackie was being so rude. But the man just wouldn't take a hint."

Pam laughed as she thought about the scene from the previous night.

"Don't look yet," Pam whispered to Jackie over the singer's deep voice as he crooned to the sound of his band, "but the two guys who were checking us out are coming this way."

Jackie immediately turned to look.

Pam let out a deep sigh. "Didn't I say don't look now?" She tapped Jackie lightly on the arm. "The deal is to avoid all eye contact."

Although they were not seated at a table directly near the stage, the restaurant was still noisy with other patrons laughing and talking while the band played. Everyone was having a great time, which was evident by all the smiles from the 30-and-over crowd. Everyone had obviously enjoyed their fair share of catfish and was now ready to sway to the music from the band.

"Hello, ladies," said the taller of the two gentlemen. "May we join you?"

Before Jackie or Pam could respond, he sat down in the empty chair next to them. His friend, who was still standing, opened his mouth and turned toward Pam to speak but her expression caused him to reconsider.

"I'm Roy and this is my buddy, Frank," said the taller one. Frank extended his hand and smiled. Pam shook it reluctantly, allowing only her fingertips to touch his hand.

"You must have been holding this chair for me," Roy said to Jackie.

"Oh? Now what makes you think that?" Her tone was serious.

"Let's call it wishful thinking on my part." He was all smiles as his eyes went from Jackie's hair, eyes, then to her light blue silk blouse, which had caught his attention.

"Yes, let's call it wishful thinking," Jackie said as she turned to look at Pam.

"Your top is blue?" He said it as more of a statement than a question. "I can barely tell in this light but I love the color blue."

"Yeah, I bet you do," Pam mumbled under her breath. She lightly kicked Jackie's foot under the table.

"So, what are you ladies drinking?"

He turned and looked up at his friend, "Frank, how about

going to order a round for the table?"

Frank smiled. "It would be my pleasure."

"Uh, excuse me," said Jackie, "but we really do not want another drink. Thanks, but no thanks."

"Okay. Well, I can use one more." He turned to Frank who nodded and walked away.

Pam mumbled again, "Wow, can you make him do tricks, too?"

"So, pretty lady, are you enjoying your evening?"

"Well, I was trying to enjoy it with my friend seeing that we rarely come out together," Jackie lied. She was hoping he would catch the hint.

"So, you don't come here often?"

"No," Jackie answered abruptly, lying again.

"Oh, it's the place to be on a Friday night. Good music, good food, sexy women." He then licked his chapped lips.

Jackie looked at him as if he had two heads.

"No offense," he said as he threw up both his hands, "Classy, beautiful, and sexy women. I just call it like I see it. And you fit that description and then some."

"Right," Jackie said. She did not wish to appear rude but she really did not want to be bothered. All she wanted was to listen to the band and the singer on stage whose deep voice could melt butter. She and Pam had been all too happy to learn that this particular band would be playing all evening.

"You wouldn't mind if I just call it like I see it, would you?" Jackie gave the guy a half smile. Pam took another sip of her drink. She was trying to keep herself from laughing out loud.

"I am sure, Roy," she placed emphasis on the 'R' in his name, making her lips part in a unique manner. It was unintentional but he found it delightful. "I am sure you are a nice man and all, but I—we," she pointed to Pam and then back to herself, "really would rather hear the band."

"I love the way you say my name." He smiled as if he'd not heard anything else she'd said.

"I can say it again if you'd like," Jackie said. "But this time it won't sound so pleasant."

"Try me," he said.

"Now, see? He's just asking it for it," Pam leaned over and whispered to Jackie. "Get him, girl!" She sat back in her chair as

she watched Roy, who kept his eyes fixed on Jackie.

"May I offer you a breath mint, Roy?" Jackie reached into her small purse.

Pam laughed, this time out loud.

"Aw, man," he replied. "Now, sister, that's just cold." He looked around the restaurant. "Where is Frank with my drink?" he mumbled. He stood up to leave. "You know you wrong, right?" he asked Jackie. But he wasn't really looking for a response as he quickly walked away.

"I wasn't being rude," said Jackie as she picked up a strip of turkey bacon, "Shucks, he caught me on a good day." She wiped her mouth with her napkin and continued, "His hot breath was making my hair sweat."

Her girlfriends all laughed. They could usually count on Jackie to come up with something silly to say.

"Girl, sometimes I forget that you are a principal of a high school," said Val, pointing her fork toward Jackie.

"Speaking of chosen professions," Pam reached for her glass of orange juice, "I could never be a dentist." She took a sip and then laughed.

"Why not?" Tricee asked looking slightly confused as she began to drink her juice.

"Because I would have a hard time telling somebody they had funky breath."

Tricee laughed, nearly choking on her juice.

"I know, right!" said Val. "Can you imagine telling a patient, 'Uh, I think there might be a problem.'" She was near tears from laughing. '"Your breath is fun-*ky*!'" She placed emphasis on the second syllable.

Pam, near tears, as well, tapped Val on the arm, "Girl, Jackie offered the man a breath mint last night. Now, see? She's just too bold!"

"No, I was not bold. It was heartfelt," Jackie chimed in. "I was trying to save him before he approached someone else."

"You guys are nuts," Tricee said, waving her hand. "I think all three of you missed your calling as standup comediennes."

She was still feeling unsettled over the phone call she'd had with her mother the night before but she was enjoying the moment with her friends. Meeting them for breakfast had helped to distract her thoughts. At least for the moment.

"So what did you and Cory end up doing last night?" Pam asked Val as the four of them caught their breath from laughing. Their waitress, a petite blond, approached their table. She looked to be in her early 20s. She wore a necklace that appeared to be some sort of an antique.

"Would you ladies like anything else?" She displayed a warm smile.

"I'll have another glass of orange juice, please," said Pam.

"I'll have another glass, as well," Tricee smiled.

"Sure. And cute top, by the way." She complimented Tricee on the black and white ruffled tank top she was wearing.

"Thank you," Tricee smiled. "Nice necklace."

"It's an antique piece handed down to me by my great grandmother."

Once the waitress left the table, it was Val's turn to discuss what she'd gotten into on the previous night. The topic would lead to an incident from her past. "Oh," she turned toward Pam. "Cory and I went to his cousin's house last night for a get-together. About 15 people, nothing major," she shrugged.

"What kind of get-together? Was it someone's birthday or just 15 black folks hanging out?" Jackie teased. Val cocked her head to one side.

"Yeah, we sat around and sang 'We Shall Overcome.'" Her remark elicited giggles from her friends as she continued. "Afterwards, we went home and enjoyed a nice, quiet evening."

Val still smiled like a teenager in love whenever she spoke about her husband of close to 12 years. They had been high school sweethearts who'd married a year after she graduated from college. They'd broken up sometime around her first year of undergrad and, during that time, Cory impregnated another woman. He was a junior in college and became a father at the tender age of 21. His son Sean was now 14 and loved Val as much as he loved his biological mother. He would say on occasion, "I have two mothers." And when he wanted something, he'd say, "I have two very special mothers."

"I think it's sweet how you and Cory still manage to squeeze in those quiet moments," said Pam with a warm smile, "You're so blessed. Cory's a good man." She picked up her fork and dived into what was left of her breakfast.

"And you're so good with Sean. He's crazy about you," said Jackie as she picked up her last strip of turkey bacon.

"Yes, I'm blessed," said Val after swallowing the last of her pancakes. She paused before reflecting on a moment from the past. "But Lord knows my faith has been tested." She smiled as she recalled an incident that had taken place close to 15 years ago. "When Cory and I broke up, I was devastated." She laughed. "It was the worst time to have a breakup. I was only in my first year of college!"

Pam chimed in, "*He* broke up with *you*, remember?"

Val suddenly stopped laughing and shot Pam an evil look.

"Please! Did you have to remind me?" She rolled her eyes at Pam. "Good grief!" Jackie and Tricee began to laugh.

"I'm just saying." Pam wiped her mouth with her napkin before continuing, "You were calling me practically every night crying and carrying on. I was afraid for you, being away from home having to deal with all that stress." She reached over and gave Val a one-armed hug. Val closed her eyes briefly and shook her head. When she opened them, she looked from Jackie to Tricee.

"I was a hot mess for real," she said, then looked at Pam and tapped her lightly on the arm. "But I was hurting, girl." She made a face. "I needed comfort. And who better to give you that than your best girlfriend."

As Val and Pam reminisced over her and Cory's past issues, Jackie and Tricee sat and listened intently. The expressions on both their faces showed complete genuineness.

"You don't have to explain, sweetie," said Tricee. "That's what friends are for."

"Indeed, it is. It is imperative for a woman to have that special girlfriend's shoulder to cry on," Jackie added.

"Yeah, that's true," agreed Pam. "But my shoulder was thousands of miles away!" They all laughed. "I still blame you for that 'C' I got on my chemistry test," Pam continued, giving Val the side-eye. "I was only in my second year of college, still trying to find my own self. And here you were calling and stressing me out!"

Val almost choked on her water from laughing so hard. Each time they'd meet, it seemed there was a topic that would arise that they'd never discussed. And then there were times when they'd chat about something they'd discussed a dozen times before.

"A breakup is bound to happen to everyone at some point,"

said Jackie, removing a tube of lip gloss from her purse. "Val, you said that it hadn't been a good time to experience a breakup." She applied a thin coating to her lips. "But there is never a good time to go through a breakup."

Val took a sip of water. "That might be true. But I was just starting college! He could have at least waited until a sister had one full year under her belt!" She chuckled.

Val thought back to a discussion she'd had with her husband some years after the fact. She'd told Cory that exact same thing that he could have waited to break up with her. He'd looked at her sideways and replied, "Please, Val. What difference would it have made? You would have still called me every name in the book. You women are notorious for that. Babe, you were calling me names I didn't even know existed! Here I was thinking you were this sweet, innocent little lady, and you were laying it on a brother!"

She swiped her husband playfully on the head as they reminisced over the past.

As she shared this with her friends, she wiped tears from her eyes. She had not expected to laugh so hard this morning over breakfast. What was funny now was obviously not funny back then.

"You know," Val said as the laughter amongst them settled, "I must give my sweetie credit for being mature enough to handle such a big responsibility. He managed to still complete his degree and has turned out to be a really good dad. That can't be said for a lot of guys."

"That's a very valid point," Jackie said. "My hat's off to all the guys who have done the right thing by their kids. Folks need a reminder—children don't ask to be born." Pam, Tricee and Val all nodded in agreement.

"Now, Cory's parents," Val shook her head and chuckled, "were not at all thrilled with their son when he called to tell them he'd gotten someone pregnant. He told me his father had to hold his mother back when he walked in the door." Val continued speaking though the thought of her mother-in-law going at her son made it difficult to keep from laughing. Her mother-in-law was a petite woman who stood about 5'1". She wore heels often and she wore them well, but the mere thought of this little lady reaching up to smack her son, who stood 5'10", was a little much.

"Cory laughs about it now and says he almost laughed back then when it happened. The way his mother was jumping up and down, trying to smack him on the head—he says it was one of the funniest things you could have witnessed!"

"Well, he might have thought it was funny," Pam chimed in, "but I bet you he's glad his dad was there to hold his mom back!"

"I know that's right!" Jackie said. "Or your hubby would be walking around this very day with a big knot!"

After more discussion about work, their plans for the remainder of the day and a few meaningless topics, Pam looked at her watch and sipped her water. She glanced around the restaurant and noticed that it was filling up and that there were twice as many people than when they'd first arrived. Pancakes 2 Go was definitely the place to be on a Saturday morning. *Why don't more people just stay home and cook their own breakfast? Maybe it's because they're like me and don't know how to cook very well. Until my sister told me, I had no idea that the skillet needed to be hot before you tossed in the bacon. Oh well.*

After entertaining her own private thoughts, Pam delved back into the conversation, bringing up Cory and Val once more. "Cory's parents really like you, Val. They were so happy when you two got back together and then married later on." Val nodded. "Not to say they dislike Desiree, Sean's mom. I just believe they were happy that he did not rush into anything."

"Something he would have regretted later," Jackie finished Pam's thoughts. "I am of the opinion that when you marry out of obligation, you end up with terrible results."

"I just think it's so romantic when high school sweethearts marry," Tricee said. "And stay married."

"You know, in spite of it all, I have to give Desiree credit." Val's three girlfriends turned to look at her. "I mean, she could have given up and dropped out of college for good." She noticed that her girlfriends were still staring at her as if she'd just admitted to something shameful. "But she went back after Sean turned a year old and finished. Now she's happily married with Sean and an adorable 4 year-old daughter." Val smiled and picked up her fork, as if to say, "so there."

Her friends all looked at each other. Tricee put her head down to hide the smirk on her face. Jackie and Pam both reached over and touched her hand.

"What?" Val asked.

"Aw, you're just so sweet. Not too many sisters—"

Jackie interrupted before Pam could finish, "Not too many women—period!"

Pam nodded. "Right—not too many women would utter such kind words about their husband's ex."

Jackie pointed her fork toward Val. "You're good. Better than me," she laughed.

"All things work out for good," Val said.

Pam began to chuckle. "Girlfriend, you have a fairy tale life."

They'd all been friends for several years now with Pam and Val having the longest friendship in the group, having attended high school together. The two had been through a lot together and, over time, they'd shared some of their stories with Jackie and Tricee. These stories would have them laughing so hard that on one occasion, Tricee lost control of her bladder. She'd made them all promise to never, ever, share her unfortunate incident with anyone else.

"Girl, now who would we tell?" Jackie had inquired, "You can trust that only the three of us will ever know that you peed on yourself."

Whether it was hearing stories about Val and Pam, sharing stories about other things, or just enjoying a girls' day or night out, the four women would easily find themselves laughing and having a wonderful time together. Of course, there were serious moments and conversations that did not necessarily end in laughter, but if there was one thing they agreed upon, it was that life would be no fun without girlfriends, your true friends.

Pam spoke after the waitress came by to refill their coffee and juice. "You have in-laws who adore you, a stepson who thinks you're really cool, a good-looking husband who cherishes the ground you walk on, and a friendly relationship with your stepson's mom. You, my dear, are a rare find." The women laughed but agreed with Pam's words.

"I have learned that it's best to remain optimistic, even when it rains harder than you'd like. No one has a perfect life." Val shrugged. "But it's best to keep your peace and your sanity."

"Here, here!" Jackie said, raising her cup of coffee. "Tell it like it is, Val! That was well said!"

A few minutes later they were all looking at their watches. Val spoke first. "I need to get going. Speaking of being this wonderful stepmom, I promised Sean I would drive him and his friends to the mall. We're supposed to have pizza afterwards." She patted her now full belly. "But, goodness, I can't even think about pizza right now."

Tricee would be the next one to speak. She hadn't planned to blurt out what she was thinking, her words just sort of came forth. "My mother is coming for a visit in two weeks. She called last night to tell me." She shrugged and continued, "But it doesn't matter because I won't be here on that particular weekend."

There was complete silence. Gone was the laughter and the chatter from only seconds earlier. It seemed as if the food—what was left of it—was now more important than any discussion. Jackie was chewing on what was left of her turkey bacon, Pam was nibbling on a very small piece of banana pancake that she'd pushed to the side of her plate, and Val was spreading grape jelly on a slice of half-eaten wheat toast as if her life depended on it. Tricee understood their silence. They weren't sure how to respond; her statement had taken them by surprise. They were well aware that Ruby had never been to Chicago to visit.

Tricee had consumed six banana pancakes, three strips of turkey bacon, two scrambled eggs, a plate of fruit (that she shared with Pam) and two glasses of orange juice. But Pancakes 2 Go served as more than a place to go for a great breakfast. It provided comfort, and she'd wanted to remain there with her three closest friends a while longer. Once they parted ways, she'd have to face the issue once again back at her condo. She would be alone with her feelings and she wasn't ready to deal with the uncertainty of what lay ahead. Her happy moment with friends had come to an end. She glanced around the restaurant, taking notice of some of the other patrons.

The young white couple seated behind them was engrossed in a conversation about a nightclub. She overheard the young woman mention to the young man that the DJ was an acquaintance. The black couple seated across from them would look up at each other every few seconds over their omelets and smile. If Tricee had to guess, she'd guess that they hadn't been dating for very long. They seemed to have that I-think-I-really-like-you expression on their faces. There were two women seated behind the newly dating couple, both with accents. They were either Jamaican or from another island. Both women wore their hair in braided styles that

Tricee found absolutely gorgeous. It caused her to consider, briefly, having her own hair braided. She noticed an African family walk in, followed by a middle-aged Latina with adorable twin girls. It was definitely a diverse atmosphere on this side of town; one of the reasons Tricee had chosen the north side of Chicago in which to reside.

As she observed the many different faces, overheard some of the lighthearted conversations, and smelled the aroma of the different foods, she now felt that she could easily spend another hour at the restaurant, even without the company of her friends.

For Jackie, Pam, and Val, the waitress' appearance was timely. It eased the tension that had filled the air.

"May I get you anything else?" the waitress asked.

"Our check please," Jackie and Pam replied at the same time.

Tricee noticed their behavior and released a light chuckle. "I'll be fine, really. No need to worry about me." Her tone was sarcastic.

Jackie gave her a sympathetic look. "Are you sure? I mean, if you need to talk, we could—"

Tricee cut her off. "I'll be fine. I have your number, all of your numbers, if I need to talk." She gave them each a so-you-better-answer-if-I-call-you look.

Pam took some money from her purse as she spoke. "Tricee, it might not be such a bad thing, you know."

Tricee shrugged. "Yeah, well. No use in giving it too much thought." *Easier said than done.*

They walked to the parking lot where hugs were exchanged. After Jackie and Pam drove off in their respective vehicles, Val and Tricee remained in the parking lot. Val needed this moment alone with her dear friend.

"I could sense that something was bothering you," she said as they stood near Tricee's car. "And I knew it had to be more than you just being tired."

"Well, I did have a rather sleepless night."

"Why don't you call me later? I am wondering why you won't be here the weekend Ruby is coming. But I know now is not a good time to get into all of that." Val surveyed the now crowded parking lot.

"Wow, Val, is it that obvious?" Tricee forced a smile.

"I don't know if it's that obvious, I just know that you're no good at fibbing."

After a hug and a kiss on the cheek from Val, Tricee climbed into her car and headed for home. She was more tired mentally than physically. And as she thought about Val's optimistic approach to life and what Pam had said about it not necessarily being such a bad thing if Ruby visited, she wanted to believe that maybe, just maybe, Ruby coming would yield some positive results. But Tricee knew that only time would tell.

7

Friday: August 16th

"What?!" Tricee screamed so loudly her wall mirror appeared to rattle. "How could you do this? What made you think that this would be okay?" The tears were streaming down her face and onto her white silk blouse. She was not only angry, she was confused. It had been a long time since her emotions had spun so out of control. She was not prepared for the turn of events that would cause her to experience one of the worst weekends of her life.

Ruby and Tricee had just returned to Tricee's home from dinner. They'd both been mostly quiet during their meal. Tricee, who was trying her best to make the most of an uncomfortable situation, initiated some small talk.

After her mother had arrived at the airport, she called Tricee to inform her that her traveling companion had arranged for her brother to meet them. Ruby had not bothered to ask Tricee why she would not be available to pick them up. When she listened to her daughter's message, she shook her head and wrote it off as her only child behaving selfishly—again. Tricee's message had stated that she would be out of town. But the next day she called Ruby again and said that there had been a change of plans. She said she would be in town after all but so busy that she wouldn't be able to make it to the airport. Ruby chose not to stir the pot and let the matter drop. "She's never been good at fibbing," she mumbled after hanging up the phone.

Ruby might not win a prize for being the world's greatest mother but she had what all mothers possessed and that was mother's intuition. Mothers had a way of knowing things about their children that their own children didn't know about themselves. It was as if God had given them something special on purpose.

She knew that one of the topics over dinner would be why Tricee had lied. But Ruby had decided that, no matter how her visit turned out, she'd try to correct the wrongs. She only hoped it wasn't too late. As far as she was concerned, Tricee was being immature. It wasn't the first time and it might not be the last.

Back home in St. Louis, as Ruby prepared for her trip, she

found herself thinking about the past. One incident that was still fresh in her memory had occurred when Tricee was in the 5th grade. Tricee had become upset after talking to her 5th grade teacher, Ms. Lambert. Ruby liked Ms. Lambert and felt that she was one of the most caring teachers a child could have. She never understood why her then 10-year-old daughter had taken such a disliking toward the woman. She recalled how Tricee had remained silent on the last day of school after a discussion she had with her teacher.

"How was your last day of school?" Ruby asked a frowning Tricee after she'd climbed into the family's white, four-door Oldsmobile.

"Fine," Tricee mumbled.

"Ms. Lambert told me she needed to talk to you after class. She says you did very well this school year." Ruby was partly smiling but Tricee did not feel there was anything to smile about. Furthermore, she'd always thought that her mother had not learned how to make her face form a complete smile, even when they were discussing something positive.

"She says that as long as you keep up the hard work and continue your reading over the summer, you'll be prepared for the honors class in 7th and 8th grades."

Tricee stared out the window as Ruby spoke.

"It's too bad they don't have an honors class for 6th grade. But Ms. Lambert did mention something about a reading and math program for 6th grade students who perform above average. She suggested that I look into it when school starts in the fall."

"Is daddy meeting us at the diner?" Tricee asked, not at all interested in any conversations that had taken place between her mother and Ms. Lambert. As far as Tricee was concerned, she couldn't quite figure out the personalities of either woman. She felt that Ms. Lambert was just odd and that Ruby was moody. One day she was happy and the next she was unhappy. And even on her happy days, her joy was more evident when she was with her friends. Tricee believed that neither she nor her father was ever the cause for any of Ruby's sun-shiny days. As far as Ruby was concerned, she believed her daughter had no reason to complain about anything since she had everything a 10-year-old could possibly want. She felt Tricee was just too ungrateful. And she wasn't even a teenager yet.

Ruby's half smile turned into a complete scowl. "No.

Daddy's not meeting us at the diner."

"Why not?"

"He's busy, Jentrice." Ruby's answer was curt.

From her mother's facial expression, Tricee knew better than to ask any more questions, especially if it involved her father.

Ruby and Tricee went to the diner for a quick meal and afterward they went to the movies. Later on that evening, Tricee headed straight to her bedroom and Ruby sat alone in her living room. She thought about the discussion she'd had with Ms. Lambert a few days prior to the last day of school. It hurt her feelings to hear what her daughter had said to the whole class. And it hurt even more to have to hear it from another woman, a woman Ruby respected. She now wondered what Ms. Lambert thought of her. Ruby decided not to bring the issue up with her daughter even though a part of her wanted badly to discuss it. That evening she'd discussed it with her husband and, somehow, the discussion led to an argument.

"That's all in the past now," Ruby said under her breath as she closed her luggage. Her visit was not to cause any more bitter feelings. She knew that her news was bound to cause some discomfort for her and Tricee but she felt certain they'd get past it. It turned out that Ruby had not been as prepared as she would have liked. Being at a loss for words over dinner was out of character for Ruby. And she'd remained quiet on the drive from the restaurant except to ask Tricee if her place of employment was in the downtown area, and if it was anywhere near the hotel where she would be staying for the next three nights.

Ruby was curious about her daughter's life. She wanted to know specific details: How did Tricee like living in such a big city? Did she date often? How were the people on her job? Did she plan to remain in Chicago? But she wasn't sure if this particular visit would be the appropriate time to ask a million questions.

She'd asked to be taken back to her hotel after dinner using fatigue as an excuse. It had been a long day indeed, and initially, she'd felt tonight was just not the time to share her news. But Tricee suggested that they go back to her place. She also suggested, with some reluctance, that her mother stay overnight. But that was not about to happen. Tricee's unexpected invitation to her condo placed Ruby in somewhat of an awkward situation.

"Jentrice, what do you want me to do? Do you think that this is any easier for me?" Ruby was sitting on the sofa with a cup of tea in her hands, shaking nervously. A few moments ago, Tricee had been sitting in her recliner but she was now pacing the floor.

After allowing her daughter to release her frustration and anger, it was now her turn to vent. "Do you think this was something that I planned?!" Ruby was becoming angry.

"You know, I am starting to believe that this was an intentional move on your part. Why didn't you tell me this sooner?" Although the heavy crying had ceased, Tricee still had tears streaming down her face. She walked into her kitchen.

She had gone shopping earlier in the day and a few of the items she'd bought had been left in a brown paper bag on her kitchen table. She'd been preparing anxiously for her mother's visit, still trying to figure out Ruby's real reason for visiting. She woke that morning when her alarm went off at 6:00 AM, the time she got out of bed every weekday morning. Fortunately, she'd gotten a good night's rest.

But now, as she fought hard to keep more tears from falling, Tricee could not fathom how or why any of this was happening. She was dealing with several emotions all at once, none of them positive. She had always associated being strong and in control of her emotions with her independent nature.

Tricee had left home at 18 to attend college and had not once regretted her decision to attend college in a different state. It seemed that her relationship with her mother was tolerable as long as they lived apart. But still, that did not seem normal to her.

Once she left home she would not ever return, at least not for good. But many of her friends had returned home to their parents until they were able to find employment. That was not a viable option for her. She did believe that leaving home at such a young age had groomed her to be the young adult that she was today. But on this day she had no idea who she was. It was just all too confusing.

As Tricee walked back into her living room, she observed her mother wiping away her own tears. Tricee had no memory of the last time she'd seen Ruby cry. At one point she did not believe that her mother was even capable of producing any tears. As soon as Ruby saw her enter the room, she stood up quickly and wiped the last traces of her tears. She straightened her posture and cleared her throat as if she was preparing to make an important speech.

She smoothed her black, knee-length skirt with her hands before placing them on her hips. She might have been nervous earlier and had even worked up some emotions herself, but now it was time to show her grown daughter who was in charge. Ruby was one of those people who believed that you were only supposed to let your guard down for a brief moment. To do so for any longer meant that you were opening yourself up to being vulnerable. And she was not about to allow that to take place.

"Look, Jentrice," Ruby shook her finger, pointing it toward Tricee, "I am still your mother." Her expression could have melted butter. "You might not like the recent turn of events, but let us not forget," Ruby pointed her finger into her chest and then back at her daughter, "I gave birth to you, baby doll, not the other way around."

Tricee stood staring at her mother as if she had lost her mind. She attempted to speak but Ruby cut her off.

"It's getting late and this has been a long day for the both of us." She threw up both her hands.

Tricee was amazed at her mother's dramatic behavior.

"I need to get back to my hotel." Ruby reached for her black leather purse and pulled out her cell phone.

"That sounds like a good idea," Tricee replied, making sure to say it as softly as possible. She jumped and immediately took a step back when Ruby turned around. "I can call you a cab," she blurted out nervously.

"Bev's brother will come and pick me up," Ruby said as she looked Tricee from head to toe. She then turned her back and began talking on her cell phone.

It would have been a difficult drive to endure but, for reasons Tricee could not explain nor fully understand, she wanted Ruby to need her, if only for that moment. It was Ruby's first time visiting and she was not too familiar with the big city. And Tricee did not know anything about this Bev or her brother. But now was clearly not the time to express her feelings about her mother's friends.

Tricee was now becoming upset at the way Ruby had managed to turn things around, as if she was the victim. She was fuming after Ruby left. And she had no idea what her mother's plans were for the remainder of her visit. Nor did she care. She could make no sense out of what had just occurred and how she'd ended up being dealt such a blow. The Holy Spirit would surely have to step in and take care of this one. It was too much of a burden for even the strongest Christian to bear.

Tricee tried hard to fight back the tears as she drifted off to sleep. She hoped that Ruby would decide to shorten her visit—she'd caused enough damage in just one day. She saw no reason for the two of them to spend any more time together during her stay.

8

"My goodness." Jeff shook his head. "You are a real vision of beauty."

Pam was dressed in black slacks and a turquoise sweater with a matching scarf. Her new black ankle boots, which were lined with fur, had a two-inch heel. Not exactly the kind of boot that was suitable for Chicago winters—except for the fur. But Pam preferred these particular boots whenever she went out. She considered them her "jazzy" pair and loved the way they looked on her. Obviously, Jeff did, as well. He noticed them right away when he picked her up. "I like your boots. They are definitely you." Pam could not help but to blush.

The day had started off with the two of them having lunch at a new restaurant that Jeff had suggested and they both decided that it was definitely worth another visit. It was the best Thai food that Pam could remember eating in a very long time. The atmosphere had been cozy and warm. But they could have eaten in a shack on the side on the road. For Pam, that, too, would have felt cozy and warm. It was Jeff's company and the way he was able to carry on a conversation that made her gush like a teenager. He was enjoying his Saturday with her, as well.

He'd complimented her on how nice she looked and told her how much he loved her hair. Her short hair really complimented her face—he'd said that at least twice. His behavior was indicative of a gentleman who harbored warm feelings for the woman he'd spent his entire day with.

Jeff had also mentioned during lunch how relaxed he felt whenever they were together. And that he was experiencing "less stress" since they'd started spending time together. Pam was quick to notice his choice of words: spending time together. He had not said that they were "dating," which is what she would have preferred. She hoped their status would change soon but, for now, all she could do was go along with the flow.

It had only been three months since they'd begun seeing each other. But still, she did not feel that dating was too strong of a word to use. She'd allowed her analytical side to surface and would find herself questioning Jeff's every move and every word that came out of his mouth.

In the past three months they'd managed to see each other occasionally during the week. And they'd gotten together just about every weekend. They would see each other when it was most convenient for Jeff. Pam understood that people led busy lives. Her full-time position as a sales representative for a pharmaceutical company allowed her only a limited amount of time for fun, but she made time in her schedule for friends and for the special guy in her life, whoever that happened to be at the time. Fortunately, her sales territory consisted of Chicago-land and its surrounding area. In the past she was required to travel more widely within the U.S., and that was how she'd met Jeff.

Being the sales director and vice president of a small pharmaceutical company required a lot of Jeff's time. He'd made that perfectly clear. He'd also made it clear that he was not ready for a committed relationship. Pam reasoned that if it weren't for the fact that he kept such a busy schedule, they'd spend a lot more time together. Her patience was wearing thin but she was willing to wait it out, trusting that, in time, they would grow closer.

She'd almost blurted out over lunch, "So where do you see us going in this relationship?" The mood had seemed perfect for such a discussion. But she remembered what had happened the last time she asked a guy that question. He stopped calling. No explanation given. What made this particular circumstance even more difficult was the fact that they were getting along so well. She was convinced that he was the one.

As she sat across from Jeff over lunch, her father's words of wisdom had been another reason she decided to forego asking the million-dollar question. He had offered his advice to Pam and her three sisters on more than one occasion. This particular day, she and her two sisters had stopped by their parents' home for what was supposed to have been a brief visit. Pam's youngest sister still lived at home and was busily entertaining herself, bobbing her head to the music in her headphones. She couldn't hear all of what was being said but found her three older sisters' behavior quite comical.

"Don't ever ask a man how he feels about you or the relationship. When you do that, you make him feel pressured." Her father puffed on his pipe and looked at his daughters over his reading glasses. The summer breeze made for a perfect evening to sit out on the front porch.

"Dad, you've told us that already." Pam waited until her

father looked down at his newspaper and rolled her eyes. Her sister, Terri, made a face at him, which caused laughter to erupt. Her father looked up from his paper, ignoring the laughter from his daughters. He also shared with them how their mother had asked him that very question after one date and how he could not wait to take her home. Afterward, he said he tossed her number in the trash as soon as he got home.

"I was not going to call her again," he stated. "That woman almost caused me to have an ulcer—asking me that question."

"So why did you marry mom after only one month of dating?" Pam asked.

"Right?" added her sister, Terri. "It seems that question made you make your move, daddy-O." Pam gave her sister a high-five as they continued laughing at their dear old dad.

Her sister, Lynn, normally tried to keep her laughter under wraps, not wishing to gang up on their father. But this time she added her two cents. It was no secret to anyone in the family that he and his daughter Lynn, the dietician, shared a special bond. It wasn't favoritism; it was just that she seemed to be more like him than his other four children: funny at times, yet she could get into one of her very serious moods. Lynn and their father could spend hours discussing the books and magazine articles they'd read. And just like their father, she was more of a homebody who preferred eating at home as opposed to going out. She preferred cooking her own meals because, that way, she knew exactly what she was eating. In their father's eyes, Lynn could do no wrong.

"Dad, you knew you would lose ma if you didn't make your move. Tillie scared you into a proposal." By this time, Cassie, the youngest, had removed her headphones to join in the laughter. A few seconds later, their mother walked out onto the porch. She placed a tall glass of ice water on the small glass table next to her husband.

"What is all this cackling about?"

Pam stood up to walk inside. "We were just asking dad why he married you after only one month of dating." Her mother shot her a look. "Not that there is anything wrong with you, Ma." Pam responded immediately. She laughed as she went inside to use the bathroom. She could still hear the muffled conversation and laughs.

Her mother wiped her forehead with the dishtowel in her hand. "It wasn't after one month. And it was a courtship. Something a lot of men these days don't know anything about simply because so many women don't require it." She then turned to look at her three daughters, her gaze landing on her youngest daughter.

"What?" Cassie asked, with a what-did-I-do expression.

"Just keep that in mind," their mother stated.

"You know," their father held his pipe next to his mouth, "You should learn a lot—having three older sisters and a wise old man for a father." He winked at his youngest daughter and went back to reading. Their mother chuckled as she turned to walk back inside.

"Girl, I feel for you," Terri remarked, "having to live here with him." She laughed as she tilted her head toward their father. Then she coughed to get his attention. When he ignored her she spoke up.

"Dad," she walked over to where her father was seated. "What made you, just out of the blue, mention men anyway?"

Pam came back outside just in time to hear her sister's question. "Yeah. We were on a whole other topic and you just start talking about what not to ask a man." Pam made a face. Her father looked up at her and then back at his other daughters.

"As long as I have daughters I will give them guidance." He stood up from his chair causing Terri to quickly move to the other side of the porch. Pam and her other two sisters burst into laughter at Terri's reaction. Their father raised his hand as if he was going to give Pam a backhand slap. This was a playful gesture he did often.

"Well, we appreciate it, but enough already." Terri remarked from the other side of the porch.

Pam appreciated her father's words of wisdom—most of the time. But that didn't mean she always heeded his advice. She decided to just go with the flow and enjoy the remainder of her evening with Jeff. The night wasn't over yet. There was still a chance that he would broach the subject of their relationship himself.

As she sat across from him in his living room, admiring his beautiful and spacious two-bedroom townhome, she couldn't help but stare at him when he wasn't looking. There was nowhere else she'd rather be on this cold, wintry Saturday evening. It might have been cold outside, but inside of Jeff's home she felt only warmth and comfort. The handsome gentleman with the caramel complexion was slowly making his way to her heart.

Jeff was easy on the eyes and, though the saying "Beauty is in the eyes of the beholder" might ring true, Pam was certain that most women would agree that Jeff was fine. There was something unique about the 5'11" ex-amateur boxer. His light-brown eyes alone could spellbind you if you looked into them long enough. He had eyelashes that many women would pay to have. His hair was cut very low, his goatee neatly trimmed. His straight, white teeth were a plus and an absolute must for Pam. She had only one absolute on her list: Her man had to have perfect teeth. Her friends thought that was shallow but respected it just the same.

Jeff's voice was deep and sexy. Some men had either a deep or a sexy voice. But Jeff had both. In fact, his voice was deep, sexy and smooth. It seemed as if his words just oozed down to his lips and then out of his mouth. And oh, his phone voice! It was even more enticing. The first time he and Pam spoke over the phone she was practically wiping sweat from her forehead. After she hung up she ran into the bathroom and splashed cold water on her face.

"Did you enjoy the shrimp gumbo?" His question caught her off guard and she didn't answer immediately. He leaned over and lightly touched her arm. "I hope it wasn't too spicy."

"It was delicious. Couldn't you tell by the way I was smacking?" Pam answered with a light chuckle, using humor to relax her nerves. "Where did you learn to cook such a wonderful dish?"

"Well, when a man grows up in a house full of women, it is inevitable that he learns to cook." Jeff smiled, obviously pleased that she'd enjoyed the meal.

"But I must confess," he sat back in his chair, "I prepared it very early this morning so all I'd have to do this evening was heat it in the oven. I usually prepare most of my meals that way." Pam was impressed. She had not met nor dated a man as precise as Jeff appeared to be.

"Well, it looks like you have this cooking thing down to an art. You obviously had some really good teachers. You also learned the proper etiquette for neat and tidy because your home is immaculate." Her nervousness gave way to her flirtatious nature. If there was one thing Pam could do well it was turn on the charm. She knew how and when to allow the charming side of her personality to surface, a knack she possessed that many men loved.

"Yes. I guess you could say that." Jeff blushed. "But it helps that I'm a quick learner."

As she sat and listened to him, allowing her sense of smell to take in the aroma of his cologne, she wondered what type of relationship he shared with the women in his family. Pam had only one brother and he cherished the ground his sisters walked on. It has been said that the way a man treats his mother is a good indicator of how he will treat the special woman in his life. As far as Pam was concerned, the way a man treated his sisters, if he had any, was a good indicator, as well. She had her own personal experience to draw upon.

Pam's brother was very protective of his mother (even though she had a husband) as well as his four sisters. However, over time, he grew much more protective of his three younger sisters. Pam was older than her brother by five years. Even as a child she had a strong will and an independent nature that would soon lead her brother to believe that his big sister didn't need a protector. Although he would not readily admit it, there wasn't anything he would not do for his beloved big sister.

It was way too soon for any prospect of meeting Jeff's family but Pam entertained the thought. If he didn't offer to introduce her to his family after at least six months, she'd have some serious thinking to do.

She looked around his living room, giving his home the once-over. A picture of Jeff surrounded by four women sat on his entertainment center. Pam could tell by the strong resemblance that the women in the picture were his sisters. The other giveaway was the word "family" at the bottom of the silver frame.

She picked up the glass of white wine that Jeff had poured for her and took a sip. "Thanks," she smiled. He stared at the liquid that formed on her lips.

"You're welcome," he smiled.

It was Pam's first time seeing his place. The only other time she'd been close was when he'd come back after picking her up to grab some documents for work that he needed to send out immediately. Pam had waited in his vehicle while he went to retrieve the documents. Initially, she'd felt a little annoyed that he had not invited her up, but she considered the circumstances and let it go. She had thought about lying, saying she had to use the restroom badly, but she decided against it. He was rushed and she could tell he was also a little distracted. In time, she figured, there would be an opportunity to not only visit but to spend some time alone there and go through his stuff.

But tonight was a different deal. As he leaned in and gently touched her hand again, Pam was convinced that Jeff was well aware of his sexiness. He had to know the effect he had on women. He was so nonchalant about it all, which made him all the sexier. He was not the aggressive type—Pam had encountered enough of those in the past. Jeff was very secure in himself and it showed.

Before he spoke, he leaned back in his chair and picked up a small gift bag that had been placed slightly under the chair. Pam had not noticed it, which was exactly the plan.

"That's a pretty bracelet you're wearing." He smiled a mischievous grin.

"I'm not wearing a bracelet." Pam looked puzzled as she looked down at her wrist.

"You are now," Jeff replied with a light chuckle. He removed the bracelet from its black, velvet-lined box, setting the box on the coffee table. He then took Pam's wrist and fastened the small tennis bracelet around it. Her mouth flew open. He began to laugh.

"As I said before, that is a very pretty bracelet you're wearing."

"Jeff, this is so beautiful! Thank you, I love it!" She leaned over and kissed him once lightly on the lips. He'd said earlier that he had a surprise, and he'd successfully delivered on his promise. The night seemed to get better and better. Pam was thinking to herself how this had been one of their best times together in their three months of "seeing each other."

"It looks good on you. Just as I imagined it would."

Pam was trying not to read too much into the evening. However, she couldn't help but to wonder what Jeff was thinking. There was just so much she wanted to know and ask. For instance, Jeff had not met any of her friends, nor had she met any of his. She had met a couple of his colleagues once when she agreed to meet him one evening after work. He had been very attentive to her then and had introduced her as "my friend Pam." He seemed unfazed by the presence of his colleagues. Pam realized that they were not his friends, which was why it was no big deal. Being around his friends would tell another story. And she was waiting for that day to arrive.

Furthermore, when she'd suggested once that he meet her and her girlfriends one Friday evening, he stated that he would love to. He'd mentioned a dinner meeting with a client but reiterated that he'd make every attempt to join her. As it turned out, his dinner meeting lasted much longer than he'd expected. Her girlfriends had remained silent when Pam informed them of his reason for being unable to join them. But when Pam excused herself to go the ladies room, it was Jackie who offered her opinion. "Hmph. A Friday night meeting with a client?" she remarked sarcastically. "Well, I hope he closed the deal."

He had called Pam at least three times that evening. She surmised that the phone calls were likely his way of reassuring her. They were in the same business and she knew that sometimes a Friday evening meeting was necessary. She'd had dinner meetings with clients on a Friday, but that was very rare. A lunch meeting on a Friday was far more common. She decided not to hold the incident against him. His phone calls had worked, along with the excuse she'd come up with for him: They'd only been seeing each other for about a month when she invited him to meet her friends. That, somehow, made it all the more acceptable.

Jeff had mastered the "make it up to you" better than any other man she'd gone out with. The following day she received a dozen red roses with a nice note. It had been a great way to start a Saturday.

Earlier, after they'd eaten lunch, Jeff had spoken with one of his colleagues. He'd made the call and allowed the conversation to take place over the speakerphone. Pam tried not to appear too interested as he spoke about a work-related project. She flipped through a magazine while Jeff had his conversation. When they made it back to his place a few hours later, he excused himself to make another phone call. She became curious and feelings of insecurity crept into her consciousness. As soon as he disappeared into his bedroom she called Tricee. But when she heard Jeff coming back into the living room, she informed Tricee that she had to go. Pam made a mental note to be sure to call Tricee tomorrow and let her know that she was okay. She realized that the abruptness of her phone call might have caused Tricee to become concerned.

Jeff's cell phone rang shortly after he'd given Pam the bracelet, interrupting their flirtatious moment. But this time, the gift he'd just given her helped to overshadow any feelings of insecurity she might have. When he stated that it was a "business call," Pam acknowledged him with a nod. *People do make business calls over the weekend.* She entertained the thought silently and went back to admiring her bracelet.

"Hang on for a second." Jeff spoke to the party on the other end but kept his gaze on Pam. He placed his cell phone on his shoulder, turning it away from his mouth.

"My dear, I need to take this call."

"Okay," Pam smiled.

He reached over and picked up the remote from the entertainment center. "Here's the remote if you want to turn on the television. Make yourself comfortable." He flashed his pearly whites and disappeared down the hall.

Pam could hear his voice but could not make out any parts of the conversation. She turned on the television and sat the remote on the sofa next to her. She had no interest in watching television. "I don't even watch my own television on a Saturday night," she mumbled. She reached into her purse to retrieve her cell phone. There were two missed calls and one voicemail message. She returned Jackie's call without listening to the message first.

Pam got up from Jeff's sofa and walked into the kitchen as she dialed Jackie's number. She felt the kitchen made for more of a private area, making it less likely for Jeff to hear much of her conversation in the event he came out of his bedroom while she was on the phone.

She glanced around the immaculate kitchen with the white counter tops. There was a round, white kitchen table with four matching chairs. A light blue medium-sized vase was set in the center. A blender, food processor, and a microwave were neatly arranged on the counter. She thought the white wall clock with a pair of boxing gloves on its face was interesting. She glanced out of the kitchen doorway to ensure that Jeff had not finished his call.

"Hi, Pam." Jackie was relaxing in her bedroom. "I was hoping you'd call before it got too late."

"Sorry, but this is the first chance I've had all evening to return your call."

"So you're not at home?" Jackie flipped through the new issue of *Essence* magazine.

"I'm out with Jeff. I'm at his place so I can't talk long." Pam peeked around the corner once more.

"Okay, you're at his place so where is he?"

"He's on a business call in his office, bedroom or whatever."

Jackie stopped turning the pages. "Hmm. Red flag alert."

"Jackie, don't start please."

"I'm just saying. This business call couldn't take place in front of you?"

Pam thought back to earlier when Jeff allowed his phone call to take place on his speaker phone. "I heard the whole conversation earlier," Pam remarked, taking a seat at Jeff's kitchen table.

That was earlier, we're talking about now. Not wanting to sound negative, Jackie let the matter drop. "All right then." She tossed the magazine onto her bed. "Be sure to check out his bathroom."

Pam looked at her cell phone. "What?" She stifled a soft laugh after she thought about Jackie's comment. "Why would I want to do that?" She'd used his bathroom earlier but had given no thought to checking it out. It was spotless, just like the rest of his home, with toilet paper on the holder. That was all that she needed to see.

"To check out his medicine cabinet," Jackie laughed. "Girl, get with the program! He might be on some type of medication or something."

Pam had to keep herself from laughing out loud. Jackie continued her spiel. "I can't believe you don't know this stuff. I can see I have to teach you a thing or two."

"Well, if he is on medication that's his business." Pam shook her head.

"And if he turns out to be off his meds while you're there, then it becomes your business."

"You are crazy. Look, I have to go. And, yes, I am still coming to Alesia's play. I'll see you in the morning."

"It starts at 10, so I hope you plan on going home tonight," Jackie teased.

"I plead the fifth," Pam chuckled.

"Girlfriend, whatever you do, remember that your body is a temple." Jackie proceeded to recite the scripture from 1 Corinthians 6:19.

Since when did she start memorizing Bible scriptures? "You're starting to sound like Tricee." Pam allowed Jackie's comment to sink in. She repeated it silently to herself.

"I'm just giving you a friendly reminder." Jackie smiled as she stood up from her bed. "I'll see you in the morning."

Jackie may have been half joking but she hoped Pam would take heed. Pam was a grown woman and Jackie realized she could make her own decisions, nevertheless, she also knew how much Pam liked Jeff. Jackie had her own opinion about Jeff based on some of the things Pam had shared, and her opinion—at least until she'd met him—was not too favorable.

As Pam stood up, Jeff walked into the kitchen.

I hope he didn't hear any of my conversation. Pam looked Jeff over from head to toe. He'd changed into a navy blue t-shirt and a pair of jeans, looking just as fine as he had earlier. Pam could not help but to wonder if he looked this good first thing in the morning. She smiled as he approached her. He noticed the cell phone in her hand but did not acknowledge it. He smiled and winked at her instead. For Pam it was an awkward moment.

"I had to return a phone call," she held up her phone. "My girlfriend's daughter is in a play tomorrow."

"That sounds like fun." He came and stood directly in front of her with his arms crossed.

"How old is her daughter?" He bit down on his bottom lip. Pam rubbed the back of her neck. She was blushing and not sure exactly why she was starting to feel nervous. It wasn't as if she'd never been alone with a man before. There was just something about the moment that caused her feelings of anxiety.

How does it go? The spirit is willing but the flesh is weak. "She's 13." Pam glanced around the kitchen. She looked for something, anything to comment on. The clock, she'd ask him about the clock. Her brother was a huge fan of boxing. Maybe she'd try to find him a clock with boxing gloves on its face.

Jeff noticed her reaction and began to chuckle. He seemed to pick up on her nervousness.

"Do you like plays? And I don't bite."

Pam exhaled and broke out into a grin. "I do enjoy plays. It should be fun. I haven't seen her daughter in a while." He nodded as she spoke. She was pleased that Jeff seemed genuinely interested in what she had to say.

"I'm sure you'll have a good time. I like plays as long as they don't bore me in the first 10 minutes." He touched her on the arm lightly before walking over to his fridge. Pam was trying her best not to stare, but his muscular physique made it nearly impossible. Jeff wasn't too muscular; he was just the right kind of muscular. Pam imagined that his muscular arms resulted from a combination of working out along with much practice punching on a punching bag. He still indulged in the sport every now and then, just to maintain his skills, though he no longer boxed for an audience. Pam had asked him once if he'd ever considered going pro. He'd laughed and stated, "only when I was a kid. I wanted to be the next Muhammad Ali."

She tried to shift her gaze anywhere but on his body. She wanted to ask him to go and change into a pair of shorts, just so she could have a full view. Pam was getting caught up in the moment. She knew if she looked him in the eyes, it would likely cause her heart to palpitate. So when he came and stood next to her, holding a bottle of wine, she focused on the bottle.

"Let's go back into the living room." Jeff tilted his head toward the kitchen door. "Ladies first," he said, as he allowed Pam to walk in front of him.

"When was the last time you saw a play?" Pam asked. She knew exactly where his eyes were.

"Huh?" his focus was elsewhere.

Pam then turned around to face him stopping in front of the sofa.

"Oh," a mischievous grin spread across his face. "It's been a while. Maybe we can check one out sometime." He set the wine on the coffee table.

"Yes, that would be nice." Pam answered and sat down, giving him the I-know-you-were watching-my-behind look.

"I guess you need to find out when the next play you want to see is playing. But a grown-up play, not the kind you're going to see tomorrow," he teased. That was another thing she liked about Jeff. He had a good sense of humor.

"Yeah, I sort of figured that," she laughed.

This time he sat next to her. Pam was starting to feel more relaxed. She and her friends had always said that a woman needed to exercise control over any given situation, whenever possible. So when Jeff offered her another glass of wine, she accepted, but two would be her limit. Pam and her friends had seen some women get wasted at a club and then leave with some man they'd just met. They'd felt that the one big mistake any woman could make was to go out and get drunk. And it didn't matter if she was with someone or by herself. It was essential that women remained in control, especially while in the presence of the opposite sex. The one exception—and Val had pointed it out for clarification—was unless she was married. "A woman should be able to let her hair—weave or natural—down in front of her own husband," she'd said.

Jeff had stated that, though he rarely drank it, white wine was the only kind he purchased. They shared a glass over dinner with Jeff looking at her every time he raised the glass to his lips. It was his way of being comical after she'd caught on to the fact that he was merely being playful.

Pam inhaled the scent of the three candles that Jeff had placed throughout his living room. He'd lit them and turned on some soft music while Pam was in the kitchen on her cell phone. He seemed to have found the perfect timing in setting just the right mood. She had taken off her boots at the front door as soon as they'd arrived at his home, which made Pam feel all the more comfortable. She was secretly hoping that a foot rub would take place at some point during the evening, though she dared not ask.

As she sat and reflected on the entire day she'd spent with Jeff, she wondered how good it must feel for men not to ever feel vulnerable. So what if she'd just sized Jeff up from head to toe in his kitchen? And so what if she wanted to see his calves and thigh muscles? Men still didn't have the same concerns that women had. They never had to keep their guards up when they were out on a date. They didn't have to worry about and ponder whether the woman sitting next to them was out for only one thing. Her brother, along with some of her male cousins, had said otherwise.

"Men have to be just as careful as women, believe that," they'd said. "You never know if they really like you or if they just want you to spend your money. Some women like to keep a 'male friend' on the side just in case they break up with a boyfriend. You'd be surprised how many times a woman has called me after midnight asking me to come over. For some women, they want you around only when it's most convenient for them." These were a few of the things Pam had heard from the men in her family. But she still could not fathom any of that. She still believed that women had it harder, especially when it came to their desire for a committed relationship.

"Are you comfortable?" Jeff ran his fingers along the back

of her hand.

"Hmmmm," Pam answered softly.

"I'll take that as a yes." Jeff set his glass on the coffee table. He watched as Pam sipped the rest of her wine. He poured her another glass, but not as much as before this time.

"Oh, no, I'm good," she protested with a wave of her hands.

"One more won't hurt. And I didn't pour as much."

There goes the two limit rule. "How kind of you," Pam said softly. "You're not having another one? Oh wait, don't answer that. I forgot you have to drive me home."

"Well, yeah." He continued to lightly rub her hands. He was hoping she'd stay over. "I'm not much of a wine drinker, remember?'

"Are you sure you're okay after two glasses?" Pam asked. She leaned over and placed a cracker in her mouth. Jeff had placed snacks on the coffee table earlier while he was heating up dinner.

"I think I can handle two glasses of Chardonnay without losing my head."

They both laughed as they continued to chat. He was enjoying her company just as much as she was enjoying his and it showed. He was glad that Pam seemed more relaxed. As far as he was concerned, the night was still young and he didn't care to entertain the thought of driving her home. He'd kept the lamp beside the sofa dimmed on purpose. Along with the candles and the soft music, he wanted everything to feel just right. He'd planned the whole day and evening carefully. He wanted Pam to feel special. He didn't do this for just anyone.

Pam was impressed. Jeff was not only the type of man who kept a tidy home, he'd taken the time to create the right mood just for her. He was romantic, and he obviously wanted Pam to know that this side of him existed. This could only mean one thing: There was something special going on between them. Why else would he have gone through the trouble? Pam was feeling confident and she knew that her sex appeal was evident in this mood. She could tell by Jeff's body language that there was no one else he wanted beside him. A woman's intuition was a powerful asset.

Jeff's voice, as if on cue, interrupted her thoughts. "You don't have to sit here with that scarf wrapped around your neck, you know." He touched the silk scarf that matched her sweater. It was as if he'd been in on her thoughts. Not about the scarf but about his body language. “Besides, it’s sort of hard to see that beautiful neck of yours.”

Pam took the bait and slowly removed her scarf. “I never thought of my neck as being beautiful, but thanks, I’ll take that.” She placed the scarf beside her. She moved in and positioned herself so that she was snuggled closer to him. “Are you always this romantic or was this a carefully planned evening just for me?” Pam was flirting. The ball was in her court, she knew that for sure.

“It’s all about you, my dear. I wanted you to have a really enjoyable visit your first time here. That way, you’ll be more apt to accept my next invitation.”

“So it’s all about presentation, huh?” Pam nodded. *He’s slick.* She leaned over to pick up her glass of wine.

“Yes. So am I on the right path so far?” He waited until she had finished sipping. He held the hand that held the glass before taking it from her and placing it back on the coffee table. He gently kissed her neck, allowing his lips to slowly make their way to hers. “You are a very sexy and beautiful woman,” he whispered.

Before, whenever they were out, Pam would not hesitate to return his kisses. But tonight was a different story with a different scene. This was a sofa, not the front seat of his BMW. Nor was it right inside the front door at her home, where they’d shared a few long and pleasant good night kisses in the past. Her body was saying one thing, but the thoughts in her head that seemed to come from nowhere were saying something else. Only seconds earlier she was snuggled next to him waiting to feel his soft lips.

Pam sat back and pulled herself away from his embrace. She wanted to slow it down, ask some questions. Jeff’s breathing told her clearly that he wanted to continue the kissing. He’d once commented after one of their kissing sessions that he liked her “carefree and easy-going” attitude. Unlike some of the women he’d known in the past. Pam had been flattered by his comment at the time, but now she analyzed that statement in her head. Was he saying he thought I was easy? Why had he said that right after we were done kissing?

“Jeff, we need to talk.” Pam reached down and smoothed out her sweater. It was subconscious on her part since it seemed that a woman’s top was the first piece of clothing to be removed. It would have taken effort for Jeff to remove her sweater but, nevertheless, Pam needed to make sure she was not exposed.

Jeff sighed. "We need to talk," he repeated her words. "What, right now?" He sat back on the sofa, closed his eyes and then rubbed his forehead.

Why do men seem to make that gesture when they're frustrated? "Yes. I have some things weighing on mind."

"You think too much." He picked up a throw pillow and placed it behind his head. Pam remained sitting on the edge of the sofa. She had to turn slightly to look back at him. Jeff almost looked like a kid who'd just been told he could not have a treat. Pam could not help but notice the hint of disappointment that showed on his face.

The irony of it all was her lack of interest in Jeff when they first met. She had stated that he was "not her type." Three months later she still had no reason why she initially felt that way. The only thing she could think of was that she thought he might have been the arrogant type.

They'd met at a conference in Atlanta that they both had tried to get out of attending. But it was mandatory for them both. Their bosses had demanded that they attend. She had teased Jeff afterward, the first time she agreed to go out with him. "You're the vice president of the company. Surely, you could have found a way out." He was immediately attracted to her charming personality and her sense of humor. And he was not shy about letting her know that her physical attributes were what had captured his attention. And now, at this very moment, Pam wondered if her physical attributes were the driving force behind Jeff's motives. It was probably not a good time to over-analyze things but she couldn't help it.

"I need to ask you a question," Pam said. She saw no reason not to just come right out and express what was on her mind.

"Is it a multiple choice question?" Jeff attempted to use humor to ease the tension. He wondered why women had such a need to ask a lot of questions. And why did they have such poor timing? Out of all of the times today that Pam could have asked her questions, she'd chosen now. It had to have been a deliberate move on her part for sure. Then again, he thought about the times he'd had a couple of other women pull this same stunt. He decided not to hold it against her. Women just didn't know any better. Perhaps, Pam would be different and learn this valuable lesson: Timing is crucial for a man when it comes to conversation. He hoped she would learn this. He couldn't imagine having to go through this the next time she came over.

"Ask away," he spoke again, allowing Pam the opportunity to speak her mind. He was interested in what she had to say. When she failed to respond, he scooted up next to her. "Is everything okay, my dear?" He took her hand in his.

"Everything is fine." Pam sighed. Their gaze met and she saw sincerity in Jeff's eyes. Maybe now wasn't the right time to ask him how he felt about her. He'd probably give the same reply that most men would give: I'm with you here now so I must like you. Maybe her father was right. And maybe the sun would shine tomorrow. Pam thought about the song from *Little Orphan Annie*. No one knew just how much she liked that song. Her friends would laugh at her for sure. She couldn't help but to stifle a laugh. Jeff didn't bother to ask what she was laughing about, he just smiled.

Jackie's words of advice hadn't left her either. It was one thing to have Tricee lecturing about saving yourself for marriage, but quite another when one of your other close friends decides to follow suit. Maybe this was happening for a reason. One thing was for certain; Jeff definitely had expectations about how he hoped the evening would end. No big surprise there.

Jeff wanted to ask Pam once more what was on her mind, but he decided to let the matter drop. She would likely give him the long version of her answer and, though he cared how she felt, he wasn't really feeling up to it. He'd learned that unless a man was prepared to hear a lecture, it was better to leave the questions for another time. Still, he just didn't get it. Why couldn't women understand that if a man spent time with you, that meant he liked you. How hard did it have to be? What did they need men to do, draw a picture?

They'd enjoyed the whole day together. After lunch, they'd even gone window shopping for a little while along Michigan Avenue at her request. He'd parked several blocks away and paid close to $25 to park for under an hour. They might have stayed out a little longer had it not been so cold. The money he'd paid to park was no issue; Pam was well worth it. But apparently, she couldn't put those little things together. If she could she would realize that he had done this because he wanted to. Some men would have easily frowned upon window shopping, especially in the cold!

They had even laughed and joked about some of the couples they'd seen together: Who do you think wears the pants in that relationship? How long do you think those two have been married? How did he end up with her? It had all been in fun. On the drive back to his place, she even laughed hard at some of his corny jokes and told a few corny—but funny—jokes of her own. And then there was the dinner he'd prepared—not bought, but prepared. And the surprise gift he'd given her that she had squealed over. *Oh Jeff, it's so beautiful!* He mimicked a woman's voice in his mind. *What did I miss between all of that and now?*

"Well, I guess I should have you drive me home. I'm sort of sorry I didn't drive my own car. Now you have to –"

"That is not a problem." He kissed the back of her hand. "You know better than that." He stood up. A few seconds later Pam stood, as well.

"I guess I'm just feeling uncertain about some things. But I'll be okay." Pam picked up her scarf and placed it back around her neck.

"Well, the last thing I want is for you to feel uncomfortable." Jeff bit down on his bottom lip. Pam noticed that this was a habit of his. He looked so sexy when he did that.

"I'll get your coat." He began to walk toward the closet by the door, then he suddenly stopped and turned around to face Pam.

"You know I don't fully understand you yet." The expression on his face this time was one that Pam could not read. He was serious, though not in a scary way. It was just a different look than she'd seen all evening.

Pam tried her best to ignore that look along with all the other concerns that swam around in her head, but she couldn't. She suddenly thought about the comment Jackie had made earlier about checking his medicine cabinet, though she realized it was not meant to be taken seriously. Calling out to Jeff as she walked down the hall, "I need to use your bathroom before we go."

9

Saturday evening: August 17th

"What kind of mother would do such a thing?" Tricee sobbed as Val and Pam tried their best to console her. Neither of the two women had ever witnessed their friend being this upset. Tricee was sobbing so heavily that they were starting to become nervous.

Ever since their friendship began several years ago, they'd always known Tricee to remain in control of her emotions. Nothing appeared to disconcert her. Sure, she had her issues like everyone else but she had always appeared more laid back. Even before she became born again, she would refer to Bible verses when one of her friends needed encouragement or if she needed to be uplifted. She'd become more adept at explaining certain Bible scriptures when referring to the Word as a guide. For the most part, they'd become used to her quoting scriptures, even during one of their day-to-day conversations.

Pam and Jackie would confess that they sometimes felt as if they were being preached to but it never got to the point of being unbearable. Val didn't mind it so much since she, too, was saved. Unlike Tricee, however, she rarely attempted to witness to others. She would only do so when she really felt a strong tug from the Holy Spirit.

Now, as Val watched Tricee bawling her eyes out, she thought the timing was most appropriate for a verse or two. She rubbed Tricee's arm as she spoke.

"Sweetie, the Word tells us that His mercies are new every morning." It was the first verse that came to mind. Pam, not as familiar with the Word, only sat and listened. It wasn't morning but she knew better than to take the verse too literally. Pam did know enough about Him to know that He was merciful throughout the entire day. But just out of curiosity, she made a mental note to ask Val one day soon to elaborate on that particular verse.

Val and Pam, along with Jackie, were all aware of Tricee's inconsistent relationship with her mother, Ruby. Tricee had shared a few details with them over time but she'd never said that she hated her mother. As far as her friends were concerned, with the exception of a couple of things she'd shared, they believed Tricee's relationship with her mother was pretty normal. They hadn't experienced some of what she'd gone through with their moms, but they still reasoned that things between Tricee and Ruby could have been much worse.

For the first time during their friendship, Val and Pam were thinking they could better comprehend Tricee's feelings. But not wanting to pass judgment or speak ill of her mother, they kept their thoughts about Ruby to themselves. They could not imagine being in Tricee's shoes nor did they want to.

"Can you believe this?" Tricee dabbed at her eyes with Kleenex. "My best friend since 3rd grade is my half-sister. How do you keep this information from your own child?" Tricee's voice was feeble. She was crying and shaking her head back and forth, causing Val and Pam to look at each other with the look of despair. Whenever Tricee thought about the email she'd received from Annette only a week prior to Ruby's phone call, she sobbed even harder. Apparently, Annette had known nothing about this secret either because her email had not mentioned it. She wondered now if Annette had since been informed.

"Tricee, we are so sorry you have to go through this." Val rubbed Tricee's back as she fought back tears of her own. "But, sweetie, you're going to make yourself sick. Just try to stop trembling so much." A tear made its way down Val's face. Pam turned her head to look away. A few seconds later she walked over to Tricee's dresser and pulled a few tissues from the box. She wiped away the tears that had fallen down her cheeks.

They were sitting in Tricee's bedroom trying to make sense of a situation that would send anyone over the edge. After Tricee called Val crying and upset over what her mother had revealed, Val did not hesitate to drive right over to the north side. Tricee tried Pam but only got her voicemail. Instead of leaving a message, all she could do was burst into tears. Pam could hear the weeping when she retrieved her messages. She immediately dialed Tricee's cell phone number but got her voicemail. She chose not to leave a message, choosing instead to try Tricee on her home phone. No answer. The answering machine picked up. Worried, Pam called Val after being unable to reach Jackie. Val gave a brief explanation of the situation. Pam immediately stated, "I'll meet you over at her place." She was just as ready as Val to offer some consolation. But

Pam found herself at a loss for words as she witnessed Tricee's sorrow. It turned out to be more than she could bear.

Pam walked into the kitchen for water, not only for Tricee but for herself. *I could use more than a glass of water right about now.* As she reached into the fridge, she paused. It suddenly dawned on her that this surprising revelation would not only affect Tricee, it would affect Annette, as well. Pam wondered if and how Annette had received the news.

She became lost in thought, unaware that she was standing with the refrigerator door wide open. Although she was more concerned for Tricee, Pam realized that several lives would be altered. There would be questions from both Tricee and Netta, and Pam was not so sure that Ruby would have all the answers. And even if she did have the answers, would she be fully prepared to give the answers? Not likely. Then there was J.P., Tricee's father. Pam wondered what he would have to say, given that he was a huge part of the problem.

Pam shook her head and let out a sigh. The thought of a parent trying to explain a secret they'd kept for over 25 years was implausible. How do you not tell your child—in Tricee's case, your only child—that her best friend is her half- sister? She pictured her parents gathering her and her four siblings around the kitchen table for a family discussion. The task would be extremely difficult. Pam felt it was unfair that Ruby had to be the one to break the news. Was it because women had inherited some special trait when it came to matters of the heart? She now felt sympathy for Tricee's mother as she pondered the situation.

She grabbed two bottled waters and closed the refrigerator door. She was convinced that, irrespective of the explanations, this situation would likely become more complicated. Life could be so unfair and Pam wondered why something of this magnitude had to happen to someone like Tricee. It could be a good thing, however. Tricee now had a sister after thinking she was an only child. But Pam realized that a lot of emotions would have to pass before Tricee could see the situation as a "good thing."

Tricee was such a sweet person and had a strong faith. She treated others kindly—well, most of the time. You'd know if you stepped on her toes. She'd politely put you back in your place. Her friends had observed her in action a couple of times, and Pam always got a big kick out of it. "I wish I could be nice when telling somebody off. Girl, that is a gift," she'd said once. For unlike her and Jackie, when they told you you'd crossed the line, it wasn't too pleasant. Both Tricee and Val had a kind way of dealing with people in general. They rarely allowed anyone to upset them. "When you become born again, you learn how to deal with people from a different perspective," Val had once stated. Pam's reply had been simple. "Well, I'm not even *close* to being at that point."

"It's going to take a whole lot of praying and faith for Tricee to get around this mountain. Lord, you'll have to remove it or at least make it smaller," Pam mumbled under her breath. "I don't mean to be rude but I'm so glad it's not happening to me, thank you," she added and looked toward the ceiling. It had been a long time since she had chatted with God. Now she found herself doing it in Tricee's kitchen of all places.

As she began walking back to the bedroom, she suddenly noticed a plaque on the kitchen wall. She'd not noticed it before and wondered if it was something that Tricee had gotten recently. It was rather plain with only a mountain as the picture. Below it, printed in bold black letters, was: *Lord, you don't have to move the mountain, but I trust your strength to get me around it.* Pam reread the words, her eyes opening wide. She began to feel a little uneasy. *Okay, is this some sort of sign?* She turned and glanced around the kitchen, a frightful expression plastered across her face. Feeling that someone else was now in the kitchen, she walked back to the bedroom, her steps long and steady. Val looked up as Pam entered the room.

"Are you okay?" Val gave her a quick once-over. "You look like you've just seen a ghost."

"I'm fine," Pam exhaled as she set the bottle of water on the nightstand. She opened the other bottle and took a long sip. *Probably not a good time to tell Tricee there's some sort of spirit dwelling in her kitchen.* She looked around the room and then sat on the chair across from the bed. Val gave Pam a look as she reached over and handed the bottled water to Tricee. It was what Val said next that would cause Pam to gasp.

"You know," Val set the water back on the nightstand, "God doesn't give us more than we can handle." Tricee placed both her hands on her face as Val spoke. "Do you remember the words to that song you love by Mahalia Jackson? The one she sings about the Lord not moving the mountain?" Val patted Tricee on the knee as she spoke. "He will give you the strength. You have to believe that."

Tricee moved her hands from her face and nodded. She then repeated the words to the song in a feeble voice. When she was done, Pam stood to her feet. Tricee and Val both looked over at Pam, each one wearing the same puzzled expression.

"Pam, what's wrong?" Tricee asked softly. She'd stopped crying but her eyes still welled with tears.

"Do you need more water?" Val asked.

Pam drank the rest of her water and stammered before speaking. "N-no. I just feel –"

"What? What is it?" Val asked, not too surprised by Pam's sudden change of behavior. Pam could be so dramatic at times, but this evening was all about Tricee. Whatever Pam was feeling would have to take a backseat. Tricee was the top priority.

Tricee excused herself and went into the bathroom. As soon as Pam heard the door close, she walked over and sat next to Val on the bed.

"Val, I feel like someone is trying to tell me something," she whispered.

"What are you talking about?" Val gave Pam a there-is-always-something-with-you look.

Pam hesitated and let out a sigh. "Maybe God is trying to tell me something." She looked around the corner of Tricee's bedroom door. "Is that possible?"

Val had not ever recalled seeing Pam look so uneasy before. It was quite comical. Val almost started laughing. "Yes, that is very possible. He is always trying to talk to His children."

Pam wanted to share with Val what she was feeling. How she had read the words on the plaque after saying close to the same words herself, and how Val had then repeated similar words to Tricee. Pam wondered if God was trying to get through to her by way of Tricee's dilemma. If so, He sure did have an interesting way of doing things. Tricee had suggested to Pam on several occasions that she should give her life to Christ, but Pam had only mumbled a "Yeah, I will one day" and left it at that.

Tricee emerged from the bathroom. Pam would have to share more with Val some other time. "We'll talk later," she whispered softly to Val.

Tricee sat on the bed with her two friends.

"Have you spoken with your mother?" Pam asked, both out of concern and curiosity. She'd allowed Val to do most of the encouraging by way of words the whole time they'd been there. Speaking up now was a good way to keep her distracted from her own thoughts. "She is still in town, isn't she?"

"Yes, she is still here," Tricee managed a weak response. "She's not leaving until Monday. But, no, I have not spoken with her since last night." Tears formed again in Tricee's eyes. "She hasn't even made an attempt to call me today. Can you believe that?" The question was directed at no one in particular. "I have spent all night and all morning trying to make sense of this whole situation. But it just doesn't make sense."

The empty box of tissue on the nightstand had been replaced with another one by Val. As Tricee reached for more tissue, Pam looked away. Watching Tricee start up again was beginning to take its toll. It seemed as if Tricee had gone through 10 boxes of tissue. It had been a long time since Pam had seen anyone shed so many tears. She'd shed a few of her own as she witnessed her friend's sorrow, but she was determined to remain strong for Tricee's sake. Therefore, she would withhold her tears.

"Have you tried to call her?" Pam asked. She did not want to ask too many questions, but to remain silent would only result in her breaking down.

"No. I am not going to call her." Tricee shook her head vigorously. Pam had excused herself earlier to keep Val and Tricee from seeing her cry. She just wasn't used to being in a situation such as this and she had no idea how to react. Val had remained calm. She'd cried some, too, but had been able to offer more encouragement.

For Pam, the set of circumstances now surrounding Tricee had stirred something within her but she could not quite put a finger on it. Pam was feeling confused. And since it was now after 8 PM, she decided it was time for her to leave. There was nothing else she felt she could say, and she and Val had both been there for several hours. First, she would ensure that Tricee was going to be okay.

"Tricee, I am here for you, you know that. Is there anything I can get for you?" Pam asked as she stroked Tricee's hand.

"I'll be just fine. Thank you two so much for coming over." Tricee then placed both hands over her face, bowed her head and closed her eyes. Val and Pam glanced at each other, both wearing the same expression and thinking: *I wish there was something more that I could do.*

As Val wiped away yet another tear, Pam looked on. *Oh, now here she is crying again.* Pam's thoughts were interrupted by the words that flowed softly from Tricee's lips.

"I guess I'm supposed to give thanks, even in this situation." She blew her nose and continued to speak, "easier said than done."

"Take His strength and not your own. Tricee, you will be just fine." Val spoke as she dabbed at her eyes with a tissue. Pam sat and observed both of her born again friends crying and listened to their exchange of words. She recognized that some of their words had come right from the Bible and she wanted so much to comprehend what the two of them had been able to grasp: Lean upon Him. Or at least learn to lean upon Him during difficult times.

As Tricee had stated easier said than done, Pam could surely relate to those four words. But unlike Tricee, whose faith would likely withstand even this test, Pam's trust and faith had a tendency to waver. She did believe that there was a God but that was the extent of it.

"I already let Cory know I was staying over." Val's statement brought Pam a sense of relief. It was her cue that she could now leave. She needed to go and deal with what had been started within her.

Tricee smiled at Val and then glanced over at Pam. Pam could sense that Tricee would have loved for them both to stay but that was not an option. There were too many other things Pam now had to figure out. But she was grateful that Tricee had Val to keep her company for the remainder of the evening.

Tricee's expression was a good indicator of how happy she'd felt to not have to spend the rest of the evening alone. However, the last thing she wanted was to inconvenience Val. "You don't have to stay over. Besides, you have a family to attend to."

"No. Not tonight I don't. And I have already told you that Cory is aware of the fact that I am spending the night here."

Tricee felt thankful to have such wonderful friends. But she couldn't help but wonder just how much information Val had shared with her husband. As Val walked over to retrieve her large purse, which she'd placed on a chair, Pam stood, as well. Val then turned back to Tricee and looked at her as if she had read her mind.

"I only mentioned to Cory that you had some things going on and that I needed to come over. He asked if you were alright and I told him that you were, but that I thought it would be a good idea if I stayed over." Tricee was satisfied with that explanation.

She trusted her friends and knew they had her best interest at heart. She just wasn't sure if she was ready for anyone else outside of her three closest friends to know the details of the awful truth. Cory and Val were husband and wife, she realized that, but now was not the time for him to know of her unpleasant and surprising new set of circumstances.

Tricee glanced over at Pam who was now standing, holding her purse in one hand and a very thin, light blue jacket in the other. Although it was a warm August evening, Pam had the habit of carrying a light jacket, especially whenever she ventured to the north side. A warm evening could easily turn into a partially cool one. Not to mention the building where Tricee lived was right on the lakefront. There was also the four or five blocks of walking she'd have to do to get back to her car.

"You're leaving, Pam?" Tricee asked.

There was a moment of hesitation. The evening had certainly been filled with surprises, not only for Tricee but for Pam, as well. Tricee, Pam realized, was still the one with the bigger issue to deal with.

"Yeah, I think I'll go on home. But please call me if you need anything, okay?" She gave Tricee a hug while softly patting her on the back. Tricee could sense that Pam was near tears so she decided not to utter another word. She put her head down as Pam walked toward the bedroom door.

"I'll be right back, Tricee," Val said. "I'm going to walk Pam out to the elevator." Tricee nodded as she managed to keep more tears from falling.

Val put the latch in the door to keep it open. At the elevator she reached over and gave Pam a hug.

'Thanks so much for coming over. I'll call you tomorrow." Val could read people very well. It was obvious to her that something was eating at Pam besides Tricee's dilemma. And it was not only because Pam had mentioned it to her earlier, it was the vibe she was getting. Although each of the four women friends was known for their perceptiveness, Val, arguably, was the most astute when it came to evaluating a situation.

She would allow Pam to speak on it first as opposed to broaching the subject herself. She knew Pam well enough to know that it would only be a matter of time before she blurted out what was on her mind. Val quickly counted backwards in her head: five, four, three, two, one, and on the count of one, Pam started talking. Val tried her best to hide her smirk.

"Val, I feel so bad for Tricee. I hate having to see her like this." Pam's words came out fast.

"I know. But we are here for her and she knows that." The elevator had now reached the 14th floor but they allowed it to close as Pam didn't move. It was obvious that she needed more time to talk.

Val glanced at Pam as if she knew exactly what would come forth next. Pam was a sweet person, in her own way. But if you didn't know her well, you'd think she was a bit selfish and believed that everything turned out, somehow, to be about her. Her friends knew her well enough to know that self-absorbed was not truly one of her traits. Pam exhaled.

"I feel like the Man upstairs is trying to get my attention."

She waited for Val to comment but when she failed to do so, Pam shot her a look. *Well, say something*, she willed her silently. Val smiled instead. When Pam noticed that her friend was allowing her to have the floor again, she exhaled again. Val sensed Pam's annoyance but remained silent. Tricee was the one going through a tough dilemma, not that Pam's feelings— whatever it was that she was feeling—was unimportant. But Val was willing to bet that Pam was not even close to experiencing what Tricee was feeling.

"I saw a plaque on Tricee's wall that I never noticed before, with words about God and His ability to move mountains." Pam spoke as Val listened intently. "And the funny thing is I was just saying to myself before I saw that plaque how God would have to move this mountain for Tricee."

A tall gentleman wearing a white t-shirt, a Cubs baseball cap and blue jeans then emerged from one of the apartments and walked over to wait on the elevator. He gave a half-smile and stood behind Val. The elevator arrived again and Val stepped aside, allowing him to enter. Pam then held the elevator with her hand.

"I already told you what I feel," Val said in an attempt to give Pam something to think about. "He delights in speaking to His children. It's up to us to listen." *Now get going, Missy.* She almost blurted her thoughts out loud.

"Hmmm." Pam tilted her head to one side. "Maybe He is trying to tell me I need to learn to listen." Val shrugged. She believed it was more to it than that but she dared not say so. "Okay." Pam responded as if Val's shrug had been verbal. "Well, girl, I'll call you later. I'll call you as soon as I am home." Pam stepped into the elevator still holding the doors and turned to face Val, the tall guy standing behind her.

"You'll keep me updated on things." Pam said, more of a demand than a question.

Val, not wishing for Pam to think that she was uninterested in her feelings calmly replied, "Yes, of course. And we'll discuss more about what you're feeling, too. Just let us help Tricee to get past this."

The gentleman let out a sigh loud enough for them both to hear. It was obvious that he was ready for Pam to release the elevator doors. If Pam's looks could kill, he wouldn't have made it to the lobby.

Val laughed at the glare Pam gave the man. She went back inside Tricee's condo. Tricee smiled, something Val hadn't seen all evening.

"What?" Val asked, not realizing that it was her smile from laughing at Pam that Tricee had picked up on.

"You're smiling," Tricee shrugged. Val then explained the look Pam had just given the guy on the elevator.

"I'll sleep on the sofa. You can have my bed," Tricee said. Val observed the white sheet, two pillows, and a colorful blanket that Tricee had placed on the sofa. She also observed the whole wheat bread, sliced turkey, lettuce, and the light Miracle Whip on the kitchen counter. It hadn't dawned on Val that she hadn't eaten anything since earlier in the afternoon.

"Girlfriend, I am not taking your bed. I will sleep on the sofa. Besides, your big-screen is in here." Val pointed toward the television. They both chuckled as they proceeded into the kitchen.

"Well, I just figured it's the least that I can do. Val, I really appreciate –"

"Don't mention it, Tricee." Val replied before Tricee could finish her statement. "You know I am here for you. That's what friends are for."

That was all that needed to be said as Val's words and her company would make the remainder of the evening a little less tense.

Tricee could not bear replaying in her mind all over again

yesterday's incident with Ruby. It had started out as a pretty good day and dinner had gone fairly well. But the bomb that Ruby dropped last night was something out of a dream, not real life.

Val and Tricee washed their hands before they prepared to make sandwiches with all of the fixings.

"I hope you don't mind turkey sandwiches. Feel free to look in my cabinets and my fridge to see if you'd like to make something else," Tricee said softly. Val could see that Tricee was trying her best to feel better.

"A sandwich is fine with me. But since you mentioned it, I'd like to make a small salad to go with it," Val said.

"Oh, go right ahead. You can use whatever you like. I have tomatoes, olives, banana peppers—I don't have to tell you to make yourself at home."

"Thanks. Would you like one, as well?" Val offered. "I could make us both one."

"No, I think I'll just have a sandwich. But thanks anyway."

After Tricee made herself a sandwich, she walked to the refrigerator to retrieve a pitcher of iced tea. Though she was feeling a little better, she was starting to feel tired. She hadn't eaten much, either, with the exception of a banana nut muffin she'd eaten around Noon. She hadn't had much of an appetite when she woke up this morning. And as for feeling tired, that was more mental than physical. Even though she was now very hungry, feelings of despair overcame her feelings of hunger. As Val joined her at the table, Tricee couldn't help but comment on the salad Val had prepared.

"Wow, Val! You sure know how to create a salad. That looks good!" Tricee's emotions had gone back and forth all evening. It was funny how the sight of food, if only for a moment, took her mind off her troubles. One minute she felt dejected and the next she was capable of emitting a chuckle. They both chuckled as Val surveyed her creation.

"Girl, I am the queen of salads! In my house we have a salad with dinner at least three times a week." She opened the plastic bottle of raspberry salad dressing. "I'll repay you," she said as she held up the now empty bottle. Tricee managed another chuckle, feeling even more thankful for Val's company.

"Sometimes just a salad is all we'll eat for dinner. I will usually add either grilled chicken or lots of turkey breast, though, since Cory doesn't believe men can eat a plain old salad." The conversation between the two women over dinner helped take Tricee's thoughts elsewhere, if only for a little while.

For a while it seemed that the incident with Ruby had not taken place. It was a relief since Tricee had hoped to put this all to rest, at least for the night. She'd hoped that by morning, she'd have a better grasp on her emotions.

As Val walked over to the fridge for more iced tea, Tricee gathered the plates to place them in the sink. They took their glasses of iced tea and headed for the living room. Val set hers on the coffee table. "I should check in with Cory."

"You need privacy?" Tricee asked, partly serious and partly joking.

"I need to grab my purse. No privacy needed." Val laughed as she walked into Tricee's bedroom. She changed into the oversized t-shirt she'd brought to sleep in, keeping on the Capri pants she'd worn that day, then dialed her home number. Her stepson, Sean, answered. Val walked back into the living room where Tricee was seated in her recliner. The sight of Val on her cell phone caused Tricee to pick up the remote. She turned down the volume as Val sat on the sofa to indulge in conversation with her family.

"I need for your friends to leave by 10:30, Sean."

There was slight annoyance in the voice on the other end. Val was unfazed.

"I don't care, Sean, if it is a Saturday night. By 10:30. You know the rules." And then followed a plea that only a teenage boy could make.

"Oh snap, Val! I almost forgot to tell you! I ironed your outfit for church tomorrow. The skirt and blouse you had laid out across your bed."

Val was unfazed. "Thanks, Sean. I appreciate it."

Another plea followed. "My dad ate the rest of your chocolate mint cookies so I went to the store and bought you some more."

Val remained unimpressed. "Thanks, Sean." She waited to see if there were any other pleas. "Okay, well your friends have only a few minutes left. It's almost 10:30. And don't eat all of my cookies!"

Defeated, her stepson grumbled and then called his dad to the phone. Val looked over at Tricee and winked. Tricee smiled thinking how nice it must be to have such a tender moment with a family member.

She picked up a magazine that Val had brought with her and flipped through its pages. *Information Technology*, a publication that Val read on a regular basis since technology was her field. Tricee did not understand too much of anything that was written on the pages but it provided a great diversion from the events of the evening.

Val's husband had apparently come to the phone as Tricee noticed a change in her tone. It was still laced with tenderness but more so now than several minutes earlier. After several minutes, Val placed her cell phone on the coffee table.

"A woman's work is never done. Had I not called home, Sean's friends would stay until midnight." She took a sip of her iced tea.

Tricee placed the magazine beside her, reached for the remote and turned the television to the evening news. Due to a nighttime baseball game, the news broadcast was on a little later than normal. Val was now standing and spreading the sheet across the sofa, preparing her place of rest for the night. As Tricee sipped the rest of her tea, she proceeded to listen to the news team recap what was going on in and around the Windy City. She was so engrossed in the story of a 7-year-old girl who'd been fatally struck by a hit-and-run driver that she failed to respond to Val's question.

"Tricee, this blanket is beautiful. Where did you buy it?" Val was admiring the light blue, thin blanket with the red and yellow pattern on it. Orange strips were sewn along the outer edge of the blanket; the colors made the blanket really stand out. It was such a beautiful piece. Val was a little surprised that Tricee would allow company to use it.

"Tricee," Val repeated. She was sitting on the sofa with the blanket spread across her lap.

"I'm sorry, girl. I was so into this story about the little girl." Tricee shook her head. "It's a shame how so many children are either run down or gunned down." She turned the volume down on the television. "What were you asking me?"

Val rubbed her hand across the blanket. "I know what you mean. It is sad. It seems that every day we read or hear about some innocent child being a victim of violence. It's ridiculous." Val stood to go into the kitchen. "Do you need anything?"

"No, I'm fine."

After pouring herself a glass of water, she came back into the living room and resumed her position on the sofa. "I was asking where you got this blanket. It's very pretty and I love the colors." She ran her hand over the fabric. "It's so soft and not too thick. It's just right for the summer."

Tricee's expression changed into one of discomfort and her eyes were now filled with sadness. She put her head down as she spoke. "My mother made that blanket. She also made me one for my 30th birthday with even more colors than this one." A tear rolled down her left cheek. "This one has been around for a long time, since I was a teenager." Tricee kept her gazed turned away from Val. "My moth –," she paused, "Ruby repaired it and created another pattern for it."

Val noticed how Tricee had caught herself and said "Ruby" as opposed to "my mother." She listened intently as Tricee continued. Hearing the pain in Tricee's voice, she now regretted even asking about the blanket.

"Ruby was going to try and sell it to one of her friends back in St. Louis but I talked her into keeping it. I asked her not to sell it because I really liked it." Tricee then turned toward Val. "I talked her into making another one to sell instead."

Val reached over and handed Tricee some Kleenex. "Thanks," Tricee said softly. "You know, when I went into my closet to grab it, my mind was so distracted. I thought I was grabbing just another blanket."

"I can see how that would happen," was all Val could manage to say. Words were not necessary.

"I rarely, if ever, use the one that she made me for my birthday, unless it's a special occasion." Tricee wiped away the last traces of tears but the sadness in her eyes remained. "I use this one sort of regularly because it reminds me of when I was younger and because it's light enough to use in the summer." She glanced over at the blanket, the words that came out of her mouth next made Val shed a tear.

"What I can't understand is how a woman, my own mother, could sew such beautiful things yet not have the same beautiful heart to match."

Although reluctant to speak, Val felt it was now time to offer her friend words of encouragement. "Oh, Tricee, sweetie, please don't think like that. I mean, if your mother didn't care, she wouldn't have made this trip." Val could understand Tricee's unpleasant feelings, but she was not convinced that Ruby was a woman with a heart of stone.

"I have to believe that your mother does have a beautiful heart. But, right now, it's hard for you to see that because of what has transpired between you two."

Tricee listened as Val spoke and was none too surprised that what she had to say made perfect sense. Nevertheless, what she was feeling toward Ruby was not what one would normally feel toward a mother. It wasn't hate because Tricee despised that word altogether. She didn't think it was possible to hate anyone. But, right now, she felt disdain for her own mother and she didn't see that changing anytime soon.

As Tricee stood to go into the bathroom she let out a sigh. She held back the tears as she spoke. "Val, I am not sure what the outcome of all of this is going to be, but for the moment, a part of me is wishing that I had been born to someone else."

Val sat silent as Tricee walked into the bathroom. In time she believed that this would all be resolved. She had to believe that Tricee's faith would win over her inability to see her mother as a loving human being. No matter how this was going to get resolved, it was all just another trick of the enemy—to kill, steal, and destroy.

While Tricee was in the bathroom, Val removed her Capri pants. It had been a long day and an even longer night. All there was left to do was get a good night's rest. Her intention was to attend church tomorrow, so she would have to wake up fairly early. The drive from the north side back to Forest Park was at least 45-minutes. And she'd promised her husband that she would arrive home early enough to attend church with the family. She would have no problem coming back to Tricee's place sometime tomorrow if needed.

When Tricee emerged from the bathroom, she, too, was now dressed for bed. Her thin, white linen robe was secured around her body with a white belt. A pink slip was visible near her neck where the robe didn't close.

"Do you plan on attending church tomorrow?" Val asked as she slid under the blanket.

"I'm not sure. I want to go but I guess it depends on how I am feeling when I wake up," Tricee said.

"Well, I will probably leave around 6:30 or so. If you are not yet awake, I'll be sure to lock the door from the inside."

"That will be fine. But I'll probably be awake by that time anyway."

Just as they said good night, Tricee's home phone rang. She walked over to look at the caller ID and saw that it was Pam calling.

"It's Pam." Tricee looked over her shoulder at Val, then picked up the phone. "Thanks for calling to let us know you made it. You must have made a stop first?" Tricee only asked because Pam had left at least two hours ago. Pam said she'd stopped by her sister's house on the way home.

"I'll call you tomorrow. Get some rest," Pam stated calmly. "Tell Val I'll talk to her later."

Tricee could tell by Pam's voice that she was just as tired as she was. And Pam could tell Tricee was beyond tired. She knew Tricee's intent was to make it seem as if she had it all under control, but Pam knew better.

Tricee hung up the phone, turned out the light, then proceeded to her bedroom. As soon as she walked into her bedroom, the phone rang again. Val sat up to turn on the lamp beside the coffee table. Tricee walked back into the living room.

"Maybe its Pam calling back," Val said. Tricee checked the caller ID to see that it was the front desk calling from downstairs.

"It's the doorman calling." Tricee looked over at the clock. "It's after 11 o'clock. Why on earth is he calling?" She looked puzzled but picked up the phone. "Hello?"

"Ms. Miller you have a guest here. Ruby Miller and – " She heard the doorman ask the other party his or her name. "It's Ms. Ruby Miller and Bev Sanders. Would you like for me to send them up?"

Proverbs 3:5 – Trust in the Lord with all thine heart; and lean not unto thine own understanding.

10

"This sure is an old looking building for an elementary school. If I was a parent, I would think twice before sending my child here."

Pam's comment caused Tricee to stop in her tracks. She thought about giving Pam a comeback but decided against it. The day had just begun. It was too early for complaining and much too early to have to hear it. Tricee took a deep breath and resumed walking. *Father, please place a bridle on this tongue of mine.*

The elementary school, located on the north side, was one of the oldest schools in the area. The dark brown building had two floors and a basement. The stairs in the front of the building were gray and narrow, and led to a set of double doors. The smell of disinfectant greeted you as soon as you walked into the building and stayed with you as you walked down the long and narrow corridor. It was obvious the maintenance crew kept the inside of the school clean. The cafeteria was located in the school's basement along with the gym. The classrooms for the 6th, 7th and 8th graders were all equipped with computers; the library also had three computer stations. And the other classrooms, which housed Kindergarten through 5th grade, were very tidy and had many books on their shelves, many of them new.

Although Tricee and Pam were there to spend time with the older children, they were given a tour of the two preschool classrooms. These two classrooms were located in the back of the building, separated from the other classrooms by a set of double doors. The doors, however, were to remain open at all times, except in fire drills. The children in the pre-K program attended for a half day, from either 9:00 AM to 11:30 AM or from noon until 2:30 PM. There was a teacher as well as an assistant in each class. The learning materials were plentiful and both classrooms also contained a small fridge. The children appeared to be very comfortable with their teachers and, from their behavior; you could tell they were enthusiastic about being in school. In fact, they were likely waiting for the day when they could attend school all day. Kindergarten was something to look forward to.

The teacher's lounge was located in the front of the building. There were three medium-sized tables with chairs, a small lounge sofa, a copier and a computer. Inside of the main office was a framed poster with the words: *Children Are Our Future. We Hold the Key to Their Success.* And right outside of the school's office, in plain view, was another framed poster: *Excellence is in Our Future; Knowledge is Power.* The administrators, teachers, and the other staff members all seemed to enjoy what they were there to do and that was to serve the children.

"It seems to have everything that a school needs to function properly and the employees all seem to love what they do," Tricee remarked as she and Pam left the pre-K classrooms. The pre-k teacher of one of the classrooms had provided the brief tour, while her assistant happily and effectively managed the children. Tricee could not find anything negative to say—not that she was looking for anything in the first place. She'd wanted to make a point with her positive statement to counter-attack Pam's negative statement a half hour earlier.

They had come to the school to participate in Career Day, an event that the administrators from the various schools throughout the city organized once a year. Jackie was on the committee. Tricee and Pam were there to discuss the importance of staying in school along with various professions available to young adults. Although Jackie was the principal of a high school, she, along with some of the other high school principals, all agreed that this event would be valuable to the younger children, as well. The elementary and middle schools used to be part of the program but, five years ago, someone with the school district decided it was only beneficial for the high school students. Well, Jackie, along with six more determined administrators, challenged the system. And two years ago, the elementary and middle schools were placed back on the agenda. Success! Great things happened when you worked as part of a team.

Jackie had asked Pam and Tricee (actually she'd asked Tricee, she practically had to beg Pam) if they would volunteer their time for the day. The slots for the high schools filled pretty quickly. The need was greater for the younger students. Val had been one of the volunteers to speak at one of the high schools. Incidentally, she had an uncle who was also a high school principal who served on the same committee as Jackie. When asked by her uncle to participate, Val did not hesitate to say yes. When Jackie called to ask her to speak, Val joyfully responded, "Girlfriend, I'll be there. My uncle beat you to the draw." Jackie thanked Val and stated, "Oh, why can't it be this easy with Pam? Good grief."

For the first part of the morning, there had been a brief tour of the school and then a meeting for all those who had come to participate. There were at least 20 adults, more than the principal had expected. He had more than enough working adults to spread out among the different classes. After the meeting, the adults were split into groups of three and four to speak to the various classrooms. There was a 45-minute lunch break, then everyone was to resume at 12:45 PM. By 1:00 PM they were all given their assignments for the remainder of the day. The volunteers all enjoyed being able to speak to the various classes. It allowed them an opportunity to meet with the various age groups. The meeting was held in the school's auditorium, located on the second floor. But it did not go over without a complaint from Pam.

"It's cold in here. Geez, I guess it takes the school's old furnace a while to heat up first thing in the morning." Pam and Tricee sat near the front. It wasn't as cold as Pam made it seem. Tricee offered Pam her wool scarf. She declined and rubbed her hands together. "I hope I don't have to keep my gloves on all day."

Tricee turned and spoke to the young lady who had taken a seat beside her. After the meeting they went to their respective classrooms. Tricee, Pam and an older gentleman were in the same group. They spoke to a 6th grade class and answered the many questions from the curious 11-year-old boys and girls. Lunch followed with ham and cheese or turkey sandwiches, and a salad.

"It was considerate of them to feed us," Tricee stated with smile.

Pam forced a smile, grunted, then proceeded to try to open the small packet of salad dressing. "Can you open this for me?" she asked Tricee. Tricee gave her a look. "Please." Pam knew that look all too well.

"Sure." Tricee opened the packet and handed it back to Pam.

"Thanks," Pam mumbled.

The next assignment was a special education classroom. The students ranged from 5th to 7th grade. It went well. One of the students, a 7th grade girl, shyly asked Pam if she liked her new dress. "Oh, it's very pretty. Do you think I can wear it?" The girl giggled. Pam was genuinely kind. Tricee was not surprised by her kindness toward this particular student. She just hoped Pam could keep that demeanor until 2:30 PM.

Now, as they walked toward the school parking lot, it was obvious that Pam had not enjoyed Career Day as much as Tricee and Val. Once they reached their vehicles Pam let out a sigh.

"I am so glad that is over." She looked the building over once more. "And I still think they could do something to make the school look more inviting."

Tricee didn't agree so she said nothing. She just wasn't up for battle with Pam today.

"People do judge by outer appearances, whether it's a person or a building." Pam continued talking as Tricee tried her best to ignore her. She focused instead on some of the teachers who were now walking to their own cars. She could imagine that they were looking forward to the weekend. One of the teachers smiled and waved goodbye as she climbed into her white Lexus GX.

"You know teachers complain about not making enough money. Funny how some of them are able to afford fancy cars." Pam was on a roll and, at this point, Tricee couldn't help but to laugh. As much as she'd tried to not give Pam any satisfaction, it had become impossible.

"You are a walking complaint! What is it, PMS?" Tricee remarked.

They were supposed to meet Jackie in Hyde Park at a local café but Tricee was starting to have second thoughts. She wasn't sure if she could take any more of Pam's negativity. The snow had pretty much melted and it wasn't as cold as it had been for the past several days. This alone caused Tricee to feel hopeful. She was looking forward to getting out some this weekend.

Tricee decided she would meet with Jackie and Pam for about an hour. She had other plans for later on in the evening. But if Pam planned to complain for that one hour, it would be an hour she'd gladly do without.

"No, I am not having a bout of PMS. I just have a lot on my mind." Pam unlocked the doors of her vehicle. "And I'm very tired."

"Well, the weekend's here and you can relax," Tricee said.

"I have some work to do tomorrow from home. Since I did not go in today, I have a little catching up to do."

"Welcome to the club girlfriend." Tricee was parked right next to Pam. She unlocked her car doors and then tossed her purse on the passenger seat. "You know, we shouldn't allow our careers to prevent us from giving up some of our time. That's just my opinion. As long as we are getting the work done, our employers should be pleased."

"Yeah, well I guess that all depends on who you're working for." Pam glanced at her watch. "Well, let me get going. I'll see you at the café."

Pam's expression, as well as her abruptness, indicated that she was either very tired or just having a bad day altogether. She had not allowed her mood, however, to interfere with the task of speaking to the children. She was able to reserve her negative comments for only Tricee to hear. She had remained pleasant to *almost* everyone else she encountered at the school. Tricee had even noticed how some of the 8th grade girls had taken a liking to Pam.

Pam was not known to take out her frustrations on children. Even though the day hadn't brought her the same satisfaction as Tricee, she had not totally regretted participating in the day's event. Tricee was convinced that once they all met later on at the café, Pam would be back to her old self.

Pam and Tricee both drove off in their respective vehicles—Tricee heading north and Pam heading south. Since she only lived a few miles from the school, Tricee decided to stop off at home first. She put in one of her gospel CDs and couldn't help but to smile at the singer's comforting words. *I wish I had been blessed with a beautiful voice.* She thought about her Aunt Janice who had a voice that would put many of today's artists to shame. She suddenly remembered that calling her aunt was on her "To Do" list for the weekend. When Tricee was about 10 minutes from home, her cell phone rang.

"Hello?"

"Hi, Tricee, it's Val. Are you driving?"

"Yes. But I'm close to home and I have my earpiece in. What's going on?" Val was opposed to people using their cell phones while driving, even if the person was using an earpiece.

"Call me back when you have a moment."

Tricee laughed. Val's three girlfriends all knew how she felt about cell phones and driving. They felt the same way and always used an earpiece, but that still wasn't good enough for Val.

As soon as Tricee walked in her front door she called Val. She looked through the mail as she spoke, remaining conscious of the time.

"How did you like Career Day?" Val asked.

"It went very well and I really enjoyed talking with the students and the teachers."

"I enjoyed it, too. But I guess you know that already from the text that I sent you."

Tricee glanced over at her home phone and noticed that the answering machine indicated that there were three messages. She walked into her kitchen, washed her hands, rinsed an apple, took a bite, and then proceeded to open one of her pieces of mail. It never ceased to amaze her how women could multitask so well.

"Yes, I got your text. I am glad you enjoyed it. Were the students really into it?"

"Yes especially the seniors. They had a ton of questions! They asked me if I enjoyed being a computer programmer, and many of them expressed an interest in technology."

After tossing the junk mail into the trash bin, Tricee gathered some clothes from her bedroom and tossed them into the laundry basket. She then changed into a different blouse, maneuvering the phone.

"The children at the school where Pam and I volunteered had their share of questions. But they were also quick to give their opinions." Tricee laughed.

"Well, it sounds like you ladies really enjoyed it! That's good. Maybe we'll do it again next year."

Tricee chuckled at that thought. "Oh, I don't know about that. I would be willing but I don't know about Pam."

She bent down to tie the laces on her boots, then reached for her sweater and coat. The conversation continued as she locked her door.

"What? Did Pam not enjoy it?"

"Let's just say she had her share of complaints. But I can say that the sister didn't allow the kids or the teachers to see her dark cloud."

As soon as she reached her vehicle, Tricee realized that she had forgotten to check the messages on her home phone. Oh, well. It would just have to wait. She wanted to get on Lakeshore Drive before it got too crowded and she was probably already too late.

"What was she complaining about? I can't say that I am surprised." They both knew how Pam could be, which is why they were able to discuss her and enjoy a laugh or two. Theirs was a friendship of respect and love. If there was ever a serious issue amongst them, they would call whomever the issue was with directly. Fortunately this was a rare occasion.

Tricee began to speak before backing out of her parking space. “The school looked too old and they need to spend the money to make it more appealing,” she mocked Pam’s complaint and tossed her head back and laughed. “And the furnace is too old. The auditorium, according to her, was freezing. She has to work from home tomorrow since today’s event caused her to fall behind. And let me see, what else? Oh yeah! The teachers are not allowed to drive nice vehicles since they complain about being underpaid.”

“Oh, how dare those teachers! Spending money on nice cars with their hard-earned money,” Val was laughing as hard as Tricee. “They need to be ashamed of themselves.”

“You know!” Tricee remarked.

“Tell girlfriend I said to chill out.” Val was unable to join them at the café. “It’s the weekend. She needs to let her hair down.”

Val and Tricee could still hear each other laughing as they hung up from their call. Val regretted not being able to join them for an early dinner, but she’d already made other plans. She was often teased by her three closest friends. If she’d remained single as they’d managed to do, she’d be able to hang out more.

I am sure that once Pam is at the café with Tricee and Jackie she’ll be back to her old self again, Val mentally echoed the same thoughts Tricee had earlier.

Whatever it was that was bothering Pam was obviously not serious enough to make her forego meeting with Tricee and Jackie. In fact, she was likely looking to use their time together to discuss whatever her issues were.

The Small Plate Café where they had agreed to meet was located near the H and P University campus where Tricee was employed. The décor was pleasing and the price of the food was very reasonable. Many of the students from the nearby campus frequented this café but today was an exception. There were only three students present—you could tell by the books and the book bags. It was likely that many of the students were still getting settled into the new semester. The only other person present when Pam arrived was an older black gentleman reading a newspaper. He was quite handsome and looked rather distinguished. His thick salt and pepper hair made him appealing. Had it not been for the hair, he might not have been considered very attractive. He was definitely not the type who could pull off the bald look.

As soon as Pam was within view, he stopped reading and set his paper on the table. He said hello, obviously hoping that Pam would smile and say hello in return. But this was not an I-feel-like-flirting sort of day for Pam. Unfortunately for him, he'd caught her on a bad day, so he would have to get his attention from another pretty lady. Better yet, perhaps he could get some attention from his wife. Pam noticed his wedding band. But he could have been single and on a Chicago most eligible bachelor list—it would not have made any difference to Pam. The half-smile she returned was indicative of her feelings. After being shot down by Pam's half - smile, the man picked up his paper, walked over to the cashier and paid for whatever it was he'd just consumed.

"Yeah, take your ego and that newspaper somewhere else, buddy," Pam mumbled under her breath. She picked up the hot cup of green tea she'd just ordered and took a sip. She did not care much for the taste. Her sister swore that it was too healthy for her to pass up and that was the problem with many of us black women. Her sister's exact words were: "Some of us sisters do not take out the time to conduct research on nutrition to learn what is healthy for us."

Pam's sister, Lynn, was seven years younger than she was. She'd been allowed to skip her junior year of high school, which made her the youngest person in her senior class. She'd graduated at the top of her class and was chosen as the valedictorian. Pam could still remember the day the family attended Lynn's high school graduation. Although she'd seen her mother cry on many occasions, it was the first time she had witnessed tears fall from her father's face. He'd stated that he was just so proud of his daughter because she had worked so hard all through school. She'd been the most serious of his five children when it came to schoolwork, preferring to study or read a book as opposed to hang out with her friends.

Her position as a registered dietician was one that she loved and she has stated that she could not see herself doing anything else. Pam loved her sister dearly and they were very close, but sometimes she felt that Lynn was something of a know-it-all. And please do not let her get started on the topics of fitness and nutrition. She'd used terms such as "conducting research" when trying to explain to black women the importance of adopting better eating habits and acronyms such as BMR, RDA, RDI, and DRV. Pam once told her, "Lynn, no one really talks like that. A person would need to carry a dictionary to keep up with your conversation." But she'd chosen to follow Lynn's advice and found herself sipping on green tea even though she despised the taste. She wished she'd ordered an iced caramel latte with whipped cream instead.

As Pam waited for Tricee and Jackie to arrive, she pulled an *Ebony* magazine from her large purse. As she began to read the young lady working behind the counter approached her. She began to wipe the tables, including the one where the older gentleman had been seated. But what happened next was enough to send Pam over the edge.

"Excuse me, Miss. But I am supposed to give you this." An outstretched brown arm appeared before Pam's face and in the young lady's hand was a business card. When Pam looked up, the young lady was grinning from ear to ear. She was very attractive and looked to be in her early 20s. She was likely a student at the nearby university. Her nails were well-manicured with red nail polish and her dark brown curly hair was pulled back off of her face. Looking at her, one would assume that between studying and working at the café, she probably spent a lot of time in the gym. Pam reasoned that this young lady could possibly go head-to-head with her sister, Lynn, on the topic of fitness and nutrition. The young lady tilted her head to the side.
"I'm sorry I didn't bring it over sooner but I was busy waiting on customers."

There had been several more people to enter the café but they had gotten their orders to go. A middle-aged woman and a young man who looked like he might have been her son were now seated near the window, and the same three college students were still present. Pam reluctantly took the business card. After reading it she inhaled and then exhaled.

"Oh, no he didn't! Oh, no he didn't!" Pam pounded a fist on the table. "He has some nerve!" The young lady, who was still standing next to Pam, nodded her head for emphasis as Pam spoke.

"Oh, yes he did, girl! Yes, he did!" Seeing Pam's reaction had been the highlight of this young lady's day and she was loving every minute of it. She began to laugh.

She was the only one working the cash register as her co-worker was preparing the food. They were the only two employees there and business for the day—with the exception of the last 10 minutes—had been rather slow. The manager was not in at the moment but, even if he had been, the young woman would have still laughed at Pam's reaction because she wouldn't have been able to help it.

"He told me when he paid for his food to 'give this to the pretty lady sitting alone.' I didn't want to bother you but I'm just relaying a message."

The business card had a hand-written phone number on the back of it with the word "cell" written above it. Pam ripped the card up and tossed it on the table.

"Give this to the lady sitting alone," Pam mumbled. "Jerk."

The young woman picked up the tiny pieces. "I'll toss it in the garbage for you."

As the young lady walked away from the table, Tricee came walking in. And it was a good thing because Pam was ready to leave.

"Hey, girl. I hope you weren't waiting too long. I would have gotten here sooner but you know how Lakeshore Drive can be." Tricee was removing her coat just as Jackie came strutting in, looking as if she owned the place. She was obviously happy about something.

"I'm glad somebody is having a good day," Pam remarked.

As Jackie removed her coat you would have thought she was auditioning for a movie. Her behavior was more sophisticated than usual. She placed her coat delicately across a chair.

"Hello, ladies! So what are we having? I'm buying."

After taking their order, the young lady looked at Pam and smirked, then walked back to the counter.

"Do you know her?" Tricee asked.

"No," Pam answered.

Jackie observed Pam's demeanor right away but that did not stop her from asking about career day. She was genuinely interested in hearing all about it.

"I enjoyed it," Tricee said.

"So did it turn out as you'd expected?" Jackie sat back in her chair as the young lady set their drinks on the table. "Mmmm, perfect." She closed her eyes briefly. "Nothing like a nice hot cup of java to stimulate your senses."

"It's just coffee." Pam rolled her eyes. Jackie was behaving as if a $2.00 cup of coffee was the world's greatest invention. She ignored Pam's eye roll and comment.

"What did the students think about your sales position? Did they ask a lot of questions?" Jackie was facing Pam as she spoke and Tricee couldn't help but notice the way she was glowing. Something was up.

As they ate their sandwiches they discussed the events of the day. Tricee shot a glance at Pam's iced caramel latte with whipped cream as she sipped on her hot cup of ginger tea. She was a little surprised that Pam had ordered a cold drink.

"Yes, some of the students asked questions. Too many, if you want to know the truth." Pam placed a forkful of chicken salad in her mouth.

"I spoke to Val. She said the students were really into it. As you know, some juniors and seniors are enrolled in at least two college-level courses. Once a week they attend a community college where the courses are taught. They loved the idea of being in a," Jackie put up her hands and made air quotes, "college environment." Jackie beamed with pride as she spoke. As a high school principal, the students' determination to succeed brought her great joy and satisfaction.

Tricee was relieved to hear that Jackie had spoken to Val. She was certain Val had mentioned how Pam had acted throughout the day and her attitude. That must have been why Jackie didn't seem any more concerned about Pam's demeanor than she was about the price of tomatoes.

She'd thought about calling Jackie herself to give her fair warning. But she realized it wouldn't be the first time they'd witnessed Pam having a bad day. Everyone had their days, some just more than others.

"I was even surprised with the way the younger students were willing to participate. They might have a few years yet before they even apply to college but, given their enthusiasm, I'd say most of them are looking forward to it." Tricee wiped her lips with her napkin before continuing. "I only hope their parents remain involved." Jackie nodded in agreement. She and Tricee shared the same motto: Education is the key to one's success.

The young lady appeared from behind the counter. "May I get you ladies anything else?"

"I might order something to go. Could you leave a menu,

please?" Jackie was finishing the rest of her turkey sandwich.

"Surely," the young lady replied.

"And I'll take another cup of coffee, please." Jackie moved her cup toward the edge of the table.

The café had not been busy for a Friday. The atmosphere would be different once the semester got under the way, however. Tricee had been there on several occasions when it was packed with students from the university.

"You know, I think I might order something to go to," Tricee said.

The young lady came back to the table, refilled Jackie's cup, and set the menu down. She then looked at Pam wondering if she, too, would make an order to go, but Pam just sipped the rest of her latte and kept quiet. The young lady was looking as if she would burst into laughter at any moment. Pam reminded her so much of her boyfriend's sister. Her boyfriend's sister was one of those don't-mess-with-me types. But at the same time she was the most caring woman you'd ever want to meet. The young lady imagined that Pam was very similar—a tough outer shell with a soft interior. The outer shell served as a barrier to keep from being hurt by others.

"Pam, would you like another latte?" Jackie asked, noticing the expression on the young lady's face.

"No, I'm fine."

Tricee was all too familiar with the menu. She looked it over briefly and set it down. "The tuna salad on pita bread is really good." She directed her comment at no one in particular. She was praying quietly to herself that Pam would lighten up and share whatever it was that was bothering her.

"I would order the tuna but I don't want to have tuna breath for my date this evening," said Jackie.

"Oh, so that's what's up with the gleeful mood!" Tricee squinted her eyes as she waved her finger at Jackie. "I knew there was a reason you came bouncing in here like you'd just hit the jackpot!"

Jackie clapped her hands together and laughed. Pam tried not to laugh but watching Tricee wave her slender finger while making that face made it difficult.

"Okay, let me clarify." Jackie put her hands up as if protesting. "It's not a date. It will be at least five or six of us and he will be in the group."

"You guys will probably end up talking to each other at some point," Tricee said. She noticed that Pam had managed to chuckle a few seconds earlier and was glad she'd been able to make that happen.

She felt even more at ease when Pam decided to chime in. She could sit there and watch her two girlfriends have all the fun or she could have some fun, too. Maybe if she joined in, it would take her mind off of her troubles.

"I have a better idea," Pam said, setting her glass of water on the table. "Why not order two tuna sandwiches so you and him both can have tuna breath." She'd made this remark with such a straight face that Jackie and Tricee did not comment. But after several seconds, they burst out into laughter.

"Does this *he* have a name?" Pam asked.

Jackie wiped a tear from her eye and cleared her throat. "This is only our second time seeing each other. Even if I had mentioned his name, you ladies would not have known who I was referring to."

"Actually, you did mention him to me before," Tricee blurted out.

"When did I mention his name?" Jackie leaned back, placing one arm on the chair and the other hand on her hip. "I do recall telling you how tall he is. I just love tall men. He's 6'3"." She could not stop grinning. "Alesia's dad is tall. I guess I just have a thing for tall men. But then again, I'm 5'9"."

"Yeah and blah, blah, blah," Tricee laughed. "You mentioned his name when you told me one of your colleagues introduced you to this 'fine specimen of a man'—your words exactly!"

"He can't be too important if you can't remember mentioning him to one of your friends!" Pam said. Although there was still a hint of sarcasm in her tone, Pam's mood had changed slightly.

"He's alright." Jackie smacked her lips together. "We'll see how things turn out this evening. If I'm lucky, maybe he'll ask me to hang out with him after the group has parted for the evening."

"Yeah, maybe," said Tricee. "But please don't turn your lips up like that." The three women laughed. "Let him ask you. If you ask him you might send the wrong signals." Tricee commented. Her mind quickly fell on her male friend whom she was meeting later on this evening.

"What's wrong with wrong signals? Sometimes they are a necessity," Jackie challenged.

They were enjoying each other but it was now after 5:30 PM. The café was beginning to fill up. Some of the students were sipping their drinks, skimming through textbooks, and looking over papers as if their lives depended on it. There were two middle-aged ladies sitting at a corner table engrossed in what appeared to be a very serious conversation. The one doing most of the talking was dressed in a dark blue, conservative pant suit and the one listening intently was wearing an oversized red sweater and jeans. It was unclear what their conversation was about but whatever it was, the one doing the listening was soaking up every word.

There were now two more employees at the café—a young man who was working at the front counter along with the young lady who'd served them, and a woman who looked to be in her early 30s who was helping to prepare the sandwiches. Tricee looked at her watch and then pulled a $20 bill from her purse.

"This will be my midnight snack," she motioned toward the container that held her tuna on a pita.

"I told you I'm buying." Jackie removed her debit card from her purse.

"I'm having dinner in about an hour. It'll be tomorrow by the time this tuna is eaten."

Jackie glanced over at the young lady who'd waited on them earlier. It must have been close to her quitting time because she'd looked at her watch three times in the past 40 minutes. Jackie was about to go over to the counter to pay until their server came walking to the table. She handed Jackie and Tricee a bag for their containers of food.

"May I suggest that since you will be eating the tuna sandwich later on, you have it with the pita bread on the side? It will taste much better that way."

Jackie and Tricee glanced at each other. "Thanks," Jackie said with smile. After the young lady walked away, Jackie leaned in toward Tricee and Pam and whispered, "She must have heard our whole conversation."

"All the more reason why we need to learn to speak more softly," Tricee whispered in return. They chuckled, wondering just how much of the conversation she had heard.

"Oh, Jackie, I forgot to tell you! I did get the pictures of Alesia that you emailed me. She looked so pretty!" Tricee suddenly remembered what she'd wanted to tell Jackie.

"Thanks! My baby did such a wonderful job in her play. I am so proud."

"Yes, it was a really good play. I enjoyed it," Pam said smiling.

Although Pam was now smiling, Tricee was not convinced that she was over whatever it was that had her bothered all day. Jackie was not too concerned. For her, Pam's attitude had softened enough, so any topic for the remainder of the time spent in this café was fair game. She still wanted to know if Pam had gotten some satisfaction from Career Day. There was some talk from the committee of possibly planning to have a similar event for the summer school session, but nothing had been finalized or agreed upon just yet. In the event the plan was put into motion, she wanted to ask her friends if they would be willing to volunteer again if their jobs allowed. It was Jackie's slick way of determining if Pam was game or not.

"So Pam, what did you like most about Career Day?" Jackie peeked at her cell phone. It was ringing on silent but she chose not to answer it.

Pam was caught off guard with the way Jackie just eased back into the subject. Tricee glanced over at Jackie. *Why did you even have to go back there?* Jackie shot Tricee a look right back. *I got this.*

After several minutes Pam began to speak. Since Jackie had caught her off guard, she had to ponder the question before replying.

"I did enjoy speaking to the students in the special education class." Pam thought about the student who asked if she liked her new dress. Tricee grinned.

"But there was this kid in one of the 6th grade classes …" Pam clenched her teeth and balled up her fists, "Ooooh, I just wanted to – "

Tricee knew exactly who she was speaking of. She had to keep herself from laughing.

"Oooh!" Pam repeated.

Tricee covered her mouth. Jackie looked at Tricee and then back at Pam.

"He had the nerve to say that he was going to become a

businessman and that all of the women would work for him and be his secretaries! I almost went off!"

Jackie found it rather amusing. She figured the kid was probably just trying to be funny, that he had no idea what he was really saying. Besides, by the time he was older, Jackie was sure he'd have a completely new perspective. She couldn't wait to hear more. Pam could be a real riot at times and Jackie welcomed the laughs. She also knew that Tricee was close to wetting her pants.

Pam went on to explain the situation, oblivious to Tricee's attempt to keep from laughing. "I had to first explain to him that the term secretary has long been replaced by the term administrative assistant. And then I had to break it down for him by explaining that women are heading businesses and owning corporations."

Pam rocked back and forth one good time and clenched her teeth once more. "Girl!" She had her fists balled up and was moving them up and down. Tricee couldn't contain her laughter much longer as she watched Pam's body language.

"Someone needed to teach him how to use a comb! Here he was in 6th grade and didn't know how to comb that head! He'd better be glad I'm not his teacher!"

Jackie was beside herself. Pam watched as Jackie and Tricee enjoyed another good laugh. She was too annoyed to laugh. Jackie had re-opened a can of worms. Tricee recalled the situation from earlier that day.

Tricee watched the expression on Pam's face as the student spoke. Although Pam had done a good job of masking her mood, she was obviously not aware of the look she was giving this student. He appeared unfazed as he continued to speak. Tricee looked around the room, hoping, really hoping that the two teachers who were in the classroom had not noticed Pam's expression.

"Many women today are in charge of running large corporations. And there are quite a few men who are administrators." Pam looked directly at the student as she spoke.

"I don't know any man who'd want to become a secretary." The student turned to look at his classmate for confirmation.

Okay. He is one of those kids who likes to show out, Tricee thought to herself. She smiled as she watched the exchange between the student and Pam. He was a cute kid but, oh, that hair! She almost wanted to slip a note into his bag, asking his parent to take him for a haircut. As for his opinion, he wasn't being disrespectful;

he just seemed to like attention.

"It is the administrators who make the jobs of the businessmen—or businesswomen—much easier. And again, an administrator can be a man as well as a woman." Pam then quickly turned her attention to another student. "Let's take a question from someone else." She then shot the kid one more nasty look.

Tricee changed the subject. She'd had enough talk of Career Day. "So what are you doing this evening?"

Tricee and Jackie had plans to go out, but Pam hadn't said what she was up to on this Friday evening.

"Yeah, are you getting together with Jeff? You haven't said much about your date with him last weekend." Jackie just had to probe deeper.

Tricee immediately turned to look at Pam. While it was true that Pam had not discussed her date with Jeff, Tricee hadn't really thought twice about it. Pam had explained why she'd called Tricee that evening when she was out with Jeff and why she'd had to suddenly hang up. It was no big deal and Tricee was just glad that nothing had been wrong. Furthermore, she'd learned that, usually, if a woman chose not to discuss her date with her friends, she probably had a good reason why. It could be for a number of different reasons.

"No! I am not seeing Jeff tonight!" Pam hissed.

Okay, a nerve has been struck. Tricee observed the look in Pam's eyes. *That was obviously the wrong question to ask. But how was Jackie to know?*

"Oh, so that's what's bothering you," Jackie stated.

And before Tricee had realized it, she blurted out the words, "That figures."

"What's that supposed to mean, Tricee?" Pam turned toward Tricee almost with the same look she'd had a few minutes ago when talking about that 6th grade student.

Tricee sighed and responded, "It doesn't mean anything." She looked over at the counter to keep from looking at Pam. The hour she meant to spend with Jackie and Pam at the café had come and gone at least 20 minutes ago, and she was expected to be back on the north side by 7:00 PM.

"What it means is, "Jackie answered for her, "When women are having a bad day, it usually has something to do with some man."

Tricee wished that Jackie would have just kept her mouth shut. Whether or not it was an accurate statement for Pam's circumstance, it did have some validity to it. But Pam would not readily admit it. Pride could be such a terrible thing.

"My having a bad day has nothing to do with Jeff or any other man for that matter." Pam thought about the earlier encounter with the older gentleman.

"Okay. If you say so. It was just a wild guess on my part." Jackie began to put on her coat. Tricee thought about offering Pam an apology but, at this point, she figured why even bother? Her comment had slipped out and she had meant no harm.

"Well, I need to get back to the north side." Tricee began to put on her coat and hat. She glanced over at Pam and offered a smile but Pam's expression did not change. Tricee's cell phone rang. She ignored it.

"Who was that?" Jackie asked.

"I didn't ask you who was calling you when your phone rang, Nosy Rosy."

Jackie laughed. "That's true. But may I ask what your plans are for the evening because something or someone has you anxious to get back to the north side."

"I'm meeting an acquaintance. He has some software that I need, which is keeping me from having to buy it. Thank God for small favors. And we might grab a bite to eat later."

"Would this be the same acquaintance whose call you did not answer when I stopped by last Saturday?"

"Maybe."

"The one from your church?" Jackie was really probing now.

"Possibly," Tricee shrugged.

"Okay, Tricee. You win." Jackie sighed and shook her head. "But you know, girlfriend, one day you're going to have to open up and stop being so private."

Tricee laughed and stole another glance at Pam who was busily applying lip gloss.

After Jackie paid the bill, they proceed to the door.

"I appreciate it," Pam said with a serious expression.

"No problem at all. Anytime," Jackie uttered.

"My treat the next time we get together," Pam said, then added, "at this café. I know the prices here."

Jackie nodded. “That’s fair.”

A woman wearing a long, tan winter coat who looked to be in her 30s spoke to Tricee as they were leaving.

“Hey, Tricee!” The woman was all smiles. “I see you can’t get enough of your favorite café.”

Tricee stood staring in silence at the woman as she continued to talk.

“How did the meeting go today with the Dean of Student Activities? I had to miss another day of work because my baby has a bad cough. I am seriously thinking of taking him out of that daycare because he just seems to keep getting sick.”

Tricee was still staring and the woman’s mouth kept moving.

“I hope my assistant remembered to go to the meeting because I need to know how I am supposed to move forward with my plans if my department is not given adequate funds. But since I brought this up in the last meeting, I think I’ll be able to move forward.”

It wasn’t until the woman mentioned their workplace and the specifics of a former meeting that Tricee realized who she was. The mention of the Dean’s name made Tricee recall the way the woman had stood firm in her request.

“Oh. I‘m sure the way you spoke up in that last meeting, you will not have a problem getting the Dean to approve your department for the funding that you need.” Tricee could not believe she could not place the woman’s face sooner. “I actually did not go in today. I attended a Career Day at one of the grammar schools.” She then introduced Jackie and Pam.

The woman smiled and complimented Jackie on her coat. “Nice to meet you both” she said, then removed her tan winter hat, exposing her mane, which was pulled back in a ponytail. It was a hairstyle Tricee had not seen on her before.

“I am sure your boss attended the meeting,” the woman remarked.

“Oh, I am sure she went, kicking and screaming. But she was aware that I had already agreed to participate in Career Day. She agreed that it was for a good cause, so I’m assuming my absence was bearable.”

After several more words were exchanged, they said their goodbyes. The woman proceeded to one of the tables near the back and began to look at a menu that had already been placed on the table. The trio was now standing outside the café'.

"What was that all about? Girl, you were looking at that woman like she was out of her mind when she spoke to you." Jackie was laughing and, actually, so was Pam.

"Dang, Tricee," said Pam. "If someone had looked at me the way you looked at her, I would have just walked away."

Tricee was not sure how she'd looked at the woman. All she knew was that she had not recognized her right away. Jackie and Pam had to do all they could to keep from bursting out laughing when the woman was talking. The way Tricee had just stared was a camera moment.

"Was I looking that bad? I just did not know who she was without her makeup on."

"Now that's just horrible!" Jackie was holding her side from laughing.

The shift ended for the young lady who had waited on them earlier. She smiled as she walked past them outside the café. She hoped to one day experience moments like that with her friends. She'd witnessed how Jackie, Pam, and Tricee seemed to really enjoy each other's company. Pam's mood had been a little less upbeat, but she realized it was probably due to the older gentleman's audacity. It was obvious that these three black women, whom she'd observed for the past hour and 20 minutes, shared a sisterhood that could not be broken.

"Does the sister look *that different*?" Pam was wiping her eyes from laughing so hard. Her demeanor had taken a 180-degree turn. "Well, I hope I don't look that different without my Fashion Fair on. And if I *ever* begin to look that unrecognizable, please have the decency to tell me. I would have to get that fixed."

"Whew!" Jackie reached into her purse hoping to find some Kleenex. "Girl, I know that's right." She put her head down and shook it. That laugh had made her evening.

"That's what happens when you wear too much makeup," Pam explained. "Your makeup becomes your regular face."

"Ladies, come on now," Tricee interjected. "It's not nice to say such things about others."

Tricee felt slightly embarrassed that her facial expressions could often give her away. Her uncle once told her, "Babygirl, you would make a terrible poker player."

But she had to admit, even if it was only to herself, that the incident that had occurred a few minutes ago had been pretty comical.

"You're right. It's not nice to say such things about others. And sometimes women can be so critical of other women," Jackie said.

"Sometimes?" Pam blurted out. "What about most times!"

"Let's work on that, ladies," Tricee said, smiling.

Jackie gave them both a hug and headed for her car. "Okay. I promise I will." There was no mistaking her smirk as she turned and walked away.

Pam and Tricee walked in the same direction toward their respective vehicles.

"The temperature has dropped," said Tricee.

"Well, I'm sure your friend from church will keep you warm."

"Very funny." Tricee was glad to see that Pam was in a better mood, even though it had been at her expense.

"Oh, that's right. You only date churchgoing men and they don't do that type of stuff."

"Exactly," Tricee said. She secured her wool scarf around her neck. "They don't do that type of stuff unless it's with their wife."

Pam made a face. "Please, spare me. They are men first." She folded her arms across her thick, black winter coat.

Tricee had gotten used to her friends teasing her when it came to her dating life. Well, she didn't really have one, but her friends believed that any outing with a man constituted a date.

She and Pam reached their cars. Tricee proceeded to unlock her doors and then climbed in. She turned to place her food in the back on the floor. She had noticed a faraway look in Pam's eyes as they walked back to their cars but refrained from asking if everything was okay. Pam's mood had gone back and forth between despondent and happy, and Tricee figured that Pam would decide when and if she wanted to discuss it. Now was certainly not the time. She had to get going. She started her car and when she saw that Pam was still standing by her vehicle, she pushed the button to roll down her car window.

"Get home safely," she said to Pam.

"Tricee, may I ask you a question?"

"Sure. But aren't you just a little cold, girlfriend? Standing out there?"

"I'm fine." There was hesitation before Pam continued.

"I need some advice on how to handle my situation with Jeff."

Tricee knew that was coming. And she was not surprised that Jeff's name had been included in the same sentence with the word advice. Pam had not shared any details of her weekend with Jeff. The only thing she'd mentioned to Jackie, during the play last Sunday, was that she'd had a nice time and that Jeff had given her a very beautiful bracelet. Jackie looked to see if Pam had worn it but she hadn't.

"It's at home. I was sort of in a hurry and forgot to put it on," she'd stated when Jackie inquired about it. This was not the whole truth but it sounded believable. Jackie was too busy being a proud mother, watching her daughter perform the lead role in her first play. She was not in the least interested in prying any further.

Tricee figured that no matter what, she'd have to keep the conversation brief.

"I don't really know your situation with Jeff." She knew that Pam had her share of doubts when it came to relationships. But she'd already told Pam, over and over again, that it didn't have to be so complicated if she would just allow God to intervene.

"I need practical advice. Not advice from a biblical perspective."

Pam watched Tricee's mouth curve into a frown. She continued speaking as Tricee just sat there looking at her with an, *I don't know what to say*, expression.

"What I mean is, if you tell me something from a biblical perspective, I might not fully understand it." Pam seemed to have read Tricee's thoughts.

"Okay," was all Tricee could muster. *Lord, this morning she worked my last nerve. And now she wants my advice but not my spiritual advice. Sprinkle some of your patience down on me, Father.* Tricee tilted her head to one side.

"Well, are you going to say something or not?" Pam asked.

"I'm still waiting for you to tell me what the issue is."

Pam let out a sigh. Tricee knew Pam had to be cold because she could see her breath as she spoke.

"I want a long term relationship," Pam uttered.

"And you want this with Jeff?"

"No, Tricee. I want it with the homeless man who hangs out at the park all day. Of course, I want it with Jeff. Who else are we talking about?" Pam's tone rose a little.

Tricee took a deep breath. She gave Pam a can-we-talk-about-this later look?

"I am just bothered by the fact that he doesn't seem to be ready for a committed relationship." Pam was looking for understanding. "I'm ready, and we spend time together and enjoy each other's company. So what's his problem?"

"Pam, Jeff is just not looking for anything serious." Tricee just came out with it. "That's my feeling anyway."

"Duh! I think I just said that he seems to not be ready for a committed relationship. Thanks, girlfriend, but I think I might have that part figured out already."

"Okay. So now that you know that, you need to decide what it is that you want."

"I just told you what I want. I am ready for a committed relationship." *Girl, are you paying attention to me?*

"What I mean is you need to determine if you're willing to settle for what Jeff is dishing out. You are the best one to make that decision. Otherwise, you'll find yourself letting him have the upper hand. Not good."

Pam thanked Tricee for her practical advice and then bent over and gave her a peck on the cheek. As Pam turned to walk away, Tricee called after her. Pam turned around, a grin plastered across her face.

"Read the book of Ruth and see what God can and will do when you trust in Him." Tricee quickly rolled up her window and drove off, before Pam had a chance to respond. From her rearview mirror, Tricee could see Pam's mouth hanging wide open.

11

Maybe I shouldn't have told Pam that Jeff doesn't want anything serious, Tricee thought quietly as she drove back to the north side. *I don't know him. I only know what Pam has told me about him. And from where I sit, Jeff doesn't seem to be looking for a serious commitment.* Her new Donald Lawrence CD played on her sound system. She reached over to turn up the volume as she turned off of Lakeshore Drive. *Oh, I just love his music.*

She arrived at the coffee shop 10 minutes late to meet her friend, Paul, who was sitting near the front by the window. Paul stood 6'1" with a slight, yet muscular build, medium brown complexion and kept his dark, black hair cut very short. He had no facial hair, which made him look closer to 28 than his actual age of 38. His thin, wire-framed glasses gave his face more of a conservative look. He sang in a group and performed at various events with his sister and one of his friends, a gentleman he'd known since they were teenagers. The three of them had truly been blessed with nice voices and they used their gifts well. The churches throughout the city were forever inviting the group to sing.

Paul's position as a systems analyst with an information technology firm, along with his Bachelor's degree in computer science, had provided him with a good income. He was a good-looking man with a nice personality. When you put it all together, everyone—at least everyone Tricee knew—considered Paul to be "a catch." Tricee had problems with that term. She felt it sounded like people were being referred to as some species of fish.

But while Paul was considered a catch for the right woman, Tricee had not entertained the thought of him being anything more. Paul had invited her once to hear him and his group perform, and he had even invited her to dinner afterward, but he'd never expressed a romantic interest in her.

They'd met at a bookstore in Evanston but it would not be until eight months later that they would run into each other at church.

The meeting at the bookstore had been a brief conversation as they skimmed through a couple of books. They'd exchanged email addresses but, for whatever reason, they had never corresponded. *I guess it wasn't meant to be*, had been Tricee's only thought and she hadn't given the matter another one.

One Sunday, Paul decided to visit Life Ministry Church, where Tricee was already a member. The following Sunday, he was so moved by the sermon that he decided to join the church. He saw Tricee in the parking lot after service was over. He'd not seen her at church the previous Sunday, but he remembered her pretty smile from eight months prior.

"Where do I know you from, or I should ask, where have I seen you before?" Paul looked at the woman standing before him with her Bible tucked underneath her arm. A puzzled look was on his face.

"Buy for Less Bookstore in Evanston," Tricee replied. She'd been described by her friends as being direct and to the point. This moment in the parking lot proved to be a good example. Paul had to smile. Tricee had said it with such a straight face. It was as if she had said, "How can you *not* remember me?"

They chatted briefly and then went on about their business. The following Sunday, Paul asked if he could give her one of his business cards. Tricee shrugged. She was not interested in being the initiator. She believed that the man should be the one to initiate communication with a woman; it didn't matter if it was only a friendship. Paul was able to pick up on her lack of interest in taking his card so he tried another approach. He asked if it would be okay if he called her sometime. They exchanged contact information and Tricee joked by stating, "Maybe this time I'll get an email." She was a little surprised that she'd allowed that to come out. Paul called her the following day and they'd enjoyed a friendship ever since.

As Tricee parked her car, she thought once more about Pam's request for practical advice. She smiled as she recalled the look on Pam's face when she'd suggested that she read the book of Ruth.

"What are you smiling about?" Paul pulled out her chair and waited for Tricee to be seated.

"Oh, just something that happened earlier with one of my girlfriends." Tricee removed her coat. She noticed that Paul was drinking something cold, just as Pam had ordered a cold latte earlier. Tricee felt that cold drinks in the winter were a bit unusual, but everyone had a right to their own preference.

"I'm sorry I'm late. I met a couple of my girlfriends earlier, and we ended up spending more time together than we'd planned."

"I'm not too surprised." Paul let out a chuckle. "Women seem to have a lot to talk about."

"Watch it, buddy." Tricee smiled as she removed her hat and her scarf. Her whole body felt a lot more relaxed than it had earlier. Her evening was sure to be more pleasant than her morning and afternoon had been. "We met at that café in Hyde Park; the one near the university." Paul resided in Hyde Park so he was very familiar with the café Tricee was speaking of.

"Yeah, I go there every now and then. They make good sandwiches." He stood up from his chair. "What would you like to drink?"

Tricee paused, then out of curiosity, asked what he was drinking.

"This is an Italian soda. Even though it's cold out, I'm not a fan of hot drinks." It was as if he'd read Tricee's mind.

"I'm a hot tea drinker, especially when it's cold. I'll have a raspberry tea, please." Tricee had spent many days and some evenings in this coffee shop, reading books or going over documents for work, so she knew the various flavors of the teas that were offered.

As Paul went to order her tea, she thought about how down to earth and laid back he was. This was only their third time interacting face to face but Tricee could tell that Paul was the type who did not allow much to bother him.

They'd had several phone conversations and would chat sometimes at church after the service. They'd gone out to dinner once but Paul's sister and his friend from their singing group had dined with them. The only other time Tricee and Paul had gotten together was during the week at a deli downtown. They'd met to discuss the software program that Tricee needed. It was more a desire than a need. The software would come in handy for completing some work-related projects at home.

Tricee was happy that she and Paul had been able to meet this evening. They were supposed to get together a few weekends ago but Paul had to cancel. Tricee had done a really good job of keeping her disappointment to herself. When he'd attempted to call her a couple times last weekend, she was in no hurry to return his calls.

"Women should not be so available," is what she'd been taught by her Aunt Janice. Tricee was only in her teens when she'd first heard those words from her aunt, but it was not until she'd reached her 30th birthday that she would fully comprehend the importance of her aunt's message. It took her a while, however, to practice what her aunt had preached. But three years ago, at 32, she'd finally succeeded. She had it down to an art now, thanks to seeking the Holy Spirit and allowing Him back into her life. *It doesn't matter if he's pursuing you or if he's just a friend—don't make yourself too available.* She could still hear her aunt's voice in her head. She would definitely remember to call her this weekend.

While Paul was ordering her drink, Tricee couldn't help but to wonder why some folks had a hard time accepting that friendship could exist between a man and a woman. She concluded that perhaps it was because of *their* inability to maintain a friendship with the opposite sex. Well, that was their issue. One shouldn't limit their options when it came to cultivating friendships. As for the whole dating thing, she was no expert on relationships but she felt her views made perfect sense.

In college, jumping into dating without allowing herself the opportunity to get to know the person first had seemed normal and fun. But that soon got old—well, sort of. After college, Tricee tried the dating thing again, fearing she was missing out on all the fun. It was a little easier as there was no longer the pressure of balancing dating with studying, but she would soon learn that it wasn't so much the balancing act as it was her choices in the men she was dating. It wasn't as if any of the guys were downright horrible or perverted in some sick sort of way. They were just not the type of men she could see herself settling into a long term relationship with. Some of the men Tricee had encountered after her college days—graduate school included—had exhibited some of the same traits as the men she'd dated during college. She'd expected to find something different, believing that men in their 30s would display a higher level of maturity.

It was no longer complicated for her at 35. Anything was possible and, being human, she could always revert back to her old way of thinking. But Tricee would try her best not to go backwards in her thinking. As long as she did not allow flesh to take control she would do just fine. Her interaction with the opposite sex was much more tolerable now. Choosing to take the steering wheel out of God's hands would only lead to more foolish choices. Tricee could not conceive of that happening.

She and Paul were enjoying their conversation over hot raspberry tea and Italian soda. They were both two young adults who had arrived at a good place in their lives. They loved the Lord and enjoyed an inner peace they'd not known before. They had talked on the phone once for close to two hours about how some men and women viewed relationships.

"When we realize that we are created whole, we're able to embrace ourselves as unique individuals. Women, especially, need to get a hold of this concept," Tricee had stated.

Paul chimed in. "I agree. I know some guys who'd rather be with a woman they know is not good for them as opposed to being by themselves."

"It can really wreak havoc on your self-esteem," Tricee said. "I have heard women say they would rather have any man than no man at all."

"And I have known men who believe that any warm body is better than an empty bed."

Even though they'd shared such an in-depth conversation about relationships, Tricee wasn't certain if Paul was involved with anyone; she'd never asked. Likewise, he had yet to ask her if there was someone special in her life. What she did know was that he certainly did not appear to be the type who dated more than one woman at a time. For all she knew, Paul might have preferred the term courting over dating, just as she did. If that was the case Tricee couldn't blame him. For a man of God, a woman of noble character should be a top priority.

Tricee could not forget the words she'd once heard from a minister on television: *A woman should desire a mate who loves God more than he loves her*. She'd clapped her hands and shouted an *Amen* at her big-screen television in agreement. And her pastor had once given a sermon on being single the Lord's way: *I believe many women settle for far too little. Until a woman realizes who she is in Christ, she will continue to accept less than what God has for her. Some women spend more time trying to please a man than trying to please their Father in heaven. If the man you're seeing right now does not have a relationship with God, you need to break it off. I don't know who I'm talking to this morning but you got that one for free*. There had been laughter and a bunch of *Amens* shouted from the women in the congregation that Sunday morning. After the service, Tricee had chatted briefly with one of the church members.

"My husband would not have had a chance had he not been a saved man," she'd said. Tricee would remember that Sunday as confirmation that she was doing something right.

Paul removed his glasses and set them on the table. "How's the tea?"

"It's very good. It's only my third cup of hot tea today."

"Well, you can have more for dinner if you'd like. I was thinking we could try that Thai food place right up the street on Sheridan Road. Unless you have a taste for something else."

Tricee paused before answering. "Let's see. I want some collard greens, homemade macaroni and cheese, sweet potatoes, snap beans, fried and or smothered chicken with gravy, and some peach cobbler for dessert."

Paul stopped drinking his Italian soda and started laughing. "Now you know we're on the wrong side of town for that." He picked up his eyeglasses. "There aren't any soul food restaurants on the north side. We'd have a better chance of seeing two of the Chicago Bulls come through the doors of this coffee shop than finding some soul food in Edgewater."

"I know, but it sounds so good!" Tricee appreciated the way Paul could laugh with her, just like her girlfriends would do.

"And did you say snap beans?" Paul was tickled by Tricee's description for green beans.

"Yes, I did." Tricee sat back in her chair and laughed, "That's what I've always called them. I used to help my grandma Eda snap beans all the time."

"You are *country*!" Paul was enjoying Tricee's company. He knew she was a beautiful person both inside and out. She had put out such a good vibe. He'd misplaced the email address she'd given him when they first met at the bookstore and hoped that she would email him but she never did. He was elated when they ran into each other at church, even if it was eight months later. It was no coincidence. For Paul, it was meant for them to meet.

They finished up their drinks and left the coffee shop.

"We can take my car. Where did you park?" Tricee was trying to ignore the woman who had stared at Paul as she entered the coffee shop. They reached her vehicle, which was parked right on the side street near the coffee shop.

"You got lucky," Paul said, oblivious to the woman's stare. "I had to park three blocks away. See? This is why I don't live on the north side. There are no soul food restaurants and the parking is terrible," he teased.

Paul was wearing a black skullcap and a black coat. As he removed his gloves from his coat pockets, Tricee could understand why the woman had stared. Paul was very easy on the eyes. But to stare just seemed rude. Tricee noticed how Paul did not seem to notice the woman at all. She figured he was either just playing it off or he really had not seen her. Men were not as astute as women when it came to things like this. Tricee managed to keep her smile from being too obvious. *Men can be so unaware at times*, she thought to herself.

Paul suggested that they walk to the restaurant but Tricee wouldn't hear of it. "You'll be driving around, looking for a parking space for at least an hour, and by that time the place will be closed," Paul said with a grin spread across his face.

"We're in my neck of the woods so let me worry about parking." Tricee unlocked her car doors. "I'll just drive you back to your car after dinner. Besides, it's too cold to walk several blocks."

Paul sighed. Tricee could tell he was trying to give her a hard time. "I guess I can take you at your word," he teased as he climbed into her four-door, maroon Ford Taurus. A nice black sports car pulled up behind them and waited patiently for the soon-to-be available parking space.

Tricee drove toward the restaurant noticing how quiet it seemed for a Friday night. There were usually more cars than this driving up and down the streets on a typical Friday night. She also noticed that the grocery store parking lot where she sometimes shopped was half full. This wasn't unusual. She knew several people who preferred to do their grocery shopping on a Friday evening, especially in the winter, so as to avoid the Saturday shoppers. Her boss was one of these people. "I prefer to do my grocery shopping on Friday evenings so I can sleep in on Saturday," she'd said. "That is my only day to relax. And who wants to get up out of their bed to run errands on a cold Saturday morning?" Tricee had to agree with her on that one. If there was one thing they had in common it was their aversion to cold weather.

Paul noticed the tiny dove hanging from Tricee's rearview mirror. He also noticed the nice scent that permeated her vehicle.

"You know what?" He caught Tricee somewhat off guard.

"What?" She looked over at him as she pulled up to a stoplight.

"You strike me as the type of lady who would drive a Jaguar."

"Is that right?"

"Yes. You just have this smooth and cool way about you." Paul began to chuckle.

"Oh, how nice of you to say?" Tricee laughed. "I am smooth and cool, and that's why I'm pushing this 2009 Ford Taurus." Tricee drove past the restaurant and circled the block, looking for a parking space. "I take it the Jaguar is your favorite car?" she asked Paul.

"Yes. It is one of my favorites."

"I like them, too, but right now my pockets can't afford one. Besides, my Ford has all the extras."

"Yeah, it's nice." Paul nodded. "You've done well, lady."

"Thank you." Tricee circled the block again, giving Paul a reason to say 'I told you so.'

"See? You should have listened to me. I told you parking – "

"Oh, wait a minute!" Tricee cut him off. "What do we have here?" She pulled into a parking space one block from the restaurant. She then looked over at Paul as she unfastened her seat belt. "Oh, excuse me for cutting you off. But you were saying?" A smirk was plastered across her face.

"Okay. You win." They laughed as they got out of the car and walked toward the restaurant.

A woman was leaving the restaurant just as Tricee and Paul were about to enter, and if you didn't see her, you certainly heard her.

"Paul!" the woman squealed. "Oh my, how long has it been?"

She was a black lady with a medium complexion who looked to be about the same height as Val, maybe a little shorter. She was probably around 5'3" if Tricee had to guess. She looked like she could be in her late 20s or early 30s—it was hard to tell. Her white, even teeth were hard to miss because she was smiling from one end of the block to the next. She was wearing a brown fur coat with a matching hat. Tricee wasn't into fur and frowned subconsciously.

Her long, brown hair came right past her shoulders and when she unbuttoned her coat her thin frame came into view. Tricee couldn't help but notice that although she was thin, she was heavy on top. Her red sweater displayed a little cleavage and Tricee discreetly glanced over at Paul to see where his eyes were. *Why is she unbuttoning her coat when she's leaving the restaurant?* Tricee wondered. She couldn't believe what she was witnessing. She had to step to the side to avoid being hit by the woman's big brown purse when she jumped up to hug Paul around the neck. Her legs were dangling in the air. She looked like a pendulum swinging back and forth. You had to have been there!

Paul looked uncomfortable, not knowing how or where to place his hands. Tricee knew he had to have been a little embarrassed. He was relieved when the woman finally released his neck.

"Paul, I have not seen you in—what, two years?"

"Uh, this is my friend, Tricee," Paul said, not really concerned with when the last time had been.

The woman ignored Paul's attempt to make introductions, choosing to keep her gaze fixed on him. Her smile and her big eyes seemed to grow wider by the minute. From her expression, she looked as if she'd been waiting to run into Paul for the past couple of years. Tricee was beginning to find the situation quite amusing. She could see that Paul seemed to get his share of attention. She thought about the woman at the coffee shop earlier. But this, what she was seeing now, was a little over the top.

"Do you still shoot ball every Saturday morning? I recall that I could never get you to go to breakfast with me because you were always anxious to get to that basketball court!"

Paul grimaced and removed his skull cap. Poor thing. Tricee tried to offer some assistance by clearing her throat but it was no use. Ms. Thing proceeded to fully open her mink coat and hold it open with both hands placed on her hips. She stood with one leg extended further back than the other. Her black pants, which were probably only a size two, were tight. She had on a pair of black boots with a two-inch heel. And unless Tricee was imagining things, the woman was standing with her back very straight, which made her chest protrude even more.

"Well, we should get inside. It was really good seeing you." Paul nodded toward the door and Tricee reached for the handle.

They'd stood in the restaurant's vestibule for what seemed like more than 10 minutes.

"Oh, let me give you one of my cards." She fiddled around in her purse and pulled out a yellow business card.

"You know, I think I'll have to pass on the card," Paul smiled. "Take care now," he said as he followed Tricee inside.

They found a table near the back. Once they were seated, the waitress, an Asian woman with shoulder-length black hair, brought over two glasses of water and two menus. She smiled. "I will give you a few moments to look over our menu."

"Thank you," Tricee said as she observed Paul let out a sigh. He set his eyeglasses on the table.

In addition to Tricee and Paul, there were two women sitting together and an elderly white man sitting alone. Tricee had been to this restaurant several times as it was located near her condo. This was the first time she'd seen so few people in it, though. The food was very good. It was so good that even Paul stated that he would sometimes drive there from Hyde Park just to indulge in his favorite dish.

"I already know what I want," he said after glancing at the menu.

"So the north side is good for something?' Tricee teased.

"You got me. Yes, the north side has its pluses."

Tricee wondered if he was still embarrassed over what had just happened. It could sometimes be a little awkward running into someone you used to date when you were out with someone else. Not that she knew any details about Paul and the woman at the door. Nor did she really care to know. But something similar had happened to her a few years prior.

She was out with a gentleman she was really starting to like when they ran into a guy she'd only gone out with twice. This guy was someone she hoped to not ever run into again. A big city allowed you that luxury—or so she thought.

In fact, Tricee had heard that this particular guy had relocated elsewhere, so it was even more surprising and awkward when she saw him that evening. She'd tried her best to pretend she didn't see him as she and the gentleman she was with headed out of the restaurant.

"Tricee!" He'd called out her name loudly and rushed over to her and her date before they could make it out the door. He looked at her from head to toe as if trying to determine if she was real. He made a few smacking sounds with his lips when he spoke.

"How you been? It sure is good to see you." Tricee couldn't help but notice her date's expression as the guy spoke. His habit of smacking his lips had been one of the reasons she had declined his offer of a third date.

Afterward, her date asked with his eyes opened wide, "Who was he?"

It had been Tricee's quick wit that saved her from appearing embarrassed. She'd replied, using a tone that was fitting for a teenage female, "Aw, you know. That's just my baby daddy." Her date was beside himself with laughter. Her expression and the way she'd said it had been very comical. Her date called her later on that evening and told her how he'd laughed all the way home.

Paul ordered Pad See Ew and Tricee decided to follow suit. "Is this one of your favorite dishes, too?" she asked Paul after the waitress had taken their orders.

"I love it. It must be good for me to drive from the south side of Chicago."

"Are there not any Thai food restaurants in Hyde Park that you like?"

"Yeah, there are a couple of places but I like this one better."

Tricee took a sip of her hot tea. Paul sipped his Diet Coke. He appeared to be back to his regular level of comfort as he and Tricee chatted over dinner. The waitress smiled as she refilled their drinks.

"Is it me or has she been smiling the whole time we've been here?" he joked.

"It's not you. She's always smiling," Tricee said.

It might have appeared that they were a couple. Tricee noticed that one of the two women she'd noticed when they arrived looked in her and Paul's direction. She then whispered to the other woman. Without even trying to appear discreet, the other woman turned around and looked at her and Paul. If the women wanted a show, Tricee was prepared to give one. She reached over and touched Paul lightly on the arm. She gave him her most flirtatious smile.

"It might not be collard greens and chicken, but it sure is hitting the spot." Paul laughed.

"It sure did. I am full."

The woman who'd done the whispering frowned. When they got up to leave, the one who'd whispered made sure to look directly at Paul as they walked past. Paul was oblivious once again. Tricee just smiled and shook her head. It had been some evening hanging out with Paul. She hoped they could do it again soon.

Paul had enjoyed his evening with Tricee. He enjoyed having her friendship and was grateful that there was no pressure for him to pursue anything more. He noticed that Tricee seemed just as pleased with having him as a friend. He figured that, for a woman, it had to have felt nice to be able to enjoy a nice dinner with a member of the opposite sex without all the pressure.

An Asian gentleman who might have been the manager asked if everything had been okay. "You have come in here before. I recognized you," he said to Tricee. He was very pleasant as he chatted with Tricee and Paul before heading back to the front.

"He didn't say that to me. I've been here a couple of times," Paul said jokingly.

"I'm prettier," Tricee smiled as she reached into her purse and pulled out a $50 bill.

"Yes, you are," Paul smiled. "Put your money away."

"Oh. Well, thank you very kindly." Tricee was not at all surprised by Paul's thoughtfulness, but she was prepared to pay for both their meals. It was what Paul said next that took her by surprise.

"That woman we saw earlier was somebody I went out with a few times."

Tricee proceeded to put on her coat and hat as she listened to Paul's explanation of the incident. She really hadn't thought more about it. She'd been curious but didn't think it would look right if she probed. Paul placed a tip on the table and then removed his coat from the chair. He stood there holding his coat and hat as if expecting Tricee to comment.

"Paul, it doesn't matter." Tricee buttoned her coat and removed her gloves from her coat pocket. "No need to explain who she was." *She just doesn't seem like your type,* she thought.

They walked to Tricee's car, happy that she'd found a close parking space. It was after 10:00 PM and the temperature had really dropped. She allowed her car to warm up before pulling out of the parking space. She began to laugh as she turned toward Paul.

"What's so funny?"

"I was just wondering why girlfriend was wearing her matching fur set. Maybe she was on her way to a fancy event, huh?"

Paul laughed. "I guess so." He hesitated and then said, "She's a nice woman but I knew we weren't going anywhere." Tricee wanted to hear more but accepted Paul's willingness to share a few minor details. As she turned right on Sheridan Road, she pointed out where she lived.

"That's where I live. That's why I wasn't too concerned about parking," she smiled.

"So you had a plan all along?"

"I knew I could always park in my building if we couldn't find a parking space near the restaurant. We would have had to walk a couple of blocks, but we still would have been closer than where you're parked."

She yawned as she pulled up behind Paul's vehicle. He glanced at his watch.

"I kept you out too late."

"No, not at all. I'm just a little tired." She yawned again. "I'm sorry," she laughed. "I am really not that sleepy, just ready to go sit in front of my television and let it watch me."

"I'm just boring, admit it," Paul teased. He went to his car to retrieve the software program. "If you need any help with this, just call me."

"Okay. I don't think I'll have any problems."

"I will be traveling for work and will be gone for about 10 days. I leave on Sunday so I might not make it to church. My one request is that you say one for me."

"Of course. Consider it done already. Keep me in prayer, as well."

As Tricee sat in her car with Paul leaning in on the passenger side as they talked, she was thinking how glad she was that they were not a couple or out on an actual date. She knew that she was not looking her best and had to be looking every bit of tired.

"Thank God for men who make for cool friends," she mumbled.

"What was that?" Paul asked.

"I was just saying you're a cool friend." Tricee yawned once more.

Paul laughed. "Get home safely, Ms. Tricee. I had a nice time. Are you going to be okay driving home?"

"I only have to drive about six blocks. I'll be fine. You be careful driving back to the south side." She wanted to ask Paul to call her once he'd made it home but she didn't want him to think she was keeping tabs. "Good night, Paul. And thanks again for the software and for dinner."

Tricee parked her car in her parking space, but instead of going through the back doors to take the elevator, she came around to the front of the building instead.

"Good evening, Ms. Miller. Did you have a good day?" The doorman asked. Felipe was an older Latino gentleman who worked part-time only. Unless he was asked to cover for one of the other doormen, Tricee would only see him on Thursday and Friday evenings. And unlike the doorman who everyone referred to as Tate—the one Tricee and Jackie thought sounded like the late singer Lou Rawls—she had not decided whose voice Felipe's was similar to. All she knew was that she liked his accent and that he was very nice.

Tricee had met Felipe's wife and daughter once and they, too, had been very friendly. Felipe, his wife, and his daughter were all very attractive; his wife could easily pass for someone in her 40s. When she told Tricee her age, which she'd volunteered, Tricee's mouth fell open.

"What is your secret? Because I want to look as good as you when I hit my 60s!" Tricee asked.

Felipe's wife blushed and responded, "Drink plenty of water and eat a lot of fruit and vegetables. Don't go to bed wearing a frown and don't hold grudges. When you do that it will eventually began to show." Tricee had received that advice with pleasure.

"I had a good day, Felipe, but a very busy one." Felipe smiled.

Tricee walked over to her mailbox only to open it and find that there was no mail. Then she remembered that she'd checked it earlier. "Okay, I must really be tired," she said out loud.

Once inside her condo, Tricee showered, got into a pair of pajamas and turned on the television in her bedroom. After watching television for about 15 minutes she was fast asleep.

She was soon startled by her cell phone, which she had failed to turn off.

"Hello?" She was way past tired.

"Tricee, I'm sorry to wake you. It's Paul."

Tricee sat straight up in her bed. "Paul, is everything okay?" She reached for the bottled water on her nightstand.

"Yes, everything is fine. I just wanted to be sure you made it home okay."

Oh, how sweet, she thought. She smiled through her tiredness. "I'm glad you called. I wanted to know you'd made it home safely. I was actually watching TV until I dozed off."

"Well, you did say you were going to get in bed and let the TV watch you," he said.

"Life and death is in the power of the tongue." Tricee quoted one of her grandmother's favorite scriptures.

"That's right. Hey, look—I don't want to keep you up. But you know what? I have a taste for some greens and smothered chicken."

Tricee burst out into laughter.

"You mentioning soul food earlier has my taste buds on alert!"

"I'm sorry. I did not mean to torture you." Tricee plopped a pillow behind her head. "So are you going to cook you some greens tomorrow to satisfy that taste?"

"Actually, I was thinking maybe you and I could go to Clara's or to that soul food place on the west side. I haven't been to either one in a while." Then before Tricee could respond, he added, "That is if you'd like to."

"Oh. I think that would be fine. I'll take a look at my schedule. I know the next few weeks for me will be pretty hectic."

Paul was sitting in his dining room wearing a white t-shirt and shorts as he looked over his planner. "Would it be okay if we try to pick a date after I return from my trip?"

"Yeah, that would be okay."

Tricee smiled as she drank the rest of her water and reached over to turn out the light. *Paul is going to make someone a really good mate.* This was the last thing she remembered thinking as she drifted off to sleep.

1 Timothy 5:2 – The elder women as mothers: the younger as sisters, with all purity.

12

Late Saturday evening: August 17th

"What is she doing here?!" Tricee slammed the phone back into its base. "I can't believe she would show up this late without calling!" Val sat up on the sofa. She was just as surprised by Ruby's unexpected late night visit as Tricee.

"Tricee, calm down. Just go down and talk to her and find out why she's here." Val put on her Capris. She wasn't sure if Tricee intended to invite Ruby and her friend upstairs but she wanted to have her clothes on just in case. At this point, Val was not too sure what was about to transpire. She'd hoped that Ruby and Tricee would give each other some much-needed time to digest all that had happened, at least until tomorrow.

Tricee put her pants back on without removing her night slip. "I'm going to go down there and tell her she has no right coming here this late without calling me first!" She angrily pulled her blouse on over her slip. Val could see beads of sweat on her friend's forehead. All she wanted right now was for this night to come to an end. Sunday could not arrive quickly enough.

Tricee walked toward the door with Val following close behind. As Tricee grabbed the doorknob with one hand, Val managed to grab Tricee's other hand. When Tricee turned toward Val, she gave her a nasty look. *If you don't let go of my hand ... !* Val had never seen Tricee look this angry before, but she was not about to allow a mean scowl to keep her from reasoning.

"Tricee, please. I just don't want you to go down there and say something that you will only regret later."

Tricee was ready to give a mean retort until Val cut her off.

"I know your situation is unlike anything I've ever experienced, but I would give *anything* to have my mother back. I know this is difficult for you and I won't even pretend to act as if I know how you feel. But, sweetie, you *still have* a mother. The only way I can deal with knowing that my mother is no longer here with me is to remind myself that I'll see her again in spirit. I would love to be able to call her just to say 'I love you' or just to talk. But I'll never be able to do that again. Do you realize how painful that is?"

Ouch! Tricee had not expected Val to go there. Her words felt like a blow to the stomach. She could feel the nerves throughout her body dancing all over. Although it had hurt, Tricee knew that Val's words were meant for good and not harm. With everything that was happening between her and Ruby, Tricee had forgotten that Val's mother had passed away four years ago. It happened one week after Val's 30th birthday, which is why Val told her friends that turning 30 was one of her darkest moments.

Val's family had always been extremely close. Her and her brother, who is one year younger than her, shared a sister and brother bond that could never be broken. And they were very close to both of their parents. When their mother died, they were devastated—as any child would be over the loss of a parent. But they were even more heartbroken for their father. He'd married their mom when he was 22 and she was only 19 and pregnant. Val's parents had shared with her and her brother how they had been planning to wed anyway, even prior to their mom becoming pregnant. They'd stated that her becoming pregnant just moved things along a lot faster.

Val's parents began to like each other during high school, but because Val's mother was only 15 and not yet allowed to date, Val's father decided to ignore his feelings and pursued another girl in his senior class. But there was just something about the sophomore girl with the smooth brown skin and the pretty, almond-shaped, dark brown eyes. He'd found her hard to erase from his mind. She was not only beautiful but smart, and mature for her age. And that smile of hers! He'd once told his children that his heart would beat faster and faster every time he saw her smile.

Once he graduated from high school, he left and moved to another state and eventually lost contact with the girl who'd captured his heart. Fortunately, thanks to a family member, they were able to reconnect. He returned home and the rest is history. "I had to move back home to chase the woman I knew would be my wife," he would say. "She is the sugar in my coffee and the icing on my cake!" Val and her brother would get a kick out of their father's terms of endearment for his wife.

They had the most loving friendship and marriage that two people could have. And even though he lost his wife when she was only 49, Val's father thanked the Lord daily that he had been able to share close to 30 years with the woman he loved with every fiber of his being.

Val and her brother would remind each other of the years their parents had been blessed to spend together. That helped to ease some of the pain. And to see both of her children happily married had given their mother great pleasure. Interestingly, just as their parents had been high school sweethearts, in an indirect sort of way, both Val and her brother also married their high school sweethearts. "It must be a Cooper family tradition," they would often joke.

Now, as Val witnessed Tricee's obvious anger and feelings of resentment toward her own mother, she couldn't help but to conjure up memories of her deceased mother. She would never forget the day she called her mother crying after Cory called and told her he needed a break from dating.

"Lynn," Val's family always called her by her middle name," just give him some time. He'll come around. I'm not saying put your life on hold, but Cory will be back. Watch and see what I'm telling you." Val never shared this conversation she'd had with her mother with anyone else. But Val's husband had teased her once by saying, "The only reason I married you was because your mother told me I would turn up missing if I didn't." Cory had absolutely adored his mother-in-law and had taken her death just as hard as her two children.

Tomorrow was not promised. Val's goal was to keep Tricee from lashing out at the woman who would always be her mother. Ruby could leave the north side tonight and not make it back safely to wherever she was staying while in town. In spite of the wedge that had now been placed between them, this was still the woman who'd clothed her, fed her and provided for her until she went out on her own. Ruby might not have been the perfect mother in Tricee's eyes, but she still deserved credit for all that she'd done right. Tricee had turned out to be a very fine young lady and surely Ruby was partly responsible for that.

There was complete silence. Tricee glared at Val as she slowly eased her hand from her friend's firm grip. She opened the door and walked toward the elevator.

"Tricee," Val called after her, but her voice would go unheard as Tricee got on the elevator. Val shook her head as she went back inside. *I hope no one notices that her slip is hanging out of her pants.*

The lobby, with its huge chandelier, was always brightly lit, even at night. The red carpet with beige stripes was spotless. When Tricee stepped off of the elevator, she noticed Ruby right away sitting in one of the big black chairs. There were two, one on each side of the doorman's desk. Bev, Ruby's friend, was happily chatting with the doorman who looked to be at least 15 years her junior. He was fairly new and, other than hello and good evening, Tricee had never held a conversation with him.

Ruby and Bev were dressed as if they had gone out for the evening and, Tricee had to admit, her mother still looked good. Ruby had always been one with an eye for fashion. Tonight she was wearing a pair of pastel blue, linen pants and a sheer, though not see-through, white blouse. It was a V-neck top with three-quarter sleeves. Tricee was thankful that the blouse wasn't see-through and she'd never cared for tops that showed too much of her mother's arms. At least her outfit had been acceptable to her only daughter. Tricee noticed the thin silver chain she'd bought her mother as a birthday gift a few years prior. And Ruby's white sandals with their two-inch heel displayed a perfect pedicure done with white polish.

Bev was wearing a knee-length, beige dress that showed off a pair of shapely calves. She had the kind of "big legs" that most black men adored. Her dress tied at the waist, which accentuated her waistline and her beige sandals went well with her dress. Her dress was very pretty but Tricee thought it showed way too much cleavage. The doorman, however, didn't seem to mind. There were a couple of occasions where he'd have to call someone to inform them that they had a guest, but all the while he never took his eyes off Bev.

Ruby looked up as Tricee came walking quickly toward her. She noticed a young white male walking behind her daughter with a grin on his face.

"Excuse me," he said to Tricee before leaving the building, "your nightgown is hanging out of your pants." He laughed, obviously intoxicated, as he walked through the revolving doors and got into a waiting red mustang.

"What are you doing here?!" Tricee angrily adjusted her slip, tucking it into her pants. "You should have called me first, Ruby!"

Ruby had made it known to Tricee on several occasions, how much she disliked it when she called her Ruby. But apparently, her daughter would not take her feelings into consideration. Although still upset with the way things had gone down the night before, Ruby maintained a calm demeanor.

"Jentrice, we need to get together tomorrow and talk. I leave on Monday and I am not leaving until you and I can discuss things like adults." She'd completely ignored her daughter's question as to why she had not phoned first. But it really wouldn't have mattered. Tricee still would not have been willing to discuss anything with her. The audacity of Ruby just showing up only seemed to make the wound deeper.

"Why didn't you call first?!" Tricee asked again. "And I'm not ready to talk tomorrow!" Tricee walked toward the set of double doors that led to the elevators she had just come out of. Ruby followed her.

"I knew that if I called you probably would have not answered," Ruby answered, trying to keep her voice from sounding weak. She was tired and the last thing she wanted was to come here and fight with her daughter.

Ruby and Bev had gone out to dinner with Bev's brother who had talked them into accompanying him to hear a blues band. Both women were reluctant at first until Bev's brother divulged more details about the establishment. "It's a classy place where the more mature crowd likes to go for live entertainment, primarily to hear the blues," he'd said.

After her spat with her daughter, Ruby wasn't so sure if she was up to hearing anybody's blues. But once they arrived they ended up having a really nice time. The crowd was a good mixture of folks from different backgrounds though the majority was black. And from what they could tell, the minimum age of the clientele was late 40s. Ruby and Bev had pretty much based their observation on the crowd's mannerisms as well as physical appearances.

They had even met an older black lady who was 80! She could have easily passed for 60. "You know what they say—black don't crack!" she'd joked after proudly revealing her age. She'd worn a white pantsuit—perfect for a summer evening—with a pair of white, sling-back flats. She'd talked with Ruby and Bev for most of the evening as they listened to the band. The woman had been downright hilarious. She'd kept Ruby and Bev in stitches.

She shared how she had outlived two husbands, raised six children and still volunteered at her great grandchildren's school whenever she felt like it. Her last boyfriend, according to her, had broken up with her after learning that she had no intention of being intimate. "I guess he thought he'd wait around as long as he could to see if it would ever happen. So when he finally asked I told him I wasn't getting it on with anybody! Not ever! I told him I wasn't giving up *nothing* but a cup of coffee and a piece of dry toast!" Ruby and Bev had to keep from falling out of their chairs from laughing. They ended up enjoying themselves immensely.

The laughter was now over. Ruby was hoping she could talk reasonably with her daughter. Tricee's half-sister, Annette, had taken the news much better than Tricee, though she had been stunned initially. After hearing Ruby's revelation, Annette attempted to call Tricee. But she knew Tricee well enough to know that, more than likely, her call had gone ignored because Tricee was not prepared to chat.

Ruby was pushing her luck, but she believed that coming over to ask her daughter to join her for dinner tomorrow had been the right thing to do.

"What time are you done with church? We can have a late lunch or an early dinner. I can have Bev drop me off or you can meet me – "

Tricee abruptly cut her mother off. "Excuse me, but aren't you being a little too presumptuous right now?" Her tone had gone up an octave.

Ruby was taken aback. "Jentrice, who do you think you're talking to like that?" Ruby's tone was now louder than before.

The doorman and Bev looked in their direction simultaneously. For the sake of privacy, Tricee closed the double doors that led to the elevator. At least this way, on the other side of the doors, they were out of earshot from the doorman and Bev. Fortunately, there weren't too many people coming in and out of the building. Either way, standing in the lobby of her building and going at it with her mother felt like nothing more than a repeat of Friday night. The only thing that was different was the location. Tricee wished she'd told the doorman to send Ruby and Bev away.

When Ruby noticed Bev and the doorman looking in her and Tricee's direction, she turned to Tricee with a solemn expression. She wasn't looking to make her daughter's personal business a public affair. She realized that Tricee was just as much of a private person as she was.

Ruby had hoped Tricee would have calmed down by now. She had not attempted to call because she wanted to give Tricee the opportunity to digest all she'd been told. She wasn't expecting a miracle, only another chance to talk before leaving town. On Monday morning, Ruby and Bev would board a plane back to St. Louis but Tricee would remain here in this building where she was known. Ruby wanted to respect that.

"I'll give you a call tomorrow." Ruby sighed as she removed a couple of aspirin from her purse. She had said all that she came to say. There was no use trying to say anything more. She was still none too pleased with how Tricee had spoken to her, but it was after midnight already. Tricee was just as strong-willed as her mother. For as long as Ruby could remember, she and Tricee did not see eye-to-eye on anything and their personalities just seemed to clash.

As Ruby turned to open the double doors, Tricee glanced over at Bev and the doorman.

"I hope you haven't picked up that habit." Tricee watched as Bev handed the doorman a small piece of paper. Ruby couldn't care less. She and Tricee had bigger issues and Bev handing out her phone number was not one of them.

"Bev's a grown woman, Jentrice." Ruby sighed as she pushed through the doors.

"All I'm saying is that we're known by the company that we keep," Tricee uttered.

"I'll call you tomorrow when I think you might be home from church," Ruby said, ignoring Tricee's comment. "I'll leave a message if I get your voicemail and I do expect a return phone call." She then turned and left the building with Bev.

"Your daughter is very pretty," Bev commented as her brother drove her and Ruby back downtown. He'd remained in the car and said nothing when he saw the expression on Ruby's face.

"So you're going to dinner with her tomorrow – ," Bev then glanced over at the time, "I mean today." She was all smiles as she'd just enjoyed an unexpected yet very nice conversation.

"After church tomorrow," Ruby replied. She wasn't interested in sharing any other details concerning that stubborn daughter of hers.

"Oh, that's nice," Bev replied with all sincerity. She could tell by Ruby's body language that it was best not to probe any further.

Ruby didn't know what Sunday would bring but she knew someone who did. *Father, I know I haven't done everything right but I'm trying to fix what has been broken. Have your way, Lord, because I cannot do it without you.*

13

"Why did you cook so much food? Are you guys expecting company?" Pam asked her mother as she stood with the refrigerator door wide open.

"We do have to eat seven days a week. And close my refrigerator. You're letting all the cold air out."

Pam had stopped by her parents' home for a brief visit. When she arrived her father was watching television in the bedroom and her mother was in the kitchen preparing Sunday dinner. Whenever she was in the mood, Pam's mother spent Saturday evening preparing a big meal for the following day. If she wasn't in the mood she'd just whip up something quick after church. Pam and her sisters would often joke about how their mother seemed to spend the majority of her time in the kitchen.

The 20-inch, wall-mounted television in the kitchen was a gift from Pam's brother to his parents but Tillie Rhodes claimed it as hers. She enjoyed sitting in her beautiful kitchen, which her four daughters had helped to decorate. The yellow wallpaper with birds was too bright for her father's taste. But since her mother would be the one in the kitchen most of the time, she'd won the battle on what colors to use. The three-bedroom home with two-and-a-half baths had been ideal for Pam's parents and Cassie, her younger sister who would graduate from high school in a few months.

Pam's parents purchased the home five years ago upon reaching an agreement that they were ready to downsize. A two-story, five-bedroom home with three full baths and a huge basement had been the home where Pam and her four siblings lived since she was a small child. The Kenwood area on Chicago's south side was lined with beautiful homes. Pam liked the area so much that she'd purchased her own home there. Her mother, however, had been ready to flee the city and had found the perfect home in Matteson, Illinois. Her parents were both enjoying suburban life.

With the exception of the big, brown recliner that sat in the corner, her parents still had much of the same furniture from their first home. The recliner had been purchased specifically for Mr. Rhodes, but Pam's niece and nephew would fight over who got to enjoy the big, comfortable chair first. In addition to the television in the kitchen, there was one in her parents' bedroom, her sister's room, and one in the basement. According to Mr. and Mrs. Rhodes, four televisions were more than enough for one household.

The family pictures—and there were a lot of pictures—were displayed on the walls throughout the house and on the mantle. The dining room consisted of an oval-shaped, cherry wood dining room table with four chairs that had been given to Pam's mother by a great aunt. Fortunately, it had kept her parents from having to purchase another one. They'd given theirs to Pam when she'd purchased her home. The long, tan table with the white top had come with six unique-looking chairs. It had been in her parents' home ever since Pam was small. She had always thought it was a pretty set, so since she was the oldest, she believed that when and if her parents decided to part with it, it should go to her. And so it did.

Unlike the home where Pam grew up, there was no upstairs. The laundry room was on one side of the basement along with a half bath. A sitting area with a television was situated on the other side. This was primarily where her youngest sister would entertain her friends. No young men were allowed, not even her sister's boyfriend. When he came to visit he was expected to remain in the living room at all times. At 18, Cassie thought her parents were being unreasonable. "When you turn 40 and are married the rules will be different. But as long as you're 18 and living under my roof, these are the rules." Mr. Rhodes had stood firm. But what he and his wife didn't know was that when they'd been out of town, Cassie's boyfriend had, indeed, spent a little time in the basement, as well as in her bedroom.

Pam's parents had worked hard to provide a comfortable life for their children. Her father received his B.A. in accounting and has worked as a CPA for more than 30 years. Her mother works part time as an LPN. Mrs. Rhodes decided that she'd worked full time long enough, and that since she was close to 60, it was time for her to slow down. Besides, she had other things she was involved in, such as volunteering at a children's hospital, which she did at least three times a month. She felt this was what God had called her to do. Furthermore, it was such an unpleasant circumstance to witness the agony of a sick child's parents. She wanted those parents to know that she cared. And her time volunteering had made a difference. Many of the parents would thank Mrs. Rhodes and the other volunteers for giving of their time, and for giving their children a reason to smile.

With five children of her own who were all born healthy, Pam's mother realized that she was blessed, and this was something she never wanted to take for granted. She had instilled in her children the importance of giving your time to the less fortunate. Pam's mother also volunteered at one of the local churches once a month, handing out food to the elderly.

"So how long have you been seeing this guy that you're going out with this evening?" Pam's mother asked as she wiped the kitchen counters.

"Would you mind if I stopped by tomorrow for Sunday dinner since you've cooked so much?" Pam attempted to ignore her mother's question. She removed a container of potato salad from the fridge.

"You know I don't mind. Why are you eating potato salad? Aren't you going out to dinner?" Mrs. Rhodes could tell when her oldest daughter was trying to dodge her questions.

Pam had not mentioned much about Jeff to her mother. In the past she would share some details of a current boyfriend, but with Jeff, since she was uncertain as to where things were going, she'd opted to remain mum. Not that she'd known exactly where things were going with other guys she'd dated, but past boyfriends had not been as closed as Jeff.

"I'm eating potato salad because I love the way you make it. And, no, I'm not going out to dinner." Pam scooped up a forkful of potato salad from the saucer. She'd used a saucer because, yes, she was going out to dinner later, but she wasn't in the mood to discuss her plans with her mother.

"It is Valentine's Day, Pam," her mother smiled as she sat down at the kitchen table next to her daughter, "and you're dressed like you're going on a date, so there's no use in you trying to be coy with me."

Pam was still in awe of her 59-year-old mother. At 41 she'd given birth to her fifth child. There was a 17-year age difference between Pam and her youngest sister. It had taken Pam time to adjust to the concept since she could not envision herself having a child at 41. She'd stated on several occasions that if she had not given birth by the time she was 33—give or take a few months—then having children was out of the question. At 35 and still single, Pam had resigned herself to remaining childless. Marriage, however, was still a big part of the equation.

"I am not being coy, mother. And how do you know I'm not meeting my girls for a night out?" Pam wiped her mouth with a napkin. "Mmmm, you put your foot in this potato salad! It's delicious!" She licked the fork and then placed it on her saucer.

Pam thought about her date later on with Jeff as she walked over to the fridge for something to drink. The last time she'd seen him had been a few weeks prior, when he'd given her the bracelet. Their evening together had ended on sort of an unpleasant note. Though she wasn't exactly sure if Jeff had felt the same as she'd felt, she did know that he seemed annoyed that evening. Once they left his place, neither of them said much on the drive back to her house. Jeff had not even bothered to walk her to her door. "I'll call you tomorrow" was all he'd said before Pam got out of his car.

He had kept his word and called the next day but Pam didn't take his call. He called a couple more times before Pam finally relented and answered. Their conversation had been brief and although she still felt unsettled over how their evening had ended, Jeff appeared as if he'd not given it a second thought. He seemed so in control of his feelings and that was scary for Pam.

"A woman chooses an outfit based on the occasion." Pam's mother spoke as she walked over to the kitchen sink. "And from that form-fitting red sweater along with those black slacks, you're not going out with your girlfriends."

"Oh, mother, please." Pam poured some iced tea into a glass. "This outfit is perfectly okay for a girl's night out. What sort of outfits did you wear when you would go out with your girlfriends back in the day?"

Pam's mother's back was facing her as she stood at the kitchen sink washing a few pots and pans. "I kept it simple with a pair of pants—not tight—and a simple blouse."

"And what kind of outfits did you wear when you were dating dad?" Pam sat back down at the table.

Mrs. Rhodes turned to face her daughter, her hands still immersed in suds. "I didn't wear any outfits whenever I was around your father. That's how I ended up with five kids."

"Ugh!" Pam set her glass on the table. "Ma, that's just gross. I'm sorry I asked!" Pam frowned and scrunched up her face.

Pam's mother was a no-nonsense type of woman. She was known to say things that would sometimes catch her children off guard. She could be funny but, when it came to work and volunteering, she was all business.

"Let's change topics. What did you and dad do today for Valentine's Day? I take it you got your usual box of chocolate-covered cherries?" Pam watched as her mother busily went about her duties in the kitchen while still holding a conversation.

"Yes, I did. But I told your father not to buy me any more candy. He knows I can't eat chocolate like I used to. And we went to lunch earlier and had the best seafood I've had in a while. That was pretty much it. But I made all of his favorites for Sunday dinner tomorrow."

"You got him to take you out to lunch?" Pam asked, surprised. They all knew that going out to eat wasn't their father's cup of tea. "I bet that was like pulling two bad teeth, huh?" Pam laughed. She was pleased that she'd managed to successfully steer the conversation toward something besides her and Jeff. Her emotions were still in a state of flux so she wanted to avoid any discussion of her dating dilemmas.

"Your father has never been one to eat out much. I guess that's the price I pay for being such a great cook." Mrs. Rhodes smiled as she joined Pam at the table.

Pam could see why people often told her that she looked a lot like her mom. Her mother's wrinkle-free, brown skin was only a tad bit lighter than her daughter's. The other difference was the hair. Pam preferred short hair whereas her mother's thick, salt and pepper mane came well past her shoulders. She wore it pulled back into a bun and was forever receiving compliments on how good it looked.

"I ran into Cory, Val's husband. I knew it was something I wanted to tell you." Pam's mother poured herself a glass of iced tea. "I was out in Oak Park yesterday visiting Ms. Alma. You know Ms. Alma—she attends church with me sometimes."

"I was just about to ask you what you were doing in Oak Park." Pam had been out to visit Val on numerous occasions. She and her husband lived in Forest Park, a suburb right next to Oak Park. But she had never known her parents to have any friends out that way.

"Yes, I know Ms. Alma. What, is she living out there now?" Pam asked with a puzzled expression.

"She is only going to be out there for a few weeks to help her granddaughter out. Her and her husband just had their first child."

"Oh, I see. So where did you see Cory?"

"He was in that men's clothing store at the mall. I figured, since I was out that way, I'd go in there to pick up something for your father."

"Oh, okay," Pam replied as her mother stood up from the kitchen table.

"You know, Cory is such a smart and handsome young man. He tells me he is considering going to law school. The police department will pay for his schooling."

Pam thought back to how elated Val had been when she learned that her hubby would no longer have to work patrol. He loved it but wanted to gain experience within the department. For the past four years he had trained new recruits at the police academy, and every now and then he was chosen to perform administrative duties within the department.

"I do recall Val mentioning that to me. He initially was going to pursue a Master's degree but he decided he would apply to law school instead."

"Doesn't he have his B.A. in criminal justice?" Pam's mother asked.

"Yes, he does. And with the experience he has with the police force, I think he would be an ideal candidate for law school. If I were on a school's admissions committee, his application would be on top. But you never know what they are looking for other than an LSAT score. Personally, I don't think that score should be the main determining factor."

Pam was enjoying this time with her mother as her father had yet to emerge from the bedroom. Pam couldn't help but notice how, lately, it seemed he would make an appearance just as she was leaving. If he did not come from his hiding place within the next 10 minutes, she would go in and interrupt whatever he was watching. Pam still got a kick out of her father and his many ways.

"I still remember when you and Val met." Pam's mother looked pleased as she recalled the memory. Pam, one year older than Val, was already a sophomore when they met in high school. "I thought she was one of the sweetest girls you brought home for me to meet. I didn't care for too many of those other girls you called yourself being friends with." Her expression went from a smile to a slight frown, "I recall two girls in particular who were just too fast." She shrugged, "but I had to trust your judgment and allow you to choose your own friends."

Pam smiled remembering quite well her mother's reaction to the two girls in question. But Val had been a totally different story. Pam could still recall how her mother had smiled when Val said her full name: Valerie Lynn Cooper. Mrs. Rhodes just felt there was something so warm about the freshman girl standing in her living room. "Oh, that's a very pretty name. Did Pam tell you she has an 8-year-old sister with your middle name?" Val had responded shyly, "Yes, ma'am."

Pam's mother removed a box of yellow cake mix and some chocolate frosting from the kitchen cabinets.

"May I help with anything?" Pam asked after checking her watch for the time.

"Thanks, but I have it all under control—unless *you* want to bake this cake," Mrs. Rhodes teased.

"Uh, maybe next time," Pam uttered. Baking was not Pam's thing and everyone in the family knew it.

"You might meet a great guy like Cory soon," Pam's mother said as she opened the box of cake mix and poured its contents into a large bowl.

Oh, really? Pam turned around and stared at the back of her mother's head. As her mother added a couple of eggs and water to the cake mix, Pam wondered where this next topic was headed.

"Ms. Alma's son is still single." Pam's mother poured the batter into a cake pan. Pam crossed her arms and continued staring at the back of her mother's head. Mrs. Rhodes was unaware of the look on her daughter's face. Ms. Alma's son was gay. That was his prerogative and Pam had no problem with that, but apparently her mother was not aware that Pam was not Ms. Alma's son's preference.

"Ms. Alma's son is gay, mother."

Pam waited for her mother to respond but she just placed the cake into the oven and remained silent.

"You heard me, right?" she asked.

When her mother failed to respond Pam smiled. *I bet that will keep you off me for a minute.* She walked over to the microwave cart and picked up a magazine. After several minutes

Mrs. Rhodes replied, "Well, there are still some great guys left, regardless of what folks have to say about there being a shortage of available black men."

Before Pam could respond, the front door slammed and her youngest sister's voice boomed through her parents' home.

"Ma, did I get any phone calls? I left out of here and forgot my cell phone," Cassie yelled as she walked into the kitchen.

"I am not your personal assistant and stop all that yelling," their mother answered.

"Oh, was I yelling? Sorry." Cassie paused and gave Pam the once-over. "Hey, big sis, look at you. Go 'head, girl. You know you wearing that red sweater." She bent over and gave Pam a hug. "That's the color a woman should always wear on a Valentine's Day date, something red."

Why are they assuming I'm going out on a date? Pam was ready to scream.

"I might want to borrow that sweater. And I like that bracelet, sis—that is so pretty. Whoever this guy is must be really special for you to get all dolled up," Cassie teased Pam playfully.

"Cassie, someone from your dentist's office called to confirm your appointment for Monday." Mrs. Rhodes spoke before Pam had an opportunity to address her sister's comments. "And forget about borrowing that sweater because it's not appropriate for you."

Cassie stuck her tongue out at her mother's back. Pam began to laugh. "Girl, you are crazy."

"I am not going back to that dentist. He has bad teeth." Cassie eyed the empty cake mix box on the counter.

"A dentist with bad teeth. Now that's messed up." Pam laughed.

"Tell me about it. I told my future husband that he needs to find another dentist to go to. He referred this dentist to me but I'm not going back." Cassie walked over to the refrigerator.

Pam thought it was cute how her little sister referred to her boyfriend as her future husband. Mrs. Rhodes just shook her head. Pam only hoped that heartbreaks would be few and far between for her youngest sister.

"Ma, you're baking a cake from the box? Aw, you should have made one from scratch." Cassie tossed the box into the trash. "Your cakes made from scratch are the bomb!"

"If you want a cake from scratch, my dear, then I suggest you get in this kitchen and bake it yourself," their mother responded.

As Pam sat and chatted with both her mother and youngest sister, she thought about how different she'd been at Cassie's age. Her little sister was a riot and was always giving her parents a hard time. This was something that Pam and her siblings had done, too, but not nearly as much as Cassie.

"Ma, I was just teasing about the sweater." Cassie gave her mother a squeeze on the shoulders and a peck on the cheek. "But I am 18 and getting ready to start college in six months. So don't be surprised if my wardrobe changes a little, alright?"

Mr. Rhodes suddenly appeared in the kitchen. "You know you need to make another appointment with the university. You need to spend a full day on campus and even try to sit in on a class." He addressed his youngest daughter and then turned to Pam. "Big date tonight?"

Pam sighed. "Hello to you, too, Pops." She stood and gave her father a hug.

"That's a good idea, Cassie," Mrs. Rhodes remarked. "H&P University is one of the top schools in the country. Oh, how we thank the Lord you won that scholarship."

Pam beamed with pride. They were all so proud of Cassie.

"Oh, I'm not going to H&P. I changed my mind."

Pam was shocked at Cassie's news and even more shocked that neither of her parents appeared fazed by what she'd just announced.

"You're not going?" Pam glared at her little sister and then at her parents.

"I'm going to school out in Los Angeles instead." Cassie opened a bag of Cheetos and began crunching.

"Over my dead body," Mr. Rhodes responded as he walked over to the fridge.

Cassie stopped eating her Cheetos, stood up, and walked quickly over to where her father was standing. Looking him right in the eye, she pointed her finger at his nose and repeated the words just like the character Celie had in the move *The Color Purple*, her voice sounding exactly like hers.

Pam just about lost it! She laughed so hard she was practically on the floor. Mrs. Rhodes was trying her best not to laugh but Cassie's comical behavior often made that very difficult.

The Color Purple was Cassie's favorite movie. She'd seen it at least 15 times and knew just about all of the lines. One day last summer, Pam, her parents and four siblings, along with her sisters' husbands, all gathered at her parents' home to watch it. Cassie would not keep her mouth closed as she explained what was going to happen in every scene. Their brother finally had enough. "Cassie, put a lid on it already! *Please!*" They'd all seen the movie already but still wanted to be able to enjoy it without their sister's commentary. Finally, their father got up and went up to his room. He left his family sitting in the basement as he could no longer tolerate Cassie's inability to keep quiet.

Mr. Rhodes finished his water and waved his daughter out of his face. "Girl, go on away from me." Pam noticed the grin on her father's face as he walked back into his bedroom.

"Whew," she wiped the tears from her eyes. "Girl, you done lost your mind for real. I'm going to pray for you."

"Please do," their mother said as she shook her head, laughing.

Pam gathered her things as she prepared to leave. She wasn't sure what was going on with her sister's sudden change of plans for college but something told her that the discussion had already taken place in the Rhodes household. She would find out more later, but for now, she had to get moving.

"Let's talk soon. I'll be over tomorrow for dinner," Pam told her sister. It then dawned on her that Cassie's boyfriend might have something to do with this whole college situation. "I'll tell you what, though," Pam decided to leave her sister with some food for thought, "It would be crazy to pass up a scholarship. A lot of your peers would love to be in your shoes."

Cassie stood to walk to her room. "Yeah, well sometimes life can make you do some crazy things. Hey, I better go change. We're going to a movie tonight. Have fun on your date," she winked at Pam and disappeared.

Pam would place her bet on their father. She knew there was no way he'd allow his daughter to pass up such an opportunity. Cassie had been awarded a full scholarship to one of the top schools in the nation. There was no way she was going off to L.A. to attend a college where she'd have to take out loans. Cassie was sadly mistaken if she thought for one second that she would win this battle. *Father Knows Best* was not only a television series. As far as Pam and her other siblings were concerned, it had always been pretty much the rule in the Rhodes household. Cassie had yet to catch on.

Pam walked out of the bathroom applying lip gloss. Seeing Jeff in about an hour had her excited though she remained hushed about her plans for the evening.

"Where do you want a man to look, Pam, when you're out on a date?" Her father was standing near the kitchen. Pam thought he'd gone back into his room but he wanted to talk to his oldest daughter before she left.

Oh, here we go again, Pam thought and cracked a smile as she buttoned her coat. *I don't care where they look. What's important is that they listen.* Mr. Rhodes waited for his daughter to respond. He was interested in her views.

"I hadn't given it much thought to be honest with you, dad." Pam's father's expression told her he was waiting to hear more of a reply than she'd just given. And who was she fooling? The last time she saw Jeff she'd wondered if her physical attributes were more on his mind than her intelligence.

"Pamela." Pam disliked it when her father called her by her full name. "You want to be sure that a man is looking at you when he is talking to you. That's important." Mr. Rhodes patted Pam on the arm. "You should never have to guess at a man's intentions. Enjoy your evening."

"Okay." Pam turned and walked out of the kitchen. She got her father's message loud and clear. When a woman wears form-fitting clothes, she has to expect for a man to give her a certain kind of attention. There was nothing wrong with looking nice, but she should be mindful of what she chooses to wear. This is how she summarized her father's words.

There was no denying the way Jeff looked at her whenever she'd wear a sexy outfit. It was enough to almost make her want to go home and change—almost, but not quite. It just seemed sort of coincidental that her father would say what he'd just said.

"See you, mother." Pam gave her mother a peck on the cheek.

"Okay, see you tomorrow. Feel free to invite your friends to dinner." Her mother was putting the finishing touches on her homemade banana pudding.

"Okay. Not sure if they have other plans, but I'll ask." Pam reached the back door and then stopped. With her hand on the doorknob she turned around and faced her mother.

"Ma, you ever read the book of Ruth?" Pam knew the answer to that question was yes.

"Yes, ma'am. Why do you ask?" Her mother picked up the remote and turned down the volume on the television. She was a little surprised by her daughter's inquiry.

Pam shrugged. "I was just curious."

"You should read the book of Esther, as well. It's another powerful Bible story about another woman from the Old Testament."

"Okay. I'll have to do that. Love you." Pam closed the door behind her.

She climbed into her 2004 Mercedes and picked up the new small Bible that was on the back seat. She placed the bookmark where the book of Esther began. Pam mumbled as she placed the Bible back down on the seat, "Read the book of Ruth, read the book of Esther. Am I wearing a sign that says 'I need Jesus?'" She backed out of her parents' driveway. "I'll get around to it. But when that might be, I have no idea."

Esther 4:14 – For if thou altogether holdest thy peace at this time, then shall there enlargement and deliverance arise to the Jews from another place; but thou and thy father's house shall be destroyed: and who knoweth whether thou art come to the kingdom for such a time as this

14

With her Buju Banton CD playing as she drove along the expressway, Pam moved her head to the beat of the music. "Destiny" was her favorite song on the CD, even though she couldn't make out all of the lyrics. She loved all types of music—with the exception of country, rock and roll, and classical. Reggae was her preference when she was in an upbeat mood. Some reggae music was difficult to understand but the beat just made you want to stop whatever you were doing and get up and dance. No small wonder a lot of folks enjoyed dancing to its fast rhythm.

The visit with her parents had left her with a few thoughts to ponder. It was some of what had been said that made her brain switch to overload. But once she reached the expressway and turned up the volume on her car's stereo sound system, the tension slowly escaped from her body. Now, as she headed to the reggae club on Chicago's north side, where she and Jeff had agreed to meet, all she could think about was the evening ahead.

This reggae club was one that Pam had frequented only a couple of times. It had been a while since she'd gone out to listen to reggae. She looked forward to allowing the rhythm to overtake her thoughts. She even hoped to get out on the dance floor. She wasn't exactly sure if Jeff even liked to dance. She did know that he enjoyed various types of music, though.

This would be their first time out in a club together. Pam thought it would be a good idea to try something different. She wanted to check out Jeff's demeanor in a different setting. It would make for a great way to get to know someone better. As much as Pam wanted to be able to say that she knew Jeff well, nothing could be further from the truth. It was definitely a part of her plans to change all of that. The unfortunate thing was that Jeff moved to his own timetable and was not the type to be easily swayed. Even in the midst of their spending time together, she'd felt that he somehow felt he had to have the upper hand.

When Pam suggested they meet at the Til Midnight reggae club located in Wrigleyville, Jeff had stated that his plans were to have dinner at his favorite Italian restaurant. He was certain that she'd love it. After dinner, his plans had been to see a movie, a new action-packed film that had just been released. Pam had turned up her nose at the mention of an action-packed film, but since their conversation was taking place over the phone, Jeff couldn't see her pained expression. Jeff had stated that he'd already made dinner reservations. That was fine with Pam but she insisted on the reggae club as opposed to the movie. Jeff had finally relented.

"Maybe we can have dinner and then go to the club," Pam had said.

"Let's just meet at the club first and take it from there," had been Jeff's compromise.

Pam thought about asking him to cancel the dinner reservations but felt it wasn't worth getting into a debate over. It had been this particular discussion that led her to believe what she kind of already felt. Jeff liked for things to go his way. Nevertheless, Pam had been proud that she hadn't given in completely to his plans. In fact, she'd insisted that they drive their own vehicles, which caused Jeff to raise an eyebrow.

"Why? I can just come and pick you up," he'd said.

Pam replied, "I just prefer to drive my own car this time."

When Jeff hung up the phone, he sighed heavily, thinking, *This woman is being hard on a brother.* He couldn't refrain from smiling.

Pam laughed silently thinking how she intended to play her cards close to her chest. Her cell phone rang, interrupting not only her thoughts but her grooving to her CD, as well. Wearing her earpiece she answered the call.

"Hello?" She smiled when she heard the voice on the other end.

"Hello, lovely lady." His voice caused her to shiver.

"Hi, Jeff." Pam turned down the volume on the stereo.

"I was calling to let you know that I'm running a little late, but I'll be there so don't take off."

Pam laughed. "Have you had that happen to you before?"

"Yes, a long time ago." Jeff let out a chuckle. "And it was embarrassing."

"Well, as long as you don't have me waiting for 30 minutes or more I promise to stay put." Pam teased. She was beginning to feel more relaxed by the minute.

"Alright, that's fair enough. See you in a bit."

Pam disconnected from the call. "Laugh if he wants to but I'm serious," she said under her breath. It had not been easy for her to ignore Jeff's calls. And it had been even harder to wait a couple of weeks before agreeing to see him again. When he'd asked to get together the week following their last night out, Pam told him she was too busy. The fact that they would be together on the evening of Valentine's Day was coincidental, but Pam was sure glad it had worked out this way. There was no way a diva would be caught alone on the most romantic evening of the year.

Her three closest pals had plans of their own for the evening. Val, of course, was spending it with Cory. Lucky lady, she would always have a date lined up on this special day. Jackie was going out again with *that* guy, the same gentleman she'd mentioned when they all met up after Career Day. His name was still a mystery, but Jackie sure did seem to glow whenever she mentioned him. And Tricee was at a Beach Boys concert out at the Rosemont Theater with a few of her white colleagues. Pam had given her the side-eye on that one.

"The Beach Boys, Tricee? Are you serious? Girlfriend, you are going to be the only black person in that crowd."

Not only did Tricee have to try to convince Pam that she knew some black people who were into the Beach Boys, she also had to convince her that it was acceptable for a saved person to go and hear them sing.

"The pearly gates are not going to slam shut in my face just because of a concert."

"Well, you'd better get on them knees and pray as soon as you get home, just in case."

Pam exited the expressway at Armitage Avenue to make a sharp right. As soon as she got to Ashland Avenue to turn left she was caught by a red light. She looked to her right only to see a very handsome Latino in a white, two-door Chrysler with dark hair and eyes that were smiling at her. He waved and she smiled back. *Jeff better get it together.* This man had to have been the sexist man driving through the city streets. Pam had never dated anyone other than black men but she could easily imagine how that could all change. What a difference a few seconds at a red light had made. He made a sad face as Pam made her left turn. She couldn't help but to laugh out loud. *Note to Pam: Accept date if ever asked out by a fine, sexy, Latino.*

Before she got out of her car she ran her hand through her hair and touched up her makeup. She closed the pressed powder compact and walked the few blocks to the club. The DJ was blasting reggae music from several different artists. The Montego Bay Boys, the reggae band who was to perform, would be playing sometime around 10:00 PM or a little after. It was now just after 9:00 PM and the crowd was slowly increasing. By midnight she figured the place would be jam-packed. There were several people on the dance floor, including a few women dancing alone. Pam observed the crowd as she removed her coat. She noticed the guy at the door who'd collected the cover charge staring in her direction. His expression indicated that he'd contemplated letting her in for free. Pam looked away to avoid eye contact and decided to move further in and nearer the back wall. This way she could still see Jeff when he entered.

As she scanned the crowd and her surroundings, she noticed that the place looked pretty much the same as it had during her last visit, with the exception of a few round tables that now sat in the middle of the floor. There were two bar stools to each table. One young man attempted to move a stool from one of the tables to where he was seated with two other people but a staff member of the club quickly corrected him. There were several pictures hung throughout the club, including two of the late Bob Marley that were placed on opposite walls. The only way you could miss them when you walked into the club was if you were looking down at the floor. On the far back wall was a picture of Montego Bay with the words 'Yeh Mon' printed across the top of it in bold, black letters.

"May I buy you a drink?" Pam's eyes grew wide at the peculiar-sounding voice behind her. It sounded a lot like Herman from *The Munsters.* Although she'd grown up watching the popular television sitcom, she was almost afraid to turn around. She would laugh hysterically at Herman's antics on the show but she had not come out expecting to run into his look-alike.

She tried to ignore his offer by pretending the music had drowned out his voice. She slowly moved her shoulders up and down hoping he would see that she was into the music. She even took a few steps forward, accidentally bumping into the woman standing in front of her.

"Excuse me," she said to the woman.

"No problem," the woman replied and went back to wiggling her shoulders and hips.

"Maybe you didn't hear me. I asked if I may buy you a drink." The man's voice caused Pam to squirm. He was obviously one of those persistent ones. Pam cautiously turned around. She strained her neck to look up at the guy. He had to have been close to 6'7".

"No, thank you. I don't drink," Pam answered politely and, trying to get away, turned to make her way through the crowd. The man was right behind her.

"So what's your name? How about a cranberry juice?"

Come on, Jeff. I need for you to walk through those doors any minute now. Pam stopped walking and, with much hesitation, turned toward the guy once again. "I'm waiting for my boyfriend." He wasn't a bad-looking guy at all and he smelled nice. But his voice was scary.

"Oh. Well, that's all you had to say. I meant no harm at all," the man responded. "Just let me talk to – "

Before he could finish, the woman Pam had accidentally bumped into came walking over. She touched Pam lightly on the arm. "Girl, I thought that was you!" the woman said excitedly.

Pam gave the woman a look with a raised eyebrow. The woman then leaned in and whispered into Pam's ear. "I'm trying to save you, my sister. Flow with it."

After several seconds Pam caught on. "Hey, girl! You changed your hair! I didn't recognize you!" Pam squealed. She and the woman embraced.

"Come on, I want you to meet someone." The woman tugged at Pam's arm.

"Have a good evening," Pam said to the tall gentleman as the woman led her away.

Once they reached the back of the club and safety they both laughed. The young woman looked around once more before she spoke.

"I could tell that you were being held captive when you bumped into me. I sort of figured you were trying to get away from him. I saw him trying to talk to you, and then he had the nerve to follow you!"

"Well, let me thank you first and foremost for saving me from Herman. I didn't want to be rude but you'd think a man would just accept no for an answer and move on to the next one," Pam said.

"Not possible. Some of them—well, many of them have a hard time with that. You know that ego thing and all. His name's

Herman?" The woman sipped the rest of her orange juice from the small plastic cup. "So you know him?"

Pam chuckled. "Herman—the character from *The Munster's*"

"Oh no!" The woman cringed and then laughed. She extended her hand. "I'm Melody. And if you think he looks like Herman, you have every right to run."

"I'm Pam." Pam shook the woman's hand. "No, it's just his voice—he sounds like Herman," Pam said with a frown.

"Oh, okay." Melody laughed at Pam's facial expression. "So do you come here a lot?"

It was 9:35 PM and Jeff still had not arrived. But Pam was at least thankful that she now had someone to talk to while she waited.

"No, I don't come here too often. It's been a while since I was here last. What about you?"

Melody was still wearing her long, grey coat but it was unbuttoned. The majority of the crowd was dressed casually, many of them wearing jeans. There were a few women wearing short skirts with long boots. One woman had on a one-piece bodysuit that had short sleeves. It was a cute outfit but it seemed more appropriate for the summer. Pam could see Melody's outfit through her open coat. She was dressed casually in a pair of jeans and a grey sweater. She wore a pair of big, hoop earrings that complimented her round face and the twists that were pulled to the top of her head. She was a pretty woman who Pam thought resembled the singer Lauryn Hill.

"No, I'm not a regular," Melody said laughing. "I came here with my friend." She looked toward the dance floor to see if she could point her friend out to Pam. "See the one wearing the jeans and the v-neck black sweater, dancing like it's nobody's business? That's my friend Van, short for Vanessa."

Pam looked through the crowd and took notice of Melody's friend. "It looks like she's having a ball!" Pam commented. "I'm not mad at her."

Pam noticed the ring, which was hard to miss, on Melody's left hand and couldn't help but wonder why she was here on Valentine's Day at the Til Midnight club and not out with her husband.

"Van knows how to party," Melody said. "Would you like a drink?" she asked.

"Sure, how about a white wine spritzer, I could sure use one."

As they headed for the bar, Melody and Pam had to ignore the comments from a few of the guys they passed in the crowd.

"Excuse me, but heaven must be missing two beautiful angels," said a dark-skinned man who stood all of 5'5".

"Please tell me you left your man at home."

"May I dance with you until the place closes?"

With drinks in hand, Pam and Melody walked to the center of the club. It had become so crowded they decided not to force their way to the back. Pam looked toward the door and was still able to see who came in and who went out, so they were in a good spot. As Melody looked toward the door she noticed two white women and a white man entering. None of them were wearing coats and, to make matters worse, one of the women had on a short-sleeved blouse.

"You know, I don't believe white folks get cold," Melody said, chuckling as she tilted her head toward the trio. "It's either that or the three of them just didn't get the memo." She made a shivering sound. "It is still winter."

Pam laughed. "They can take the cold much better than we can."

Melody took a sip of her drink. "So are you meeting someone here?"

"Yes. I'm … " Pam paused, "meeting the guy I'm dating, my guy friend." She shrugged. "I don't know how to refer to him. Isn't that awful?"

Melody smiled. "I understand. I know where you're coming from. But I'm so glad I'm not dating anymore."

Melody seemed so laid back and, from the way she'd responded, Pam felt it would be harmless to ask how long she'd been married. She took a sip of her drink and then acknowledged Melody's ring. "How long have you been married, if I may ask?"

Melody grinned. Her smile could light up a room. "Yes, you may ask. We've been married going on seven years. My husband's in New York on business. He asked me to meet him there but, you know, I told him we could celebrate V-day when he returns."

Pam was all ears and listening intently.

"We have a one-year-old," Melody continued. "So for the past year, my life has consisted of nothing but baby talk, potty training and baby food." Melody laughed. "He is such a blessing and our bundle of joy, but mama needed a night out!"

Pam was all smiles as she listened to the new mom talk about her baby and her life. For a brief moment she allowed herself to go there in her own mind. Pam adored her niece and nephew and thought back to when both of them were still newborns. Melody removed her coat and laid it across her arm.

"I just wanted to get out and have some 'me time.' My mother-in-law was all too thrilled to babysit."

Pam noticed a guy staring at Melody as she was speaking.

"When Van called and asked me if I wanted to go out, I hung up the phone and ran to my closet to look for an outfit."

Pam laughed. She was truly enjoying their conversation, thinking how it felt as if they'd known each other for more than 20 minutes.

"I don't blame you. Everyone needs some 'me time' every now and then," said Pam.

"Yeah. And Van is my only single friend who didn't blow me off when I got married. So it was like an honor that she asked me to join her. She just broke up with her boyfriend so she might just be using me for tonight to keep from having to spend the night alone," Melody laughed. "But I don't care. Shucks, use me!"

Melody had a great sense of humor and her friendship with Van made Pam think about her friendship with Tricee, Jackie, and Val.

"Well, I am glad you are out and having a good time because that is all that matters," Pam replied. The two then raised their cups to a toast.

Just as Pam was ready to excuse herself for the ladies room, she saw Jeff walk in, a pair of eyes trailing him. A white woman with bright red hair stopped talking to her blond-haired friend as soon as she saw Jeff. A black woman with long, black hair—Pam was sure it was a weave—forgot all about the guy she was talking to. The guy just stared at her in disbelief. And a young, black female with a ponytail who looked to be in her early 20s also gave Jeff a quick once-over

"Ms. Rhodes, I am glad you didn't give up on me." Jeff planted a peck on Pam's cheek. "And you look really nice."

Jeff smelled good, as usual, and he looked good in his button-down, long-sleeved shirt, which was tucked inside his jeans.

He carried his short, black jacket, which he'd removed as soon as he walked into the club.

"My mother is Ms. Rhodes. And I was this close to giving up on you." Pam placed her thumb and her forefinger together.

"Oh, okay. Ms. Pam. I would have been deeply hurt had you left." He placed his hand over his heart.

Seeing him now made Pam forget that she'd been perturbed with him, and not having seen him in a couple of weeks made her heart flutter. She wasn't sure if she'd want to make him wait a couple of weeks again.

"Oh. Jeff, this is Melody." Pam turned toward Melody.

"My pleasure, Melody," said Jeff, smiling as he extended his hand. "What are you ladies drinking?" Pam took note of his good manners.

Melody shifted to one foot and tugged at her purse strap. "Actually, I need to go to the little girls' room," she said. "But thanks just the same."

"You know, I was on my way to the restroom, too, before I saw you coming in," Pam said to Jeff.

"Okay. Well, I could use a drink. I'll meet you back here." Jeff watched as Pam and Melody turned and headed for the ladies room. *I wonder why women always travel in pairs when they go to the restroom.*

"Hi. Are you having a good time?" The blond woman asked Jeff as he stood at the bar. "My friend wanted to know if you'd like to join us for a drink." She motioned toward the redhead.

"I am having a good time, thanks." Jeff smiled. "But, no thanks. If you'll please excuse me." He turned and walked to a spot near the far end of the bar. The blond went back to where her friend was seated, whispered something to her and then shrugged.

Jeff was hoping that Pam was still in the ladies room and had not witnessed him being approached. He didn't think she would cause a scene over something so trivial—he believed she was much bigger than that—but she was already filled with questions about their relationship. No use in giving her one more thing to over-analyze.

"May I have a club soda, please?" Jeff ordered his drink.

"Sure thing, man," the bartender replied.

He was about to take a sip of his drink when the black female with the ponytail came over to where he was standing.

"Hi, you look familiar," the young woman said.

Jeff looked at the woman and realized that she looked familiar to him, too. She stood before him with a puzzled look on her face.

"No disrespect and this is not a come-on, but I think I have seen you out in Schaumburg—a grocery store somewhere, a bank, something …"

After several seconds it dawned on Jeff where he'd seen her before. "Do you work at the Bank of Schaumburg?" he asked. *Either she worked at the bank or she had a twin.*

"No, that's my twin sister."

Jeff coughed as he removed his drink from his lips.

"I'm just teasing," the woman replied. "I work there part time as a teller. I knew I had seen you from somewhere."

"I guess it is a small world after all, huh?"

"I guess it is," the woman said. "Well, good seeing you. I hope you enjoy the band, they are good. I've heard them play before."

As the woman turned to walk away, Jeff observed a very tall guy ask her to dance. She happily obliged him and they made their way to the dance floor.

Dude has a very unique-sounding voice, Jeff thought to himself as he walked back to where Pam was standing.

"Girl, look at Herman." Melody tilted her chin toward the tall guy who'd tried to talk to Pam earlier. "He done found himself a dance partner."

Pam laughed as she watched the woman's ponytail swing back and forth as she and the very tall guy got their groove on. The DJ was playing hits from Beenie Man and the dancing crowd was in full force.

"Work it, Herman!" Pam said.

"Girl, leave Herman alone! He is working that tall frame!"

Both Melody and Pam were in stitches.

Jeff made his way back over to Pam and Melody. "What's so funny?" he asked Pam.

"Nothing," Pam replied. "We're just people watching."

Jeff saw Melody's grin and followed her eyes to the woman he'd just spoken to and her dance partner. He knew then why Pam and Melody were laughing.

"He is just a little too tall to do that dance," Melody said to Pam, though Jeff heard her, too.

Dude does look a little out of place. But, hey, he looks as though he's having a good time. Jeff had every intention of enjoying this evening with Pam. He had another surprise for her. He'd purchased tickets for them to see a Maxwell concert next weekend. Surely, Pam would be all over him with kisses after this surprise, just as she'd been when he'd given her the bracelet. He didn't know too many women who didn't like Maxwell. Most of the men he knew would go out of their way to get tickets to a Maxwell concert simply because they were all aware of the singer's popularity with the female crowd.

Jeff looked forward to getting to know Pam better and, although they still had a lot to learn about each other, he saw no reason to hold off on buying gifts he knew would make her happy. This wasn't moving too fast, especially for someone he really liked. Pam was unique. There was something special about her that Jeff couldn't quite put his finger on. And sex appeal—it just oozed right out of her. He liked making her happy. That's what he would do for any woman he enjoyed being with. But all the questions she'd been asking recently would have to stop. Jeff wanted Pam to just go with the flow. He felt that her questions were just another way of keeping him on his toes. He didn't mind playing by some of her rules, but she could think again if she thought he would play by all of her rules.

And this driving their own vehicles to the club. Jeff wasn't sure what was up with that. He didn't know how Pam planned for the evening to end, but he knew how he planned for it to end. He was either staying over at her place tonight or she was staying over at his. If she thought they would both drive their cars back to their own homes after dinner, she was mistaken.

"Well, love, we should get going," Jeff whispered to Pam after they'd heard one song from the band.

"Already?" Pam asked. "Don't you want to dance before we leave?"

"I don't fast dance, I slow dance." Jeff helped Pam put on her coat. It was hard to miss the twinkle in his eyes. Pam wasn't sure if they were still going to the Italian place for dinner or if Jeff had made other plans. But she did know that after dinner, she would be driving her car back to the south side. She would love to slow dance with Jeff and thought that maybe, just maybe, she'd have an opportunity for one dance at her place tonight. But if Jeff thought they would spend the entire night together, he could think again. He'd tried that the last time. Pam still had questions, but tonight she would not allow him the upper hand.

"Well, Melody, it's been a pleasure. You have my contact info."

"It has been fun, Pam." Melody then whispered to Pam as Jeff was putting on his coat, "Take it slow. Don't allow yourself to feel pressure. Men like the hunt, remember that." Melody winked as Pam nodded and smiled.

"You want to just take my car?" Pam asked as she and Jeff stood next to her vehicle.

"Why not just follow me to the restaurant? I don't want to leave my car parked on the north side. The restaurant where we're going for dinner is downtown."

"Okay, but then afterwards – "

Jeff leaned in and kissed Pam on the lips before she could finish her sentence. "Just go with the flow, babe, okay?" He smiled and brushed Pam's cheek with the back of his hand.

"Okay. Go with the flow. I can do that," Pam blushed. "I do have one question though."

"One question," Jeff repeated. "Go ahead."

"What did Marcia want?" A silly grin was plastered on Pam's face.

Jeff looked perplexed. "Marcia? Who's that?"

"The blond who approached you when you were at the bar," Pam said, pressing her lips together trying not to laugh. "Yeah, I saw that."

"I didn't ask her name, though," Jeff responded, still confused.

Finally Pam laughed. "Marcia Brady!"

After several seconds, Jeff began to laugh. "Woman you are something."

He waited until Pam was in her car and then walked the one block to where he was parked. Yes, this Pam was quite a woman: funny, sexy, smart, and that red sweater. Jeff could not think of any other woman he'd dated who made a red sweater look that good! He'd tried his best to keep his eyes on her face when they were in the club. Over dinner he'd make sure he focused on her eyes when she spoke, though he knew it would take much restraint.

The night is still young, Jeff thought silently as he fastened his seat belt. *And filled with all kinds of possibilities.*

15

Sunday afternoon: August 18th

"Before she travailed, she brought forth; before her pain came, she was delivered of a man child. Shall I bring to the birth, and not cause to bring forth? saith the Lord: shall I cause to bring forth, and shut the womb? saith thy God. Translation: A woman does not give birth before she feels the pain. She does not give birth to a son before she feels the pain of birth. In the same way, I will not cause pain without allowing something new to be born, says the Lord. If I cause you the pain, I will not stop you from giving birth to your new nation, says your God."

The pastor's sermon that morning remained etched in Tricee's mind. She believed it had been a word just for her. Although she still wasn't 100% sure what the Lord was trying to tell her, the sermon based on chapter 66 of the book of Isaiah had been powerful.

One of the things Tricee liked about Pastor Downey was his use of The Good Word Bible. He taught and preached from The King James Bible but would often refer to The Good Word Bible, which was broken down into plain English. This made it easier for those who did not yet understand the Bible and its Hebrew phrasing. Pastor Downey was not only a preacher he was a teacher of the word. And for Tricee and so many others in the congregation, that was important.

While she had grown in her walk with Christ, Tricee still had so many unanswered questions. And now with her current dilemma, she had a lot more questions for God. She understood His power, but what was beginning to be hard for her to accept was why He'd allowed some things to happen in the first place. What she was going through right now was very painful and she'd asked the Lord over and over—why? As she sat in her kitchen with her Bible open in front of her, the words just seemed to jump out at her: *I will not cause pain without allowing something new to be born.* Tricee thought about a question she'd posed to her grandmother when she was much younger.

"Grandma Eda, why can't the Lord just come down at night while we are in the bed and sit across from us and talk to us? It sure would make things easy!"

Grandma Eda chuckled at her 6-year-old granddaughter's inquiry. "Honey love, if the Lord gave us all of the answers directly then we wouldn't go to Him as much. He wants us to keep depending on Him for what we need. See this way, it keeps us going back to Him over and over again, which makes us grow closer to Him."

Lord, I sure do wish you could just come down and sit across from me and tell me what to do right now. I'm feeling like that small child again, Tricee prayed silently. She closed her Bible and let her mind drift back to the night before.

After her discussion with her mother, Tricee had gone back upstairs where Val was sound asleep. She'd felt badly that Val was having to witness her drama. When she awoke this morning, Val was already gone. She'd left Tricee a note explaining that she did not wish to wake her and that she would call her later on today. But Tricee felt that Val was more than deserving of a break. The last thing she wanted was to use up any of Val's time today talking about her problems.

Tricee had overslept and been late for church. She thought about just missing church altogether but realized that would have been exactly what the enemy wanted. She arrived just before the worship service ended. She knew she'd missed some great singing but the sermon had fed her well. She was just about to change out of what she'd worn to church when her home phone rang. It was Jackie and she was talking non-stop.

"Tricee, are you okay? I am so sorry I missed your call. I'm in Milwaukee for a leadership conference and it lasted longer than I thought it would. We had a speaker during breakfast and then went right into the workshop. Then after that it was one session after another. Last night we had to attend a mandatory dinner, which included having to listen to another speaker. He went on and on." Jackie paused, exhaled, and continued. "By the time I got back to the hotel it was late and I didn't want to call you. I tried calling you on your cell this morning but you didn't answer. I figured you were in church. Pam called me and left a message. She said something about your mom and you having some discussion and that you were very upset, but that I should really let you give me all the details."

Tricee decided it was time to jump in. "Jackie, girlfriend. Please put your brakes on and slow down."

She was amused at Jackie's obvious concern. And there was no telling what Pam had said in the message she'd left. Tricee thought about Pam and the strange way she had behaved yesterday. She knew Pam had probably only shared so much with Jackie for the sake of her privacy.

"I'm fine. It's a long story but you've probably figured that out already. And I had forgotten about your business trip to Milwaukee," said Tricee.

She held her cordless phone between her ear and shoulder as she changed into a gold t-shirt and a white pair of shorts. She had decided to forego meeting Ruby for dinner, opting to take a stroll along the lakefront instead. Her intention was to have a peaceful afternoon and evening alone to process all that had taken place this weekend, and her dinner companion would be God Almighty.

"When are you leaving Milwaukee? Are you still in your hotel room?" she asked Jackie as she plopped down on her bed.

"I'm in a coffee shop, of course."

"Yeah, I guess I should have known," Tricee replied. It was a known fact that the first thing Jackie would do whenever she traveled was locate the nearest coffee shop.

"I'm leaving here shortly. I arranged for a late checkout and decided to browse at a few of the stores."

"Have a safe drive home. I will talk to you later on this evening."

Tricee sounded like she was ready to hang up but Jackie wanted to hear some details. The urgency in Pam's voice when she left her message had Jackie wanting to at least know what had transpired between Tricee and her mother.

"So what are your plans later on?" Jackie asked Tricee.

A frown formed on Tricee's face and she became silent.

"Hello?"

"I'm still here." Tricee sat straight up on her bed. "I just had an unpleasant thought."

"Oh?" Jackie could sense that Tricee's mood had suddenly changed.

"My mother wants to have dinner this evening. She believes it's crucial for us to get together and discuss this issue before she leaves tomorrow." Tricee walked over to her closet and pulled out her sandals. “But I don’t see how a chat over dinner is going to resolve anything.”

Jackie sipped her coffee and flipped through the pages of a book she’d just purchased. She listened intently as Tricee spoke.

“How much has Pam told you?”

“Huh? Oh.” Jackie closed her book. “She really didn’t go into details.” She waited for Tricee to reply.

“My best friend from 3rd grade is my half-sister. Annette the attorney. We have the same father.” Tricee wiped a tear from her eye. The same words that had caused her so much pain now flowed easily from her lips: *Annette is your half-sister*. But the pain she felt was still the same.

Jackie’s mouth flew open and Tricee could sense that her sudden silence meant she was at a loss for words.

“Oh, well. I should go. I have some things to figure out.” Tricee walked back into her living room.

“Tricee, I’m so sorry,” Jackie finally spoke, moving her coffee cup to the side.

“I know. It’s a sorry situation,” Tricee uttered. “I guess I should be happy, right? I mean after all, I now have a sister. I’ve always wanted one. I’ve never been happy about being an only child.”

Jackie knew Tricee was being cynical. After being away for the entire weekend and away from her daughter, Jackie realized that she’d have a lot of catching up to do. It would be a few days before she and Tricee would be able to speak in detail. The two-and-a-half-hour drive from Milwaukee back to Chicago’s south side would have her thinking about nothing else but Tricee’s well-being. But Jackie could not help but think of how this was affecting Ruby.

“I can’t imagine what your mother must be going through right now.” Jackie’s words came out before she could stop them.

Tricee stopped suddenly in the middle of her living room. “Excuse me?” She wasn’t sure she’d just heard Jackie correctly. “You can’t imagine what Ruby is feeling?”

Jackie sighed, regretting that she hadn’t kept her big mouth shut. “I’m sorry. I didn’t mean to make it sound like that.”

“You can’t imagine what Ruby is going through?” Tricee repeated her words. She realized Jackie had meant no harm but still, her words had cut deep. “How can you feel badly for Ruby? I would think you would feel badly for the person who had the misfortune of hearing such surprising news."

"I do feel bad for you, Tricee. I guess I was looking at it from a mother's perspective." Jackie glanced at her watch. "I *am* a mother, and I cannot imagine having to tell my daughter something like that."

"But you are not the one telling your daughter *something like that.*" Tricee was trying not to get angry. The enemy had used Jackie to do his dirty work. Tricee closed her eyes, rubbed her temples and took a few deep breaths.

Jackie removed a few one dollar bills from her purse. She knew by Tricee's tone that it was best that they end their phone call. An older, white gentleman who looked to be around 80 strolled into the coffee shop walking with a cane and wearing a stained white t-shirt. The words *Proud Republican, hear me roar* were written across the front of it. He looked over at Jackie and made a face. Once he sat down with his coffee he waved at her.

"Weirdo," Jackie mumbled under her breath. "The least you can do is put on a clean t-shirt." Jackie refocused on her conversation. "I apologize, Tricee. It was a poor choice of words on my end," she replied as she walked out of the coffee shop."

"Right," Tricee responded softly. "I know you didn't mean it to be hurtful."

"Let's talk later, okay?" Jackie climbed into her silver Volvo. The little white teddy bear with the words *I love mom* had been given to her by her daughter. She could not even begin to imagine her and Alesia having a strained mother-daughter relationship like Tricee and Ruby.

"Yeah, let's just talk later." Tricee was definitely ready to hang up. A stroll along the lake would help clear her head.

"You know what my aunt used to say." Jackie tossed her purse and the small, brown paper bag onto the passenger seat.

"What's that?"

"There is a prayer for all seasons." Jackie smiled as she recalled her mother's deceased oldest sister. "She used to say that God expects for us to go through changes just as we go through the different seasons."

Tricee listened as Jackie continued.

"Isn't it comforting to know that, no matter what season we're in, God is right there to hear our every call?"

Jackie didn't attend church regularly but she read her Bible on a semi-regular basis. Tricee wasn't surprised by what Jackie had just shared.

"Yeah, that is very comforting."

Jackie decided to go one step further. She exhaled and hoped that Tricee would not hang up on her. She was only sharing what she'd felt led by the spirit to share.

"I think you should have dinner with your mother, Tricee."

Tricee heard the words but she didn't respond.

"You both owe each other at least that."

Tricee was ready to protest but Jackie continued.

"I am sure you're not the only one hurting, sweetie."

After their phone call, Tricee stood still in the middle of her living room. She was going through so many emotions. A part of her wanted to believe that Pam had shared more than Jackie had let on but, then again, Tricee trusted her friends and knew they respected her privacy. Even if Pam had shared more details with Jackie, it would not have made any difference.

Between Val and Jackie, Tricee had received the same message: Don't be so hard on Ruby. Well, that was easier said than done. Pam had been the only one to not express too much of her feelings. Either way, Tricee could not erase the pain. Forgiving her mother would not come easily.

"I just need peace of mind, Lord." She sighed and walked into her kitchen. "Some fresh air would do me good."

As she was leaving to take her walk, she grabbed a bottle of water from the fridge. She picked up her Bible from the kitchen table to take it into her bedroom and noticed the church bulletin peering from its pages. After service, one of the church members had approached her as she was walking to the parking lot. She'd wanted to invite Tricee to attend a speaking engagement featuring a female pastor who was known for her candid sermons. The church member had written the information about the event on the bulletin and Tricee, not being in the mood to chat, had nonchalantly inserted the bulletin inside of her Bible.

She opened her Bible to remove the bulletin and saw that it had been placed in the book of Matthew, Chapter 18. Tricee silently read the two highlighted verses, 21 and 22. She'd highlighted them during a Bible study session. The fact that she had been led to those two scriptures at this very moment gave her pause.

Okay, Lord. I hear you. I know what you're trying to say. But forgiving Ruby is just not going to be easy.

Tricee reached the lobby only to find the same doorman from the previous night, the one who'd been mesmerized by Bev, standing behind the desk. She hadn't realized it was so close to 3:00 PM, the time the shift changed for the doormen on staff. When she reached the doors that led outside, he looked up at her, smiled and said hello. She mumbled a quiet "hello" without looking at him and walked out of the building.

Once at the lakefront, Tricee exchanged greetings with a few of the people she recognized and then found an empty bench. A middle-aged man and a little boy followed behind a young woman and a little girl. They were, no doubt, a family; Tricee could see the strong resemblance in their faces. When they reached the bench where Tricee was sitting, they stopped to allow the little girl to tie her shoe. Afterward, as they continued their walk, the little girl turned around and waved. The little boy, however, turned to Tricee and stuck out his tongue. Tricee chuckled. *That's why I want a little girl when I start my family.*

After several minutes had passed, Tricee let out a sigh and removed her cell phone from her small handbag. She scrolled through her phone numbers until she reached her mother's number.

"Hello, dear. I was just about to call you." Ruby answered in a joyful tone.

Tricee uttered softly, "What time do you want to meet for dinner?"

16

"Tricee, are you sure you're saved?" Pam asked from Tricee's bedroom, the one that had been transformed into an office. After she chose a Maxwell CD from Tricee's collection, she joined Tricee in the kitchen and named a few of the other artists she'd found in her collection.

"Barry White, Chaka Khan, Janet Jackson, Jay-Z, KRS-One, Naughty by Nature, Geto Boys—what would your pastor think if he saw your selection of music? I never knew you had so many CDs."

Tricee had well over 100 CDs on the CD rack alone. Several others had been placed in the two-tier bookshelf that sat across from her computer. And due to her need for organization, they were grouped according to type of music.

Pam picked up some cheese and crackers from the serving plate. "You have all of my favorite old school hits by some of my favorite artists: Aretha Franklin; Ashford and Simpson; the Four Tops; Melba Moore; Regina Bell; the Temptations; Earth, Wind, and Fire—is there anybody you don't have?"

Pam, along with Jackie and Val, were gathered at Tricee's condo. They would finally meet Kenzie, Tricee's friend from college, who was in town this week on business. Kenzie was leaving Friday morning and Thursday evening had been the best day for the women to meet.

When Tricee informed her three girlfriends the previous week that Kenzie would be in town, Pam had been the only one who needed to be reminded who she was. Tricee, Val, and Jackie had all met at Pam's Kenwood home last Friday evening, enjoying take-out for dinner.

"I invited Kenzie to join us next Thursday for dinner. She'll be in Chicago on business for a few days." Tricee scooped some of the beef and broccoli from the container.

"Who's Kenzie?" Pam scooped several helpings of shrimp fried rice onto her plate.

"My friend from college," Tricee replied. "I told you about her."

Pam shrugged. "I don't remember." She then pointed her fork at Val and Jackie. "You must have told these two."

"No, she mentioned her to all of us," Jackie stated.

"Yeah, her white friend who belted out Dr. King's speech during their sophomore year," Val added with a chuckle.

Pam made a face. "I would have remembered something like that."

"I know I mentioned her to you. You probably just forgot." Tricee helped herself to another shrimp egg roll.

"Why?" Pam asked, turning to face Tricee. Val and Jackie stole glances at each other and shook their heads.

"Why?" Tricee asked. "What why?"

Val laughed. "'What why?' I love it."

Pam's interrogation began. "You guys weren't close or anything. Why are you inviting her to dinner?"

"Actually, Pam, Kenzie and I were *pretty close. She was one of the few young women I'd met in college that I could relate to." Tricee excused herself and went into Pam's kitchen.*

"Is she getting an attitude just because I asked if they were close?" Pam whispered.

Tricee returned to the living room with two glasses of water. She handed one to Jackie and resumed her place on Pam's brown, leather sofa.

"Are you offended because I asked you that?" Pam placed her plate on the coffee table.

"It would take more than that to offend me, Pam." Tricee picked up her plate and finished the rest of her meal. After she chewed and swallowed she turned back to Pam. "But what I do want to know is why you are so against me inviting Kenzie to hang out with us?"

Pam took a sip from her glass of diet iced green tea. She wiped her mouth with her napkin. "I'm not against her hanging out with us."

"Well, it sure seems that way," Tricee said.

Jackie and Val were seated across from Pam and Tricee. Jackie sat in the chair that matched the sofa, her feet propped up on the ottoman. Val was seated on the floor, leaning on a couple of huge brown pillows. They both looked back and forth from Pam to Tricee as the two women spoke. You would have thought they were watching a tennis match.

"Let me ask you a question." Pam leaned back on the sofa.

Jackie, Val and Tricee all looked at her in anticipation of what she was about to say.

"Oh, forget it." Pam stood up. "Who wants apple pie?" She then walked toward her kitchen to retrieve the store-bought pie.

She could hear the muffled snickers behind her. When she returned she saw the smirk on Tricee's face.

"What's the giggling for?" Pam looked at Tricee, then at Val and Jackie.

Val cleared her throat. "We just want to know why you're so opposed to integrating our sister circle." Jackie and Tricee tried to contain their laughter. "You do realize that segregation is a thing of the past, right?"

"Whatever, Val," Pam uttered.

"The look on your face when Val mentioned that Kenzie was white said it all," Jackie chimed in.

"Oh, she was *white? What—is she not white anymore?" Pam asked sarcastically. She popped a huge bite of apple pie into her mouth.*

Tricee was amused at the banter between her friends. She couldn't help but wonder what Pam was going to ask before she headed into the kitchen for the pie.

"What were you going to ask me?" Tricee cut a slice of apple pie.

Pam stopped eating. She picked at the crust of her pie with her fork. "Would Kenzie invite you to hang out with her and her friends if the situation was reversed?"

"Yes, she would," Tricee replied matter-of-factly.

Pam grunted.

"You know what, Pam?" Jackie stood up from the chair. "You can have such a pessimistic outlook sometimes."

Val nodded but quickly stopped when Pam turned to look in her direction.

Jackie walked over to where Tricee was seated and picked up Tricee's glass of water. "Is this glass of water half empty or half full?" she asked Pam. She looked as if she was auditioning for a commercial, standing there with one hand on her hip and the other holding out the glass.

When Pam did not respond, Jackie repeated the question. "Come on. Is this glass of water half empty or half full?"

"You know what?" Pam stood and walked over to Jackie. "I was only asking her a question about her friend." She reached for

the glass of water but Jackie held it away. "But you three are making a big deal over nothing."

Val stood and walked over to Jackie and Pam. "I'll answer. I see it as half full." She then turned to Tricee. "What about you, Tricee? Half empty or half full?"

"I'm an optimist. I say half full."

Pam couldn't keep from laughing much longer. "It's half empty. Now look at the time." She walked over and pointed at her wall clock. "I think it's half time for all three of you to get up out of my house."

As Tricee continued to get everything ready, she grew more and more excited at the thought of seeing Kenzie again. It was hard to believe that they'd managed to stay connected yet not physically see each other in all of these years. Kenzie would send a X-mas card every year to Ruby's address, and Ruby would make sure that Tricee received it. When Tricee relocated to Chicago, she gave Kenzie her address, and although Kenzie could now send the card directly to Tricee, she still made sure to send one to Ruby.

"First of all, my pastor wouldn't see my R&B music collection because I'd make sure he only saw my gospel CDs." She placed the bowl of coleslaw into the fridge. "Then again, who knows? Pastor just might want to get up and dance once he saw all of that old school music."

Jackie and Val joined Pam and Tricee in the kitchen. They'd overheard some of their conversation.

"*You* have a Geto Boys CD?" Jackie asked, taking a seat at the kitchen table.

"I didn't see any gospel music in there," Pam said to Jackie.

"That's because I keep my gospel CDs in my bedroom."

"In case you wake up in the middle of the night needing to get your praise on," Val teased.

"Exactly. And the Geto Boys CD is not mine." Tricee waved her big mixing spoon toward Pam and Jackie.

"Oh. Then whose it?" Pam inquired.

"It must have been left here by somebody." Tricee eyed her Maxwell CD, which Pam had brought to the kitchen. But before she could say anything, Jackie and Val started singing the lyrics to one of the Geto Boys' songs and dancing in Tricee's kitchen. Pam stood up and joined in. A few seconds later, Tricee waved her big spoon in the air as she began to sing. It was moments like these that reminded the four women why they were such good friends.

"Whew!" said Val as she sat back down. By now all four women were practically out of breath. "That was fun. I can't believe we remembered all the words to that song."

Tricee laughed. "This is true, that was fun. But we're supposed to set a good example." Tricee glanced at Jackie and Pam.

"I saw that," Jackie said, laughing.

Tricee stuck out her tongue at Jackie, then she turned to Pam. "No, you cannot borrow my Maxwell CD, so don't ask."

Tricee looked at the clock. It was 6:45 PM and Kenzie was due to arrive any minute. She'd said she was really looking forward to seeing Tricee and meeting Jackie, Val and Pam. Tricee had instructed Kenzie to call her once she boarded the train at the Howard Street station. From there it would take less than 15 minutes to arrive at Tricee's condo. Kenzie had tried to object when Tricee informed her that she'd give her a ride back to her hotel in Evanston, but Tricee wouldn't hear of it. She explained to Kenzie that Evanston was very close to where she lived.

"Oh, come on! You don't even listen to it that often," Pam pleaded.

"No," Tricee repeated. "You can play it and enjoy it while you're here, but my CDs are not to leave my home."

Pam playfully tapped Tricee on the arm. "Okay, okay," she uttered.

Pam really didn't see what Tricee and Kenzie could possibly have in common. And she just knew that Kenzie would arrive and put on a fake I-am-so-happy-to-meet-you smile. Unlike Tricee, Pam could not name one white person with whom she was friends, and that was perfectly fine by her. Being in sales, Pam met and worked with all types of people, but that was the extent of it. She made no effort to include any of the white women she'd met or worked with in her circle of friends. And frankly, she was convinced that they were just as disinterested in becoming friends with her. Unlike Tricee and Val who had attended universities where students of color were in the minority, Pam and Jackie had attended HBCUs for their undergraduate studies. This was by choice. Pam had attended her father's alma mater in Tennessee, which had made him proud.

She'd liked it so much, she decided to remain and pursue her graduate degree there, as well. She had told her parents, "I love it here. Being around so many of my own people in this academic setting is a liberating experience." There were blacks from various socioeconomic levels. Pam had met students whose parents didn't have much, as well as students whose parents were wealthy. The students were hard workers and very bright. It was obvious that the parents had worked really hard to send their kids to college, and had instilled in them a sense of worth and value. Pam didn't consider herself prejudiced, she considered herself a proud black woman—proud of her heritage and proud of all that her ancestors had endured and accomplished.

When Tricee's home phone rang, Pam watched a smile flash across Tricee's face and assumed it was Kenzie. She thought about what her mother used to tell her and her four siblings: If you can't say anything nice to or about someone, then don't say anything at all. With those words etched into her thoughts, Pam's mind was made up for the evening. When Kenzie arrived she would keep her words to a minimum. This was more so for Tricee's sake. She had no intention of disrespecting her friend's home.

"Hi, Aunt Janice. I, um, have been meaning to call you." Tricee laughed. "I know that's what everyone says, but it's true."

Pam overheard Tricee's greeting and realized it was not Kenzie. She went to use Tricee's bathroom as Jackie and Val made their way back into the living room.

"Oh, sweetie, that's okay. I know you have a very busy schedule." Tricee's Aunt Janice was on husband number four and had managed to remain friends with all three of her exes as well as their current wives and girlfriends. She was not only very pretty she was very unique. And the woman could sing! Everyone who ever met her always liked her. Tricee once asked her aunt, jokingly, in reference to husband number four, "Auntie Sis, is this it for you now?"

"Oh, yes, dear," Aunt Janice replied "Your auntie only has so many miles left!"

Tricee noticed the coughing as Aunt Janice spoke. When she inquired about it, Aunt Janice brushed it off saying she was just getting over a cold. *That sounds like more than just a cold.* Tricee immediately became concerned but chose not to dig any deeper. She would, however, bring it up the next time they spoke.

"What's wrong?" Jackie noticed Tricee's expression after she hung up with her aunt.

"Oh, nothing," Tricee responded unaware of her facial expression.

Pam emerged from the bathroom. "I just love this CD." She stopped in the middle of the floor, closed her eyes and moved to Maxwell's smooth and sexy voice. "I could listen to his music all day."

"You just saw him in concert last Saturday. Why didn't you make Jeff buy you a CD while you guys were there?" Jackie asked.

Pam had, indeed, enjoyed the concert but had been rather reserved when asked how her date with Jeff had gone that evening.

She ignored Jackie's question and continued to sway to the lyrics. She shifted the conversation back to the plans for the evening. "I'm hungry. Is McKenzie going to get here soon?"

Tricee sighed. "Pam, her name is Kenzie."

"Kenzie, Keisha, Kim—pick one. But is she on her way because a sister is ready to eat!"

Tricee exhaled as if she was trying to keep herself composed. Pam giggled. She could tell Tricee was starting to become irritable.

"I hope you have some lemons," Pam said to Tricee as she sat next to Val on the sofa. "You know white women only drink their water with lemon." Pam closed her eyes again and rocked her head back and forth as the song came to an end.

"You're so silly," Val said, laughing.

"What? It's true." Pam jerked her head in Val's direction. "A salad and a glass of water with a slice of lemon, that's what they order when they're out to dinner." Pam looked over at Tricee and winked. Tricee shot her an evil eye.

"Look here." Tricee pointed her finger at Pam and shook it. "I'm going to need for you to behave before I put you on the Red Line back to the south side."

"Yeah. And you rode over here with me, lamb chops," Jackie intervened. "So if you want to get back home without having to ride that train, you better behave."

Pam turned toward Val.

"Oh no, don't look at me," said Val. "When I leave here my car is headed to the suburb of Forest Park."

A few minutes later the doorman called stating that Kenzie was in the lobby. The excitement between Tricee and Kenzie was hard to miss. They embraced for what seemed liked 20 minutes when Tricee ran down to the lobby to meet her. And they embraced again back upstairs in Tricee's condo.

The kitchen table, set for six, was covered with a nice pink and white linen table cloth, one that Tricee rarely used. There were six wine glasses beside the plates. Tricee wasn't a drinker but Pam had brought some white wine and mineral water. Jackie had brought iced tea and soda along with a cheesecake. And Val had prepared some of her delicious Cajun brown rice at Tricee's request.

Pam noticed that the table was set for six when she walked into the kitchen but made no comment. She did, however, comment on the two chairs that did not match the other four, which had come with the table. "Tricee must have borrowed these two chairs," she said to no one in particular. It was Val who responded.

"Yeah, she borrowed the chairs from Karen. She should be here sometime this evening."

"Karen?" Pam's expression was one of surprise. Tricee had introduced Karen to Pam, Val, and Jackie but Pam's and Karen's personalities had clashed.

But Tricee wanted Karen at her dinner that evening. She figured that Pam and Karen could at least tolerate each other for a couple of hours. Besides, it would be nice if new friendships were formed this evening. Tricee sure hoped so. Val and Jackie were aware that Karen and Pam didn't really get along but they made no big deal of it. It wasn't as if Karen hung out with them on a regular basis.

"Let me take your coat. Nice! I like it" said Tricee, admiring the belted, light blue, knee-length wool coat.

"Oh, this old thing?" Kenzie laughed as she handed her coat to Tricee.

Kenzie's blond hair, which was pulled back into a ponytail, looked darker than Tricee remembered it, but other than that, she looked pretty much the same. When standing next to Jackie, the two women looked to be the same height, but Kenzie's boots had a heel which made her taller. In college, she and Tricee had been the same height.

After the introductions, they headed back into the living room. Pam went over to the entertainment center and put in another Maxell CD.

"Oh, I love his music!" Kenzie exclaimed.

Oh really? Pam glanced at Kenzie and Tricee glanced at her.

"Yeah, he's popular with the women." Jackie chimed hoping Pam would remain silent.

"It is so nice to finally meet you ladies. Tricee has told me so much about each of you. But I only believe half of what she has shared," Kenzie teased.

After a little small talk, the five women headed into the kitchen. Val could tell already that Kenzie was easy to get along with and that she possessed a sense of humor.

"Well, we don't believe all of what Tricee has shared about you, either. I mean, you ladies sounded like you were pretty wild back in college."

Kenzie's expression became serious as she turned to face Tricee. "You didn't tell them everything did you?" After several seconds of silence, Kenzie began to laugh, causing the other women—except Pam—to laugh also. Tricee removed the pitcher of iced tea and a few cans of diet soda from the fridge.

"No. I only told them how we used to sneak into the guys' dorm rooms. And how we used to sneak whoever we were dating back into our rooms. But that was normal stuff."

Pam took in Kenzie's appearance. She was dressed casually in a pair of dark gray slacks and a white, button-down blouse that was tucked inside her pants. And she couldn't help but notice the beautiful diamond on Kenzie's left finger.

"So Kenzie, you're in public relations?" Jackie asked as they were passing the food around the table. She, too, thought that Kenzie seemed really nice and down to earth.

"Yes," Kenzie said after sipping a glass of Diet Coke. "I'm the director of media relations for Channel 8 news in Denver. I enjoy it but, like with everything else, it comes with its own set of problems." She put a fork filled with Cajun rice into her mouth, swallowed and continued talking. "And you're a high school principal, right?"

The baked chicken and coleslaw that Tricee had prepared was delicious. The whole meal had been quite filling. Tricee was proud of the way her baked chicken with parsley had turned out. The coleslaw with raisins was something new but everyone seemed to enjoy it. After several more minutes, there was a knock at the door. Tricee excused herself to answer it.

"Yes, I'm a high school principal at a public school. And I have to say that I do enjoy what I do. But let's not even talk about the problems," Jackie laughed.

It seemed that almost everyone knew about the challenges of working for the school system, but Jackie remained optimistic. And she would be the first one to come to the defense of the teachers. If she'd said it once, she'd said it many times before—she had excellent teachers who worked hard at her school. And the system was filled with teachers who really cared about the children. Although her daughter attended a private school, a decision that had been made by both her and her ex, Jackie had faith in all that the public schools had to offer.

"She also holds a Ph.D. in educational leadership. She doesn't share that with others," Val leaned over and whispered softly to Kenzie.

"That's wonderful," Kenzie said. "It takes much discipline to pursue a Ph.D. I'd love to go back to school, but right now just doesn't seem to be the right time."

The women continued to talk about their careers, their hobbies, and their future goals. Pam would join in every now and then but for the most part she didn't say much. She did, however, manage to drink two glasses of white wine spritzers.

As Karen and Tricee walked into the kitchen, Pam stood up.

"Hi Karen," Jackie spoke cheerfully in an attempt to diffuse the sudden tension that had filled Tricee's condo.

"Hello ladies," Karen spoke, acknowledging the four women. Pam mouthed a soft "hello" and went into the living room.

It's going to be a long evening. Karen shook her head and turned to Tricee. "I'm hungry. I hope you saved some for me." She giggled as she handed Tricee a brown paper bag.

"I put a plate aside for you." Tricee retrieved the plate that was wrapped in aluminum foil from the stove top. She glanced toward her living room where Pam was now standing by the entertainment center, sipping on her third glass of wine.

"That dinner was delicious. I think I'll try that baked chicken recipe." Val walked over to where Pam was standing.

"Yeah, who knew that Tricee could bake a chicken like that," Pam responded.

"You know what I don't understand?"

"What's that?"

"Why someone as attractive and nice as Tricee has yet to meet that special someone."

"What, are you interested?" Pam smirked. She knew Val could only have one reason for approaching her while the others remained in the kitchen.

"Oh, she's a comedian now." Val began to laugh. The one advantage she had over Jackie and Tricee was the extended period of time in which she'd known Pam. Even though there was a great deal of comfort between the four of them, Val could say some things to Pam that Jackie and Tricee would have to think twice about first.

"I'm just saying she has a lot going for her. She can cook, she loves the Lord, she's smart, and she knows how to treat others. She has all the qualities that men look for in a woman."

Pam was prepared to ask Val exactly where this sudden praise for Tricee was coming from and, more importantly, where it was going.

"First of all," Pam looked at Val sideways, "You and I both know—a lot of men are not looking for born again women." Val nodded. "But as for the other qualities, I'll give her that. But why did she have to invite Karen without telling me first?"

"You know her intentions were good," Val said. "Tricee tries to see the good in others."

Pam grunted and sipped from her wine glass.

"Pam, all I am saying is, in order to make the best of this evening –," Val paused. "If you give Kenzie and Karen a chance you might just find you have some things in common with them."

"Other than purchasing feminine products, I doubt it."

Val laughed loudly causing the other women to look in her and Pam's direction.

"Just relax and enjoy the evening." Val shook her head as the others joined her and Pam in the living room.

Each of the four women carried a glass in their hand; Jackie was the only one with a plate of food. She was often teased about how much she could eat yet remain so slender.

"So, Karen, my sister," Jackie looked over at Pam. "Do you always drink your water with a slice of lemon?"

Tricee laughed as Jackie and Val began to chuckle.

Karen was rather chic in a pair of black pants with a dark raspberry blouse and a short blazer to match. She was wearing a black pair of flats with a pointy toe. Pam noticed the pretty necklace around Karen's neck. It was sort of similar in design to the bracelet that Jeff had given her last month.

Karen's position at a large engineering firm allowed her to do a great deal of traveling, and Pam had reached the conclusion when they first met that Karen likely came into contact with a variety of men. She was convinced that Karen was the type to date various men at one time and that she only dated men who were very well off. As Karen turned to Jackie and began to speak, Pam cringed at the sound of her voice.

"Yes, why do you ask? I always drink my water with lemon," Karen answered, oblivious to the motive behind the question but noticing the laughter between Jackie and Tricee.

"Oh, I just didn't know sisters did that, that's all," Jackie said, laughing.

A few drinks of soda, iced tea, and white wine spritzer helped to ease some of the tension as the evening progressed. Val and Kenzie were the only two married women in the group. Jackie was the only divorced one. Pam, Tricee, and Karen discussed the hopeful possibilities of marriage in the near future. Karen stated she was in no hurry.

Pam mumbled, "Why doesn't that surprise me?" but it was loud enough for the others to hear.

Each of the other five women looked at Pam who was smiling, obviously very pleased with her comment. The white wine spritzers were taking over her ability to think before she spoke.

"I have something for you." Kenzie turned to Tricee. She didn't seem to notice any friction, not even with how Pam had commented on some of her comments. She only knew she was having a great time.

"It's beautiful, Kenzie! Thanks! You didn't have to." Tricee held up a small, white pin in the shape of a dove.

"Yes, she did," mumbled Pam.

Tricee ignored her. "Remember that big poster of a dove that I had hanging on my wall in college?"

Kenzie nodded as she reached into her bag and removed a box of chocolate, "I remember."

"Is that Godiva chocolate?" Jackie asked excitedly.

"It is!" Kenzie announced. "You can't have a meal without Godiva as a dessert!"

"Oh, now you're talking," said Val as Kenzie opened the box and passed it around.

"Ah, yes. The end of the month and chocolate is just what I need." Val took a piece from the box and handed it to Jackie.

"Oh, yummy. I don't think I have to explain this craving."

"No need to explain. I'm right there with you, girlfriend. Once a month, chocolate is a girl's best friend!" said Val, closing her eyes as the flavor filled her mouth.

"Why do you think I bought it? Oh my. This is pure delight," said Kenzie as she chewed on the tasty sweet.

Karen and Tricee laughed as they watched the three women devour a few pieces of candy.

"Are you ladies going to be okay?" Tricee asked.

"That's what I was about to ask," Karen laughed.

"Oh great," said Pam. "I'm stuck in a room where half of the women are experiencing a bout of PMS." Pam then turned and looked at Kenzie. "So, Kenzie, are you partial to dark chocolate *and* white chocolate?"

Tricee gasped, but Kenzie was able to hold her own. She smiled as she gave Pam a reply. "As a matter of fact, Pam, I do like them both. What about you?"

Tricee shot Pam a look that said, *You asked for it.*

As the evening came to a close, Kenzie pulled out her wallet and shared photos of her husband. The women all agreed—except Pam—that Kenzie's husband was very handsome. His dark hair and eyes made him very appealing. Tricee, Val and Jackie all agreed that he resembled the late actor Robert Urich.

Kenzie pointed out to Jackie that she could sense that she was in a fairly new relationship. She based her assessment on the number of times Jackie left the room to chat on her cell phone.

"Okay, I admit—I'm feeling like a teenager again," Jackie commented after she'd hung up from her last conversation with Lem.

"Well, it took you forever just to tell us his name. I was beginning to think you'd made him up." Pam said.

"No, he's real! Very real!" Jackie placed her hand over her heart. "And I think I am falling in love."

"Oh, new love is so wonderful. But just wait after, say, six months. It's going to start to wear off," Val teased. Kenzie nodded.

Kenzie had noticed the rock on Val's left hand as soon as she'd arrived, but Tricee had already shared that Val was the only one of the four who was married. Both women had been married for more than 10 years and both admitted they were still madly in love with their spouses.

"Well, after only one month of dating, I guess you'd know," Pam laughed but her tone was serious. It was a jab at Jackie but Jackie ignored it. The other women all turned and looked at each other.

"Love at first sight happens in real life, you know," Jackie responded. She was not bothered by Pam's comment. But Tricee was. She had just about had enough of Pam's snide remarks.

"Pam, I am sure Lem is falling for her, too. It's obvious that Jackie has met someone she's compatible with. Can you say the same?"

"Oops." Jackie turned to Val and swung her hand in the air. "I didn't see that ball coming? Did you, Serena?"

Val, Kenzie and Karen were practically on the floor laughing. Jackie hadn't expected for Tricee to come to her defense but it sure was funny.

Karen felt that Pam deserved that one. She'd tried to remain pleasant all evening. It was good to know that someone had put Pam in her place, because a few more minutes and one more white wine spritzer and she would have gladly done it herself.

"That's game, set and match!" Karen laughed so hard she was near tears.

Kenzie was red from laughing. Val was trying her best to stop laughing but found it difficult. She got up and ran into the bathroom.

As the women all gathered their things and prepared to leave, Jackie commented on Karen's necklace. "That's a pretty necklace, Karen. Pam it looks similar to the bracelet you just got."

Pam rolled her eyes. She'd noticed Karen's necklace earlier but wasn't about to admit that it did, indeed, look similar to her bracelet.

"It doesn't look similar."

"Oh, okay." Jackie shrugged as she put on her coat.

Karen hadn't shared any details all evening about her dating life, only that she was "seeing someone." When asked by Kenzie if her necklace was a gift from that special guy in her life, Karen responded with a laugh.

Val emerged from the bathroom. "This has been fun. We have to do it again sometime.

"I agree," Kenzie added. "The next time I'm in town, I'd like to treat you ladies to dinner. I have really enjoyed meeting you guys."

"I am so glad you had a nice time," Tricee said. "What time is your flight tomorrow?"

"10:45 AM, which means I need to be at the airport by 8:30."

"I will have you back in Evanston in no time."

"No hurry, I am used to being an early riser."

Val chimed in. "I am taking a vacation day tomorrow. I need to get some things done at home and the schools are closed tomorrow. Sean is coming over to help me with some home projects."

"Yeah, it's teacher institute day for the city schools too," said Jackie, "we should be able to get a lot accomplished since the students will be out."

"Well, this girl is going in. I have a lot on my plate," Tricee said. "What about you Karen? Are you working tomorrow?"

"No, I am off to the Dominican Republic for business in two weeks. I need to prepare for that so I am taking tomorrow off. I'm going upstairs, putting my big girl panties on, having me a cocktail and watching some television."

"Your big girl panties and you weigh all of 140 lbs," Tricee laughed.

They all said their goodbyes to Karen as she boarded one elevator and they waited on the other. Pam then turned to Kenzie.

"May I ask you a question, Kenzie?"

"Sure, Pam." Kenzie turned to Pam and smiled, which made Val chuckle.

Tricee looked directly at Pam. *This woman doesn't believe hot water will scald.* She waited for Pam to ask her question.

"Never mind." Pam waved her hand in frustration.

Jackie turned to Pam. "If you don't behave on the drive home, I will do to you what Tupac did to Janet in *Poetic Justice*."

"When he made her get out of that truck and walk?" Val blurted out.

Once inside Jackie's vehicle, Pam fastened her seat belt and began to speak.

"Tricee better think twice – "

"No talking." Jackie cut her off. "Hush."

"She could have told me Karen was – "

Jackie placed her finger to her lips. "Hush!"

But Pam was determined to talk. "Jackie, I'm not about to sit here – "

"Shushhhhhh!" Jackie allowed the word to roll off her lips.

Pam finally gave up and sat back in her seat. With her lips poked out and her arms folded across her chest, she remained in that position until Jackie got her home. She didn't even say goodnight when she got out of the car.

"You have a good night, too," Jackie uttered and drove off.

The following day, Jackie called Tricee. "You would have thought I was in the car with a 5-year-old. I had to endure a 35-year-old woman pouting all the way back to the south side." They both chuckled.

Both women agreed that the evening had been enjoyable, with the exception of Pam's mouth. New friendships had been formed between the other four women. Tricee remained hopeful that all was not completely lost for Pam.

17

Tricee was walking out the door when her home phone rang. She hurried back inside and looked at the caller ID. It was her Aunt Janice.

"Hello, favorite aunt," Tricee said, excitedly. "I trust all is well." She removed her purse from her shoulder and sat on her recliner.

"Hello! And congratulations!"

"Thank you. Thank you very much," Tricee replied in her best Elvis voice.

As Tricee spoke to her aunt, she was relieved that Aunt Janice was not coughing like she had been when they spoke last month. Aunt Janice's husband had told her about Tricee's promotion. She was out when Tricee had called. "They should have put you into that position a long time ago." Tricee had grinned from ear-to-ear at her uncle's kind words.

On March 15th, Tricee was promoted to Director of Strategic Partnerships & Programs. There had been other opportunities for this same position at other institutions of higher learning, but she'd declined those offers. With her M.B.A., Tricee realized she could have been promoted to a director's position sooner than the five years it had taken at H&P University. But H&P had paid her a very good salary as Associate Director and she enjoyed working with the students and the faculty members. H&P University was the best employer Tricee had worked for. It was rated as one of the top 20 places to work.

After speaking briefly with her aunt, Tricee went into the bathroom for one more check in the mirror. *Okay, now I can leave.* When she reached the lobby, the doorman, Tate, commented on how nice she looked.

"Thank you very much," Tricee blushed. She paused before walking out of the building. "Tate, has anyone ever told you how much you sound like the late singer Lou Rawls?"

Tate smiled. "Yes, Ma'am. I hear it all the time."

"Well, I hope you take it as a compliment," Tricee smiled as she turned and walked out of the building.

A resident of the building came walking in just as Tricee was leaving.

"Hi, Tricee. You're looking good!" The woman looked Tricee over from head to toe. "You must be going out on a date."

No. I'm on my way to bake cookies for the residents at the nursing home. Tricee gave a warm smile. "Thank you. I'm meeting friends for dinner." She glanced at her watch. "And I am already running a little late. It was good seeing you."

"Enjoy your evening." The woman stood for several seconds looking at Tricee as she turned and walked away.

There had been a few occasions when she and this neighbor had spoken at length, and each time, this woman had nothing but negative things to say about the opposite sex. Everyone had a right to their opinion, but Tricee just could not tolerate all the male bashing. That wasn't something she and her girlfriends were into.

As far as this woman was concerned, men were out to get you and couldn't be trusted. One of the things that Tricee felt was rather interesting was that anytime she'd see this woman with a man, it was a different man from the one last seen with her. One of the men Tricee had seen her with was wearing a wedding band and, based on their body language, he wasn't a relative. A few days after seeing this neighbor with her married friend, Tricee ran into her again in the laundry room. The negative comments started up again.

"Men are just out to get what they can. I say get them before they get you."

Tricee took a few deep breaths before responding. She had held her breath long enough.

"You know, I don't stand to judge anybody, but many times we women need to learn to make better choices. Yeah, you have some men who are liars and cheaters, but you also have some women who lie and cheat. How can a woman or man expect to meet a good mate when their own integrity is in question?"

After saying what was on her mind, Tricee went back to her laundry while the woman just stood there, not able to respond.

Tricee could feel the woman's eyes on her as she walked away. *Maybe my lecture has given her something to think about,* she thought silently as she headed for the coffee shop. The springtime air felt good against her skin. Her hair was pulled up out of her face, allowing her neck to feel the breeze. Tricee inhaled and exhaled, taking in the springtime season. The 70 degree temperature was just what she and all of the city of Chicago had been waiting anxiously for. Many of the people out on this Saturday evening, primarily the men, wore short sleeves. Although spring had officially sprung in the Windy City, there was still a chance for snow.

Tricee was meeting Paul at the coffee shop and was taking advantage of the nice weather by walking instead of driving. Paul was perfectly fine with doing the driving. He'd volunteered to pick her up but Tricee suggested that they meet instead. After meeting at the coffee shop, they were going to dinner at Sweet Greens, the popular soul food restaurant on the west side.

Tricee's dark blue slacks were one of her favorite pair—and one of her most expensive pair. The black shoes she was wearing were also a bit on the pricey side, but she couldn't resist them. It was as if the shoes were calling out her name when she saw them in the store's window on display. She wasn't one to spend a fortune on clothes unless it was something she really liked.

Her red blouse brought out her complexion and her short, black, suede jacket was perfect for the evening. She had it laying across her arms now but figured she'd probably need to put it on later. Her small hoop earrings completed her ensemble, giving her a jazzy and casual look. There were a few heads that turned to look in Tricee's direction. Her black purse, which was strapped across her shoulder, contained a book she'd been reading. She decided to bring it with her to read while she waited for Paul. She'd intentionally arrive earlier than their designated meeting time.

When Tricee reached the intersection of Thorndale and Sheridan, she felt her cell phone vibrate in her purse. She reached in and answered before crossing the street.

"Hey, Jackie. What's going on?"

"Hey, lady. What's up with you? I tried to call you earlier but it went straight to voicemail."

"I know. I was busy getting ready and couldn't talk." The light turned green and Tricee crossed the street.

"Oh, you're going out this evening?"

"I'm just on my way to meet Paul. We both finally found some time to meet for dinner."

Due to very busy schedules, Paul and Tricee had not been able to meet for dinner anytime during the whole month of February. They'd managed to have a couple of brief phone chats but that was about it. When Tricee shared her promotion via an email message, Paul felt it was imperative that they celebrate. And what better way to celebrate than over greens and candied yams. He was also scheduled to sing the following Sunday with his group and had invited Tricee to attend. Jackie had been made aware that Paul was Tricee's friend from church, the one she'd been so secretive about before.

"Oh, that's nice. Where are you guys going?" Jackie asked.

"Sweet Greens on the west side," Tricee replied as a young man who looked to be in his 20s winked as he walked past.

"I haven't been there since last year. But Alesia told me her dad took her and his girlfriend there recently."

"Oh?" Tricee was a little surprised at Jackie's statement. Although Jackie's ex-husband was seriously involved with someone, Jackie rarely mentioned her daughter being out with her father's girlfriend. But if you sat down and talked with Jackie—even briefly, without knowing anything about her—you'd learn that she was a contented person, and she wasn't one to stew over anything, no matter how upset she got.

After going through her divorce, she had once shared with her friends that life was too short to hold on to resentment or anger. Her divorce had been an amicable one, but even in spite of that, she'd stated that it had still caused a lot of emotional pain.

As Jackie spoke, Tricee could sense the extra joy in her friend's voice. Jackie just had a way of always sounding cheerful. Tricee thought back to an incident that had taken place once while she was out shopping with her three friends. It was obvious that the sales clerk was in a bad mood and was taking it out on Jackie. But instead of addressing it, Jackie chose to ignore it. Once they left the store and the sales clerk was mentioned, Jackie responded in a way that had made Tricee proud.

"One of the things I try to remember is this: You never know what a person might be going through. Instead of making a big deal out of something that is really nothing, I'd rather just leave it alone. Besides, it's her problem not mine."

Upon noticing that Jackie had stopped walking after her comment, Tricee, Val and Pam stopped walking, as well.

"But don't get me wrong. Had she jumped at me," Jackie punched her fists in the air as she spoke, "Jackie knows how to go two to the left and one to the right." Her three girlfriends had been beside themselves with laughter.

Tricee was now only two blocks from the coffee shop. She could sense that there had been a reason for Jackie's attempt in trying to reach her before the evening came to an end. She was not, however, prepared for what Jackie would say next.

"I'm going to marry Lemuell—I mean Lem," Jackie quickly corrected herself. Her friends all knew him as Lem.

Tricee's mouth flew open.

"Are you there?" Jackie released a nervous laugh. "I know that one flew right over your head."

"He asked you to marry him?" Tricee's eyes were as big as saucers. Granted, Jackie and Lem were spending a lot of time together, but Tricee had not expected that he'd propose so soon.

"No, he didn't propose." Jackie was standing in front of a full length mirror. "These pants make me look thick."

"Forget about the pants, girl," Tricee's voice went up a notch. "What's this about marrying Lem?"

Jackie laughed at the excitement in Tricee's voice. "I just feel it."

"Okay," Tricee said slowly. "Have you told Lem this?"

"No."

"Good. Please don't."

"I know, Tricee. I still have all of my notes from your sermon on letting the man lead."

Tricee had to laugh at Jackie's statement.

"Well, if this is what you believe in your spirit then go to God with it."

"Speaking of which, Lem is in the church. I have attended with him a couple of times."

"That's good," Tricee countered.

Before they ended their call, Jackie shared one more small detail. "You're the only person I'm sharing this with."

"Okay."

"We have not been intimate. I don't plan on it and I am guessing that he's not planning on it, either."

"Well, that's great to hear. Not sure if I needed to know all that … ," Tricee teased.

"I know," Jackie said smiling. "Well, I better let you go. Enjoy your soul food."

"Have a nice evening, Jackie."

When Jackie married the first time, she was barely out of college and "madly in love" with Alesia's father. According to her, he was the finest man she'd ever met and by far the sexiest. Not to mention that he was also driven and doing quite well for a 24-year-old. He was educated, gainfully employed, tall and very romantic. She'd told her girlfriends once that he'd "charmed the skirt right off me and I had no intentions on protesting." But what she was feeling now for Lem was coming from a different place. It felt more like a spiritual connection, something Jackie couldn't really explain.

If anybody deserves to be happy it's Jackie, Tricee smiled as she entered the coffee shop.

The same young, white woman who had served Tricee and Paul the last time they were there was working this evening. Tricee hadn't been back to the coffee shop since that cold night in January. Unlike that evening there were more patrons. It was obvious that the woman was friends with the group sitting near the counter. Tricee overheard one of them ask, "Will you be able to go clubbing with us? What time does your shift end?"

The woman who'd inquired about the work shift was dressed in a purple dress with three, long, beaded necklaces around her neck, each a different color. She was wearing black tights with black combat boots, and her long, light brown hair had pink highlights. The other members of the group were dressed in similar attire.

Tricee ordered a cup of tea and held a brief conversation with the server. Afterward, she removed her book from her purse and sat at the table closest to the window, the same table where she and Paul had sat before. She had only read one page when she heard the sound of an unfamiliar male voice.

"Is that a good book?"

"Yes, as a matter of fact, it is," Tricee replied.

"I can tell. You seem to be really into it," he responded with a huge smile.

The man standing before her had smooth brown skin and a dimple in his left cheek. He had a solid build—Tricee was certain he had a gym membership somewhere—and was dressed casually in jeans and a black t-shirt. When he smiled his dimple seemed to do its own little dance. Tricee couldn't help but notice it. She'd always liked dimples and used to wish God had given her a pair.

"So are you just enjoying your Saturday evening with a good book or is it something you're reading for a class?" He titled his head trying to read the title. Tricee couldn't help but to smile. She took a sip of her tea before responding, "I'm waiting for a friend and, no, I'm not reading this for a class."

The man shrugged. "I thought maybe you were a college student."

"No, not a college student." Tricee blushed, suddenly feeling a bit shy.

"I'm Hunter," he extended his hand, "and I don't mean to disturb you."

"I'm Tricee." Tricee reluctantly extended her hand. After a few seconds of silence they both chuckled.

As many times as she'd come to this coffee shop, she'd not recalled ever seeing this gentleman. He had a book in his hand, which caused Tricee to believe that maybe he came there regularly to read. Based on his comment earlier, it was very likely. But Tricee was not about to ask. He might have been handsome but still, she didn't know him. He could have been crazy and just pretending to be nice while trying to pick up women in a coffee shop. She could have easily inquired about the book he was reading but that would have only led to a longer conversation. Besides, Paul would be arriving shortly and they would be off to dinner. Now was not an opportune time to hold a conversation, even if she'd wanted to.

"Well, Tricee, it was nice to meet you. I should let you get back to your book. But I have to ask, do you come here often?"

They both began to laugh. He lightly smacked his forehead with his hand. "That sounded like a pick up line, didn't it?"

"Yeah, it did," Tricee nodded, smiling all the while.

"I didn't mean for it to come out like that."

"It's okay," said Tricee.

He then hunched his shoulders and tilted his head. "So, do you come here often? I mean, I'm just wondering if I might run into you again. You know, just curious, that's all."

His attempt at humor was funny and Tricee released a giggle. "It just sort of depends on my mood."

"Well, I'll be here next Saturday about this time. So if you're in the mood and available … "

Lord, I think one of your angels done got loose. Tricee felt herself blushing. "It was nice meeting you, Hunter. We'll see what next Saturday brings."

"Okay, that sounds fair enough. By the way, I love your hair. The twists look really good on you."

"Oh, thank you." Tricee was flattered. She'd received compliments on her hair before, but a man had never actually referred to her hairstyle by name.

"I like natural hairstyles on black women," he went on to say. "My two sisters own To Weave or Knot, a hair salon in the Beverly area."

Tricee was very familiar with the salon. It was where Jackie would go to have her hair styled.

"My friend goes there. They do a great job," Tricee said just as Paul came walking in.

"Hi, Tricee," Paul acknowledged her and then turned toward the man standing next to him. "How you doing?"

"I'm just fine," Hunter replied, smiling, looking directly at Tricee.

"Hunter, this is my friend Paul," Tricee said, trying not to display any awkwardness.

"Nice to meet you." Paul then smiled as he looked at Tricee, "Can I get you some more tea?"

"Yes, that would be good."

Paul walked away, leaving Tricee sitting there feeling awkward while Hunter stood there smiling.

"I hope to see you next Saturday, Tricee. I'll be here."

Hunter then turned and left the coffee shop. Tricee watched him as he left. *Oh boy. Why did that feel so uncomfortable when Paul and I are just friends?* She wondered. She placed her book back into her purse. Paul soon came back to the table with a cup of tea in one hand and a glass of Italian soda in the other.

"I'm sorry I'm late. I had to go by my building. One of the renters called me just as I was leaving."

"Oh, that's right. I do recall you mentioning you had a building."

"Yeah, and it has its challenges." Paul grinned. "But it's a good investment."

"You own a condo, too, right?" Tricee asked, glad that Paul hadn't asked about Hunter. Not that he'd have any reason to ask.

Paul nodded. "I lived in my building for a while before I bought the condo. It is much better not living near your tenants. At least I prefer not to."

Tricee and Paul chatted briefly, finished their drinks and then left the coffee shop. The vehicle Paul was driving was not the same one he'd driven back in January. Tricee climbed into his SUV and fastened her seat belt.

"I love all this room. My next set of wheels will be something a little bigger than what I have now." She glanced around the interior of the vehicle. "But nothing this big."

Paul laughed. "I keep telling you, a Jaguar is what you need."

"Yeah, when X-mas falls in June," Tricee laughed.

Paul headed for the expressway as he and Tricee chatted and the CD he'd chosen played softly in the background. After a few seconds, Tricee recognized the voices she heard coming from the speakers.

"That's your group?" She'd heard Paul sing this particular gospel song when he'd invited her to hear him sing once.

"It is," Paul nodded.

"It sounds great! When you guys make it to the top, making millions off your music, don't forget about us normal people."

Paul laughed. "I won't. I don't know about the other two."

Tricee was in a very relaxed mood, which is exactly what she needed. She'd only been in her position for a couple of weeks but her work load had increased drastically. She was so busy at work, only to find herself working from home on the weekends, as well. The software Paul had given her had come in very handy.

They arrived at Sweet Greens at 8:30 PM and, just as they'd expected, the restaurant was filled to capacity. The line inside was long but it moved rather quickly. Sweet Greens was a delicatessen type of restaurant where you told the server at each station what you wanted. You then paid for it at the end of the line and seated yourself. Paul paid for their meals: catfish, corn bread, collard greens, macaroni and cheese, and a side order of sweet potatoes that Paul insisted they have. For dessert they both ordered peach cobbler.

"Well, here's to Tricee on becoming one of the best directors the university will ever have." Paul lifted his glass of 7-Up while Tricee lifted her glass of ginger ale.

"I'll drink to that."

They bowed their heads, said grace and then dug in.

"I'd give anything to be able to make my greens like this," Tricee said. "I can never get them to the right consistency."

"I'll have to watch my sister the next time she cooks some." Paul scooped up a forkful of macaroni and cheese. "She makes the best greens. But don't ever tell her I passed on her secret."

Tricee giggled, "Scout's honor."

Paul wiped his mouth with his napkin. "If she finds out I told anyone about her cooking secrets, I'll have to find a replacement because she'll leave the group."

Tricee could tell that Paul and his sister were close. She'd only met her once but it was obvious that the two had a close brother-sister relationship. Tricee looked around the restaurant, noticing that it looked the same as she'd remembered it. There were pictures of famous people and of Chicago politicians who'd dined at the popular restaurant. The back wall held pictures of various family members of the owner of the establishment, an older black gentleman in his late 80s. Sweet Greens had been around since the 70s and was originally located on Chicago's south side, right beyond downtown. But for the past 20 years, the city's west side was its home. Many patrons thought nothing of driving from the far south side to indulge in the delicious cuisine.

As Tricee and Paul enjoyed their meals, they could hear the sounds of smacking lips and a few "um, um, um, ums" throughout the restaurant. Every couple of seconds, they would look up from their meals and utter a word or two, but for the most part, they'd kept their focus on the plate of goodies before them.

After their main courses, two empty plates sat in front of them. Tricee sat back in her seat. "I am stuffed." She reached for the container that held the peach cobbler.

Paul laughed. "You still have room for peach cobbler?"

"Oh, yeah," Tricee said, laughing.

"Woman, you can sure put it away." Paul smiled as Tricee bit into the cobbler. "I'll have to take mine home."

"Not if I get to it first," Tricee teased.

"We'll be up in here boxing if you touch my peach cobbler." Paul laughed and stood up.

"I need some water. Would you like one?"

"Yes, please." Tricee watched as two women leaving the restaurant looked over at her and Paul and smiled. She figured they probably assumed that she and Paul were a couple. Tricee smiled and went back to enjoying her cobbler.

She wasn't sure if Paul had plans for them to go elsewhere after dinner. He was dressed casually but looked really nice in his dark slacks and navy blue shirt. Tricee thought back, briefly, to the last time they were out. She'd wondered if Paul had completely erased the incident of bumping into an ex, from his mind. She was enjoying his company and thought it would be nice to hang out a while longer.

Paul sat down and placed the bottled water in front of Tricee. He opened his bottle and took a long sip.

"Thirsty?" Tricee asked.

Paul smiled. "I tend to need a lot of water after eating rich foods."

"Soul food is not rich." Tricee grinned as she gathered her purse. "I'm done. Ready when you are."

Paul grabbed his container of peach cobbler. "Folks are still coming in."

A young man who worked at the restaurant came over and cleaned their table as they were leaving. A group of four came over just as he was done.

A few minutes later, Paul and Tricee were headed back to the north side. He allowed the XM stereo system to play and they listened to Miles Davis. As they drove down the dark city streets, Paul was thinking to himself how much the area on the west side had changed. He realized that Tricee was not from Chicago so she had no firsthand knowledge of the transformation that many of the neighborhoods had gone through over the years. After some brief reminiscing, Paul glanced over at Tricee. He'd wanted to share some news with her.

"I want you to meet someone." He smiled but it was more of a nervous smile, as if he was a little uncomfortable.

"You're not trying to fix me up, are you?" Tricee asked teasingly.

"No," Paul laughed. "I don't think you need my help in meeting anybody," he replied as he thought back to Hunter from the coffee shop.

"Right," Tricee said, a little embarrassed. "So who is it?"

"I proposed last weekend to the woman I've been dating. I would like for you to meet my fiancée."

Tricee remained silent. Paul's announcement had certainly taken her by surprise. Had she known Paul was involved with someone, things would have made more sense. But for whatever other reason she had not figured out yet, she had not been expecting to hear what she'd just heard. Paul looked straight ahead.

After several minutes, Tricee managed to speak, "Congratulations. That is good news."

"Thank you."

For Tricee, the awkwardness felt similar to earlier at the coffee shop. She had no idea how Paul felt but his expression communicated that he was a little uncomfortable, too. But Tricee had to give him credit for his attempt at making an awkward moment more bearable.

"The guy at the coffee shop was really taken with you."

"I don't know about all of that," Tricee shrugged. She was genuinely happy for Paul but couldn't help but wonder why he had never mentioned his involvement with someone else.

"Trust me." Paul grinned as he looked over at Tricee. "I'm a man, remember? I know what I'm talking about."

Tricee thought about Hunter and how he had seemed so polite. His approach was not aggressive. In fact, she could tell that he was trying his best to maintain a respectful demeanor, even after Paul arrived. Even though Tricee had introduced Paul as a friend, Hunter had no way of knowing who Paul was. For all it was worth, Tricee appreciated meeting someone who had appeared very nice, though they weren't likely to see each other again.

After more small talk and an hour later, Paul pulled into the circular driveway of Tricee's building.

"Tricee, I had a nice time, of course." He turned toward her. "I hope you enjoyed the greens as much as I did."

"I enjoyed every bit of it." Tricee unfastened her seat belt and tossed her purse across her shoulder.

"Oh, yeah. I hope you can make it next Sunday to hear us sing," Paul said, reminding Tricee of the event. He hoped she would make it but he had an inkling that that was not going to happen.

"I'll let you know." Tricee smiled as she climbed out of his vehicle. "Have a safe drive home, as I always say."

Paul smiled, "I will."

Tricee walked around the SUV and was about to proceed into her building, but she paused beside Paul's window. He lowered it.

"How long have you – "

Paul listened intently as he waited for Tricee to finish her thought. But she decided instead not to ask.

"Thanks again, for dinner," she said.

Paul reached into the back seat for his peach cobbler. He held the container out toward Tricee. "Do me a huge favor and take this."

"No. I'm not taking your dessert," Tricee protested.

"Please? My sister is baking a chocolate cake tomorrow. You have to help me, Tricee."

She grinned. "Oh, okay. But just this once."

Tricee placed the cobbler in the fridge as soon as she made it up to her apt. It had been a nice evening even though there was the unexpected news. She plopped down on her sofa and turned on the television.

"I do recall saying a couple of months ago that Paul was going to make someone a great mate," she mumbled, with a hint of sarcasm. "I just was not expecting my prophecy to come to pass so soon."

18

Pam and her youngest sister, Cassie, walked through the mall looking at all of the different styles that were out for the spring season. Pam had invited her sister to lunch so they could spend some time together and so she could purchase Cassie's dress for her upcoming prom. It was a surprise that Cassie knew nothing about.

Aside from spending time together, Pam figured it would be a good opportunity to get in her youngest sister's business. Although they had not discussed Cassie's dilemma over which college she'd attend, Pam had learned from their mother that Cassie and their father were still at odds. Pam wanted to know the real reason her sister wanted so badly to attend a college in Los Angeles. And she wanted to know some other minor details about her little sister.

"This is an excellent way to exercise," Pam said as they circled the mall, "I need to do this on a regular basis."

"It's also a good way to spend money that you don't have," Cassie replied. They stopped in front of one of the more expensive department stores at the mall. Their attention was immediately drawn to the silk blue blouse hanging from the mannequin.

"Now that is off the chain!" Cassie squealed. "I would rock that with a pair of black pants or even some jeans."

"Let's go take a closer look," Pam said with a huge grin. "But don't get your hopes up. It's too grown up for you."

"I disagree," said Cassie as she followed Pam inside. "I'm trying it on."

After taking a closer look at the blouse, it took much effort on Pam's part to leave it in the store. The sales clerk did her best to get Pam to try it on, but she politely declined. She talked Cassie out of trying it on, too.

As they made their way to the other end of the mall, Cassie pointed toward the food court on the lower level.

"Let's go eat, I'm hungry."

As soon as they reached the bottom of the escalator, Cassie was greeted by two of her friends. Both young women were carrying a shopping bag and one was nibbling on popcorn.

"Hey, Cassie!" the taller one said. "We didn't know you were coming to the mall today."

"Yeah," said the shorter one with the bag of popcorn. "We could have all came together and hung out." She folded her bag of popcorn and reached into her jacket for a napkin. The shorter one acknowledged Pam but the taller one had not. Cassie, witnessing the expression on Pam's face, quickly introduced her friends.

"Meena, this is my sister, Pam," Cassie said to the taller girl. "And, Pam, you already know Staci."

"Yes, I know Staci. How's your grandmother?"

"Mama Alma is fine." Staci rolled her eyes. "She would be a lot better if she would stay out of my business." They all laughed.

"Don't count on that," Pam said. "She's a grandmother, it's her job."

Pam noticed the scowl on the taller girl's face but ignored it.

"So what are your plans after high school?" she asked Staci. "I'm sure you must be looking forward to marching across that stage."

Staci gave a half smile. "I can't wait. I am so ready to become my own person and not have to listen to my mom or my grandmother's rules."

"I'm sorry to rain on your sunshine, but there will always be somebody's rules to follow," Pam said.

Staci was always telling Cassie how she was ready to move out and into her own place. Her sister gave birth to a baby girl back in February, and ever since the birth of her niece, Staci has been in love with the idea of marriage and starting her own family. Cassie would remind her that she was still very young with her whole life ahead of her, and that she needed to not only have a Plan B but a Plan C, as well.

"So what do you – ," Pam started to ask Staci but was cut off by Meena.

"Cassie, did you buy your prom dress yet?"

"No." Cassie glanced over at Pam and then back to Meena. "I'll probably buy it next weekend."

Pam pressed her lips together. *If this girl doesn't stop with the rudeness, I'll have her picking that long face of hers up off of this floor.* She would ask Cassie later about her friend's nasty attitude, but for now she would hold her peace.

"I'm going to community college after I graduate." Staci smiled as she looked at Pam. "As soon as I save enough money, me and my boyfriend will get our own apartment."

"Sis, would you please try to talk some sense into this girl." Cassie playfully grabbed Staci's arm. "She needs to focus on herself, not some boy."

Pam released a light chuckle. "Well, I will say this. Make sure you're doing what *you* want to do and not what *your boyfriend* wants to do." Pam looked over at Cassie. "I tell Cassie all the time not to ever put a man's needs before her own."

Cassie smiled. "That's right."

Pam looked over at Meena with an attempt at being polite.

"Meena, are you graduating with Staci and Cassie?"

Meena gave a quick retort, "Yes, I am."

"Okay," Pam uttered. It was really time for Cassie to bring the conversation to a close. Pam couldn't take too much more of this girl's attitude. Cassie felt sorry for Meena, sort of. But she did not appreciate the manner in which she was treating her big sister. She would address it later on with a phone call. Pam knew nothing about Meena but Cassie and Staci did.

Meena had a hard time keeping friends because she thought she was the "hottest girl" in the senior class. No one had taught her about inner beauty. Staci and Cassie were her only two real friends at school. The other girls tolerated her when necessary but talked about her behind her back. Staci and Cassie could understand why Meena was so disliked but they never talked about her with the other girls. And Meena was jealous of Cassie. Cassie was bright, all of her teachers admired her determination, and she was more than likely going to be chosen as the class valedictorian.

There had been one incident that caused Cassie to reconsider her friendship with Meena. Meena had shared with Staci what she thought about Cassie's boyfriend. Although he attended a different high school, Cassie's friends had met him on a few occasions. Meena thought Cassie's boyfriend was very cute and said she didn't see how he had ended up with Cassie. Staci allowed her comment to pass since she knew Meena was carrying a jealousy bone, and because most people would agree that Cassie was just as pretty as Meena was. It was her next comment that pushed Staci into calling Cassie to inform her of Meena's unkind words. "If Cassie's boyfriend went to our school, he would no doubt be my man. Cassie wouldn't stand a chance."

Staci told Cassie that she had not wished to start anything, but Meena's arrogance when she'd made that comment had made her cringe. It also made her believe that if Meena could say that about Cassie, who'd been nothing short of nice to her; there was no telling what she'd say about her. Staci would reach her own conclusion about Meena. She was a terribly insecure young woman with no clue as to how to be a real friend or a real girlfriend. She had treated her boyfriend badly by taking his kindness for granted. He eventually caught on to her and broke up with her. To make matters worse, he'd gotten back with his ex-girlfriend whom he was taking to the prom.

After Staci told Cassie what Meena had said, Cassie went to Meena's house to confront her.

"Look, Meena," Cassie had stated with a straight face. "I don't believe in allowing a guy to come between my friendships but I will not remain friends with a girl who could say such unkind things behind my back." They had been alone in Meena's bedroom.

Cassie turned to walk away and Meena began to apologize profusely, sobbing.

Cassie and Staci knew that Meena's rude behavior toward Pam had nothing to do with Pam and everything to do with Meena's own unfortunate set of circumstances.

After saying their goodbyes to Cassie's friends, Pam and Cassie went to order some Chinese food. Pam chuckled at the exchange that had just taken place.

"You saved the jolly green giant just in the nick of time. I don't mean to judge anyone," Pam removed her wallet from her purse, "but that child has issues."

"Meena does have issues," Cassie explained. "One of them being that she's not graduating with the senior class. She has to go to summer school."

Pam and Cassie took their trays of food and found a table. Pam took a bite of her egg roll while Cassie continued.

"And she's going to the prom with one of her cousins because her and her boyfriend broke up."

Pam wiped her mouth with her napkin. "Yeah, she has issues, alright."

Cassie swallowed a mouthful of shrimp fried rice and took a long sip of Coke. "I am going to let her know I didn't appreciate the way she treated you just now. I mean, she could have at least tried to be nice for those few minutes."

Pam was tempted to tell Cassie to let it pass, that it was no big deal. But the more she thought about it, the more she figured that Meena probably needed the lesson.

As they finished their lunch, three young guys approached their table.

"Cas, we thought that was you." The young man who spoke was tall and lanky. The three of them all looked to be about Cassie's age.

"Oh, hey." Cassie spoke to all three of them at the same time.

"Is this your mom?" the taller one asked as he glanced at Pam. Pam stopped drinking her soda and shot the young man a look.

Cassie laughed. "No, this is my sister, Pam."

"Oh, oh. Nice to meet you, Pam," Cassie's tall friend responded nervously. His two friends began to laugh. "You have a beautiful sister," he said to Cassie.

"It's nice to meet you, Pam," one of the other young men said.

"Yeah, Pam. It's really nice to meet you," the third one uttered.

Pam broke out into a grin. They were polite young men with good manners, even though the lanky one had mistaken her for Cassie's mom.

"It's very nice to meet you, too," she said, acknowledging the three young men.

Pam and Cassie stepped onto the escalator to head back to the upper level.

"You know," Cassie said when they stepped off the escalator, "You could have had me when you were 17. So technically you could be my mom."

Pam made a face. "I'm going to forget you even uttered such words, girl."

Cassie laughed as they continued their stroll past the stores. She was enjoying her day with Pam. Her other two sisters were both married with one child, so Cassie rarely got an opportunity to spend a lot of one-on-one time with them. And their only brother was seriously involved in a relationship. He and Cassie had gone to dinner once in the last couple of years but, unlike her sisters, her brother wasn't into holding too much of a conversation, he was more concerned with a satisfied belly. Cassie had shared some details of that dinner with her sisters. She couldn't keep herself from laughing.

"It was so boring having dinner with Walt. He didn't have *anything* to talk about. Ugh, I don't know how his girlfriend can stand it."

"Sweetie," her sister Terri had said, "men are not like women when it comes to running their mouth. I don't know what kind of conversation you were expecting."

"Really," her sister Lynn chimed in. "So you might as well get used to the silence now."

"And don't try to make them talk because it only makes things worse," Pam had said.

"Oh no, don't do that," Terri said, waving her hand. "Because then they start saying stuff that doesn't make any kind of sense."

Cassie really enjoyed the few moments she did get to spend with each of her four siblings. Now, as they walked through the mall, Pam let Cassie in on her surprise, making Cassie all the more thankful to have Pam as a big sister.

"I thought I'd buy your prom dress. It's my gift to you," Pam said as they reached a store with a variety of prom dresses.

"Oooohh! Sis, thanks!" Cassie hugged Pam as they stood in front of the store. Pam chuckled as a few people looked over at them and smiled. Others couldn't have cared less as they walked right by.

"Are you excited?" Pam teased. "Come on, let's shop!"

Cassie walked out of the dressing room looking absolutely gorgeous in a long, ivory dress. Pam had to hold back tears as she looked at her baby sister. *My, how times flies. I still remember when mom and dad brought her home from the hospital.*

They spent the next two-and-a-half hours shopping for all of her accessories, plus a pair of shoes.

As they walked to Pam's car, both of them wiped out from shopping, Pam's cell phone rang. But with her hands full of bags, she let the call go to voicemail. She and Cassie placed the bags in her trunk and then walked back to the front of the car. Pam listened to her message as she climbed into the driver's seat.

"I need to call dad back," she said before starting the engine. "He's doing my taxes. He should know by now that I always wait until a few days prior to the 15th to file."

"You mean you have to call *your* father back," Cassie opened the small bag to look at the two new tubes of lip gloss she'd bought. She opened one of them and applied a light coating to her lips.

Pam shook her head as she proceeded to talk to their father. After their call ended she pulled out of the mall parking lot. She glanced over at Cassie, not too surprised at her sister's comment.

"Oh, so he's not your father anymore?" Pam made a right turn onto the expressway.

"Nope."

"I see. Interesting. The man who has kept a roof over your head for the past 18 years is not your father?"

Cassie tossed her lip gloss back into the small bag. "Nope," she repeated.

"The man who purchased that car back home in the driveway is not your father?"

"It's a used car," said Cassie. "And, again, I say no. I'm mad at him.

Pam knew without a doubt that her sister loved their father dearly, but she needed for Cassie to understand the importance of being grateful for wonderful parents. They chatted on the drive back to their parents' house about Cassie's plans and, sure enough, Cassie's desire to attend college in L.A. had everything to do with her boyfriend leaving for San Diego after high school to join the navy.

"Cassie, have you looked at the numbers?" Pam asked after saying all that she could against Cassie's plan to leave Chicago. "You would have to take out a big loan and work just to make it. Why do all of that when you can go to school for next to nothing?"

"Have I looked at the numbers?" Cassie stopped reading the magazine she was flipping through and looked over at Pam. "You sound like dad. He asked me the same thing and I told him he was sounding just like an accountant."

"He *is* an accountant?" Pam replied, keeping her eyes on the road.

"Well, I told him I needed for him to be my father and support me in my decision, not my accountant."

Pam shook her head. "I am too through with you." She grinned, knowing that Cassie had lost this battle even before it started.

They were about 20 minutes from their parents' home when Cassie's cell phone rang.

"Hey, ma."

"Hi, Cassie. Are you and Pam done shopping?" Mrs. Rhodes asked.

"Oh, ma! Pam bought my prom dress!"

"That was very kind of her. I hope you thanked your sister."

Cassie poked out her lips and Pam laughed. "Ma, of course I said thank you. Dag! Give me some credit!"

"Good. Look here, I need for you to stop by the store to get your father some Diet Dr. Pepper."

"That's a negative," Cassie replied. She then moved her phone away from her mouth and said softly, "He's your husband."

Pam laughed out loud. She often wondered if her sister would attempt to do stand-up on the side.

"What did you just say?" Mrs. Rhodes asked.

"I said I'd be more than happy to get daddy his soda."

"That's what I thought you said. Well, I might be gone when you get home. Ms. Alma and I are going to Ms. Idella's for Bible study."

"Okay, Ma. Love you."

Pam bypassed the street to their parents' home and drove toward the grocery store instead. Their mother's mention of Ms. Alma made Cassie think about the last time she'd seen Staci's grandmother.

"I can't stand Ms. Alma sometimes," Cassie blurted out as she turned up the volume on Pam's stereo.

"Why?" Pam reached over and turned it down. "Girl what are you trying to do? Get me stopped by an officer?"

"You might meet your future husband this way," Cassie teased.

"No, thank you, and why don't you like Ms. Alma?"

"She was over to our house a couple of weeks ago and was just staring at my jeans." Cassie started flipping once more through her magazine.

"Your jeans were probably too tight," Pam pulled up to the stop sign.

"Well, she needs to not worry about my jeans. She better keep a close eye on her granddaughter, Staci. She thought she was preg – "

Cassie suddenly stopped talking. Pam glanced at her and said nothing as she pulled into the grocery store parking lot. Inside, Cassie picked up the soda while Pam reached for a few items she needed. She had planned to cook dinner for Jeff this evening at his place.

When she mentioned her plans to cook to her friends, they'd all given her a strange look.

"What are you going to cook?" Val had asked. Pam explained that she'd gotten a recipe for chicken stir-fry from her sister, Lynn.

"You must be in love because you have never cooked for a man before," Jackie added.

There had been some truth in that statement. Pam had cooked for one other guy before, but she had burned it and messed it up so badly that they couldn't eat it.

"Honey, if you mess up chicken stir-fry," her sister Lynn teased after giving Pam the recipe, "you don't need to try to cook anything else."

Pam and Cassie walked out of the grocery store and loaded the bags into the back seat.

"So what were you going to say about Staci?" Pam asked, hoping that she didn't seem too nosy.

"What did I say?" Cassie opened a bag of M&Ms.

"You were saying Ms. Alma needs to keep an eye on her."

Pam knew exactly what Cassie was going to say earlier. The letters p-r-e and g, which Pam clearly heard, were usually followed by 'nant.' But Pam could tell that Cassie was trying to act as if she didn't know what she was talking about.

"It sounded like you were going to say Staci thought she was pregnant."

Pam noticed the way Cassie winced. "It was a false alarm. Don't mention it, Pam. Okay?" Cassie pleaded regretting that she'd allowed such private information about her best friend to slip out.

"You know I'm not going to say anything. Who would I mention it to?" Pam asked.

She then looked over at Cassie and decided now was the time to be nosy and try to find out some details about her little sister.

"You are careful, aren't you, Cassie?"

Cassie popped two M&Ms into her mouth and turned to look out the window. Pam could tell she was embarrassed but it hadn't been her intent to embarrass her little sister. She was just being a very concerned big sister.

Cassie sighed. "I'm not doing anything."

Pam didn't believe that although it could have very well been the truth. "That's good. You should keep it that way for as long as possible."

Cassie finally managed to stop feeling embarrassed and allowed herself to smile. Her big sister had just shelled out a few hundred dollars on everything she would need for her senior prom. Cassie recalled the look on Pam's face earlier when she'd stepped out of the dressing room. Cassie knew that look all too well. It had been the look of a very proud big sister. She'd noticed the way Pam had tried to hold back tears. At that very moment it wouldn't have mattered if Pam had purchased only the accessories or if Cassie had had to purchase her own dress. It had been the look of love that she most cherished, and no dollar amount could have topped that.

Cassie began to chuckle as Pam drove the block to their parents' home. "You want to hear something funny?"

"I'm not sure but try me anyway." Pam could only imagine what was to come out of Cassie's mouth next. From the grin on Cassie's face, she knew it was probably going to be something silly.

"I know who is getting it on, though."

Cassie's grin turned into laughter. "Our parents are! It normally happens about once a month at the same time."

Pam shook her head and began to laugh, too. "Cassie, you're nuts!"

Pam parked in her parents' driveway and quickly unfastened her seat belt. "Girl, come and unlock this back door before I wet my pants." Pam yelled.

They were both howling with laughter as Cassie unlocked the back door. Pam ran past her father, who was sitting at the kitchen table, and straight into the bathroom. Mr. Rhodes looked up from his newspaper.

"Hey there, player." Cassie went over to the fridge. "Your eldest had a little too much to drink." Mr. Rhodes shook his head and went back to reading the paper.

Pam emerged from the bathroom. "Whew, that was close." She bent over and gave her father a peck on the cheek. "You need to have this child committed," she said pointing at Cassie.

Cassie and Pam went back out to Pam's car to retrieve the bags.

"I need to go," Pam looked at the items she'd just purchased. "I need to be on my way to Jeff's in a couple of hours to start dinner."

Cassie went into her bedroom to look at all of her things while Pam joined her father at the table. They chatted briefly with Pam promising to have all of her tax documents to her father by Sunday night. That would give her all day tomorrow. She went into Cassie's room to say goodbye.

"Thanks again, sis. I really appreciate you doing this for me," Cassie said as she put on the ivory shoes that matched her prom dress. She fastened the straps that went across the ankle and followed Pam back into the kitchen. "I can't wait to show Staci my things."

"Bye, Dad," Pam gave her father a hug. "I'll see you tomorrow."

Cassie followed Pam to the back door. Mr. Rhodes looked down at the dressy shoes Cassie was wearing.

"Pour me a glass of soda, would you?" he said to Cassie.

Pam turned to look at Cassie. Her expression said it all. Cassie got the hint, filled a glass with ice and retrieved a can of the soda they'd just purchased from the store.

"I'll have dinner ready in just a few minutes," she set the glass of soda in front of her father. "Dad, I want to show you my dress!" she said happily.

Mr. Rhodes replied with an uninterested "okay" as he began reading the real estate section of the newspaper.

Pam smiled as she walked to her car. She couldn't help but think about what Cassie said to her just before she left. *You deserve to be happy, sis. You need to ask yourself if this Jeff is marriage material. You don't want to waste your time with a man who isn't looking to move forward. He is lucky to have you.*

Pam grinned as she thought about the wise words from her 18-year-old sister. As she rang Jeff's buzzer, she could only hope that, by now, Jeff had realized that he was, indeed, fortunate.

"Excuse me, Miss. Are you here to see Jeff Mays?" he asked Pam when she made it to his door.

"As a matter of fact, I am," she smiled as she looked him over. In a white shirt and navy blue slacks he looked causal, comfortable and good, as usual.

"Well, in that case," he took the bags, "allow me."

He allowed Pam to enter first. He closed the door and walked into the kitchen where he set the bags on the kitchen table.

"The next time you're on the way up, please call me. You shouldn't have to carry bags as long as I'm around," he said.

After an embrace, he kissed Pam lightly on the cheek. He took a step back while still holding her hands. He closed his eyes for a brief moment and opened them again. "Absolutely gorgeous!"

Pam blushed, spun around and removed her jacket. "I try," she said. She had changed into a simple black top and jeans.

"Well, you don't have to try too hard."

"Flattery will get you everywhere," Pam smiled.

They chatted over dinner with Jeff complimenting Pam on the dish she'd prepared. She thanked him, pleased that she had not messed it up. He'd stated that he hoped Pam would prepare her chicken stir-fry again soon. When he offered her another glass of wine, however, Pam declined. "Two is enough," she'd said.

Ever since the evening of Valentine's Day, things were going pretty good. As a matter of fact, things were going great. But Pam still did not want Jeff to believe he had the upper hand because of one slip up she'd had.

She watched as Jeff removed a pendant from the box. She was already imagining how good it would look with her sleeveless black dress.

"What do you think of this?" Jeff asked as he held the necklace in his well-manicured hands.

"It's very nice." Pam made every attempt to curb her enthusiasm.

"I bought it for my sister for her birthday," Jeff said, oblivious to Pam's reaction.

Pam's smile quickly faded. "I'm sure your sister will like it," she said dryly. *Why are you showing me a gift you purchased for someone else?*

"I wanted your opinion," Jeff said. "I know you have good taste."

Pam mumbled, "I guess so."

Jeff placed the necklace back into the box and put it back in the cabinet. As he turned around he heard Pam mumble.

"What was that?"

"I was just saying how tired I am," Pam said quickly.

Jeff noticed the expression on her face. Then it dawned on him why she seemed a little miffed.

"Oh, love. I apologize about that." He was sincere.

"What?" Pam was hoping to let the matter drop.

"The necklace. I guess my timing was a little off. I really just wanted your opinion, that's all." He took her by the hands. "We have grown somewhat closer and, as I was shopping for a gift for my sister, I was thinking about you. How I was going to show it to you to see if you liked it."

"It's no big deal," Pam said once she realized that he'd really meant no harm.

Jeff said they'd grown somewhat closer, something he'd never said before. So for Pam, he was at least beginning to open up. He had saved himself with that explanation because she was prepared to tell him she was ready to leave.

The remainder of the evening went well. They shared a couple of slow dances and Pam even talked him into a fast dance, even though it was for all of two or three minutes.

He eventually talked her into a third glass of wine and, cuddling on the sofa, Pam began singing along to the CD that was playing.

Jeff laughed. "Don't quit your day job."

It was way past midnight and too late to drive back to the south side. After three white wine spritzers, Pam was not about to consider driving anywhere. She'd packed a pink, silk gown as a just-in-case. Jeff was pleased and it showed on his face when she emerged from the bathroom. "Nice gown," he walked toward her.

The only thing Pam could think about when she woke up to the smell of eggs and turkey sausage the next morning was that Jeff was, indeed, marriage material. She had received the answer to the question her baby sister had posed. But what Pam did not know was that there would be more questions for which she would need answers.

19

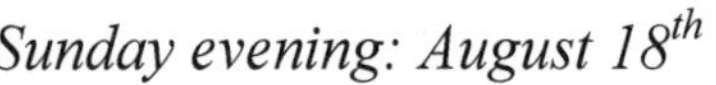

Sunday evening: August 18th

Tricee sat in her car for several minutes before pulling out of the parking garage. Ruby suggested that they meet somewhere close to her condo in an attempt to make things more convenient for her only daughter. When Tricee inquired as to how her mother would get to the north side, Ruby had stated that either Bev or Bev's brother would bring her. Tricee figured if Ruby was being dropped off, she certainly would need a ride back to her hotel downtown. But she would learn later on that Bev's brother would act as Ruby's designated driver for the evening.

It was starting to look to Tricee as if Bev's brother and her mother were more than just friends. But with all that had occurred over the weekend, Ruby's social life had been the farthest thing from her mind. With her mother's weekend stay in the big city coming to an end, now was the time for Tricee to inquire about her mother's social life or lack thereof, whichever would prove more accurate. Tomorrow morning, while Tricee prepared for the start of a new week, Ruby and Bev would head back to St. Louis and, more than likely, resume their lives as if nothing had happened.

Tricee wanted badly to believe that this whole episode between her and her mother had, indeed, affected Ruby just as much as it had her. But because Ruby rarely, if ever, allowed anything to upset her for more than just a day, Tricee was not convinced. Just as she was about to pull out of her parking space, a car horn sounded, bringing her back to reality.

Tricee's neighbor, a middle-aged white woman, waved as she was leaving the parking garage. Tricee waved back, grinning and shaking her head. Her neighbor's hair was black but two weeks prior it had been a light brown. And about four months ago it had been light brown with red highlights. Tricee concluded that it was her neighbor's way of keeping the grey away as long as possible.

She pulled out of the garage and onto Sheridan Road, hoping that her last evening with Ruby would go better than the last two. Furthermore, she had no idea if Ruby had spoken to Annette at any time over this past weekend. But something told her that it was a great possibility. Annette had attempted to call twice and had left a voicemail message, but Tricee had yet to return her calls

Ruby was already seated and waiting when Tricee strolled into the Italian restaurant. When the valet, a young Latino that Tricee had seen before, asked how she was doing "on this fine evening," she forced a smile before vaguely stating, "I'm fine". She wanted to turn around and get back into her vehicle and drive back to her condo. But realizing that it would have been rude to blow off her own mother, she proceeded to walk slowly into the restaurant. She glanced around, wondering if she would see any familiar faces, but there were none. Not even the bartender, who she knew from past conversation, was a full-time employee.

Leo, the bartender, a black man in his late 30s, was down-to-earth and just a genuinely nice guy. He was well liked by everyone who frequented the restaurant, and it appeared that everyone knew him by name. Whenever Tricee would order take-out, she'd go to the bar and order a 7-Up with cherry juice while she waited for her meal. The first time she met Leo, they'd enjoyed a pleasant and humorous conversation.

He'd told Tricee that he thought she was a college student because she looked rather young for her age, but that he wasn't too surprised when he found out she was close to his age.

"I keep telling folks it's an advantage to being born black. It's that melanin we've been blessed with," he'd said.

Tricee laughed. "I agree. I don't think I could take spending hours lying out in the sun. It looks kind of painful to me."

"My partner has a regular routine in the summer. He is out there by 10 in the morning and stays for about 40 minutes. Then he comes home and gets ready for work. He asked me one day to come to the beach and join him. I told him I'd pass. I'll just apply my Noxzema over my already brown skin to get that bronzed appearance."

Ever since that first conversation, whenever Leo would see Tricee come in to order take-out he would wave her over. "One 7-Up with cherry juice," he'd say as he set the drink in front of her. She would nod and give him the thumbs up.

Leo, while clearly gay, did not go out of his way to make his preference known. Tricee would observe how he would get hit on by men and women, and how he would remain cordial yet professional. He was, indeed, a class act.

As she passed the bar area and the various tables to join Ruby, Tricee could not help but wonder, if Leo had been working, would she have chatted with him and made Ruby wait? It was a nice thought.

"Hi, Ruby." She sat down to join her mother. Her eyes went immediately to the wig that was neatly placed upon Ruby's head. It looked okay, but it was a different look, one Tricee was not too sure she liked.

"Hello, dear." Ruby's eyes fell onto the cotton, navy blue, short-sleeved blouse that Tricee was wearing. "You know, 'Hi mother' would make for a much warmer greeting."

Tricee shrugged. Ruby rolled her eyes and glanced at the menu.

The restaurant was filled to capacity with several patrons waiting to be seated. Ruby glanced around, obviously pleased with her daughter's choice. Bev's brother knew exactly where the restaurant was located as soon as Ruby told him the name of it. He'd told Ruby that it had been there now for about three years and that it was one of a few places recently built to restore the historical Bryn Mawr district on the north side. Ruby looked over the menu, noticing that Tricee had already taken a glance at her menu and set it down in front of her.

"This is a nice place. Do you come here often?" Ruby asked smiling. Tricee noticed for the first time this weekend how radiant her mother looked when she smiled. Last night, she'd noticed how nice Ruby looked, but due to the unpleasant circumstance, it was hard to really focus on her mother's radiant appearance. There were no wrinkles, no frown lines and nothing about Ruby's face that indicated she was tired from living. She was wearing makeup but only a little, and Tricee could see how much it enhanced her appearance.

"Yes, I have been here before." Tricee gave a half smile.

The waiter appeared and set a glass of water in front of her. "Thank you. I think we're ready to order. Ruby, are you ready to order?"

The waiter went over the dinner specials. Tricee ordered the grilled salmon with steamed vegetables and Ruby ordered the chicken alfredo pasta dish. Tricee also ordered calamari much to Ruby's displeasure. The waiter could tell by the look on her face that she would not be indulging.

"You may bring only one plate for the appetizer," she said to the waiter. He began to laugh.

"This bread is delicious. I'll feast on it while I wait for my main course."

"I'll bring extra," the waiter smiled as he walked away.

Tricee had not yet allowed herself to decide how she felt about her father, who had played a big part in why they were all in this situation in the first place. She had been too busy being angry with Ruby. And because Annette's mother was deceased, she had not given her any thought. After making small talk about things that were of no importance, at least not for Tricee, she sat back in her chair.

"Why are you wearing a wig? It's not you," she blurted out.

Ruby sipped from her glass of wine. "I like the way it makes me look. And I needed a change."

"Enjoy your dinner, ladies. May I get you another glass of wine?"

"No." It was Tricee who answered.

"I believe he was talking to me. No, thank you. I'll just have water. I can monitor my own alcohol intake, Jentrice."

After she and Ruby bowed their heads and blessed their meals, there was silence between them for the first time all evening. Ruby had something she wanted to share with Tricee but was finding it rather difficult to just come out and say what had been on her mind all morning. She realized that the startling news she'd already shared had caused some distress, and now didn't seem like a good time to share any more news.

"Why did you wear that blouse to dinner, Jentrice?" Ruby finally asked. "This is such a nice place. Surely, you could have chosen a nicer top than that."

Tricee's mouth flew open.

"A cotton blouse with short sleeves is something you'd wear around the house when you're doing the dishes."

Tricee gulped down the rest of her iced tea. Ruby just stared at the expression on her daughter's face.

"You know, you look just like your father when you make that face." Ruby smiled, recalling one of a few memorable moments. "His eyebrows would turn in just like yours are doing right now when he was upset."

Tricee slowly formed a smile. She recalled how many times people had said she looked a lot like her father.

"I paid $8 for this blouse. It was marked down from $29.99."

Ruby laughed. "I wouldn't have told anybody that."

It was the first time they both actually smiled at each other all evening.

"We're even now. I don't like your wig and you don't like my blouse." Tricee wiped her mouth with her napkin, still trying to figure out how to proceed during the rest of their meal. Finally, she figured she'd just come out and ask whatever questions popped into her mind.

The waiter brought their desserts. They were sipping on tea and coffee when Tricee set down her cup.

"Why did you refer to yourself as Ms. Miller to the doorman?"

"I don't know. I guess I was trying to retain a sense of privacy. I saw no reason for the doorman to know we had different last names."

Ruby had gone back to her maiden name sometime after her divorce. She hadn't used Miller in years. But last night, when she told the doorman she was Tricee's mother, she found herself using her married name.

"The way he was looking at Bev, I would be surprised if that doorman remembers his own name. She sure had his nose and eyes wide open." Tricee took a bite of her tiramisu.

Ruby shook her head. She knew Tricee would not be able to get through dinner without mentioning Bev. But Ruby was far more interested in discussing family. She thought she'd share something that Tricee had not ever known.

"You know, your Grandma Eda did not want your father to marry me." She bit into her tiramisu. "That woman hated me."

"I don't believe that. Grandma Eda did not have a hateful bone in her body."

"She had one. And it had my name written all over it. Poor thing. I went to visit her at the nursing home last month and she didn't even know who I was."

Tricee couldn't help but to smile at the mention of her Grandma Eda. Ruby knew exactly what she was doing. Their dinner had turned out okay after all. There were still a lot of unanswered questions, but this was a huge start.

Outside the restaurant, Tricee handed her ticket to the valet.

"Have a safe flight home." She turned to Ruby.

"I will. I'll call you when I make it back to St. Louis."

Just then, Bev's brother's Lincoln Town Car pulled up to the curb.

"I'm not ready to meet Bev's brother just yet," Tricee spoke softly.

Ruby reached over and gave Tricee a hug. She was glad that she hadn't shared any other news after all.

"I understand, dear." She kissed Tricee on the cheek and climbed into the waiting vehicle.

The night might have ended on a much better note but Tricee hoped Ruby was prepared for their next conversation. The pain hadn't gone away just because they'd been able to get through dinner. Tricee was still fearful of the unknown and she was still angry with Ruby.

As Tricee drove the few blocks back to her condo, she listened intently to the words from the lady pastor on the radio. It was a scripture Tricee had repeated to herself many times before: *Psalms 34:4 – I sought the Lord, and he heard me, and delivered me from all my fears.* Tricee had repeated it several times by the time she pulled into her parking space.

20

"Ah!" Tricee winced. She'd nearly slipped as she walked to the grocery store. Fortunately, the pain in her left ankle only lasted for a few minutes and she was able to keep going. Once inside the store, she removed her grocery list from her purse and crossed off each item as she placed it into the cart: fat-free milk, wheat bread, lettuce, mushrooms, apples. A bag of blue tortilla chips, though not on the list, made its way into the cart. When she walked past the display of cake mix and frosting, she hesitated before placing one of each into the cart. *It's on sale. Why not?*

As she placed the last item on the conveyor belt, she felt the vibration from her cell phone. She removed it from her purse and smiled as she read the text message: *I am looking forward to seeing you again.* She couldn't help but think about Hunter as she walked back to her condo.

After thinking about it for a whole week, she'd decided to meet him at the coffee shop the following Saturday, after their initial meeting. It was the first time she'd ever agreed to meet someone without the benefit of at least a phone conversation first, and the thought of it all had made her kind of uneasy. But even if he hadn't shown up, a trip to the coffee shop was never wasted. By that Friday evening she'd made up her mind.

She arrived at the coffee shop at 7:15 PM. Hunter was already there. He stood as soon as she walked in.

"Hi, again. I'm so glad you decided to meet me." He was all smiles.

Tricee looked him from head to toe. "Excuse me?" She looked at Hunter as if she'd never seen him before. "I'm just here to read my book and have a cup of tea." She proceeded to place her order.

Hunter, noticing her serious expression, put his hands into his pockets. "Oh."

Tricee tried to contain her smile but his expression made it difficult. "I'm sorry, I couldn't resist. I had to make sure your sense of humor from last week was real."

"Oh, okay," he said as they took their drinks to the table. "Oh, Tricee, you really had me going. I thought you really had forgotten who I was." They shared small talk as they sipped on hot tea and juice.

"So tell me a little about Tricee." Hunter couldn't stop smiling. "I like how you have your twists down like that. I really like that hairstyle on you."

Tricee blushed. He had complimented her last week when she'd worn them up.

"Thank you. Well, let me see ... I was just promoted so I stay fairly busy. But I make time to enjoy the things that I like. On Sundays after church, I try not to do too much of anything. It's a day of relaxation, sort of. So tell me something about yourself. Do you live north?" Now it was Hunter's time to check her sense of humor.

"No, I live in the south loop. I work in education, too, but as a consultant. And I live at home with my mother." He watched the expression on Tricee's face. "That's not going to be a problem is it?"

Tricee sat back in her chair. "Uh, no. Why would that be a problem?" She couldn't believe what she was hearing but tried not to show her displeasure.

"I just know that a lot of women are put off when they meet a grown man who still lives at home." Hunter was doing a good job of stringing her along.

Tricee shrugged. "Well, I don't know you and there are good reasons why some men live at home. Is your mother ill?"

"No, she's perfectly fine. She still works every day. I just find it more economical to live with her."

Tricee frowned and Hunter began to laugh.

"Tricee, I haven't lived at home since I was 19. After I finished college I found a job and my own place. I haven't been back since."

"Oh, okay, so you were pulling my leg?"

"Yes." Hunter hoped he hadn't offended her. When she started to smile he realized that he hadn't.

"I had to get you back for making me think you were not here to meet me. And I had to make sure your sense of humor was still intact."

Tricee set her cup down after taking a sip." Well, you sure had me going."

"I can just hear you now," He placed his hand on his hip and mocked the voice of a woman, "'Ooh, girl! He still lives at

home with his mama! Child, I can't have that! Oh no! Thirty-seven and still at home, no thank you!'"

Tricee was beside herself with laughter.

Since that Saturday, she and Hunter had gotten together a couple times for dinner and found that they had much in common. Interestingly, he was also in education as a consultant, primarily for high schools. His territory consisted of mostly high schools in the suburban area, though he was called upon to go to some of the high schools in the city. When Tricee asked Jackie if she'd ever met him, possibly at her high school, Jackie had stated that his name had, indeed, sounded familiar.

Hunter attended True Word church in the suburbs where Val and her husband once belonged. He played the drums but only as a fill-in for the regular drummer. After their first meeting, Hunter made it clear that he wanted to see Tricee again. When she mentioned that she preferred the term meeting over dating, he'd smiled and asked, "When would you be available for our next meeting?"

He was very easy to talk to and Tricee found herself wondering if he'd been sent as Paul's replacement to be her good guy friend. His love for the church and playing the drums was only a couple of his passions. He believed that it made no difference whether you used your gifts inside or outside of the church, as long as you did it all to the glory of God. He'd spoken highly of his two sisters and his mother, as well as his father who was now deceased. When he shared with Tricee how it had been only the Lord's strength that helped his family deal with the loss of his brother, Tricee could see the pain in his eyes. His only brother, whom he referred to as his right-hand man and best friend, had passed away unexpectedly last year at the age of 37; he'd been only one year older than Hunter.

After Tricee put away her groceries, she replied to his text message: *How sweet...* She was looking forward to seeing him again, as well, but keeping that to herself seemed the best thing to do. This evening he was taking his mother to an early Mother's Day dinner. He and Tricee had agreed to meet for brunch tomorrow after church. When he asked if he could possibly see her after he'd taken his mother to dinner, Tricee informed him that she was meeting her friends for an early dinner and that she had a few things to do for work. They agreed to at least touch base via a phone call before the night was over.

When she arrived at the Cozy Cup Café downtown, Val and Pam were already there. Tricee could see them from outside through the café's large windows.

"Hey, look at you," Pam said as Tricee removed her jacket. "I like that outfit. I love that yellow top on you. You look all jazzy." Pam was really laying on the compliments.

Tricee gave her the side-eye. "Are you still coming to church with me tomorrow for Mother's Day or have you changed your plans?"

"Yes," Pam sounded offended. "Why did you ask?" Tricee looked at Val and crossed her eyes.

"Girl, you're crazy." Val laughed.

"I was just wondering," Tricee said to Pam.

The waiter came over to take their orders and several minutes later, Jackie came in.

"You ladies are starting the party without me." Then she looked at the waiter. "I'll have the turkey on wheat, please. And a glass of iced tea."

"Surely." The waiter turned to walk away.

"Um, excuse me," Pam called after him. "May we get a refill, please?"

"Surely. I'll bring more tea right over."

"Thank you." Pam smiled. The waiter turned and walked way. "And while you're at it can you bring a little kindness?" she mumbled. She then turned to Jackie, "You're glowing. What have you been up to?"

Tricee and Jackie exchanged a quick glance. Tricee thought about what Jackie had told her a couple of weeks ago, smiling as she recalled their conversation.

"I haven't been up to anything. I went to church with Lem a couple of times, maybe that's what you're seeing."

"Hmm, okay. Maybe I need to come to that church," Pam teased.

The waiter brought their meals. Val ordered onion rings but no one else wanted to partake.

"I was hoping you ladies didn't want any," she laughed. "I love my onion rings." She ate one and then snapped her fingers. "Oh, Pam! Did you tell them about the necklace that Jeff bought?"

Then Val quickly hunched her shoulders. “Oops, sorry,” she said in a childlike voice. Pam shot her a look. *You and your big mouth!*

The only reason she’d shared with Val what happened at Jeff’s was because she’d spoken to Val the following day. It had still been fresh on her mind but by then, she’d found it funny. She had not shared the story with Tricee or Jackie because she hadn’t given it any more thought.

Jackie and Tricee looked at Pam. “He bought you a necklace?” Tricee asked.

“It wasn’t a necklace it was a pendant.” Pam’s tone went up a notch.

“He’s bought you gifts before. What’s the big deal?” Jackie took a bite of her sandwich.

“It wasn’t for her, it was for his sister!” Val blurted out, laughing uncontrollably.

“What –,” Jackie stopped eating and looked at Pam. “You thought it was for you and it wasn’t?”

Before she knew it Jackie was near tears.

“Yeah, the mood was set and everything.” Val spoke as if she was there. “I mean, any man with only half a brain would know better than that. He would have done better by just asking you to go shopping with him, to choose a gift for his sister.”

Tricee couldn’t hold her laugh in much longer. “Talk about bad timing! His timing was way off! But then maybe he really just didn’t know.”

“Wooo, let me catch my breath,” Jackie huffed, “Let me catch my breath. Brother man Jeff is a piece of work!”

Pam yanked her hand away from Val’s but her smile did not go unnoticed. “It was no big deal.”

“Oh, I beg to differ, my sister,” Val said. “Now see, it wouldn’t be so bad except that you and Jeff are not really in a committed relationship.”

“Well, they *have* been seeing each other for—What? Six months, right?” Tricee asked.

“Seven.” Pam turned to Val. “You can’t hold ice water can you?”

“Well, that’s long enough to have some level of comfort, but still.” Jackie wiped tears from her eyes.

“Let’s say Cory had done that to me. See, it wouldn’t have been so bad because he’s my husband.”

Tricee immediately whipped her neck toward Val. "Oh, yes, it would have been so bad because Cory doesn't have a sister!"

"Girl, bye! Let's say cousin then." She clapped her hands while laughing. "It makes a big difference! I would not have been so embarrassed!"

"Pam, we're not laughing at *you.*" Jackie lightly touched Pam's arm. "We're laughing *with* you but *at* Jeff. He ought to know better than that. What was he thinking? Setting the mood and then pulling out a gift for another woman! I don't care if it was his grandmama, he ought to know better!"

"Oh, I needed that laugh." Val exhaled. "Girl, you sure can pick 'em, can't you?"

Pam just smiled. "I'm not telling you anything else." She lightly swiped Val on the arm.

As they continued their meals, two black men came in accompanied by two white women. The four women were so into their conversation that they had not paid the two couples any attention. The man with the darker complexion, however, would look over at them from time to time.

"So what's on the agenda for this evening?" Tricee asked as she finished her sandwich. "I'm going home to look over this document for work. I keep putting it off."

"Alesia and I are watching a DVD. She gets to choose, I just hope it's not animated. My brother and dad are taking my mom and me to lunch for Mother's Day tomorrow. And after we get rid of the men, Alesia, my mom and I are going shopping and then to a movie."

Jackie wanted to have some time alone with her mom to tell her what she was feeling about Lem. When her mother first met him, she told Jackie Lem reminded her of Jackie's father when he was younger. Jackie was almost moved to tears by her mother's statement.

"Jeff is out of town this weekend. I'm going home to read. I have a few sales reports that need my attention but it won't get done tonight."

"I don't have any plans." Val drank the rest of her iced tea. "Cory placed me on punishment."

"Oh?" Tricee picked up the dessert menu.

"Yeah. He accused me of being too friendly with the guy who works part time behind the seafood counter. He's having his male cycle so he's a little sensitive."

"Well, *are you* too friendly with this guy?" Jackie asked.

"Please! I mean he *is* cute … " Val blushed.

Pam laughed. "Yep, you're too friendly with him.

"I don't even know the guy." Val pushed her plate to the side. "Well, except that he's a junior in college, studying biology and plans to go to medical school, preferably in the state of Washington. He has one younger brother, a senior in high school who plays on the basketball team. He is so good that he might just have a chance at the NBA."

Jackie, Tricee and Pam stared at Val as she spoke.

"But, of course, his mother is against that. She wants his brother to go to college and says the NBA can wait. His father—his parents are divorced—is neutral. He says he can always go back to college, even after he is drafted because players do that all the time. His favorite foods are pasta dishes and meatloaf. And he has worked at the meat market for close to a year now." She shrugged. "Other than that, I really don't know too much about him."

"Boxers or briefs?" Pam leaned back in her chair while facing Val.

"I was thinking Pull-ups or diapers?" Tricee teased. "He's a young one."

"And that's what makes it flattering. At my age, I need that every now and then."

"You're 34, not 84," Jackie stated as she noticed the darker man staring. His friend then turned and looked in their direction, as well.

"So, Val, what exactly is your punishment?" The waiter cleared their plates and refilled their glasses. A few minutes later he brought their desserts to go.

"Get this. He slept on the sofa last night. When will men learn? He did me a favor. I needed a break. When he grabbed a blanket and headed for the sofa, I popped some microwave popcorn, poured myself a tall glass of Coke, went into that bedroom and watched reruns of *The Andy Griffith Show*. I had a good time laughing along with the men of Mayberry. And then at four this morning, he climbed into bed hunching me, 'Val, you sleep?' I was like, 'Yeah, I'm sleep, nutty man, it's 4:00 AM!' I did open my eyes for a quick second but then rolled over and went right back to sleep."

"I bet maybe he'll think twice the next time he puts you on punishment, huh?" asked Pam.

"And from the way it sounds, your punishment ended this morning at 4:00 AM." Jackie winked.

"I love Cory dearly and he has nothing to worry about, he knows that."

Val had never accused her husband of anything because he'd never given her a reason to. In fact, whenever Val would notice other women behaving in an overly friendly manner toward Cory she would tease him. She'd shared with her girlfriends how she liked to go to this one particular fast food restaurant near their home simply because one of the female workers had an eye for Cory. They always got extra fries. One day he suggested going someplace else. Val had told him, "No way. And miss out on my extra fries?" She would tell her friends that women needed to use their men to their advantage. "Girlfriend, do you realize how much free food you can get when you're out with your man?" she'd joked.

They gathered their purses and apple Danish pastries and walked toward the door.

"Is it me or has he been staring at us the whole time?" Tricee asked softly.

"It's not you," Jackie said. "You know, some black men—and I didn't say all—think it bothers all of us when we see them out with white women. It's as if they expect us to react badly. But what they need to realize is that we couldn't care less."

"I have way more important things to be concerned with," said Val.

"And who brothers choose to date is not on the list, good grief!" said Tricee.

"I know that's right." Pam laughed.

They left the café and walked toward their respective vehicles.

"I'm parked this way." Val pointed down Wabash. "See you ladies."

"I'm in the garage," said Jackie.

"So am I," said Tricee.

"I'm a block from the garage," Pam pulled out her cell phone, "so I can walk this way."

After they'd walked a block, Tricee shared the news about Paul. "Paul's engaged."

"Engaged?" Pam stopped walking and looked directly at Tricee. "I didn't even know he had a girlfriend. When did he get engaged and why are you just now saying something?"

Pam was more surprised by the news than Jackie.

"I don't know exactly when he got engaged but he told me back in March when we went out to dinner. No big deal."

"I think that's wonderful. Have you met his fiancée?" Jackie asked.

"No."

"If it's not a big deal then why didn't you tell us sooner?" Pam was convinced that Tricee liked Paul as more than just a friend. It hadn't mattered that Tricee had met Hunter and that she'd said on several occasions that she and Paul were just friends. Just like she and Hunter were becoming good "friends."

"Pam, please don't make a federal case out of this. And can we walk *and* chew gum because I need to get home." Jackie resumed walking.

"Humph," Pam uttered. "I'm just saying. It seems sort of odd that he's engaged when he never mentioned he had a girlfriend. I'll see you in the morning" She gave both Tricee and Jackie a hug and walked toward her vehicle.

"She has to make a big deal out of everything," said Jackie as she fished around for her car keys. "She's going to church with you tomorrow?"

Tricee nodded.

"Maybe your pastor will do a sermon on how not to overanalyze." They laughed as Jackie reached over and gave Tricee a hug.

When Tricee climbed into her vehicle and looked at her cell phone. It indicated one new message: *You deserve to hear kind words.* Before she started her engine she sent Hunter a reply: *Do you like lemon cake with lemon frosting?*

21

By 8:00 PM, Tricee had completed a budget report, a tentative agenda for two of her upcoming meetings with the Dean of the School of Education and emailed her assistant a list of things that she needed done before the end of the month. It had taken her longer than the two hours she'd allotted for the tasks but she was happy to have it all done. After checking her emails and printing out the report that she'd gone over four times, she shut down her computer. She grabbed an apple from off the kitchen counter and read Hunter's reply to her last text message: *I love lemon cake. Yum.* She was about to reply when her home phone rang.

"Hello?"

"Hello there. How are you?"

Tricee was a little surprised. She wondered why Paul wasn't out with his fiancée on this Saturday evening.

"Oh." She paused. "I'm doing fine."

"You sound disappointed," Paul chuckled.

Tricee turned down the volume on the television. "Oh, no. I was just a little distracted by the television, that's all."

"Oh. Well, I don't want to interrupt … "

"It's fine, Paul, really. How are you?"

"I'm doing well. I was just calling to see how things were going for you in your new role."

"I am even busier now, but that was to be expected." Tricee laughed. "I think I'll wait before I tell my boss that I don't want the position."

"That sounds like a good idea," said Paul. He was smiling as they spoke. He had always liked Tricee's sense of humor. His sister once asked him if he had ever thought about Tricee as more than just a friend. And she had inquired as to why Tricee had not come to hear them sing. Paul had simply stated, "She had other plans." He didn't feel up to going into any details.

"So have you set a wedding date yet?" Tricee regretted it as soon as she'd said it.

"You mean has she set a date yet?"

"Aren't you a part of the equation?" They both laughed.

"Yeah, but I'm pretty much allowing her to take over."

"That's a good practice."

"So how's the drummer doing? I am not too good with names."

Tricee smiled. "His name is Hunter and he's doing fine."

Tricee had been to church with Hunter once. She hoped she'd have an opportunity to hear him play the drums but the regular drummer was on hand. She had to remind herself that Hunter's talents on the drums were for God's glory, not Tricee's.

When they'd gone out to dinner last week, she found herself trying hard not to stare at his biceps. Although Hunter had a slight build, his biceps were bigger than she'd expected.

Jackie had teased her, saying, "Buy him a play drum set. That way he can entertain you all you want."

Just as she was about to ask Paul about work, her cell phone rang.

"Paul, this is my aunt calling. Is it okay if we talk sometime this week?"

"Sure. Have a good week. We'll talk soon." After hanging up with Paul, Tricee smiled as she spoke to her aunt.

"Hi, Aunt Janice, how are you?"

Tricee could hear the weakness in her aunt's voice. "I'm well."

Tricee was still not convinced.

"So why are you home on a Saturday evening? Are you still in the getting-to-know-you phase with the gentleman you were telling me about?" Aunt Janice asked.

"I stay out of trouble by staying in on the weekends, and yes to question two." Tricee laughed.

"That's good. He sounds really nice, Tricee."

Aunt Janice was forever entertaining the idea of her favorite niece's future wedding. When Tricee told her aunt once that marriage might not be a part of God's plan for her, Aunt Janice whole heartedly disagreed. "Nonsense," she'd replied. "God is too smart not to hook you up with one of His kings."

"He's a good friend, auntie, that's it."

"Hmmm, okay. But just to be on the safe side, I better start looking early for something to wear to the wedding."

"Okay now, Aunt Janice! Don't make me come over there!"

Aunt Janice laughed. She then proceeded to ask Tricee what she asked her every year. "So are you going to call your mother tomorrow?"

She was well aware of Ruby's and Tricee's strained mother and daughter relationship. She avoided asking Tricee a lot of questions about her older sister because she knew Tricee wasn't too fond of discussing Ruby. And they rarely, if ever, spoke about the secret that Ruby had finally shared with Tricee last year. But every year, her aunt would make sure to ask Tricee if she planned on calling Ruby for Mother's Day. It was more or less just confirmation. She knew Tricee well enough to know that she'd at least perform that gesture.

"I'll call her in the morning," Tricee answered quickly. "What are you doing tomorrow for Mother's Day?"

Aunt Janice had one daughter who lived in Portland. She only made it home to St. Louis for Christmas and Thanksgiving. Uncle Ced had three grown children, none of them living in St. Louis and—like Aunt Janice's daughter—they only visited around the holidays. When Tricee lived in St. Louis, she would treat her aunt to dinner for Mother's Day while Ruby would only receive a card.

"Your Uncle Ced wants to cook for me. He says he wants to try something different as opposed to eating out. He's at the market right now."

"Oh, that's sweet." Tricee had always like Uncle Ced. She felt that he was the best husband out of Aunt Janice's four. "What is he cooking?"

"Lamb chops. But that's all he will tell me. I just hope it's something delicious."

Tricee could tell that Aunt Janice was getting tired.

"I'm sure that whatever Uncle Ced cooks is going to be just fine. I should let you go, though, so you can rest. Have you been to the doctor for a checkup?"

"Yes, Ms. Tricee. And everything is fine."

"Okay." Tricee blew a kiss through the phone. "That's for you. I love you, Auntie."

"I love you to, sweetie."

As soon as she hung up with her aunt, Pam called.

"Hey, Tricee. I'm up north. Do you mind if I stop by?"

"No, not at all."

Twenty minutes later Pam was at Tricee's front door.

"So what brings you to the north side this evening?"

“I have to pick Cassie up from a party. She’s at this gathering at the university about five blocks from here. She didn’t drive her own car because she thought she’d want to hang out with her friends all night. But she changed her mind. I think she just wants to get home and spend the rest of the night talking to her boyfriend.’

“I remember those nights.” Tricee laughed.

Pam picked up a catalogue from the coffee table.

“Who’s that cute old Spanish doorman downstairs? I don’t think I’ve ever seen him before.”

“Felipe.” Tricee looked puzzled. “He normally doesn’t work on Saturday evenings. He must be filling in for Tate.” She kicked Pam lightly in the leg. “He’s not old.”

“Well, he’s about my father’s age, 60. Don’t you think that’s old?”

“No, I don’t. And believe it or not, Felipe is sixty … seven, I think.”

Pam stopped flipping the pages of the catalogue. “Really? He doesn’t look it.”

Tricee’s phone rang again.

“I’m popular this evening.”

Pam smiled and went back to looking at the catalogue.

“Hello?” Tricee turned away to keep Pam from seeing the big smile on her face.

“Hello, there. I trust you enjoyed dinner with your friends.”

“Hi, Hunter. Yes, I did. In fact, one of my girlfriends just stopped by.”

“Okay. Well, my mom and I had a really nice dinner. I just dropped her off. I just wanted to call and say good night. I’ll see you tomorrow at one?”

“Yes.”

When Tricee turned around Pam was looking at her with a huge smile.

“We can discuss that lemon cake you asked me about. Good night, Tricee.”

“Good night.”

Pam placed the catalogue on the table. “Was that your new boyfriend?”

“He’s not my boyfriend. He’s a friend.” Tricee started looking through one of the other catalogues.

"Okay. Don't get testy." Pam laughed. "I don't know how you do it."

"Do what?"

"I don't see how you can go without a steady man."

"I have a man."

Pam rolled her eyes. "I'm talking about a real man."

"Jesus *is* real," Tricee responded without looking up.

Pam sighed. "What about when you just want a man to hold you at night?"

"*He's* a comforter."

"What about when you have a headache and you just want someone to rub your temples?"

"*He's* a healer."

Pam sighed again. "What about when you need that special someone to talk to because you've had a rough day at work?'

"*He's* always available."

"What about your needs? And you know what I'm talking about."

"*He* provides for all of my needs." Tricee stood up from the sofa. "And *He's* so wonderful that He is capable of removing those desires so I don't have to worry about them." She started walking toward the kitchen. "So there." Tricee turned around just in time to catch the small pillow Pam had tossed at her.

Cassie soon called informing Pam that she could start heading over to the campus.

"I'll drive you to your car." Tricee grabbed her jacket. "No use in letting you walk alone out here at night."

"Thanks." Pam pointed toward the catalogues. "There are some really cute clothes in there. I might want to order something."

"It's Karen's. She left it here."

Pam quickly wiped her hands on her sweatshirt. "Yikes, I'd better go wash my hands."

"You goofy," Tricee commented as they left her apartment.

They reached the lobby and walked through the back door to reach the parking garage.

"I'm sorry for earlier, for how I responded when you told me about Paul."

"Oh." Tricee threw up her hands. "I hadn't even given that any more thought."

"Do you have a picture of Hunter?"

Tricee pulled out her cell phone. “I do.”

Pam’s eyes grew wide. “He has locs! I didn’t know you liked dreads, Tricee! I like how he has them pulled back. He’s handsome.”

“It’s not about his locs, it’s about him and his personality.”

“Okay.” Pam mumbled. “I still didn’t know you were into dreads. Have you played with them yet?”

“I’m not even going to answer that.” She hit Pam lightly on the arm. “You just try to get here by 9:15 in the morning. Service starts at 10:00 AM.

“I’ll call you when I pull up out front. I’ll drive us to church and make sure I have you back in time for your brunch date with dreadlocks.”

“You better stop.”

They laughed as they climbed into Tricee’s vehicle. She put in the CD that Hunter had made for her as she made a left out of the garage.

“That sounds nice,” Pam remarked. She then sent a text to whom Tricee assumed was Cassie. She figured Pam was letting her sister know she was on her way. Then she dialed Jeff’s number and left him a message.

“I’m sure he’s asleep by now.” Pam placed her cell phone back in her purse.

“Where is he, again?” Tricee asked as she headed down Sheridan.

“Atlanta.” She closed her eyes and moved her head back and forth to the music.

When Tricee reached the stop light after driving three blocks, she noticed Karen in the car next to her. The car was in the left lane preparing to turn onto Lakeshore Drive, but Karen was so busy laughing that she didn’t see Tricee.

“Karen is never without a date on a Saturday night,” Tricee said.

“Huh?” Pam opened her eyes.

“Karen.” Tricee tilted her head in the direction of the white BMW. Pam looked in the direction of the car that was right next to them. She squinted and then opened her eyes wide. She recognized the white BMW as well as the driver wearing the Chicago Bears baseball cap.

"That's Jeff!" she screamed as the light turned green and the BMW turned left. She immediately took out her cell phone.

"Pam, what are you doing?"

"What does it look like I'm doing? I'm calling that liar!"

"And you expect for him to answer?"

Tricee felt so badly for Pam. But she knew that calling Jeff right now was not the answer.

"So you figure you'll leave him a nasty message? Pam, please. I wouldn't even give him the satisfaction."

Tricee could only imagine the pain that Pam had to be feeling. She felt badly for her as she watched the tears fall from Pam's eyes. But what Tricee did not know was that Pam would hold her partly responsible for her pain.

22

"Jackie, why are you putting all of that sugar in your coffee?" Pam stared at Jackie intently.

"I always put sugar and cream in my coffee."

"No, you don't. You like your coffee just like you like your men, remember? Black and strong. That's what you always say."

"I need to broaden my horizons." Jackie took a sip of the coffee and frowned. "Whew! Now that's different."

They were having breakfast at a diner near Pam's home. Jackie had invited Pam to breakfast to try and discuss Pam's unkind treatment of Tricee. It had been several weeks and Pam was still upset with Tricee. They'd not spoken since that Sunday, the day after she and Tricee saw Karen and Jeff.

Jackie felt that Pam was taking out her anger on the wrong person and that she was letting Jeff off the hook way too easily. Pam could sense by the way Jackie was acting that she'd invited her to breakfast for a reason. When Jackie stirred two sugars and three creams into her coffee, Pam knew something was up. As far as Pam was concerned, Jackie could save her breath because Jeff had already explained the situation.

He'd called Pam the following day just as he'd planned. He had already informed Pam of his plans to take his mother and sisters out for Mother's Day and stated that he'd call her as soon as he was back home. When he called, Pam began her interrogation. When Jeff suggested that they talk after she'd calmed down, she became even more upset.

She gathered all of the gifts he'd given her and ran out to her car. The hour drive out to Schaumburg had been one of her worst drives ever. Her heartbeat was so rapid that she had to consciously tell herself to breathe every few minutes.

When she was 10 minutes from Jeff's place, she called her sister Lynn who tried to reason with her and convince her to turn around and go back home.

"Pam, it's 10:00 at night. You need to be at home getting ready for the start of a new work week, not driving out to Schaumburg to confront some lying man."

Pam had considered her sister's words for all of two minutes. Fifteen minutes later she was ringing Jeff's bell. He answered but instead of asking her to come up he met her downstairs. Pam immediately started to throw her hands at him. Jeff grabbed her by the wrists and led her upstairs. She was crying even harder by then.

Jeff explained that Karen was just a friend and that he'd only taken her out a few times. He stated that they'd known each other for about a year. When Pam asked why he hadn't called to let her know his trip had been canceled, he told her that he'd had a lot of work to catch up on. When she'd asked how he ended up seeing Karen Saturday night, he told her they just happened to run into each other that Friday and agreed to go to dinner Saturday. He told Pam she was jumping to conclusions. He suggested that they go out for a late night snack and, by the time Pam was in her car driving back to the south side, everything was fine between them.

"Why did you ask me out to breakfast Jackie?" Pam asked as the server set the turkey bacon and egg sandwiches in front of them.

"Excuse me. May I have another cup of coffee, please," Jackie said to the server. "You can take this, I won't need it." She handed the server the sugar and cream.

"Pam, I just think you're being very unfair to Tricee. Do you really think she knew about Karen and Jeff? You know Tricee better than that."

"Jackie, I'm not going through this. You don't know the full story." Pam took a bite of her sandwich.

"I don't think you know the full story either."

They ate the rest of their breakfast in silence. When they got ready to leave, Pam pulled a $20 bill and a $10 bill from her purse.

"Pam, *I* asked *you* out to breakfast." Jackie pulled out her debit card. "Can we not do this, please?" Jackie paid the bill and Pam angrily left the café. She got into her vehicle and drove off.

Jackie called Val who answered the phone huffing and puffing. "Hello?"

"I can't believe her! Pam is being so irrational!" Jackie could hear loud music in the background.

"I told you to expect the claws to come out. So you can't say I didn't warn you."

"She is so in the dark about Jeff."

Jackie heard Cory in the background. "Come on, Val."

"Okay," she yelled back. A few seconds later she got another call. "Jackie, hang on for a second."

"Hello?"

"Hey, Val." Pam could hear the loud music. "It's 10 in the morning, are you guys having a party?"

"No," Val laughed. "We're cleaning." She set the mop against the wall. "Cory and I like to dance on Saturday mornings when we're doing our chores. It makes the mopping and sweeping more bearable."

"Oh, okay. Well, I knew Jackie had a motive for asking me out to breakfast."

"She's only trying to be helpful, Pam."

"I didn't ask for her help."

They talked for several minutes. Val had almost forgotten that Jackie was on the other line.

"Oh, Pam! Hang on. Jackie is on the other line." Val switched over. "Jackie, I'm sorry! I forgot you were on hold. That was Pam."

Jackie heard Cory again, "Babe, come on! Cheryl Lynn's "Got to Be Real" is on. I want to dance off this. It's my old-school hit!" He put the furniture polish and the rag on the entertainment center and turned up the volume.

"We can just start the CD over, sweetie!" Val yelled out.

"Val, what are you guys doing over there?" Jackie turned off the expressway.

Val laughed. "My husband wants to dance and I have both you and Pam on the phone. You guys are not going to worry me this morning!"

"Oh, so Pam's on the other line?"

"Yes. Can we talk later, Jackie?"

"Yeah, that's fine."

Val switched over to Pam. "Pam, can I call you back later? I really need to get my cleaning done."

"So that was Jackie on the other line?" Val could hear Pam's attitude through the phone.

"Yep." Val was not about to discuss the issue, at least not now. "I'll call you later, okay?"

As soon as Jackie arrived home, her cell phone rang. She spoke with Lem for a few minutes before helping her daughter with a class project. As she started on some chores of her own, she couldn't help but think about how much different her and Lem's relationship was from Pam and Jeff's. Lem was starting to say things like "when we" get ready to do this and "when we" travel here. Jackie noticed it but would only smile and allow him to finish his thoughts. Lem was talking like a man who was preparing for something long term.

By the time 7:00 PM rolled around, Jackie was tired and ready to call it an early night. Pam had helped to deplete some of her energy. She called Tricee who was on her way to dinner with Hunter.

"Hi, Tricee." Jackie chose not to share that she and Pam had met for breakfast. "Are you busy?"

"Hunter's here. We're on our way to dinner. I had him stop by to look at my computer. It was acting up."

Jackie smiled. "Oh, so he's good with computers, too?" She recalled that Paul had been good with computers. "A lot of men are good with computers. I wonder why that is?"

Tricee laughed. "Val's good with computers. She's not a man."

"Oh, well, you know. She's the exception. Well, let me let you get back to Mr. Hunter."

Tricee's voice went into a whisper. "You know, Jackie, Hunter is so nice and understanding. I told him about Pam and how she's upset with me. He said to just give her some time, she'll come around. He says that because he has sisters, he knows what he's talking about. He is just so easy to talk to. He has proven himself to be a really good friend."

Jackie whispered into the phone. "He sounds really nice. Why are you are talking so softly? Is he standing right next to you?"

"No," Tricee laughed. "He's in my office."

"Well, enjoy dinner. And I agree with Hunter. Pam will come around soon."

Jackie sure hoped so. She loved both Pam and Tricee like sisters. It was a shame to see their friendship on the rocks over something so ridiculous.

Just as Hunter was finishing up in her office, there was a knock on Tricee's front door. Karen stood before her casually dressed in a nautical striped top and a pair of black, straight-legged pants. She had seen Karen only once or twice since the Jeff incident a couple of weeks ago but had chosen not to say anything.

"Hey, Karen." Tricee had not been expecting to see her.

"I hope I'm not catching you a bad time. I just came by to get my crock pot."

Tricee slapped her hand into her forehead. "Oh, Karen, I'm sorry. I forgot you were coming by tonight to pick it up."

Tricee invited her in. She introduced Karen to Hunter. She thought about what Pam had said, about how women mention their male friends to other women. Pam was convinced that Karen had mentioned Jeff to her, but since she knew she had told Pam the truth, she quickly dismissed the thought.

"Thanks for letting me use it." Tricee handed Karen her crock pot.

"Anytime," Karen said.

Tricee turned to Hunter. "I need to talk to Karen for just a few minutes."

"No problem." Hunter smiled and picked up the remote.

Tricee and Karen stepped out into the hall.

"We're on our way to dinner. I have a taste for Japanese cuisine."

"That sounds good." Karen smiled.

Tricee hesitated and then got right to the point.

"Karen, Pam and I saw you a few weeks ago with the guy Pam is dating. And now she is upset with me because she thinks I knew you were seeing him."

"A few weeks ago … " Karen had to ponder that as Tricee was not being very specific.

"He drives a white BMW." Tricee chose not to call any names.

"Jeff?" Tricee nodded.

"Jeff and I are not in a serious relationship. We get together every now and then." Karen's attitude was rather nonchalant.

"I just thought I'd mention it. I knew it was bound to come out at some point."

Karen released a light chuckle. "Does Pam really believe she's the only woman in Jeff's life?"

"I don't know. I just know she's mad at me. But it's not your problem. Or mine."

"Well, I'm sorry she's mad at you, Tricee. Frankly, I think she's mad at the wrong person."

Tricee had to agree. She missed Pam but she'd already put forth effort trying to call her twice. Pam had not returned her calls.

When Karen asked if she could come by sometime on Sunday, Tricee hesitated before saying yes.

"I'm not trying to put you in the middle of anything. I would just like to finish this discussion. I know you and Pam are friends and I respect that."

After their brief discussion, Tricee could tell that Pam was much more into Jeff than Karen was. She mumbled as she walked back into her apartment, "Pam needs to put that box of cereal right back on the shelf."

23

Tuesday: August 20th

Tricee strolled along the lakefront, deep in thought. The guy who rode past her on his bicycle said hello but she failed to respond. Ruby's weekend visit left her with all kinds of thoughts. When she called to inform Tricee that she'd made it safely back to St. Louis, Tricee allowed her answering machine to pick up the call. She'd listened to the message three times and, even now, she was replaying it over and over in her mind. *Jentrice, I made it home safely. Look, my dear, I know the news I shared came as a big surprise, but I really hope we can get past this. Love you. Call me when you get this message.*

Her mother's news had done more than come as a big surprise. That was putting it mildly. Tricee could sense from the tone in Ruby's voice on her answering machine that she was just as mentally drained as she was. Although dinner on Sunday had turned out pleasant enough, the pain was still there. There was only so much a person could take and Tricee was running on empty. Even though she knew she'd have to get around to eventually asking more questions, the thought of talking to Ruby right now was the farthest thing from Tricee's mind. Looking out at the lake was a better option.

Tricee had left work early, simply because she couldn't keep her focus. When she woke up yesterday morning, the Monday morning blues had taken on a whole new meaning. But she'd made it through the day, partly because she had stayed very busy.

"Are you okay? You don't look well," one of her colleagues had said to her.

Tricee responded, "I don't feel well. I think I might be coming down with something."

Later on that afternoon she'd gone into the restroom and had herself a good cry. When her boss came into her office, she could see that something was wrong. But being the kind of boss that she was, she didn't probe. She asked Tricee if she needed to take the day off and told her that she was available if she needed to talk. Tricee thanked her boss for the offer and decided to take a half day.

She came home, changed into something more comfortable and headed straight for the lake.

There were a few people out on the beach but far fewer than what she'd expect to see on the weekend. Many of the teenagers and young children were happily enjoying the beach before their summer vacation came to an end. While everyone else was enjoying the warm August afternoon, Tricee was in despair.

Ironically, both Annette and J.P. had attempted to call her last night but she still wasn't ready to talk. She wondered if Ruby had told J.P. to expect a phone call from her. As for Annette, she'd tried to call at least three times already.

As Tricee approached the bench, she sighed before sitting down. *Lord, what's the use in praying when it doesn't seem as though you're listening*, she thought. She reached into her fannie pack to retrieve a stick of gum and when she looked up, an older woman was standing before her. "Whatever it is, dear, give it to the Lord. He's knows all about it." The woman smiled, then turned and walked away. Although it was 90 degrees out, the woman was wearing a thick, grey, hooded sweater and sweat pants. Tricee watched as the woman made her way farther along the path. Tricee stood and looked out into the water once more, before heading back to her condo.

After a shower she went into the kitchen and prepared a chicken breast and sautéed vegetables for dinner. She then removed a few documents from her briefcase. The five-page report given to her by her boss was a top priority. She looked it over carefully, marked where she'd have to make a few changes and placed it back in her briefcase. After looking over the agenda for Friday's meeting, she ate her dinner while watching television. Several minutes later she was asleep on the sofa. The last thing she remembered watching was the six o'clock news. She was awakened by her home phone. She answered without bothering to look at the caller ID.

"Hello?" she answered groggily.

"Oh. Excuse me, sir. I think I have the wrong number." *Click.*

A few seconds later the phone rang again. "Hello?" she answered in an irritable tone.

"Uh, sir? I was looking for Tricee. Is this 555- … "

Tricee began to sit up when she recognized the voice. "Pam, this *is* Tricee."

"Oh! Girl, why does your voice sound like the lead singer from The Temptations? For a minute I thought you had a man over there. I was like 'I know she doesn't have a man over there' … "

Tricee sat fully upright on the sofa. Although she didn't really feel much like talking, she welcomed the distraction from her thoughts.

"I guess I don't have the most attractive-sounding voice when I'm tired. And sorry to disappoint you but, no, I don't have a man over here."

Tricee and Pam hadn't talked since Pam left Tricee's apartment on Saturday. While Tricee had noticed Pam's strange behavior, she'd thought no more about it. Pam, on the other hand, had intentionally waited until Ruby had left to go back home before she called. She'd called to check on Tricee but also to discuss what she'd felt since Saturday.

"So how are you?" Pam asked.

"I'm as well as can be expected given the weekend I just had."

"Oh. Well, if this is not a good time I can call later." Pam hoped it was a good time.

"It's just going to take some time for me to feel back to normal." Tricee glanced at the clock. "But thanks for calling."

Pam realized that Tricee was prepared to hang up and suddenly spoke up. "Tricee, may I talk to you about something? It's sort of important."

Tricee turned off her television. "Sure. Is everything okay?"

Pam exhaled. "I just have this funny feeling about something."

"What is it, Pam?"

"When I was at your place on Saturday, I felt like the man upstairs was trying to give me a sign." She felt a little uncomfortable sharing this for fear that it all sounded too weird. But ever since Saturday she couldn't stop thinking about the words on that plaque.

"Pam, what are you talking about?" Tricee was now very curious.

"Well," Pam said slowly. "I just believe God is trying to talk to me through your situation. I read that plaque on your kitchen wall. And then just as I was coming back into your bedroom, Val was telling you pretty much what was on that plaque. It just feels sort of strange. I can't explain it."

Tricee got up from the sofa and walked into her kitchen. The plaque had gone unnoticed. In fact, she couldn't remember the last time she'd paid it any attention. She stood in her kitchen and read the words. And after reading them she thought about what the woman had said earlier at the beach.

"Tricee, are you still there?"

"Yes, I'm here."

"Well, what do you think? Val says that God talks to us many times though others. Have you experienced that a lot?"

Tricee closed her eyes. "Yeah, I have. I think a lot of folks do."

"So what do you think? Why am I feeling like this?" Before Tricee could respond, Pam spoke again. "Never mind." She released a light chuckle. "You have other things to deal with and here I am asking you about my issues."

Tricee sat down at her kitchen table. "No, it's not a bother. In fact, this conversation sort of helped me see things a little differently."

"Really?" Pam was not expecting to hear that.

"Really." Tricee laughed.

"Well, now that we've got yours figured out, can you help me to see what I need to see?"

They both laughed.

"I think it would be better if you went to God and asked Him what He was trying to say to you."

"Okay. I guess I can do that. Thanks."

"You're quite welcome."

"Tricee, may I say one more thing?"

Tricee didn't respond, choosing instead to allow Pam to go on.

"I don't mean this in a harmful way, but as a Christian, aren't you required to find it in your heart to forgive Ruby? I mean, I know that what she shared was very hurtful, but if you hold on to the pain then you're only allowing the enemy to win. I know you have such a strong faith and I just don't want to see you lose that."

Tricee sat and stared at the phone for several minutes after her chat with Pam. She got up from the table and went into her bedroom where she pulled a medium-sized box from the rear of her closet. She pulled a photo album from the box and slowly began to flip through the pages. There were several pictures of her and Ruby and a couple of photos of her, Ruby and J.P. There were several photos of relatives. When she got to the last page in the album, she stared at a photo of her and Annette. The photo was taken when they were 11. Someone, Tricee assumed it was Ruby, had written the year across the top. It was the first time Tricee had looked at the photo with a different pair of eyes. She searched their faces to find any resemblance between Annette and J.P. or herself.

She could not keep a tear from falling as she dialed Ruby's number.

"Hello, dear." Ruby answered as if she had been waiting for Tricee to call.

"Hi." Tricee sat on the edge of her bed.

"Are you okay, dear?"

Tricee decided to get straight to the point. The conversation had to take place at some time and she figured it might as well be now.

"Why didn't you tell me sooner? There must be a reason."

Ruby sighed. "Jentrice, please know that I'm hurting just as much as you."

"I don't really know if that's even possible," Tricee said loudly. "What were you thinking to not tell me? I needed to know this a long time ago, not now!" Ruby allowed her daughter to finish realizing that she was speaking from a place of pain. "I'm so angry but I know I have to let it go."

"I know. And you have every right to be angry." Ruby sat back on her bed as she tried her best to explain. "We lived in a small town and your father and I just felt it was best to keep quiet."

"What about Annette's mother?"

Tricee had heard other people say that Annette's mother had all sorts of problems. But as a child, Tricee couldn't imagine someone as pretty as Annette's mother having anything short of a happy life. And she was always so nice to Tricee. In fact, Tricee remembered Annette's mother being kind to just about everyone. She'd learned after Annette's mother passed that she'd suffered from depression.

When Annette turned 10, her mother remarried and had a baby boy. But a new marriage and a new baby couldn't cure depression. Tricee recalled Annette's stepfather being a heavyset man who doted on his son and treated Annette as if she was his biological daughter. Tricee remembered him being a lot nicer than the man Annette had always referred to as her father.

Her mother passed away when her son turned five. She was found lying in the alley by two teenaged boys. The word was that she had been on her way back from the store, but there had been disputes about what really happened. After she passed, Annette's brother remained with his father and Annette was sent to live with her grandparents. By this time she was a sophomore in high school and had to be transferred to another school, but she and Tricee were determined to stay in contact.

"Annette's mother was perfectly fine with keeping it a secret. I believe it was much more stressful for her. She had so many problems but had always refused to get help. I never blamed her entirely. I blamed both her and your father. "

"Does Annette know now?" Tricee was sure she already knew the answer.

"Yes," Ruby said softly. "She knows and she was shocked but she was not nearly as upset as you are. She knew her mother's pain. I believe Annette is just trying to enjoy life as best as she can because of what she has been through. She has already lost a mother and the man she knew as her father. And to a certain degree she lost her little brother when the family was separated."

Ruby hesitated before continuing, "Until the day he died, the man Annette knew as her father thought she was his biological daughter."

"Maybe he is. It is very pos – "

Ruby could see that Tricee was hoping for a different ending. "J.P. is Annette's father, Jentrice. We know that for certain."

Tricee kept silent.

"You know, Annette and her brother are so blessed. Even though they've been through some hard times, they are both doing very well. She told me they made a pact to remain close when he entered college. They both knew they wanted a better life than their mother had and they wanted to make her proud. They believed that was really important, even after her death."

Annette's brother, at 25, is a successful architect—the youngest one at his firm. He resides not too far from Annette and remains close to his father who has since remarried.

"Yeah, she told me once about the pact they made." Tricee stood up from her bed. "Well, at least somebody gets to have a happy ending."

Ruby realized that Tricee's comment was out of anger so she let it pass.

"God doesn't give us more than we can handle. I know I made a mistake but I couldn't carry the guilt much longer."

"And that's why you told me now after all these years. Because of guilt. That sure doesn't make it any easier for me. But, you know, I have to forgive you."

Tricee was determined not to cry but she could hear muffled sounds from Ruby.

"I'm hurting but I know in time I'll heal. I'm going to take some time off in the next couple months and come home. I'll take enough time so that I can visit J.P. in Louisville before I come to St. Louis. I need closure. But please don't mention this to Annette or J.P. I want to be the one to tell them both."

"I think that's a step in the right direction, dear. I think it's a step in the right direction for all of us."

"I'm not doing it for anyone else but myself." Tricee's tone was harsh but Ruby understood.

After their phone call Ruby allowed the tears to fall freely. She'd never been exactly sure why her and her daughter's relationship had always been so strained in the first place. But she was hopeful that, after tonight's conversation, they were both on the way to watching it slowly mend. It was all such an unfortunate set of circumstances. But she'd felt as if a huge burden had been lifted. She didn't tell Tricee that Bev's brother had proposed and that she'd accepted, but she sensed deep down that her daughter might already have an inkling that she and Bev's brother were heavily involved. Her tears tonight were a mixture of joy and of pain.

Tricee closed the photo album and was about to place it back into the box when she paused. She opened the photo album again and removed the photo of her and Annette. She placed it in the top drawer of her nightstand. *It doesn't belong tucked away anymore*, she thought. Although she could not ask God to move every mountain, she expected and trusted that He would, indeed, give her a hand in getting around them.

2 Corinthians 12:9 – And he said unto me, My grace is sufficient for thee: for my strength is made perfect in weakness. Most gladly therefore will I rather glory in my infirmities, that the power of Christ may rest upon me.

24

Tricee sat alone in the university's café. Although a couple of her co-workers had asked her to join them for lunch, she declined their offers. "Maybe sometime later on in the week," she'd said. She'd needed the hour to herself. Even though it had been several weeks since the incident with Jeff and Karen, Tricee could not erase it from her mind. While she could understand why Pam had decided not to go to church with her that Sunday as planned, she couldn't believe that she would call her that Sunday evening and explode.

"Tricee, you can't tell me you did not know about Jeff and Karen!" Pam screamed into the phone.

"Pam, Karen is a very private person. She doesn't share details with me about her dating life. She mentioned one guy a couple of times but his name wasn't Jeff. In fact, I don't know if she even said what his name was!"

"I don't believe that! Two straight women don't hang out and not discuss the men in their lives! I'm willing to bet," Pam punched her fist in the air, "I just bet that you told her about Paul! He was just a friend but I bet you mentioned him!"

This is ridiculous, Tricee thought silently. "What has Paul got to do with this?"

"He has everything to do with this because I'm trying to make a point!"

"Pam, first of all, you need to stop yelling at me. Second of all, I have no reason to lie to you – "

Pam cut her off. "You have every reason to lie! You know I can't stand Karen and you know she doesn't like me. So it would make perfect sense for you not to tell me!"

Tricee took a deep breath. "As I was saying, third of all – "

"There is no third of all!" Pam's voice went even louder.

Tricee had had enough. "Pam, I'll tell you what. You call me back when you have calmed down." Click.

Tricee released a scream of her own. "Aaargh! Old crazy woman!" She took a few deep breaths. "Lord, I didn't mean to call her crazy but I'm so upset right now."

Pam was furious that Tricee had hung up on her. She was still fuming with her cell phone in her hand. "She hung up on me and she calls herself a Christian!"

Tricee attempted to call Pam back to apologize for hanging up on her but her phone call was ignored.

Not only had Tricee not been able to erase her and Pam's exchange but her conversation with Karen had been rather interesting. Unlike her conversation with Pam, there had been no yelling. In fact, she and Karen had shared a few laughs. As she finished the last of her Greek salad, her mind went back to her and Karen's discussion. They'd agreed to meet at a restaurant near their building at 4:00 PM. Tricee had arrived at 3:50 PM while Karen had arrived fifteen minutes late.

"Sorry I'm late." Karen tossed her brown Coach bag onto the seat next to her.

"No problem. Have you been here before?" Tricee looked around at the fairly new restaurant. She'd walked past it several times but had never been inside.

"Yes, a couple of times." Karen glanced at the menu. "They make good omelets. They serve breakfast all day."

"I think I'll just have the turkey club." Tricee placed the menu on the table.

The waitress took their orders and, a few minutes later, was back with their juice and iced tea.

Karen sipped her orange juice and then set down her glass.

"Like I was saying last night, Tricee. Jeff and I are not in a serious relationship."

Tricee could appreciate Karen being so direct.

"My guess is that Pam is looking for something more." Karen shrugged.

"Karen, I don't want to get too personal, but I take it you're okay with not being in a committed relationship with Jeff."

"Jeff is not the only man I see. But let me clarify," Karen pointed her index finger, "I don't sleep with every man I date. I know Jeff's type. It's obvious that he's not looking for a long-term relationship, at least not now. We haven't been intimate so he is enjoying the chase. I don't know about Pam but that was not hard to figure out."

"Well, some women can't grasp that." Tricee sipped her iced tea.

"I know. Don't get me wrong—Jeff is a nice guy in his own way and we have a good time together, but he knows I am not pressed for dates."

The waitress brought their meals.

"Thank you," said Karen. "May I have a glass of water, please?"

Tricee took a bite of her sandwich and, being satisfied with the taste, knew she'd soon become a regular customer. She was glad that Karen had suggested the place.

From her demeanor, Tricee sensed that Karen posed something of a challenge to Jeff. "Karen, I get the impression that you're not afraid to ask a man a lot of questions."

"No, I'm not. That's the only way to find things out. Some of them might not tell the truth but you can usually tell when that happens. Sometimes, we as women only hear what we want to hear. If I get a vague response from a guy, it's up to me to decide how far I want to go from there."

Their topic of conversation wasn't just about Pam and Jeff but relationships in general. Karen shared a couple of other details about Jeff before their meal was over and, while Tricee felt badly that he'd not been honest with Pam, she took comfort in knowing that she had been.

"I agree. I had one guy tell me that I asked too many questions. I was only asking basic stuff and he got all offended."

"See, that right there," Karen pointed her toast at Tricee, "makes it look as if he was hiding something. I hope you told him where he could go after that." She took a bite of her toast and then carefully wiped her mouth. Even the way Karen wiped her mouth had been comical to Tricee. Her demonstrative behavior made Tricee want to laugh but she held back.

"I told him nicely, but I told him." Tricee took a bite of her pickle.

"But you know," Karen began spreading jelly on her toast, "there are some slick women out here, too. I have a cousin who is very skilled at not being truthful. She can put some men to shame. When they ask her something she doesn't want to answer, she'll make something up or—get this," Karen was now on a roll, "—she'll start an argument and make the man so upset he'll want to either get off the phone or end their evening. That's expending way too much energy for me." She set her toast back on her plate. "I had a guy get mad at me for asking him if he was married. He said that he was and then asked me why that was a problem. I let him

have it. I told him I didn't know who he was used to dealing with but that I was not the one. Why are you laughing, Tricee?"

Tricee put down her fork. "I was trying not to but, Karen, I have never known any other woman who can move her neck the way you do. I am beginning to think you invented the neck roll."

Karen laughed. "I guess it's just force of habit. I have to make my point."

"I'm glad we had this chat." Tricee pushed her plate away.

"So am I." Karen paused before continuing, "I bet Jeff took Pam to see Maxwell back in February, didn't he?"

Tricee nodded.

"He asked me to go but I told him I had other plans."

"I can't say I'm surprised."

"You know that necklace I had on when your friend from college was in town, that night we had dinner at your apartment?"

"Yeah. Actually that would have been some time after the Maxwell concert."

"Jeff bought that for me. He had a bracelet, too, but I didn't accept it. I just didn't want to. I do have limitations."

Tricee immediately thought about the bracelet he had given to Pam. They finished their meals and stood from the table.

"How Pam chooses to deal with Jeff is her business, but I hope she decides to stop being mad at you." Karen removed her credit card from her purse. "It's my treat. It's the least I can do for being late."

Tricee had to give Karen credit. Although she had a totally different perspective on relationships than Karen, Karen at least was not in the dark about Jeff like Pam was. Tricee thought about the quote from Maya Angelou: "*The first time someone shows you who they are, believe them.*" It was one of her favorite quotes. Unfortunately, this had been something Pam had failed to heed in her dealings with Jeff.

The remainder of the work day had gone by quickly and Tricee was actually able to leave her office at 5:00 PM. As soon as she arrived home she checked the messages on her home phone.

"Hi, Tricee. It's your Aunt Janice. Call me when you can, sweetie. I am just calling to see how you are doing."

"Hello, pretty lady. It's Hunter. I thought I'd leave you a nice message on your home phone to make you smile after what I am sure was a long and busy day."

His mission had been accomplished. Tricee smiled as she walked into the kitchen.

She prepared a chicken breast with sautéed spinach, mushrooms and carrots. While waiting for the chicken to bake, she went into the living room to watch the news. Her cell phone rang and she was surprised to see the name Cassie Rhodes on the caller ID.

"Hello?" Tricee raised an eyebrow.

"Hi, Tricee. It's Cassie."

"Hi, Cassie. Is everything okay?" Tricee could not recall the last time Cassie had called her. It certainly had not been anytime in the last year.

"Oh, yes. Everything is fine. Am I catching you at a bad time?"

"No, not at all. I am just watching the news while I wait for my dinner to get ready."

"Oh, okay. Well, I am sure you have heard that I'm attending H&P this fall."

"Yes and congratulations! I am sure you will have a great experience at H&P."

"You have to say that, you work there."

Tricee laughed at Cassie's comment. "Well, I am a little biased."

Tricee sensed that Cassie was calling for some other reason, not just to share news about where she would be attending college in the fall. But she allowed Cassie to lead the discussion.

"You have a right to be biased. Hey, Tricee, look—I just wanted to tell you that I think Pam is way out of line in how she is treating you. When she picked me up that night I could tell that she was all upset. But when I asked what was wrong, of course, she didn't want to talk about it."

Tricee listened carefully, choosing not to comment. She didn't want Cassie to misconstrue anything she'd have to say.

"I asked her again a couple days later and she told me what happened. When I asked her if she had spoken with you, she told me to mind my own business. But she didn't say it so nicely."

Tricee chuckled. *I can only imagine.*

"I told her she was wrong for holding anger against you and that I didn't think she was setting a good example for me. I told her she was blaming you for something that isn't your fault. And after I said all of that I ran."

Tricee was still laughing when she hung up the phone.

Jackie called an hour later. "Are you in bed already? It's not even 10:00 yet."

"I knew I should have turned off my cell phone," Tricee teased.

"Ouch."

"I'm kidding."

"I know that. So what's up with you?"

"Cassie called me."

Jackie was a little surprised to hear that. "She did? What did she want?"

"Basically to tell me that Pam is behaving badly."

"Bless her sweet heart." Jackie, Tricee and Val had always liked Pam's youngest sister. They all thought she was very smart and downright hilarious!

"Well, everyone can see that Pam is in the wrong. Anyway, I was calling to ask if you and Hunter wanted to go to dinner next weekend. I was thinking we could triple date."

"Triple date?"

"Yeah," Jackie said slowly. "That's when three couples get together and go out and have fun. It'll be Lem and I, Cory and Val, and you and Hunter."

"I'll have to see. I don't want to rush into anything. Besides, I wouldn't qualify us as a couple. It's only been close to two months."

"But who's counting," Jackie teased. "Tricee, it's not rushing just to ask him to join your friends for dinner. And you know that man is really into you. We won't bite him if that's what you're concerned about."

"You'd better not bite him," Tricee smiled. "I'll get back to you about it."

As soon as Jackie came back to her room after checking on her daughter, her phone rang. She'd just opened a new book and was about to start reading. It was Pam.

"Hi, Jackie. I was calling to get some info on the upcoming summer program at one of the high schools. I promised my cousin I'd call you to get the details."

"Well, everything hasn't been finalized yet but I expect it to be in a couple of weeks-by the middle of June. I'll have more information then. If I find out anything sooner, I'll call and let you know."

"Thanks, I really appreciate it."

After inquiring about the summer program, Pam decided to take the conversation elsewhere.

"Jackie, may I ask you a question?"

"Sure." Jackie closed her book.

"If Lem was seeing a woman that one of your friends knew about but didn't tell you, wouldn't it bother you?"

"Pam this is not about me."

"I'm just asking a question."

"Yes, it would bother me. But, fortunately, I don't have friends that would do that."

"So you think." Pam tossed her blouse on the chair.

She glanced at the beautiful pink and white flowers Jeff had given her last night after dinner. Karen was history. He'd shared everything he could at Pam's insistence and she saw no reason to not believe him.

"Pam, if Jeff was actually involved with Karen, wouldn't it bother you?"

"Jackie, I thought we went over this already."

"No." Jackie was shaking her head on the other end. "We haven't. Let me assure you that Jeff and Karen are still involved. You might want to keep that in mind while you continue to make Tricee suffer. And rest assured that he has spent time with Karen since you and Tricee saw them together."

Tricee had shared with Jackie the conversation she'd had with Karen. And like Tricee, Jackie was not surprised that Jeff was seeing Karen and Pam at the same time.

Pam angrily hung up the phone. She walked over to her dresser and picked up the flowers. She walked into the kitchen and tossed the flowers, along with the vase, into the tall silver garbage can. She cried in the shower, allowing her tears to fall with the water. She changed into her night gown and climbed into bed. She was soon startled by the doorbell.

She reached for her robe and walked to the front door. She peeked out of her window and was surprised to see a white BMW parked in front. She opened the door slowly, moved to the side and allowed Jeff to come inside.

"Jeff, what are you doing here?"

"I was missing you. I had to see those beautiful eyes before I closed my own eyes tonight."

Pam's frown turned into a smile. Jeff's surprise visit caused Pam to suddenly forget all about the conversation she'd just had with Jackie.

25

Tricee quickly wiped the tears from her eyes, careful not to allow the other patrons in the restaurant to see her. Her worst fears were now a reality. Aunt Janice was very ill and the doctors were giving her less than three months. There had not been much discussion about her illness, only that she had been diagnosed with a rare condition. The condition had spread to her lungs and caused her to feel weak all over. Tricee was livid to hear that the doctors had not been able to give this condition a name.

Uncle Ced was making travel arrangements to take Aunt Janice on a one-week cruise, something she'd always wanted to do. Initially, Tricee did not think this was a good idea for fear that her aunt was too ill to travel for an extended period. But after spending an hour on the phone with her uncle, Tricee hung up convinced that he had everything under control.

Tricee stared out of the window of the Thai food restaurant as she contemplated leaving. She had already ordered her meal but wasn't too sure if she would enjoy it.

The waitress set her shrimp fried rice in front of her. "May I bring you anything else?"

Tricee jumped. "Oh, yes. I would like more tea, please."

"I'm sorry. I didn't mean to scare you." The waitress smiled.

"I was daydreaming."

"How have you been?" She was the same waitress who had waited on Tricee and Paul on that cold Friday evening in January.

"I'm fine." Tricee forced herself to smile. "Thanks for asking."

After taking a few bites of her meal, she set her fork on the table. Her appetite was just not cooperating. When the waitress came back to her table to refill her tea, Tricee asked for a container.

She walked back to her condo silently, holding a conversation with God. It all had seemed so unfair. Aunt Janice was only 53. Tricee had always expected that her aunt would be one of those people who lived to see their 80s. It just wasn't right. But as much as she was in despair, she knew she had to accept God's will.

When she mentioned her aunt's condition to Hunter, he told her to try to focus on all of the fond memories. Tricee smiled as she recalled his words. Although it was much easier said than done, she attempted to replace thoughts of her aunt's illness with happy memories.

She pushed through the revolving doors and, with her head down, walked straight toward the elevator.

"Ms. Miller, you look so serious."

Tricee looked up. "Oh. Good evening, Tate. I wasn't trying to ignore you. I have a lot on my mind."

"I can see that," he smiled. "Well, relax and enjoy the rest of your evening."

"Thanks, Tate. You do the same."

As soon as she walked into her apartment, she looked at her cell phone and saw two missed calls, but there was only one voicemail message.

"Hi, Tricee. This is Paul. I hope all is well. I really need to talk to you so can you call, please, when you receive this message."

She hadn't spoken to Paul since he'd called asking her about her new position. She'd had every intention of calling him back since their conversation had been cut short, but she just hadn't gotten around to it. As she listened to Paul's message again, she sensed a bit of urgency in his voice. She turned on the television as she dialed his number.

"Hello there." The way Paul had answered his phone, Tricee could tell that he'd known it was her.

"Hi there. I'm just retuning your call. How are things?" Tricee had no intention of being on the phone long. All she wanted right now was a hot bath, a warm cup of something, and the comforts of her warm bed.

"I'm well. I was wondering if we could discuss something."

Tricee kicked off her slippers and sat back in her recliner. "Sure."

"I am beginning to have second thoughts about getting married."

Tricee's eyes went wide. "Oh."

Paul laughed. "I guess that was not what you were expecting to hear."

"Not exactly," Tricee chuckled. First it was her fall out with Pam, then her aunt's illness, and now Paul calling to tell her he was having second thoughts.

"Uh," she was at a loss for words. "I'm not sure what to say."

"I know. A face-to-face discussion would have been more appropriate. I'm sorry for calling and springing this on you." He'd expected that his news would take Tricee by surprise. He knew he'd be a little uncomfortable, initially, but to put off telling her how he felt would not have made things any easier.

"Maybe you're just having cold feet. It's normal."

Although she and Paul had once been able to chat about just about everything, Tricee was surprised that he'd called her. They hadn't hung out since their last dinner together back in March, three months ago. A lot had changed. Well, not a lot, but enough.

"I don't think so. It is much deeper than that."

"Paul, may I ask you a question?" Tricee decided not to beat around the bush.

"Of course you can. I called you with my issues remember? And please don't think I expect for you to solve all of my problems tonight." Paul chuckled.

"Thanks," Tricee smiled "That makes it a lot easier. Why didn't you ever mention that you were involved with someone?"

"I guess I just thought it wasn't important."

He heard Tricee sigh and realized she was looking for an explanation other than the one he'd just given.

"I guess I thought had I told you sooner, you would have allowed that to keep us from being friends."

"You should know me better than that. But I understand." Tricee thought about how difficult it must have been for Paul to call her expressing how he felt. "You don't have guy friends that you could have shared this with? I mean, I'm just asking."

"Tricee, men are not like women. We don't really share deep emotional stuff."

They both laughed.

"I'm glad you felt comfortable enough to share it with me. Just pray on it and I know you'll allow God to lead you."

"That's wise counsel. See, that is why I called you."

Tricee didn't really want to ask the next question but she did anyway.

"Have you spoken with your fiancée about how you feel?"

Paul hesitated. "No. But I plan to. I just need to make sure I am clear on my feelings first."

"I know that whatever you decide, Paul, it will be the right thing."

He and Tricee stayed on the phone for another 30 minutes. She told him about her aunt, which made him feel guilty. He'd stated that had he known about her aunt, he would not have gone into his issues. Tricee reassured him that he had no reason to feel badly. Interestingly, he had not asked about Hunter.

Hunter called just as Tricee was climbing into bed.

"Good evening. I wanted to call to check on you."

"That's encouraging and much appreciated." Tricee was all smiles.

"Would you be up for a meeting tonight? I know there is that 24-hour diner on Devon."

Tricee wanted badly to say yes but she was just too drained. And then she thought about when Pam had said to her, before they'd fallen out: *What about when you need a man to rub your temples, etc.* She decided that she could use that right about now and that Hunter would be the perfect man to come over and rub not only her temples but also her feet. She smiled at the thought. And then of course, there was Aunt Janice's voice in her head: *Don't be too available.*

"I'll tell you what. How about you attend church with me tomorrow, since you haven't been to my church yet, and we can go to the diner afterwards?" *If you only knew how much I want to say, 'Yes, come right over.'* Tricee blushed, hoping Hunter was okay with her idea.

Hunter grinned. "I'd love to go to church with you tomorrow. How about if we do what you just suggested and still go out for dinner. You do have to eat lunch and dinner, right?"

"That's right." She and Hunter were both smiling when they hung up the phone.

Tricee sat in bed and conjured up fond memories she'd shared with her aunt. Her aunt's laughter and her beautiful singing voice was the last thing on her mind when she fell asleep. The next morning, Tricee could recall every detail from her dream.

Aunt Janice was standing at the front of a big church. There was a strong gust of wind as the rain fell hard outside against the windows. A white dove sat perched upon a windowsill. As her aunt sang the lyrics to a song unfamiliar to Tricee, the bridal party stood smiling at the radiant bride, a stranger Tricee had not seen before, as she walked alone down the aisle. But when she reached the front of the church, the bride was no longer a stranger. It was Tricee standing next to a bridegroom whose face she could not make out.

Suddenly, the wind and the rain stopped and the dove flew away. Everyone turned to look at the bride who had closed her eyes. Aunt Janice began to sing another song, this time, one she knew. After the song ended, Tricee opened her eyes only to find Aunt Janice blowing her a kiss. Tricee blew her a kiss in return and then watched in amazement as her aunt faded away. She then turned and looked at the white dove that had reappeared.

The bridegroom touched her face lightly with his hands and whispered softly, "It's okay. All is well now." She looked into his eyes as she placed her hands upon his shoulders. She could see Hunter sitting in the front pews, smiling. Still unable to make out the face of the bridegroom, Tricee turned to walk away. She turned around and looked toward the front of the church where she could now clearly see the bridegroom's face. She watched as Paul came walking slowly toward her.

Psalms 4:8 – I will both lay me down in peace, and sleep: for thou, Lord, only makest me dwell in safety.

26

Pam wiped her forehead as she left her cousin's spacious loft. She wiped it again as she walked down Huron St. It was just the last week of June and already a blistering 95 degrees. *Couldn't it have at least waited until August to get this hot?*

She was still wearing the beige, trapeze skirt suit she'd worn to work but removed the jacket because it was so hot.

"Maybe you're having hot flashes," her cousin had teased her as soon as she began to complain about the heat.

"Please. At 35, I don't think so."

She rarely paid her cousin a visit. It seemed that whenever they were in each other's presence, their conversation, which would start off nicely, would end up in some sort of debate. Pam was beginning to feel that her cousin believed she was better than the rest of her relatives due to the hefty salary she made as an interior designer. While Pam made a nice salary in her sales position, unlike her cousin, she never saw a reason to flaunt her success.

But on the few occasions when she did visit, she would stop at the Drake hotel, which was a few blocks from her cousin's luxury apartment. The hotel's restaurant served great food and the atmosphere was very nice and classy. Since she still had about 20 minutes before she was to meet Jeff, she decided to head over to the Drake to have a drink.

As soon as she walked inside the lobby, her cell phone indicated that she had a text message: *Pam, I'm sorry. I need to cancel our dinner plans. I'm working late.* Pam read the text message and angrily tossed her cell phone back into her Michael Kors handbag. She had just gone on and on about Jeff to her cousin and now he had the nerve to cancel. Pam was starting to become fed up. Right before she reached the bar, her cell phone indicated that she had another text message: *Let's get together tomorrow for dinner. I promise I'll make it up to you."*

Pam immediately sent a reply*: I can't. Wednesdays are too busy*. That wasn't true. Wednesdays were no busier than any other day of the week.

Although she was now convinced that Tricee had not known of Jeff's relationship with Karen, Pam still had not apologized, at least not directly. She called Tricee after learning of her aunt's illness and neither Jeff's or Karen's name had been mentioned. Pam just didn't think it was proper timing. She'd called because she wanted Tricee to know that she cared. She wanted badly to ask Tricee if they could get together and chat but she'd felt a little embarrassed. Tricee was carrying a heavy burden while Pam had allowed Jeff to interfere with their friendship. She knew something had to change.

"Would you like to run a tab?" The bartender had an accent but Pam could not make out where it was from. He also had a very warm smile.

"No thanks, I'm driving. I'll just have a white wine spritzer."

"Coming right up." His friendliness almost helped Pam forget she was upset.

The restaurant was filling up quickly but Pam paid no attention as folks approached the bar to order drinks. The two bar stools next to her were empty. A middle-aged white guy dressed in a business suit sat in the third bar stool.

Pam was soon interrupted by a woman's voice.

"Pam?"

She slowly looked up at the blonde-haired, white woman who stood before her. *Do I know you?*

"Pam! I thought that was you," the woman said excitedly. "It's Kenzie."

Pam gave the woman a once-over. "Kenzie," she repeated the woman's name.

"Tricee's friend from college. How are you?"

Pam then remembered who the woman was.

"Kenzie, I didn't recognize you," Pam's tone was one of disinterest. *You look just like the three other blond-haired white women I passed on my way here,* she thought sarcastically.

"I know! We all look alike, right?" Pam was taken aback by Kenzie's comment and though she tried to contain her laughter, she couldn't.

"I have to agree with you. But you know, I thought that was what you guys said about us."

Kenzie placed her small black purse on the bar. "Well, see now there you have it. We're all humans capable of saying silly things."

"That would qualify as a very true statement," Pam said as they gave each other a hug.

Kenzie was dressed casually in a long, multicolored-print skirt, white beaded V-neck top and white LifeStride sandals. She was the last person Pam expected to see.

"What can I get you to drink?" the bartender asked.

"I'll have a glass of merlot, please. Pam would you like another drink?" Kenzie noticed Pam's glass of wine.

"Actually," the bartender looked at Pam and winked, "she's driving."

Pam smiled back at him. "I'll have a club soda with a twist of lime please."

"You got it."

"Flirting are we?" Kenzie teased after the bartender walked away.

"No," Pam chuckled. "Just being friendly. So how long have you been in town?"

"I just got in Sunday evening but I leave tomorrow. It makes for a very tired Kenzie."

"I can imagine. How's your husband?"

"He's fine. It would be nice to see more of him, though."

Pam noticed that Kenzie's tone was not the same as when she'd spoken of him back in February. But she was not about to probe, and she certainly was not about to share with Kenzie her situation with Tricee.

"Oh, shoot the moon," Kenzie blurted out.

"Shoot the moon?" Pam laughed and raised an eyebrow. She followed Kenzie's eyes to a white male who looked to be in his late 20s. He came walking toward the bar.

"My colleague," Kenzie leaned in, speaking softly. "He asked me to join him for dinner and I told him I wasn't feeling well." A few seconds later, Kenzie's colleague was standing over Pam and Kenzie at the bar.

Kenzie introduced Pam to her colleague and hoped he would not ask to join them. "This is Pam. I haven't seen her in a while and we have a lot of catching up to do."

The gentleman turned toward Pam. "It's a pleasure to meet you, Pam." He extended his right hand toward Pam.

"It always is," Pam extended her hand and the gentleman let out a howling laugh. A few of the people at the bar turned to look in their direction. Pam leaned away and slowly eased her hand from his grip. Kenzie tapped her fingers lightly on the bar.

"That was funny, Pam."

"I guess so," Pam mumbled.

"Well, I'd better let you two ladies get back to your chat. I know how it is to run into a friend." He turned to leave and then looked over his shoulder. "Kenzie, I'll see you in the morning." He sipped on whatever he was drinking and walked away.

"I hope I didn't sound rude." Kenzie turned to face Pam.

"You were not rude. You were cordial. I've seen rude." Pam laughed.

"He's a nice guy but he can be so arrogant at times." Kenzie sipped her wine.

"Well, I thought he had pulled a muscle the way he was laughing."

"Oh my." Kenzie pulled her hair back and wrapped it together into a ponytail. "I have to hear that laugh all the time."

"He's traveling back to Denver with you, I take it."

"He is. But I wear my headphones during the flight."

"Smart lady."

Pam and Kenzie laughed.

"So have you spoken to Tricee? Does she know you're in town?" The mere mention of Tricee's name coming from her own mouth evoked some emotion from Pam.

"No. I called her and left a message but I haven't heard back. But this is such a quick trip that I figured it was unlikely we'd have a chance to meet." Kenzie took a few chips from the basket. "I can imagine she must be pretty busy, with that promotion and all."

Pam looked down at her lap.

"What's wrong?" Kenzie touched Pam lightly on the arm. Pam could see the genuine concern in Kenzie's eyes.

"Tricee just found out recently that her aunt is dying."

"Oh, I'm so sorry to hear that! Is this the aunt who lives in St. Louis?"

Pam nodded.

"Well, I'll be sure to call her. In fact, once I get up to my room I'll try her again. Tricee is such an amazing person isn't she?"

Pam smiled, "Yes, she really is."

Pam and Kenzie finished their wine and Pam glanced at her watch. She had enjoyed talking to Kenzie and wondered if Kenzie had recalled how unfriendly she was back in February. Unlike then,

Pam could now see why Tricee and Kenzie were friends. They shared a few of the same traits.

"Have you had dinner yet?" Kenzie placed a few more chips into her mouth. "These are so good and I'm so hungry."

"I see," Pam chuckled. Her expression then changed. "No, I haven't had dinner yet. I was supposed to meet my friend for dinner but he canceled. I was so upset that I lost my appetite. So I think I'll stop off on my way home and grab some take-out. Some fish and chips are starting to sound pretty good right about now."

"That does sound good. I think I'll just order room service. Is this the guy you were seeing back in February?" Kenzie recalled Pam briefly mentioning a guy she was seeing.

"Yes. But I think things are coming to an end."

"If it's not working for you, Pam, then it is best for it to end."

"You're right," Pam nodded in agreement. "I'm starting to see that now. Honestly, I just didn't want to see what my girlfriends could see all along."

"If things don't change for me soon, I might have to make some difficult decisions, too."

Kenzie shared what was going on in her marriage and Pam found herself giving advice or at least trying to. Kenzie was very open about her situation.

"He's away from home so much. And then I have to travel for work, but not as much as he does. I feel that things are changing between us. I'm just ready for things to be different. I want to go back to how things were before."

"It sounds like you need to communicate this to your husband. It doesn't sound like you've done that."

"And you're right, I haven't."

"Well, that's a start," Pam laid a few dollars on the bar. "And thanks for allowing me to finally put my Master's degree in counseling to use."

Kenzie laughed. "Anytime." She reached into her purse and pulled out a business card. "The next time I'm in the Windy City, dinner will be on me."

"Okay," Pam nodded and smiled. "And you get to choose the place."

Kenzie looked Pam straight in the eyes. "Take me to a place where all the fine black men hang out," she teased.

Pam held up her finger. "Okay, Kenzie. Don't make me get ugly now."

By the time they reached the lobby they were both laughing.

"Uh, Pam," Kenzie said softly. "The guy to your left, white shirt, is staring at you. Look slowly."

Pam turned around slowly as Kenzie suggested. The guy was staring but at Kenzie not at Pam.

"Uh, Kenzie, I think he's looking at you. Look slowly."

Kenzie turned slowly and the man was, indeed, staring but at Pam.

"Okay, let's both turn and look to see where his eyes are focused," Kenzie suggested.

"Okay," Pam chuckled. "One, two three." They both turned to look at the man who was, indeed, staring at them both.

"Oh my." Kenzie was trying her best not to laugh. "His right eye is looking at me – "

"And his left eye is looking at me. I would guess it would be hard for him to pick up a woman with that problem."

Before Pam walked out of the hotel, she and Kenzie embraced. After their embrace, Kenzie suddenly had a curious expression that Pam could not help but notice.

"Pam, may I ask you a question?"

Pam raised an eyebrow. "Not if it's one of those silly white folks' questions."

Kenzie fell silent and then began to laugh. "Aw, Pam. Please, just one silly question."

They both laughed. Pam had seen in Kenzie what she had not allowed herself to see when they'd first met. She was glad they'd run into each other at the hotel.

"I'm just wondering why a smart lady like you is even dating someone like Jeff."

"Kenzie, I have asked myself that same question."

An hour after leaving the hotel, Pam was sitting by the lake on the south side near her home. The hot summer evening presented a perfect opportunity for being near the water. She exhaled and pulled out her cell phone.

"Hello?" Tricee sat up in her bed. She was already almost asleep.

"Am I catching you at a bad time?"

"No, not really. What's going on?"

"Not much. I'm sitting here on the lakefront. You know I rarely sit out by the lake."

It felt great hearing Tricee's voice and Pam realized that they had a lot of catching up to do. She didn't expect for it to happen during this phone call and she knew Tricee didn't either. Pam knew she could not last another day without calling Tricee to apologize.

A couple walked past her, the man's arm draped around the woman's shoulders. She was an attractive woman, much shorter than he was. The man was handsome and favored the actor Will Smith, only darker. The woman was about a shade lighter than he was with her hair in braids. They looked so happy. As they continued their walk along the lakefront, Pam thought about Jeff. She'd hoped that they would spend many of their summer evenings strolling along the lakefront. But that was obviously not going to happen now.

"Hey, guess who I ran into this evening?"

Tricee yawned, "Who?"

"Kenzie. She's in town but she leaves in the morning."

"Oh, right. She did leave me a message but I was just too busy to call her back. In fact, she called a while ago but I was in the shower. I'll give her a call tomorrow. How is she?" Tricee removed the phone from her ear, looked at it, then put it back. "You didn't say anything mean to her did you?"

Pam laughed. "No. I was not mean to your little friend. In fact, we had a nice chat."

"Somebody catch me, quick, before I faint!" Tricee teased.

"Very funny." Pam stood up from the bench. "Believe it or not, we actually gave each other some advice on our relationships."

"That's good to hear. Progress is a good thing." Tricee looked over at the clock on her night stand. She was glad Pam had called but hoped that their conversation would soon end. She was exhausted from a very busy day at work. It was one of those days where everything that could possibly go wrong had, in fact, gone wrong. By the end of the day, both Tricee and her assistant were running to get to their cars. As for Pam, as long as they were back to being friends, Tricee figured they could easily pick up where they left off.

She'd seen Karen this evening with Jeff but she was not about to divulge this detail to Pam. They were leaving the building as she was walking in. Apparently, they had just left Karen's apartment. Karen introduced them and Tricee noticed the expression on Karen's face.

"Tricee, I am so sorry for the way I acted. I really do hope you can forgive me. I was wrong for making you pay for my suffering."

Pam exhaled as she waited for Tricee to respond. There was complete silence. A few seconds later, Pam heard light snoring.

"Tricee!" she yelled.

"Hey!" Tricee yelled back.

"You fell asleep on me. Did you hear what I just said? I was apologizing to you."

"And I accept." She yawned again while tossing and turning.

While she accepted Pam's apology, Tricee made a mental note to speak with Pam about her behavior. If nothing else, she wanted Pam to know how much her silent treatment had hurt not only their friendship but her feelings. Christian or not, Tricee was still human and believed she had every right to discuss her hurt feelings with the person who had caused the pain.

"And you forgive me?" Pam was all smiles.

"Yes, of course. Now you have a good night and we'll chat soon."

Tricee was getting ready to hang up the phone when Pam spoke again.

"Wait, Tricee. I have one more thing to ask you. It's about Jesus."

"Pam, why don't you call Jesus directly?" Tricee frowned as she pounded her pillows, "He's up all night you know?"

"Okay, okay, I get the hint. I'll call you before the week is out."

As soon as Pam arrived home, she washed her hands and delved into her fish and chips. She opened her Bible and turned it to the book of Ruth. She'd read the four chapters twice already in the past week and wondered why it was such a short book. She'd only read the first three chapters of the book of Esther but planned to finish it in a few days. But for now, she wanted to read the book of Ruth for a third time.

She was interrupted by her home phone. She grabbed the dishtowel and wiped her hands. It was Jeff.

"Hello?"

"Well, hello there, beautiful lady." He sounded extremely happy. "Did I wake you?"

"Jeff, I'm busy." Pam closed her eyes and swallowed the small lump that formed in her throat.

"Well, I was only calling to ensure that my lady was home and safe."

Pam remained silent.

"I'm sorry I had to cancel." He looked at the black, women's watch he'd purchased earlier. "But after my meeting I had something very important to take care of."

He'd canceled his plans with Pam because Karen had insisted he meet her on the north side after his meeting. He'd only been at her condo for less than 10 minutes when she suggested they leave to go to the nearest restaurant for appetizers and drinks.

"Jeff, it was fun while it lasted but this is no longer what I need." Karen sipped the rest of her cocktail.

"What are your needs? I am sure I can meet and provide for each one."

"I doubt it." Karen placed a few dollars on the table. "There are no hard feelings. I just need to move on."

"Can I at least give you a ride back to your building?"

"No, it's okay. I'll take a cab or walk."

"He's all yours, Pam," Karen mumbled as she walked out of the restaurant.

"I have something for you. It's going to look really good on you." He placed the watch back inside its case.

Pam sighed. "Jeff, I need to go. I'm eating."

"Okay. Well, pick out your favorite restaurant for Friday night. Whatever you want to do, you call it. And I'll make it happen."

"Why don't you call Karen and see if she's available?" The lump in Pam's throat had suddenly disappeared.

"Karen and I are done, love." He paused before continuing. "Pam, you never told me what you wanted from this relationship. You assumed things without just coming out and telling me how you really felt."

"Jeff, I think you knew very well what I expected from the relationship."

"What is it? What are your expectations?"

Pam sighed heavily. "It doesn't matter now. But thanks for the lesson. I'll be sure to remember it for my next relationship."

"I can be that man, Pam. I never made you any promises because I always wanted to be fair. Please don't try to make it seem as if everything I did was wrong."

Pam remained silent as she allowed herself to process Jeff's words. He was persistent. "We can get together on Friday to talk. If you feel the same way on Friday, then fine, but we should at least discuss it."

"There is nothing left to discuss." Pam sat down on her sofa. "Besides, I'm busy on Friday. Take care, Jeff."

Pam unplugged her home phone, then removed her cell phone from her purse and turned it off.

She placed the rest of her food in the refrigerator and grabbed a yellow highlighter from the pencil holder on her kitchen counter. When she got to chapter three in the book of Ruth, she highlighted verse 18 as she read it aloud: *Then said she, Sit still, my daughter, until thou know how the matter will fall: for the man will not be in rest, until he have finished the thing this day.*

Epilogue

The guests were all gathered at the banquet hall after leaving the church where the nuptials had just taken place. It had been a small, intimate ceremony for about 50 people. Jackie and her new husband, Lem, agreed to keep it as simple as possible.

Jackie was wearing a beautiful off-white, mid-length dress with lace sleeves and Lem was dressed in a grey suit with a light blue tie and an off-white shirt. He'd chosen the shirt specifically to match his bride's dress. As he stood with his uncle, a pastor of close to 50 years who'd just married the happy couple, he looked across the room at his lovely bride and smiled. His two daughters, ages 16 and 17, were elated as they witnessed the smile on their father's face. They were very happy that their father had met someone like Jackie and felt that inheriting a little sister was an added bonus. Alesia was just as excited to be able to say that she now had two big sisters.

"Jackie, you look so beautiful." Tricee leaned in to give her friend a hug for the fifth time. "Thanks," Jackie gushed. "I feel so alive. I could complete a triathlon without getting tired." "Wow," said Val. "Whatever it is Lem has, may I have some to give Cory?" They laughed.

"Okay?" said Pam. "I hope I feel like that after saying I do."

It was a typical hot and muggy August afternoon but, fortunately, both the church and the banquet hall were equipped with air conditioning.

"Just think," said Val as she touched Jackie lightly on the arm, "seven months ago, you and Lem were merely trying to get to know each other. And now you are man and wife."

Jackie blushed. "And thanks to Lem, I have become closer to the creator."

"God knew what He was doing." Val leaned in and gave her friend a hug.

Jackie blushed as she saw her husband walking toward them.

"Thank you, ladies, for celebrating our special day with us." He placed Jackie's hand in his.

"Oh, we wouldn't have missed it for the world," said Val.

"You do realize that she comes with baggage, right?" Tricee asked as she pointed to Val, Pam, and then herself. "Three pieces to be exact."

Lem laughed. "It's three pieces of good luggage. I can live with that." He then turned to Pam. "Pam, there's someone here who wants to meet you."

"Oh?" said Pam. She looked surprised by Lem's statement. She then turned to her three friends and put her head down, but her attempt at acting bashful had failed.

"Oh, please! You're not shy," Val quipped before picking up her glass of lemonade.

"Do you mind, sweetie, if I steal Pam for a minute?" Lem asked his new bride. "Please say no because my cousin is bugging me." He laughed and then turned toward Pam. "Do you mind? Once I make the introduction you guys are on your own."

Pam smiled, ready to tell Lem thanks, but no thanks until Jackie spoke up.

"Oh, girl. It's just an introduction. And when did you suddenly become shy?"

"I agree. And if you don't like him, just run away," Tricee teased.

Pam relented and she and Lem walked away.

Val turned to see her husband, Cory, chatting with a woman wearing a form-fitting black dress. She was doing most of the talking while Cory looked as if he was trying to spot the nearest exit.

"Excuse me, ladies," Val drank the rest of her lemonade and set the empty cup on the table, "but I need to go and rescue my honey."

Tricee and Jackie both turned around to look.

"Is that a relative of Lem's, Jackie?" Tricee asked as she picked up her glass of lemonade. "You'd better hope so."

Jackie turned to look. "Wow, you're right. I sure hope she is related. But I'll you what. My back hurts just looking at what she has to carry around."

"Val, you'd better get over there and quick." Tricee set her glass back down.

"I'm all over it, sweetie." Val laughed and hurried over to her husband. Tricee and Jackie chuckled as they watched Cory scratch the back of his head. He looked terribly uncomfortable.

Now that she finally had Tricee alone, the smile on Jackie's face faded.

"Tricee, I'm so sorry about Aunt Janice. I know I've said it already but had I known I would have chosen another day to get married seeing it has only been two weeks."

"Please, don't even think that." Tricee rubbed Jackie on the arm. "We cannot control these sorts of things."

"I know." Jackie leaned in and gave her hug. "I'm just so glad you were able to be here with me. I just wish things could have been different, that's all."

"Now you know Aunt Janice would not want you to stand here and dwell on something you had no control over, especially not on your wedding day." She took Jackie by the hand.

Jackie smiled at the memory she had of Tricee's aunt. She'd only spoken to her by phone, but it felt like she'd known her forever.

"I can just hear her now. 'You need to focus on making that new husband of yours happy.'"

"Yep! That sounds like Aunt Janice," Tricee smiled. "I was hoping she could hang on just a little longer but I guess her body just got tired."

Aunt Janice had made her transition two weeks prior. And although her death had been very difficult for Tricee, she was glad that her aunt and uncle had taken that cruise. Uncle Ced had informed Tricee that Aunt Janice had done fine for the first four days of the cruise, but had spent the majority of the last three days in the bed.

Aunt Janice had told her husband that she enjoyed every minute of it and couldn't wait to do it again. She'd known that she didn't have much longer but had kept her sense of humor and a sense of hope.

Later on that evening, Val and Tricee were back at Tricee's apartment, sipping ice cold Italian sodas. Hunter was out of town but had called moments earlier to see how she was doing and, of course, to ask about the wedding. Paul had also called but Tricee had kept the conversation short on purpose. Val noticed Tricee's expression when she hung up the phone.

"So what are you going to do?"

"About what?" she asked, trying to pretend she had no idea what Val was talking about.

"You know about what," said Val with a grin. "Paul. What are you going to do about Paul?"

Tricee shrugged. "I haven't given it much thought." She had given what they'd discussed some thought but was trying her best not to entertain it.

"He's going to expect an answer at some point, you know?" Val burped after drinking the last of her soda. "Excuse me," she said in a childlike voice.

"Pig." Tricee laughed and went into the kitchen for another bottle of Italian soda.

"That was such a lovely wedding, wasn't it?" she asked when she came back into the living room.

"Yes! And Jackie was such a lovely bride. I wish I had known you and Jackie when I married Cory."

"Well, that doesn't matter. We're in your life now."

"I know. But just having all four of us together on this special day just felt so wonderful."

"At least Pam was there with you to share in your special day." Tricee took a sip of soda.

"Yeah," Val smiled. "My girl was right there with me every step of the way." Val grabbed a cookie from the platter.

"I know Jackie is going to love the gift Pam bought her."

"I know!" Tricee exclaimed. "That crystal dish is lovely. I asked her, 'What are you trying to do, make us look bad?' I almost wanted to run out and buy another gift."

"Speaking of Pam, I wonder if she's having a good time with Lem's cousin. I think she agreed to have coffee with him—or is it green tea now?—whatever she's drinking tonight." Val bit into the oatmeal raisin cookie.

"I'm sure they will find something to talk about for an hour." Tricee picked up one of the cookies. "Pam told me an hour was all he was getting. But enough about Pam." Tricee began to laugh, "I thought it was so hilarious when you, Cory and that woman got on the dance floor. Whew! I was rolling!" Tricee was practically on the floor laughing.

Val shook her head. "I guess Triple D was determined to dance with my husband. When she grabbed Cory's hand to dance, I grabbed his other hand. Girl, Tricee, I was like, I guess we're getting ready to do ring around the roses. I wasn't about to let my husband dance with her by himself."

"And you are the self-assured one. I guess you said that wasn't happening, huh, Val," Tricee was beside herself.

"You have to know where to draw the line." Val stood from the sofa and walked into Tricee's bedroom to get her purse. When she came back into the living room, she was fumbling around for her tube of lip gloss.

"Has Hunter eaten your cookies yet?" Val smiled as she applied a coat of gloss to her lips.

"Excuse me?" Tricee looked at Val sideways.

"Your cookies. Has Hunter – "

"I heard what you said. It was just the way you said it."

Val smiled as she rephrased her question. "Did Hunter have a chance to eat the cookies you baked him?" She grabbed another cookie from the platter.

"That sounds better," Tricee giggled. "And, yes, he has."

Tricee walked Val to the door. "Tricee, that's a nice picture on your nightstand. I don't think I've seen it before. Is that you and Anne – "

"It's Annette and I when we were younger," Tricee said softly. "A year ago around this time is when I found out we were half-sisters, remember? I had set it out last year thinking I was ready to look at it, but I placed it back in the photo album. A couple days ago it dawned on me that a year has passed. So I think I'm ready to look at it on a daily basis."

After Val left, Tricee thought about all that had taken place in the past few months and year. She felt she'd done a pretty good job of handling it all.

As for relationships, she never would have thought she'd end up having to choose between the man who'd captured her heart and the man who started out as a really good friend. It remained a mystery, even to her, how she would handle the situation. Paul's proposal had, indeed, taken her by surprise.

After she pushed open the window in her living room, just enough to allow the breeze to make its way inside, Tricee sat with her legs folded up under her on the sofa. She closed her eyes and listened to the CD that Hunter had given her. Track 2 was his favorite song and he'd told Tricee he hoped it would one day become her favorite, as well.

She hummed along to the words: *Forever, you and me, one day together, forever, you and me, always together, forever, together, you and me.*

Psalms 30:5 – For his anger endureth but a moment; in his favour is life: weeping may endure for a night, but joy cometh in the morning.

13903600R00151

Made in the USA
Charleston, SC
07 August 2012